Turn Coat

The problem with hunting down the traitor in the White Council was simple: because of the specific information leaks that had occurred, there were a limited number of people who could have possessed the information. The suspect pool was damn small – just about everyone in it was a member of the Senior Council, and everyone there was beyond reproach.

The second someone threw an accusation at one of them, things were going to get busy, and fast. If an innocent was fingered, they would react the same way Morgan had. Knowing full well that the justice of the Council was blind, especially to annoying things like facts, they would have little choice but to resist.

One punky young wizard like me bucking the system was one thing, but when one of the heavyweights on the Senior Council did it, there would be a world of difference. The Senior Council members all had extensive contacts in the Council. They all had centuries of experience and skill to back up enormous amounts of raw strength. If one of them put up a fight, it would mean more than resisting arrest.

It would mean internal strife like the White Council had never seen.

It would mean civil war.

Turn Coat

A novel of
the Dresden Files

Jim Butcher

www.orbitbooks.net

ORBIT

First published in Great Britain in 2009 by Orbit
This paperback edition published in 2010 by Orbit

A CIP catalogue record for this book is available from
the British Library.

ISBN 978-1-84149-689-4

Typeset in Garamond 3 by
Palimpsest Book Production Limited, Grangemouth, Stirlingshire.
Printed and bound in Great Britain by
CPI Mackays, Chatham ME5 8TD

Papers used by Orbit are natural, renewable and recyclable
products sourced from well-managed forests and certified
in accordance with the rules of the Forest Stewardship Council.

Mixed Sources
Product group from well-managed
forests and other controlled sources
www.fsc.org   Cert no. SGS-COC-004081
© 1996 Forest Stewardship Council
FSC

Orbit
An imprint of
Little, Brown Book Group
100 Victoria Embankment
London EC4Y 0DY

An Hachette UK Company
www.hachette.co.uk

www.orbitbooks.net

For Bob. Sleep well.

ACKNOWLEDGEMENTS

I would like to thank Anne Sowards, my marvelous editor, my agent, Jenn Jackson, and my poor deluded beta readers. I've been facing the kinds of problems authors only dream about having, and you all have been a tremendous help to me. With luck, I'll figure out how best to repay you for the time and effort you've all given me.

And, always, for Shannon and JJ, who like me even when I vanish into my own head for days at a time.

1

The summer sun was busy broiling the asphalt from Chicago's streets, the agony in my head had kept me horizontal for half a day, and some idiot was pounding on my apartment door.

I answered it and Morgan, half his face covered in blood, gasped, 'The Wardens are coming. Hide me. Please.'

His eyes rolled back into his skull and he collapsed.

Oh.

Super.

Up until that moment, I'd been laboring under the misapprehension that the splitting pain in my skull would be the worst thing to happen to me today.

'Hell's frickin' bells!' I blurted at Morgan's unconscious form. 'You have *got* to be kidding me!' I was really, really tempted to slam the door and leave him lying there in a heap. He sure as hell deserved it.

I couldn't just stand there doing nothing, though.

'You need to get your head examined,' I muttered to myself. Then I deactivated my wards – the magical security system I've got laid over my apartment – grabbed Morgan under the arms, and hauled him inside. He was a big man, over six feet, with plenty of muscle – and he was completely limp. I had a hard time moving him, even though I'm no junior petite myself.

I shut the door behind me and brought my wards back up. Then I waved a hand at my apartment in general, focused my will, and muttered, *'Flickum bicus.'* A dozen candles spaced around the room flickered to life as I pronounced the simple spell, and I knelt beside the unconscious Morgan, examining him for injuries.

He had half a dozen nasty cuts, oozing and ugly and probably painful, but not life-threatening. The flesh on his ribs, beneath his left arm, was blistered and burned, and his plain white shirt had been scorched away. He also had a deep wound in one leg that was clumsily wrapped in what looked like a kitchen apron. I didn't dare unwrap the thing. It could start the bleeding again, and my medical skills are nothing I'd want to bet a life on.

Even Morgan's life.

He needed a doctor.

Unfortunately, if the Wardens of the White Council were pursuing him, they probably knew he was wounded. They would, therefore, be watching hospitals. If I took him to one of the local emergency rooms, the Council would know about it within hours.

So I called a friend.

Waldo Butters studied Morgan's injuries in silence for a few moments, while I hovered. He was a wiry little guy, and his black hair stood up helter-skelter, like the fur of a frightened cat. He wore green hospital scrubs and sneakers, and his hands were swift and nimble. He had dark and very intelligent eyes behind black wire-rimmed spectacles, and looked like he hadn't slept in two weeks.

'I'm not a doctor,' Butters said.

We'd done this dance several times. 'You are the Mighty Butters,' I said. 'You can do anything.'

'I'm a medical examiner. I cut up corpses.'

'If it helps, think of this as a preventative autopsy.'

Butters gave me an even look and said, 'Can't take him to the hospital, huh?'

'Yeah.'

Butters shook his head. 'Isn't this the guy who tried to kill you that one Halloween?'

'And a few other times before that,' I said.

He opened a medical kit and started rummaging through it. 'I was never really clear on why.'

I shrugged. 'When I was a kid, I killed a man with magic. I was captured by the Wardens and tried by the White Council.'

'I guess you got off.'

I shook my head. 'But they figured that since I was just trying to survive the guy killing me with magic, maybe I deserved a break. Suspended sentence, sort of. Morgan was my probation officer.'

'Probation?' Butters asked.

'If I screwed up again, he was supposed to chop my head off. He followed me around looking for a good excuse to do it.'

Butters blinked up at me, surprised.

'I spent the first several years of my adult life looking over my shoulder, worrying about this guy. Getting hounded and harassed by him. I had nightmares for a while, and he was in them.' Truth be told, I *still* had nightmares occasionally, about being pursued by an implacable killer in a grey cloak, holding a wicked cold sword.

Butters began to wet the bandages over the leg wound. 'And you're helping him?'

I shrugged. 'He thought I was a dangerous animal and needed to be put down. He really believed it, and acted accordingly.'

Butters gave me a quick glance. 'And you're *helping* him?'

'He was wrong,' I said. 'That doesn't make him a villain. It just makes him an asshole. It isn't reason enough to kill him.'

'Reconciled, eh?'

'Not especially.'

Butters lifted his eyebrows. 'Then why'd he come to *you* for help?'

'Last place anyone would look for him be my guess.'

'Jesus Christ,' Butters muttered. He'd gotten the improvised bandage off, and found a wound maybe three inches long, but deep, its edges puckered like a little mouth. Blood began drooling from it. 'It's like a knife wound, but bigger.'

'That's probably because it was done with something like a knife, but bigger.'

'A sword?' Butters said. 'You've got to be kidding me.'

'The Council's old school,' I said. 'Really, really, *really* old school.'

Butters shook his head. 'Wash your hands the way I just did. Do it thorough – takes two or three minutes. Then get a pair of gloves on and get back here. I need an extra pair of hands.'

I swallowed. 'Uh. Butters, I don't know if I'm the right guy to––'

'Oh bite me, wizard boy,' Butters said, his tone annoyed. 'You haven't got a moral leg to stand on. If it's okay that I'm not a doctor, it's okay that you aren't a nurse. So wash your freaking hands and help me before we lose him.'

I stared at Butters helplessly for a second. Then I got up and washed my freaking hands.

For the record, surgeries aren't pretty. There's a hideous sense of intimately inappropriate exposure to another human being, and it feels something like accidentally walking in on a naked parent. Only there's more gore. Bits are exposed that just shouldn't be out in the open, and they're covered in blood. It's embarrassing, disgusting, and unsettling all at the same time.

'There,' Butters said, an infinity later. 'Okay, let go. Get your hands out of my way.'

'It cut the artery?' I asked.

'Oh, hell no,' Butters said. 'Whoever stabbed him barely nicked it. Otherwise he'd be dead.'

'But it's fixed, right?'

'For some definitions of "fixed". Harry, this is meatball surgery of the roughest sort, but the wound should stay closed as long as he doesn't go walking around on it. And he should get looked at by a real doctor soonest.' He frowned in concentration. 'Just give me a minute to close up here.'

'Take all the time you need.'

Butters fell silent while he worked, and didn't speak again until after he'd finished sewing the wound closed and covered the site in bandages. Then he turned his attention to the smaller injuries, closing most of them with bandages, suturing a particularly ugly one. He also applied a topical antibiotic to the burn, and carefully covered it in a layer of gauze.

'Okay,' Butters said. 'I sterilized everything as best I could, but it wouldn't shock me to see an infection anyway. He starts running a fever, or if there's too much swelling, you've got to get him to one of two places – the hospital or the morgue.'

'Got it,' I said quietly.

'We should get him onto a bed. Get him warm.'

'Okay.'

We lifted Morgan by the simple expedient of picking up the entire area rug he was lying on, and settled him down on the only bed in the place, the little twin in my closet-sized bedroom. We covered him up.

'He really ought to have a saline IV going,' Butters said. 'For that matter, a unit of blood couldn't hurt, either. And he needs antibiotics, man, but I can't write prescriptions.'

'I'll handle it,' I said.

Butters grimaced at me, his dark eyes concerned. He started to speak and then stopped, several times.

'Harry,' he said, finally. 'You're *on* the White Council, aren't you?'

'Yeah.'

'And you *are* a Warden, aren't you?'

'Yep.'

Butters shook his head. 'So, your own people are after this guy. I can't imagine that they'll be very happy with you if they find him here.'

I shrugged. 'They're always upset about something.'

'I'm serious. This is nothing but trouble for you. So why help him?'

I was quiet for a moment, looking down at Morgan's slack, pale, unconscious face.

'Because Morgan wouldn't break the Laws of Magic,' I said quietly. 'Not even if it cost him his life.'

'You sound pretty sure about that.'

I nodded. 'I am. I'm helping him because I know what it feels like to have the Wardens on your ass for something you haven't done.' I rose and looked away from the unconscious man on my bed. 'I know it better than anyone alive.'

Butters shook his head. 'You are a rare kind of crazy, man.'

'Thanks.'

He started cleaning up everything he'd set out during the improvised surgery. 'So. How are the headaches?'

They'd been a problem, the past several months – increasingly painful migraines. 'Fine,' I told him.

'Yeah, right,' Butters said. 'I really wish you'd try the MRI again.'

Technology and wizards don't coexist well, and magnetic resonance imagers are right up there. 'One baptism in fire-extinguishing foam per year is my limit,' I said.

'It could be something serious,' Butters said. 'Anything happens in your head or neck, you don't take chances. There's way too much going on there.'

'They're lightening up,' I lied.

'Hogwash,' Butters said, giving me a gimlet stare. 'You've got a headache now, don't you?'

I looked from Butters to Morgan's recumbent form. 'Yeah,' I said. 'I sure as hell got one now.'

2

Morgan slept.

My first impression of the guy had stuck with me pretty hard – tall, heavily muscled, with a lean, sunken face I'd always associated with religious ascetics and half-crazy artists. He had brown hair that was unevenly streaked with iron, and a beard that, while always kept trimmed, perpetually seemed to need a few more weeks to fill out. He had hard, steady eyes, and all the comforting, reassuring charm of a dental drill.

Asleep, he looked . . . old. Tired. I noticed the deep worry lines between his brows and at the corners of his mouth. His hands, which were large and blunt-fingered, showed more of his age than the rest of him. I knew he was better than a century old, which was nudging toward active maturity, for a wizard. There were scars across both of his hands – the graffiti of violence. The last two fingers of his right hand were stiff and slightly crooked, as if they'd been badly broken, and healed without being properly set. His eyes looked sunken, and the skin beneath them was dark enough to resemble bruises. Maybe Morgan had bad dreams, too.

It was harder to be afraid of him when he was asleep.

Mouse, my big grey dog, rose from his usual napping post in the kitchen alcove, and shambled over to stand beside me, two hundred pounds of silent companionship. He looked soberly at Morgan and then up at me.

'Do me a favor,' I told him. 'Stay with him. Make sure he doesn't try to walk on that leg. It could kill him.'

Mouse nudged his head against my hip, made a quiet snorting sound, and padded over to the bed. He lay down on the floor, stretching out alongside it, and promptly went back to sleep.

I pulled the door most of the way shut and sank down into the easy chair by the fireplace, where I could rub my temples and try to think.

The White Council of Wizards was the governing body for the practice of magic in the world, and made up of its most powerful practitioners. Being a member of the White Council was something akin to earning your black belt in a martial art – it meant that you could handle yourself well, that you had real skill that was recognized by your fellow wizards. The Council oversaw the use of magic among its members, according to the Seven Laws of Magic.

God help the poor practitioner who broke one of the Laws. The Council would send the Wardens to administer justice, which generally took the form of ruthless pursuit, a swift trial, and a prompt execution – when the offender wasn't killed resisting arrest.

It sounds harsh, and it is – but over time I'd been forced to admit that it might well be necessary. The use of black magic corrupts the mind and the heart and the soul of the wizard employing it. It doesn't happen instantly, and it doesn't happen all at once – it's a slow, festering thing that grows like a tumor, until whatever human empathy and compassion a person might have once had is consumed in the need for power. By the time a wizard has fallen to that temptation and become a warlock, people are dead, or worse than dead. It was the duty of the Wardens to make a quick end of warlocks – by any means necessary.

There was more to being a Warden than that, though. They were also the soldiers and defenders of the White Council. In our recent war with the Vampire Courts, the lion's share of the fighting had been carried out by the Wardens, those men and women with a gift for swift, violent magic. Hell, in most of the battles, such as they were, it had been Morgan who was in the center of the fighting.

I'd done my share during the war, but among my fellow Wardens, the only ones who were happy to work with me had been the newer recruits. The older ones had all seen too many lives shattered by the abuse of magic, and their experiences had marked them deeply. With one exception, they didn't like me, they didn't trust me, and they didn't want anything to do with me.

That generally suited me just fine.

Over the past few years, the White Council had come to realize that someone on the inside was feeding information to the vampires. A lot of people died because of the traitor, but he, or she, had never been identified. Given how much the Council in general and the Wardens in particular loved me, the ensuing paranoia-fest had kept my life from getting too boring – especially after I'd been dragooned into joining the Wardens myself, as part of the war effort.

So why was Morgan here, asking for help from *me*?

Call me crazy, but my suspicious side immediately put forward the idea that Morgan was trying to sucker me into doing something to get me into major hot water with the Council again. Hell, he'd tried to kill me that way, once, several years ago. But logic simply didn't support that idea. If Morgan wasn't really in trouble with the Council, then I couldn't get into trouble for hiding him from a pursuit that didn't exist. Besides, his injuries said more about his sincerity than any number of words could. They had not been faked.

He was actually on the lam.

Until I found out more about what was going on, I didn't dare go to anyone for help. I couldn't very well ask my fellow Wardens about Morgan without it being painfully obvious that I had seen him, which would only attract their interest. And if the Council was after Morgan, then anyone who helped him would become an accomplice to the crime, and draw heat of his own. I couldn't ask anyone to help me.

Anyone else, I corrected myself. I'd had little option but to call Butters in – and frankly, the fact that he was not at all involved in the supernatural world would afford him some insulation from any consequences that might arise from his complicity. Besides which, Butters had earned a little good credit with the White Council the night he'd helped me prevent a family-sized order of necromancers from turning one of their number into a minor god. He'd saved the life of at least one Warden – two, if you counted me – and was in far less danger than anyone attached to the community would be.

Me, for example.

Man, my head was killing me.

Until I knew more about what was going on, I really couldn't take any intelligent action – and I didn't dare start asking questions for fear of attracting unwanted attention. Rushing headlong into a investigation would be a mistake, which meant that I would have to wait until Morgan could start talking to me.

So I stretched out on my couch to do some thinking, and began focusing on my breathing, trying to relax the headache away and clear my thoughts. It went so well that I stayed right there doing it for about six hours, until the late dusk of a Chicago summer had settled on the city.

I didn't fall asleep. I was meditating. You're going to have to take my word for it.

I woke up when Mouse let out a low guttural sound that wasn't quite a bark, but was considerably shorter and more distinct than a growl. I sat up and went to my bedroom, to find Morgan awake.

Mouse was standing next to the bed, leaning his broad, heavy head on Morgan's chest. The wounded man was idly scratching Mouse's ears. He glanced aside at me and started to sit up.

Mouse leaned harder, and gently flattened Morgan to the bed again.

Morgan exhaled in obvious discomfort, and said, in a croaking, dry voice, 'I take it I am undergoing mandatory bed rest.'

'Yeah,' I said quietly. 'You were banged up pretty bad. The doctor said that walking on that leg would be a bad idea.'

Morgan's eyes sharpened. 'Doctor?'

'Relax. It was off the books. I know a guy.'

Morgan grunted. Then he licked cracked lips and said, 'Is there anything to drink?'

I got him some cold water in a sports bottle with a big straw. He knew better than to guzzle. He sipped at it slowly. Then he took a deep breath, grimaced like a man about to intentionally put his hand in a fire, and said, 'Thank y—'

'Oh shut *up*,' I said, shuddering. 'Neither of us wants that conversation.'

Maybe I imagined it, but it looked like he relaxed slightly. He nodded and closed his eyes again.

'Don't go back to sleep yet,' I told him. 'I still have to take your temperature. It would be awkward.'

'God's beard, yes,' Morgan said, opening his eyes. I went and got my thermometer, one of the old-fashioned ones filled with mercury. When I came back, Morgan said, 'You didn't turn me in.'

'Not yet,' I said. 'I'm willing to hear you out.'

Morgan nodded, accepted the thermometer, and said, 'Aleron LaFortier is dead.'

He stuck the thermometer in his mouth, presumably to attempt to kill me with the suspense. I fought back by thinking through the implications, instead.

LaFortier was a member of the Senior Council – seven of the oldest and most capable wizards on the planet, the ones who ran the White Council and commanded the Wardens. He was – had been – skinny, bald, and a sanctimonious jerk. I'd been wearing a hood at the time, so I couldn't be certain, but I suspected that his voice had been the first of the Senior Council to vote guilty at my trial, and had argued against clemency for my crimes. He was a hard-line supporter of the Merlin, the head of the Council, who had been dead set against me.

All in all, a swell guy.

But he'd also been one of the best-protected wizards in the world. All the members of the Senior Council were not only dangerous in their own rights, but protected by details of Wardens, to boot. Attempted assassinations had been semiregular events during the war with the vampires, and the Wardens had become very, very good at keeping the Senior Council safe.

I did some math from there.

'It was an inside job,' I said quietly. 'Like the one that killed Simon at Archangel.'

Morgan nodded.

'And they blamed you?'

Morgan nodded and took the thermometer out of his mouth. He glanced at it, and then passed to me. I looked. Ninety-nine and change.

I met his eyes and said, 'Did you do it?'

'No.'

I grunted. I believed him.

'Why'd they finger you?'

'Because they found me standing over LaFortier's body with the murder weapon in my hand,' he replied. 'They also turned up a newly created account, in my name, with several million dollars in it, and phone records that showed I was in regular contact with a known operative of the Red Court.'

I arched an eyebrow. 'Gosh. That was irrational of them, to jump to that conclusion.'

Morgan's mouth turned up in a small sour smile.

'What's your story?' I asked him.

'I went to bed two nights ago. I woke up in LaFortier's private study in Edinburgh, with a lump on the back of my head and a bloody dagger in my hand. Simmons and Thorsen burst into the room maybe fifteen seconds later.'

'You were framed.'

'Thoroughly.'

I exhaled a slow breath. 'You got any proof? An alibi? Anything?'

'If I did,' he said, 'I wouldn't have had to escape custody. Once I realized that someone had gone to a lot of effort to set me up to take the blame, I knew that my only chance—' He broke off, coughing.

'Was to find the real killer,' I finished for him. I passed him the drink again, and he choked down a few sips, slowly relaxing.

A few minutes later, he turned exhausted eyes to mine. 'Are you going to turn me in?'

I looked at him for a silent minute, and then sighed. 'It'd be a lot easier.'

'Yes,' Morgan said.

'You sure you were going down for it?'

Something in his expression became even more remote than usual. He nodded. 'I've seen it often enough.'

'So I could leave you hanging out to dry.'

'You could.'

'But if I did that, we wouldn't find the traitor. And since you'd died in his place, he'd be free to continue operating. More people would get killed, and the next person he framed—'

'—might be you,' Morgan finished.

'With my luck?' I said glumly. 'No *might* about it.'

The brief sour smile appeared on his face again.

'They're using tracking spells to follow you,' I said. 'I assume you've taken some kind of countermeasure, or they'd already be at the door.'

He nodded.

'How long is it going to last?'

'Forty-eight hours. Sixty at the most.'

I nodded slowly, thinking. 'You're running a fever. I've got some medical supplies stashed. I'll get them for you. Hopefully we can keep it from getting any worse.'

He nodded again, and then his sunken eyes closed. He'd run out of gas. I watched him for a minute, then turned and started gathering up my things.

'Keep an eye on him, boy,' I said to Mouse.

The big dog settled down on the floor beside the bed.

Forty-eight hours. I had about two days to find the traitor within the White Council – something no one had been able to do during the past several years. After that, Morgan would be found, tried, and killed – and his accomplice, your friendly neighborhood Harry Dresden, would be next.

Nothing motivates like a deadline.

Especially the literal kind.

3

I got in my busted-up old Volkswagen bug, the mighty *Blue Beetle*, and headed for the cache of medical supplies.

The problem with hunting down the traitor in the White Council was simple: because of the specific information leaks that had occurred, there were a limited number of people who *could* have possessed the information. The suspect pool was damn small – just about everyone in it was a member of the Senior Council, and everyone there was beyond reproach.

The second someone threw an accusation at one of them, things were going to get busy, and fast. If an innocent was fingered, they would react the same way Morgan had. Knowing full well that the justice of the Council was blind, especially to annoying things like facts, they would have little choice but to resist.

One punky young wizard like me bucking the system was one thing, but when one of the heavyweights on the Senior Council did it, there would be a world of difference. The Senior Council members all had extensive contacts in the Council. They all had centuries of experience and skill to back up enormous amounts of raw strength. If one of *them* put up a fight, it would mean more than resisting arrest.

It would mean internal strife like the White Council had never seen.

It would mean civil war.

And, under the circumstances, I couldn't imagine anything more disastrous for the White Council. The balance of power between the supernatural nations was a precarious thing – and we had barely managed to hang on throughout the war with the Vampire Courts. Both sides were getting their wind back now, but the vampires could replace their losses far more quickly than we could. If the Council dissolved into infighting now, it would trigger a feeding frenzy amongst our foes.

Morgan had been right to run. I knew the Merlin well enough to know that he wouldn't blink twice before sacrificing an innocent man if it meant holding the Council together, much less someone who might actually be guilty.

Meanwhile, the real traitor would be clapping his hands in glee. One of the Senior Council was already down, and if the Council as a whole didn't implode in the next few days, it would become that much rifer with paranoia and distrust, following the execution of the most capable and highly accomplished combat commander in the Wardens. All the traitor would need to do was rinse and repeat, with minor variations, and sooner or later something would crack.

I would only get one shot at this. I had to find the guilty party, and I had to be right and irrefutable the very first time.

Colonel Mustard, in the den, with the lead pipe.

Now all I needed was a clue.

No pressure, Harry.

My half brother lived in an expensive apartment on the very edge of the Gold Coast area, which, in Chicago, is where a whole lot of people with a whole lot of money live. Thomas runs an upscale boutique, specializing in the kind of upper-crust clientele who seem to be willing to pay a couple hundred dollars for a haircut and a blow-dry. He does well for himself, too, as evidenced by his expensive address.

I parked a few blocks west of his apartment, where the rates weren't quite so Gold Coasty, and then walked in to his place and leaned on his buzzer. No one answered. I checked the clock in the lobby, then folded my arms, leaned against a wall, and waited for him to get home from work.

His car pulled into the building's lot a few minutes later. He'd replaced the enormous Hummer that we'd managed to trash with a brand-new ridiculously expensive car – a Jaguar, with plenty of flash and gold trim. It was, needless to say, pure white. I kept on lurking, waiting for him to come around to the doors.

He did, a minute later. He was maybe a hair or three under six feet tall, dressed in midnight blue leather pants and a white silk shirt with big blousy sleeves. His hair was midnight black, presumably to complement the pants, and fell in rippling waves to just below his shoulders. He had grey eyes, teeth whiter than the Ku Klux Klan, and a face that had been made for fashion magazines. He had the build to go with it, too. Thomas made all those Spartans in that movie look like slackers, and he didn't even use an airbrush.

He raised his dark brows as he saw me. "Arry,' he said in the hideously accurate French accent he used in public. 'Good evening, *mon ami*.'

I nodded to him. 'Hey. We need to talk.'

His smile faded as he took in my expression and body language, and he nodded. 'But of course.'

We went on up to his apartment. It was immaculate, as always, the furnishings expensive, modern, and oh so trendy, with a lot of brushed nickel finish in evidence. I went in, leaned my quarterstaff against the frame of the front door, and slouched down onto one of the couches. I looked at it for a minute.

'How much did you pay for this?' I asked him.

He dropped the accent. 'About what you did for the *Beetle*.'

I shook my head, and tried to find a comfortable way to sit. 'That much money, you'd think they could afford more cushions. I've sat on fences more comfy than this.'

'That's because it isn't really meant to be sat upon,' Thomas replied. 'It's meant to show people how very wealthy and fashionable one is.'

'I got one of my couches for thirty bucks at a garage sale. It's orange and green plaid, and it's tough not to fall asleep in it when you sit down.'

'It's very you,' Thomas said, smiling as he crossed to the kitchen. 'Whereas this is very much me. Or very much my persona, anyway. Beer?'

'Long as it's cold.'

He returned with a couple of dark brown bottles coated in frost, and passed me one. We took the tops off, clinked, and then he sat down on the chair across from the couch as we drank.

'Okay,' he said. 'What's up?'

'Trouble,' I replied. I told him about Morgan.

Thomas scowled. 'Empty night, Harry. Morgan? *Morgan!?* What's wrong with your head?'

I shrugged. 'I don't think he did it.'

'Who cares? Morgan wouldn't cross the street to piss on you if you were on fire,' Thomas growled. 'He's finally getting his comeuppance. Why should you lift a finger?'

'Because I don't think he did it,' I said. 'Besides. You haven't thought it through.'

Thomas slouched back in the chair and regarded me with narrowed eyes as he sipped at his beer. I joined him, and let him mull it over in silence. There was nothing wrong with Thomas's brain.

'Okay,' he said, grudgingly. 'I can think of a couple of reasons you'd want to cover his homicidal ass.'

'I need the medical stuff I left with you.'

He rose and went to the hall closet – which was packed to groaning with all manner of household articles that build up when you stay in one place for a while. He removed a white toolbox with a red cross painted on the side of it, and calmly caught a softball that rolled off the top shelf before it hit his head. He shut everything in again, got a cooler out of his fridge, and put it and the medical kit on the floor next to me.

'Please don't tell me that this is all I can do,' he said.

'No. There's something else.'

He spread his hands. 'Well?'

'I'd like you to find out what the Vampire Courts know about the manhunt. And I need you to stay under the radar while you do it.'

He stared at me for a moment, and then exhaled slowly. 'Why?'

I shrugged. 'I've got to know more about what's going on. I can't ask my people. And if a bunch of people know you're asking around, someone is going to connect some dots and take a harder look at Chicago.'

My brother the vampire went completely still for a moment. It isn't something human beings can do. All of him, even the sense of his presence in the room, just . . . stopped. I felt like I was staring at a wax figure.

'You're asking me to bring Justine into this,' he said.

Justine was the girl who had been willing to give her life for my brother. And who he'd nearly killed himself to protect. 'Love' didn't begin to cover what they had. Neither did 'broken'.

My brother was a vampire of the White Court. For him, love hurt. Thomas and Justine couldn't ever be together.

'She's the personal aide of the leader of the White Court,' I said. 'If anyone's in a good position to find out, she is.'

He rose, the motion a little too quick to be wholly human, and paced back and forth in agitation. 'She's already taking enough risks, feeding information on the White Court's activities back to you when it's safe for her to do it. I don't want her taking more chances.'

'I get that,' I said. 'But situations like this are the whole reason she went undercover in the first place. This is exactly the kind of thing she wanted to do when she went in.'

Thomas mutely shook his head.

I sighed. 'Look, I'm not asking her to deactivate the tractor beam, rescue the princess, and escape to the fourth moon of Yavin. I just need to know what she's heard and what she can find out without blowing her cover.'

He paced for another half a minute or so before he stopped and stared at me hard. 'Promise me something, first.'

'What?'

'Promise me that you won't put her in any more danger than she already is. Promise me that you won't act on any information they could trace back to her.'

'Dammit, Thomas,' I said wearily. 'That just isn't possible. There's no way to know exactly which information will be safe to use, and no way to know for certain which bits of data might be misinformation.'

'Promise me,' he said, emphasizing both words.

I shook my head. 'I promise that I'll do absolutely everything in my power to keep Justine safe.'

His jaws clenched a few times. The promise didn't satisfy him – though it was probably more accurate to say that the *situation* didn't satisfy him. He knew I couldn't guarantee her complete safety and he knew that I'd given him everything I could.

He took a deep, slow breath.

Then he nodded.

'Okay,' he said.

4

About five minutes after I left Thomas's place, I found myself instinctively checking the rearview mirror every couple of seconds and recognized the quiet tension that had begun to flow through me. My gut was telling me that I'd picked up a tail.

Granted, it was only an intuition, but hey. Wizard, over here. My instincts had earned enough credibility to make me pay attention to them. If they told me someone was following me, it was time to start watching my back.

If someone was following me, it wasn't necessarily connected to the current situation with Morgan. I mean, it didn't absolutely *have* to be, right? But I hadn't survived a ton of ugly furballs by being thick all of the time. Generally, maybe, but not *all* the time, and I'd be an idiot to assume that my sudden company was unconnected to Morgan.

I took a few turns purely for fun, but I couldn't spot any vehicles following mine. That didn't necessarily mean anything. A good surveillance team, working together, could follow a target all but invisibly, especially at night, when every car on the road looked pretty much like the same pair of headlights. Just because I couldn't see them didn't mean that they weren't there.

The hairs on the back of my neck stood up, and I felt my shoulders ratcheting tighter with each passing streetlight.

What if my pursuer wasn't in a car?

My imagination promptly treated me to visions of numerous winged horrors, soaring silently on batlike wings just above the level of the ambient light of the city, preparing to dive down upon the *Blue Beetle* and tear it into strips of sheet metal. The streets were busy, as they almost always were in this part of town. It was one hell of a public location for a hit, but that didn't automatically preclude the possibility. It had happened to me before.

I chewed on my lower lip and thought. I couldn't go back to my apartment until I was sure that I had shaken the tail. To do that, I'd have to spot him.

I wasn't going to get through the next two days without taking some chances. I figured I might as well get started.

I drew in a deep breath, focused my thoughts, and blinked slowly, once. When I opened my eyes again, I brought my Sight along with them.

A wizard's Sight, his ability to perceive the world around him in a vastly broadened spectrum of interacting forces, is a dangerous gift. Whether it's called spirit vision, or inner sight, or the Third Eye, it lets you perceive things you'd otherwise never be able to interact with. It shows you the world the way it really is, matter all intertwined with a universe of energy, of magic. The Sight can show you beauty that would make angels weep humble tears, and terrors that the Black-Goat-with-a-Thousand-Young wouldn't dare use for its kids' bedtime stories.

Whatever you see, the good, the bad, the insanity-inducing – it sticks with you forever. You can't ever forget it, and time doesn't blur the memories. It's yours. Permanently.

Wizards who run around using their Sight willy-nilly wind up bonkers.

My Third Eye showed me Chicago, in its true shape, and for a second I thought I had been teleported to Vegas. Energy ran through the streets, the buildings, the people, appearing to me as slender filaments of light that ran this way and that, plunging into solid objects and out the other side without interruption. The energies coursing through the grand old buildings had a solid and unmoving stability about them, as did the city streets – but the rest of it, the random energies generated by the thoughts and emotions of eight million people, was completely unplanned and coursed everywhere in frenetic, haphazard, garish color.

Clouds of emotion were interspersed with the flickering campfire sparks of ideas. Heavy flowing streams of deep thought rolled slowly beneath blazing, dancing gems of joy. The muck of negative emotions clung to surfaces, staining them darker, while fragile bubbles of dreams floated blissfully toward kaleidoscope stars.

Holy crap. I could barely *see* the lines on the road through all of that.

I checked over my shoulder, seeing each occupant of the cars behind me clearly, as brilliantly lit shapes of white that skittered with other colors that changed with thoughts, moods, and personalities. If I'd been closer to them, I'd have been able to see more details about them, though they would be subject to my subconscious interpretation. Even at this distance, though, I could tell that they were all mortals.

That was a relief, in some ways. I'd be able to spot any wizard strong enough to be one of the Wardens. If whoever was pursuing me was a normal, it was almost certain that the Wardens hadn't caught up to Morgan yet.

I checked up above me and—

Time froze.

Try to imagine the stench of rotten meat. Imagine the languid, arrhythmic pulsing of a corpse filled with maggots. Imagine the scent of stale body odor mixed with mildew, the sound of nails screeching across a chalkboard, the taste of rotten milk, and the flavor of spoiled fruit.

Now imagine that your eyes can experience those things, all at once, in excruciating detail.

That's what I saw: a stomach-churning, nightmare-inducing mass, blazing like a lighthouse beacon upon one of the buildings above me. I could vaguely make out a physical form behind it, but it was like trying to peer through raw sewage. I couldn't get any details through the haze of absolute *wrongness* that surrounded it as it bounded from the edge of one rooftop to another, moving more than fast enough to keep pace with me.

Someone screamed, and I dimly noted that it was probably me. The car hit something that made it shriek in protest. It jounced hard up and down, *wham-wham*. I'd drifted into the curb. I felt the front wheels shimmy through the steering wheel, and I slammed on the brakes, still screaming, as I fought to close my Third Eye.

The next thing I knew, car horns were blaring an impatient symphony.

I was sitting in the driver's seat, gripping the wheel until my knuckles were white. The engine had died. Judging from the dampness on my cheeks, I must have been crying – unless I'd started foaming at the mouth, which, I reflected, was a distinct possibility.

Stars and stones. What on God's green earth *was* that thing?

Even brushing against the subject in my thoughts was enough to bring the memory of the thing back to me in all its hideous terror. I flinched and squeezed my eyes shut, shoving hard against the steering wheel. I could feel my body shaking. I don't know how long it took me to fight my way clear of the memory – and when I did, everything was the same, only louder.

With the clock counting down, I couldn't afford to let the cops take me into custody for a DWI, but that's exactly what would happen if I didn't start driving again, assuming I didn't actually wreck the car first. I took a deep breath and willed myself not to think of the apparition—

I saw it again.

When I came back, I'd bitten my tongue, and my throat felt raw. I shook even harder.

There was no way I could drive. Not like this. One stray thought and I could get somebody killed in a collision. But I couldn't remain there, either.

I pulled the *Beetle* up onto the sidewalk, where it would be out of the street at least. Then I got out of the car and started walking away. The city would tow me in about three point five milliseconds, but at least I wouldn't be around to get arrested.

I stumbled down the sidewalk, hoping that my pursuer, the apparition, wasn't—

When I looked up again, I was curled into a ball on the ground, muscles aching from cramping so tight. People were walking wide around me, giving me nervous side-long glances. I felt so weak that I wasn't sure I could stand.

I needed help.

I looked up at the street signs on the nearest corner and stared at them until my cudgeled brain finally worked out where I was standing.

I rose, forced to lean on my staff to stay upright, and hobbled forward as quickly as I could. I started calculating prime numbers as I walked, focusing on the process as intently as I would any spell.

'One,' I muttered through clenched teeth. 'Two. Three. Five. Seven. Eleven. Thirteen . . .'

And I staggered through the night, literally too terrified to think about what might be coming after me.

5

By the time I'd reached twenty-two hundred and thirty-nine, I'd arrived at Billy and Georgia's place.

Life had changed for the young werewolves since Billy had graduated and started pulling in serious money as an engineer, but they hadn't moved out of the apartment they'd had in college. Georgia was still in school, learning something psychological, and they were saving for a house. Good thing for me. I wouldn't have been able to walk to the suburbs.

Georgia answered the door. She was a tall woman, lean and willowy, and in a T-shirt and loose, long shorts, she looked smarter than she did pretty.

'My God,' she said, when she saw me. 'Harry.'

'Hey, Georgia,' I said. 'Twenty-two hundred and . . . uh. Forty-three. I need a dark, quiet room.'

She blinked at me. 'What?'

'Twenty-two hundred and fifty-one,' I responded, seriously. 'And send up the wolf-signal. You want the gang here. Twenty-two hundred and, uh . . . sixty . . . seven.'

She stepped back from the door, holding the door open for me. 'Harry, what are you talking about?'

I came inside. 'Twenty-two hundred and sixty . . . *not* divisible by three, sixty-nine. I need a dark room. Quiet. Protection.'

'Is something after you?' Georgia said.

Even with the help of Eratosthenes, when Georgia asked

the question and my brain answered it, I couldn't keep the image of that *thing* from invading my thoughts, and it drove me to my knees and would have sent me all the way to the floor – except that Billy caught me before I could get there. He was a short guy, maybe five six, but he had the upper body of a professional wrestler and moved with the speed and precision of a predator.

'Dark room,' I gasped. 'Call in the gang. Hurry.'

'Do it,' Georgia said, her voice low and urgent. She shut the door and locked it, then slammed down a heavy wooden beam the size of a picnic table's bench that they had installed themselves. 'Get him into our room. I'll make the calls.'

'Got it,' Billy said. He picked me up the way you'd carry a child, barely grunting as he did. He carried me down the hall and into a dark bedroom. He laid me down on a bed, then crossed to the window – and pulled and locked a heavy steel security curtain over it, evidently another customization that he and Georgia had installed.

'What do you need, Harry?' Billy asked.

'Dark. Quiet. Explain it later.'

He put a hand on my shoulder and said, 'Right.' Then he padded out of the room and shut the door.

It left me in the dark with my thoughts – which is where I needed to be.

'Come on, Harry,' I muttered to myself. 'Get used to the idea.'

And I thought about the thing I'd Seen.

It hurt. But when I came back to myself, I did it again. And again. And again.

Yes, I'd Seen something horrible. Yes, it was a hideous terror. But I'd Seen other things, too.

I called up those memories, too, all of them just as sharp and fresh as the horror pressing upon me. I'd Seen good people screaming in madness under the influence of black magic. I'd Seen the true selves of men and women, good and bad, Seen people kill – and die. I'd Seen the Queens of Faerie as they prepared for battle, drawing all their awful power around them.

And I'd be damned if I was going to roll over for one more horrible thing doing nothing but jumping from one rooftop to another.

'Come on, punk,' I snarled at the memory. 'Next to those others, you're a bad yearbook picture.'

And I hit myself with it, again and again, filling my mind with every horrible and beautiful thing I had ever Seen – and as I did, I focused on what I had bloody well done about it. I remembered the things I'd battled and destroyed. I remembered the strongholds of nightmares and terrors that I had invaded, the dark gates I'd kicked down. I remembered the faces of prisoners I'd freed, and the funerals of those I'd been too late to save. I remembered the sounds of voices and laughter, the joy of loved ones reunited, the tears of the lost and bereaved.

There are bad things in the world. There's no getting away from that. But that doesn't mean nothing can be done about them. You can't abandon life just because it's scary, and just because sometimes you get hurt.

The memory of the thing hurt like hell – but pain wasn't anything special or new. I'd lived with it before, and would do it again. It wasn't the first thing I'd Seen, and it wouldn't be the last.

I was *not* going to roll over and die.

Sledgehammers of perfect memory pounded me down into blackness.

When I pulled myself back together, I was sitting on the bed, my legs folded Indian-style. My palms rested on my knees. My breathing was slow and rhythmically heavy. My back was straight. My head pounded painfully, but not cripplingly so.

I looked up and around the room. It was dark, but I'd been in there long enough for my eyes to adjust to the light coming under the door. I could see myself in the dresser mirror. My back was straight and relaxed. I'd taken my coat off, and was wearing a black T-shirt that read 'PREFECTIONIST' in small white letters, backward in the mirror. A thin, dark runnel of blood had streamed from each nostril and was now drying on my upper lip. I could taste blood in my mouth, probably from where I'd bitten my tongue earlier.

I thought of my pursuer again, and the image made me shudder – but that was all. I kept breathing slowly and steadily.

That was the upside of being human. On the whole, we're an adaptable sort of being. Certainly, I'd never be able to get rid of my memory of this awful thing, or any of the other awful things I'd Seen – so if the memory couldn't change, it would have to be me. I could get used to seeing that kind of horror, enough to see it and yet remain a reasoning being. Better men than I had done so.

Morgan had.

I shivered again, and not because of any memory. It was because I knew what it could mean, when you forced yourself to live with hideous things like that. It changed you.

Maybe not all at once. Maybe it didn't turn you into a monster. But I'd been scarred and I knew it.

How many times would something like this need to happen before I started bending myself into something horrible just to survive? I was young for a wizard. Where would I be after decades or centuries of refusing to look away?

Ask Morgan.

I got up and went into the bathroom attached to the bedroom. I turned on the lights, and winced as they raked at my eyes. I washed the blood from my face, and cleaned the sink of it carefully. In my business, you don't leave your blood where anyone can find it.

Then I put my coat back on and left the bedroom.

Billy and Georgia were in the living room. Billy was at the window that led out to the tiny balcony. Georgia was on the phone.

'I'm not getting anything out here,' Billy said. 'Is he sure?'

Georgia murmured into the phone. 'Yes. He's sure it circled this way. It should be in sight from where you are.'

'It isn't,' Billy said. He turned his head over his shoulder and said, 'Harry. Are you all right?'

'I'll survive,' I said, and paced over to the window. 'It followed me here, huh?'

'Something's outside,' Billy said. 'Something we've never run into before. It's been playing hide-and-seek with Kirby and Andi for an hour. They can't catch it or get a good look at it.'

I gave Billy a sharp look. There weren't many things that could keep ahead of the werewolves, working together. Wolves are just too damn alert and quick, and Billy and company had been working Chicago almost as long as I had. They knew how to handle themselves – and in the past couple of months, I'd been teaching my apprentice a little humility by letting her try her veiling spells against the werewolves. They'd hunted her down in moments, every time.

'So whatever's out there, it isn't human,' I said. 'Not if it can stay ahead of Kirby and Andi.' I crossed to the window and stared out with Billy. 'And it can veil itself from sight.'

'What is it?' Billy asked quietly.

'I don't know,' I said. 'But it's real bad.' I glanced back at Georgia. 'How long was I down?'

She checked her watch. 'Eighty-two minutes.'

I nodded. 'It's had plenty of time to try to come in, if that's what it wanted.' I felt a nauseated little quiver in my stomach as a tight smile stretched my lips. 'It's playing with me.'

'What?' Billy said.

'It's dancing around in front of us out there, under a veil. It's daring me to use my Sight so that I'll be able to spot it.'

From outside, there was a sound, a cry. It was short and high-pitched, loud enough to make the windows quiver. I'd never heard anything like it before. The hair stood up on the back of my neck, a purely instinctive reaction. My instincts had been tracking this thing well, so far, so I trusted them when they told me one more thing – that cry was a statement. The hunt was on.

An instant later, every light in sight blew out in a shower of sparks, and darkness swallowed several city blocks.

'Tell Andi and Kirby to get back here to the apartment!' I snapped at Georgia. I grabbed my staff from where it leaned against the wall by the door. 'Billy, you're with me. Get your game face on.'

'Harry?' Georgia said, confused.

'*Now!*' I snapped, flinging the bar off the door.

By the time I'd reached the bottom of the stairs, there was the sound of a heavy, controlled impact, and a wolf with hair the same dark brown as Billy's hit the floor next to me. It was an enormous beast, easily as heavy as Mouse, but taller and leaner – a wolf the world has rarely seen between here and the last ice age. I slammed open the door and let Billy out ahead of me. He bounded over a parked car – and I mean *completely* over it, lengthwise – and shot toward the buildings at the back of the complex.

Billy had been in contact with Andi and Kirby, and knew their approximate positions. I followed him, my staff in hand, already summoning up my will. I wasn't sure what was out here, but I wanted to be ready for it.

Kirby appeared from around the northernmost corner of the other building. He hurried along with a cell phone pressed to his ear, a lanky, dark-haired young man in sweat pants and a baggy T-shirt. The active phone painted half his face like a miniature floodlight. I checked the southern corner of the building at once, and saw a dark, furry shape trotting around the corner – Andi, like Billy, in her wolf form.

Wait a minute.

If the whatever-it-was had taken out the local lights, how in the hell had Kirby's cell phone survived the hex? Magic and technology don't get along so well, and the more complex electronic devices tended to fall apart most quickly. Cell phones were like those security guys in red shirts on old *Star Trek*: as soon as something started happening, they were always the first to go.

If the creature, whatever it was, had blown out the lights, it would have gotten the phone, too. Unless it hadn't *wanted* to take the phone out.

Kirby was the only clearly lit object in sight – an ideal target.

When the attack came, it came fast.

There was a ripple in the air, as something moving beneath a veil crossed between me and the light cast by Kirby's phone. There was an explosive snarl, and the phone went flying, leaving Kirby hidden in shadow.

Billy flung himself forward, even as I ripped the silver pentacle amulet from around my neck and lifted it, calling forth silver-blue wizard light with my will. Light flooded the area between the complex's buildings.

Kirby was on his back, in the center of a splatter of black that could only be blood. Billy was standing crouched over him, his teeth bared in a snarl. He suddenly lunged forward, teeth ripping, and a distortion of the air in front of him bounded up and then to one side. I lurched forward, feeling as if I was running through hip-deep peanut butter. I got the impression of something four-legged and furry evading Billy's attack, a raw flicker of vision like something seen out of the very corner of the eye.

Then Billy was on his back, slashing with canine claws, ripping savagely with his teeth, while something shadowy and massive overbore him, pinning him down.

Andi, a red-furred wolf that was smaller and swifter than Billy's form, hurtled through the air and tore at the back of the attacker.

It screamed again, the sound deeper-chested than before, more resonant. The creature whirled on Andi, too swiftly to be believed, and a limb slammed into her, sending her flying into a brick wall. She hit with a yipping cry of pain and a hideous snapping sound.

I raised my staff, anger and terror and determination surging down into the wooden tool, and shouted, '*Forzare!*'

My will unspooled into a lance of invisible energy and slammed into the creature. I've flipped over cars with blasts of force like that, but the thing barely rocked back, slapping at the air with its forelimbs. The blast shattered against it in a shower of reddish sparks.

The conflicting energies disrupted its veil, just for a second. I saw something somewhere between a cougar and a bear, with sparse, dirty golden fur. It must have weighed several hundred pounds. It had oversized fangs, bloodied claws, and its eyes were a bright and sickly yellow that looked reptilian, somehow.

Its snarling mouth twisted in a way that no animal's could, forming *words*, albeit words that I did not understand. Its form twisted, changing with liquid speed, and in maybe half a second, a cougar bigger than any mountain lion I'd ever even *heard* about was hurtling toward me, vanishing into the rippling colors of a veil as it came.

I brought up my left hand, slamming my will into the bracelet hung upon it. The bracelet, a braid of metals hung with charms in the shape of medieval shields, was another tool like the staff, a device that let me focus the energies I wielded more quickly and efficiently.

A quarter dome of blue-white light sprang into existence before me, and the creature slammed into it like a brick wall. Well. More like a rickety wooden wall. I felt the shield begin to give as the creature struck it – but at least initially, it stopped it in its tracks.

Billy hit it low and hard.

The great dark wolf sailed in, teeth ripping, and got hold of something. The creature howled, this time more in pain than fury, and whirled on Billy – but the leader of Chicago's resident werewolves was already on the way back out, and he bounded aside from the creature's counter-attack.

It was faster than Billy was. It caught him, and I saw Billy hunch his shoulders against its attack, his fur being bloodied as he crouched low, standing his ground.

So that *Georgia* could hit it low and hard.

Georgia's wolf form was dusty brown, taller and lither than Billy's, and moved with deadly precision. She raked at the creature, forcing it to turn to her – only to be forced to keep whirling as Billy went after its flank.

I brandished my staff, timing my shot with my teeth gritted, and then screamed again as I sent another lance of force at the creature, aiming for its legs. The blast tore gashes in the asphalt and brought the nearly invisible thing to the ground, once more disrupting its veil. Billy and Georgia rushed toward it to keep it pinned down, and I raised my staff, calling up more energy. My next shot was going to pile-driver the thing straight down into the water table, by God.

But once more, its shape turned liquid – and suddenly a hawk with a wingspan longer than my car tore into the air, reptilian yellow eyes glaring. It soared aloft, its wings beating twice, and vanished into the night sky.

I stared after that for a second. Then I said, 'Oh, crap.'

I looked around in the wildly dancing light of my

amulet, and rushed toward Andi. She was unconscious, her body reverted to its human form – that of a redhead with a killer figure. One entire side of her body was a swelling purple bruise. She had a broken arm, shoulder, ribs, and her face was so horribly damaged that I had to worry about her skull as well. She was breathing, barely.

The shapeshifter had been *strong*.

Georgia arrived at my side in wolf form, her eyes, ears, and nose all alert, scanning around us, above us.

I turned my head to see Billy, nude and in human form, crouched over Kirby. I lifted my light and moved a couple of steps over toward him so I could see.

Kirby's throat was gone. Just gone. There was a scoop of flesh as wide as my palm missing, and bare vertebrae showed at the back of it. The edges of the gaping wound were black and crumbling, as if charred to black dust. Kirby's eyes were glassy and staring. His blood was everywhere.

'Hell's bells,' I breathed. I stared at the dead young man, a friend, and shook my head hard once. 'Billy, come on. Andi's still alive. We can't leave her out here. We've got to get her behind your threshold and get her an ambulance, now.'

Billy crouched over Kirby, his face twisted in confusion and rage.

'Will!' I shouted.

He looked up at me.

'Andi,' I said. 'Help me get her inside.'

He nodded jerkily. Then the two of us went to her. We laid my duster out on the ground and got her onto it as gently as we could. Then we picked her up and carried her back toward the apartment building. People were calling out in the buildings around us, now. Flashlights and candles and chemical glow lights had begun to appear. I had no doubt that within a few minutes, we'd get sirens, too.

From somewhere above us, there was a contemptuous brassy cry – the same tone I heard before, though modulated differently now, coming from an avian throat.

'What was that?' Billy asked, his tone dull and heavy. 'What was that thing?'

'I'm not certain,' I answered, breathing hard. Georgia was coming along behind us, dragging my staff in her jaws. 'But if it's what I think it is, things just got a lot worse.'

Billy looked up at me, Kirby's blood all over his face and hands. 'What is it, Harry?'

'A Native American nightmare,' I said. I looked at him grimly. 'A skinwalker.'

6

Georgia told the EMTs she was Andi's sister, which was true in a spiritual sense, I suppose, and rode with her in the ambulance to the hospital. The EMTs looked grim.

The cops had gathered around Kirby's body, and were busy closing off the scene.

'I have to be here,' Billy said.

'I know,' I said. 'I'm on the clock, Billy. I can't stay. I can't lose the time.'

He nodded. 'What do I need to know about skin-walkers?'

'They're . . . they're just evil, man. They like hurting people. Shapeshifters, obviously – and the more afraid of them you are, the more powerful they get. They literally feed on fear.'

Billy eyed me. 'Meaning you aren't going to tell me anything more. Because it won't help me. You think it will scare me.'

'We knew it was here, we were ready for a fight, and you saw what happened,' I said. 'If it had hit us from a real ambush, it would have been worse.'

He bared his teeth in a snarl. 'We had it.'

'We had it at a momentary disadvantage – and it *saw* that, and it was *smart* enough to leave and come back later. All we did was prove to it that it would have to take us seriously to kill us. We won't get another opportunity like that one.' I put a hand on his shoulder. 'You and Georgia stay close to Andi. This thing *likes* hurting people. And it gets off on hunting down wounded prey. She's still in danger.'

'Got it,' he said quietly. 'What are you going to do?'

'Find out why it's here,' I said. 'There's Council business afoot. Christ, I didn't mean to bring you into this.' I stared toward the knot of officers around Kirby's corpse. 'I didn't mean for this to happen.'

'Kirby was an adult, Dresden,' Billy said. 'He knew what could happen. He chose to be here.'

Which was the truth. But it didn't help. Kirby was still dead. I hadn't known what the skinwalker *was* before, beyond something awful, but that didn't change anything.

Kirby was still dead.

And Andi . . . God, I hadn't even thought about that part. Andi and Kirby had been an intense item. She was going to be heartbroken.

Assuming she didn't die, too.

Billy – I just couldn't think of him as Will – blinked tears out of his eyes and said, 'You didn't know it was going to come down like that, man. We all owe you our lives, Harry. I'm glad we got the chance to be there for you.' He nodded toward the police. 'I'll do the talking, then get to Georgia. You'd better go.'

We traded grips, and his was crushingly tight with tension and grief. I nodded to him, and turned to leave. The city lights were starting to come back on as I went out the back entrance to Will's building, down a side street, and through an alley that ran behind an old bookstore where I wasn't welcome anymore. I passed the spot in that alley where I'd nearly died, and shivered as I did. I'd barely dodged the old man's scythe, that day.

Tonight, Kirby hadn't.

My head felt dislocated, somehow. I should be feeling more than I was. I should be madder than hell. I should be shaking with fear. Something. But instead, I felt like I was observing events from a remote cold place somewhere up above and behind me. It was, I reasoned, probably a side effect of exposing myself to the skinwalker's true form. Or rather, a side effect of what I'd had to do to get over it.

I wasn't worried about the skinwalker sneaking up on me. Oh, sure, he might do it, but not cold. Supernatural beings like the skinwalker had so much power that reality itself gets a little strained around them wherever they go, and that has a number of side effects. One of them is a sort of psychic stench that goes with them – a presence that my instincts had twigged to long before the skinwalker had been in a position to do me any real harm.

Read a little folklore, the stuff that hasn't been prettied up by Disney and the like. Start with the Brothers Grimm. It won't tell you about skinwalkers, but it will give you a good idea of just how dark some of those tales can be.

Skinwalkers are dark compared to *that*. You've got to get the real stories from the peoples of the Navajo, Ute, and other Southwestern tribes to get the really juicy material. They don't talk about them often, because the genuine and entirely rational fear the stories inspire only makes the creatures stronger. The tribes rarely talk about them with outsiders, because outsiders have no foundation of folklore to draw upon to protect themselves – and because you never know when the outsider to whom you're telling dark tales might *be* a skinwalker, looking to indulge a sense of macabre irony. But I've been in the business awhile, and I know people who know the stories. They'd confided a handful to me, in broad daylight, looking nervously around them as they spoke, as if afraid that dredging up the dark memories might catch a skinwalker's attention.

Because sometimes it did.

That's how bad skinwalkers are. Even amongst the people who know the danger they represent, who know better than anyone else in the world how to defend against them, no one wants to talk about skinwalkers.

But in a way, it worked in my favor. Walking down a dark alley in the middle of a Chicago night, and stepping over the spot on the concrete where I'd almost been ripped to pieces just wasn't *spooky* enough to encompass the presence of a skinwalker. If things got majorly *Tales from the Darkside* creepy and shivery, I'd know I was in real trouble.

As it was, the night was simply—

A small figure in a lightweight Cubs jacket stepped around the corner at the end of the alley. The newly restored streetlight shone on blond hair, and Sergeant Karrin Murphy said, 'Evening, Dresden.'

—complicated.

'Murph,' I responded woodenly. Murphy was a sergeant with Chicago PD's Special Investigations department. When something supernaturally bad happened and the cops got involved, Murphy often contacted me to get my take on things. The city didn't want to hear about 'imaginary' things like skinwalkers or vampires. They just wanted the problem to go away – but Murphy and the rest of SI were the people who had to make it happen.

'I tip a guy down at impound to keep an eye out for certain vehicles,' Murphy said. 'Pay him in bottles of

McAnally's ale. He calls me and tells me your car got brought in.'

'Uh-huh,' I said.

Murphy fell into pace beside me as I turned out onto the sidewalk. She was five feet nothing, with blond hair that fell a little past her shoulders and blue eyes. She was more cute than pretty, and looked like someone's favorite aunt. Which seemed likely. She had a fairly large Irish Catholic family.

'Then I hear about a power outage,' she said, 'and a huge disturbance at the same apartments where your werewolf friends live. I hear about a girl who might not make it and a boy who didn't.'

'Yeah,' I said. It might have come out a little bleak.

'Who was it?' Murphy asked.

'Kirby,' I said.

'Jesus,' Murphy said. 'What happened?'

'Something fast and mean was following me. The werewolves jumped it. Things went bad.'

Murphy nodded and stopped, and I dimly realized that we were standing next to her Saturn – an updated version of the one that had been blown up – blithely parked in front of a hydrant. She went around to the trunk and popped it open. 'I took a look at that pile of parts you call a car.' She drew out the medical toolbox and cooler from her trunk and held them up. 'These were on the passenger seat. I thought they might have been there for a reason.'

Hell's bells. In the confusion of the attack and its aftermath, I had all but forgotten the whole reason I'd gone out in the first place. I took the medical kit from her as she offered it. 'Yeah. Stars and stones, yeah, Murph. Thank you.'

'You need a ride?' she asked me.

I'd been planning on flagging down a cab, eventually, but it would be better not to spend the money if I didn't need to. Wizarding might be sexy, but it didn't pay nearly as well as lucrative careers like law enforcement. 'Sure,' I said.

'What a coincidence. I need some questions answered.' She unlocked the door with an actual key, not the little what's-it that does it for you automatically with the press of a button, and held it open for me with a gallant little gesture, like I'd done for her about a million times. She probably thought she was mocking me with that imper-sonation.

She was probably right.

This mess was getting stickier by the minute, and I didn't want to drag Murphy into it. I mean, Jesus, the werewolves had been capable defenders of their territory for a long while, and I'd gotten half of them taken out in the first couple hours of the case. Murphy wouldn't fare any better in the waters through which I was currently swimming.

On the other hand, I trusted Murph. I trusted her judg-ment, her ability to see where her limits lay. She'd seen cops carved to pieces when they tried to box out of their weight division, and knew better than to attempt it. And if she started throwing obstacles in my way – and she could, a lot of them, that I couldn't do diddly about – then my life would get a whole lot harder. Even though she wasn't running CPD's Special Investigations depart-ment anymore, she still had clout there, and a word from her to Lieutenant Stallings could hobble me, maybe lethally.

So I guess you could say that Murphy was threatening

to bust me if I didn't talk to her, and you'd be right. And you could say that Murphy was offering to put her life on the line to help me, and you'd be right. And you could say that Murphy had done me a favor with the medical kit, in order to obligate me to her when she told me that she wanted to be dealt in, and you'd be right.

You could also say that I was standing around dithering when time was critical, and you'd be right about that, too.

At the end of the day, Murphy is good people.

I got in the car.

'So let me get this straight,' Murphy said, as we approached my apartment. 'You're hiding a fugitive from your own people's cops, and you think the guy's been set up in order to touch off a civil war within the White Council. And there's some kind of Navajo boogeyman loose in town, following you around and attempting to kill you. And you aren't sure they're related.'

'More like I don't know how they're related. Yet.'

Murphy chewed on her lip. 'Is there anyone on the Council who is in tight with Native American boogeymen?'

'Hard to imagine it,' I said quietly. "Injun Joe' Listens-to-Wind was a Senior Council member who was some kind of Native American shaman. He was a doctor, a healer, and a specialist in exorcisms and restorative magic. He was, in fact, a decent guy. He liked animals.

'But someone's a traitor,' Murphy said quietly. 'Right?'

'Yeah,' I said. 'Someone.'

Murphy nodded, frowning at the road ahead of her. 'The reason treachery is so reviled,' she said in a careful tone of voice, 'is because it usually comes from someone you didn't think could possibly do such a thing.'

I didn't say anything in reply. In a minute, her car crunched to a stop in the little gravel lot outside my apartment.

I picked up the medical kit, the cooler, and my staff, and got out of the car.

'Call me the minute you know something,' she said.

'Yep,' I told her. 'Don't take any chances if you see something coming.'

She shook her head. 'They aren't your kids, Harry.'

'Doesn't matter. Anything you can do to protect them in the hospital . . .'

'Relax,' she said. 'Your werewolves won't be alone. I'll see to it.'

I nodded and closed my eyes for a second.

'Harry?' she asked me.

'Yeah?'

'You . . . don't look so good.'

'It's been a long night,' I said.

'Yeah,' she said. 'Look. I know something about those.'

Murphy did. She'd had more than her share of psychic trauma. She'd seen friends die, too. My memory turned out an unwelcome flash from years before – her former partner, Carmichael, half eviscerated and bleeding to death on white institutional tile flooring.

'I'll make it,' I said.

'Of course you will,' she said. 'There's just . . . there's a lot of ways you could deal, Harry. Some of them are better than others. I care about what happens to you. And I'm here.'

I kept my eyes closed in order to make sure I didn't start crying like a girl or something. I nodded, not trusting myself to speak.

'Take care, Harry,' she said.

'You, too,' I said. It came out a little raspy. I tilted the toolbox at her in a wave, and headed into my apartment to see Morgan.

I had to admit – I hated hearing the sound of my friend's car leaving.

I pushed those thoughts away. Psychic trauma or not, I could fall to little pieces later.

I had work to do.

7

Morgan woke up when I opened the bedroom door. He looked bad, but not any worse than he did before, except for some spots of color on his cheeks.

'Lemme see to my roommates,' I said. 'I got the goods.' I put the medical kit down on the nightstand.

He nodded and closed his eyes.

I took Mouse outside for a walk to the mailbox. He seemed unusually alert, nose snuffling at everything, but he didn't show any signs of alarm. We went by the spot in the tiny backyard that had been designated as Mouse's business area, and went back inside. Mister, my bobtailed grey tomcat, was waiting when I opened the door, and tried to bolt out. I caught him, barely: Mister weighs the next best thing to thirty pounds. He gave me a look that might have been indignant, then raised his stumpy tail straight in the air and walked haughtily away, making his way to his usual resting point atop one of my apartment's bookcases.

Mouse looked at me with his head tilted as I shut the door.

'Something bad is running around out there,' I told him. 'It might decide to send me a message. I'd rather he didn't use Mister to do it.'

Mouse's cavernous chest rumbled with a low growl.

'Or you, either, for that matter,' I told him. 'I don't know if you know what a skinwalker is, but it's serious trouble. Watch yourself.'

Mouse considered that for a moment, and then yawned.

I found myself laughing. 'Pride goes before a fall, boy.'

He wagged his tail at me and rubbed up against my leg, evidently pleased to have made me smile. I made sure both sets of bowls had food and water in them, and then went in to Morgan.

His temperature was up another half a degree, and he was obviously in pain.

'This isn't heavy-duty stuff,' I told him, as I broke out the medical kit. 'Me and Billy made a run up to Canada for most of it. There's some codeine for the pain, though, and I've got the stuff to run an IV for you, saline, intravenous antibiotics.'

Morgan nodded. Then he frowned at me, an expression I was used to from him, raked his eyes over me more closely, and asked, 'Is that blood I smell on you?'

Damn. For a guy who had been beaten to within a few inches of death's door, he was fairly observant. Andi hadn't really been bleeding when we picked her up in my coat. She was only oozing from a number of gouges and scrapes – but there had been enough of them to add up. 'Yeah,' I said.

'What happened?'

I told him about the skinwalker and what had happened to Kirby and Andi.

He shook his head wearily. 'There's a reason we don't encourage amateurs to try to act like Wardens, Dresden.'

I scowled at him, got a bowl of warm water and some antibacterial soap, and started cleaning up his left arm. 'Yeah, well. I didn't see any Wardens doing anything about it.'

'Chicago is your area of responsibility, Warden Dresden.'

'And there I was,' I said. 'And if they hadn't been there to help, I'd be dead right now.'

'Then you call for backup. You *don't* behave like a bloody superhero and throw lambs to the wolves to help you do it. Those are the people you're supposed to be protecting.'

'Good thinking,' I said, getting out the bag of saline, and suspending it from the hook I'd set in the wall over the bed. I made sure the tube was primed. Air bubbles, bad. 'That's exactly what we need: more Wardens in Chicago.'

Morgan grunted and fell silent for a moment, eyes closed. I thought he'd dropped off again, but evidently he was only thinking. 'It must have followed me up.'

'Huh?'

'The skinwalker,' he said. 'When I left Edinburgh, I took a Way to Tucson. I came to Chicago by train. It must have sensed me when the tracks passed through its territory.'

'Why would it do that?'

'Follow an injured wizard?' he asked. 'Because they get stronger by devouring the essence of practitioners. I was an easy meal.'

'It *eats* magic?'

Morgan nodded. 'Adds its victims' power to its own.'

'So what you're telling me is that not only did the skinwalker get away, but now it's stronger for having killed Kirby.'

He shrugged. 'I doubt the werewolf represented much gain, relative to what it already possessed. Your talents, or mine, are orders of magnitude greater.'

I took up a rubber hose and bound it around Morgan's upper arm. I waited for the veins just below the bend of his elbow to pop up. 'Seems like an awfully unlikely chance encounter.'

Morgan shook his head. 'Skinwalkers can only dwell on tribal lands in the American Southwest. It wasn't as if whoever is framing me would know that I was going to escape and flee to Tucson.'

'Point,' I said, slipping the needle into his arm. 'Who would wanna go there in the summer, anyway?' I thought about it. 'The skinwalker's got to go back to his home territory, though?'

Morgan nodded. 'The longer he's away, the more power it costs him.'

'How long can he stay here?' I asked.

He winced as I missed the vein and had to try again. 'More than long enough.'

'How do we kill it?' I frowned as I missed the vein again.

'Give me that,' Morgan muttered. He took the needle and inserted it himself, smoothly, and got it on the first try.

I guess you learn a few things over a dozen decades.

'We probably don't,' he said. 'The true skinwalkers, the naagloshii, are millennia old. Tangling with them is a fool's game. We avoid it.'

I taped down the needle and hooked up the catheter. 'Pretend for a minute that it isn't going to cooperate with that plan.'

Morgan grunted and scratched at his chin with his other hand. 'There are some native magics that can cripple or destroy it. A true shaman of the blood could perform an enemy ghost way and drive it out. Without those our only recourse is to hit it with a lot of raw power – and it isn't likely to stand still and cooperate with that plan, either.'

'It's a tough target,' I admitted. 'It knows magic, and how to defend against it.'

'Yes,' Morgan said. He watched me pick a preloaded syringe of antibiotics from the cooler. 'And its abilities are more than the equal of both of us put together.'

'Jinkies,' I said. I primed the syringe and pushed the antibiotics into the IV line. Then I got the codeine and a cup of water, offering Morgan both. He downed the pills, laid his head back wearily, and closed his eyes.

'I Saw one once, too,' he said.

I started cleaning up. I didn't say anything.

'They aren't invulnerable. They can be killed.'

I tossed wrappers into the trash can and restored equipment to the medical kit. I grimaced at the bloodied rug that still lay beneath Morgan. I'd have to get that out from under him soon. I turned to leave, but stopped in the doorway.

'How'd you do it?' I asked, without looking behind me.

It took him a moment to answer. I thought he'd passed out again.

'It was the fifties,' he said. 'Started in New Mexico. It followed me to Nevada. I lured it onto a government testing site, and stepped across into the Nevernever just before the bomb went off.'

I blinked and looked over my shoulder at him. 'You *nuked* it?'

He opened one eye and smiled.

It was sort of creepy.

'Stars and stones . . . that's . . .' I had to call a spade a spade. 'Kind of cool.'

'Gets me to sleep at night,' he mumbled. He closed his eye again, sighed, and let his head sag a little to one side.

I watched over his sleep for a moment, and then closed the door.

I was pretty tired, myself. But like the man said:

'I have promises to keep,' I sighed to myself.

I got on the phone, and started calling my contacts on the Paranet.

The Paranet was an organization I'd helped found a couple of years before. It's essentially a union whose members cooperate in order to protect themselves from paranormal threats. Most of the Paranet consisted of practitioners with marginal talents, of which there were plenty. A practitioner had to be in the top percentile before the White Council would even consider recognizing him, and those who couldn't cut it basically got left out in the cold. As a result, they were vulnerable to any number of supernatural predators.

Which I think sucks.

So an old friend named Elaine Mallory and I had taken a dead woman's money and begun making contact with the marginal folks in city after city. We'd encouraged them to get together to share information, to have someone they could call for help. If things started going bad, a distress call could be sent up the Paranet, and then I or one of the other Wardens in the US could charge in. We also gave seminars on how to recognize magical threats, as well as teaching methods of basic self-defense for when the capes couldn't show up to save the day.

It had been going pretty well. We already had new chapters opening up in Mexico and Canada, and Europe wouldn't be far behind.

So I started calling up my contacts in those various

cities, asking if they'd heard of anything odd happening. I couldn't afford to get any more specific than that, but as it turned out, I didn't need to. Of the first dozen calls, folks in four cities had noted an upswing in Warden activity, reporting that they were all appearing in pairs. Only two of the next thirty towns had similar reports, but it was enough to give me a good idea of what was going on – a quiet manhunt.

But I just had to wonder. Of all the places the Wardens could choose to hunt for Morgan, why would they pick Poughkeepsie? Why Omaha?

The words 'wild-goose chase' sprang to mind. Whatever Morgan was doing to mask his presence from their tracking spells, it had them chasing their tails all over the place.

At least I accomplished one positive thing. Establishing rumors of Wardens on the move meant that I had a good and non-suspicion-arousing motivation to start asking questions of my own.

So next, I started calling the Wardens I was on good terms with. Three of them worked for me, technically speaking, in several cities in the Eastern and Midwestern United States. I'm not a very good boss. I mostly just let them decide how to do their job and try to lend a hand when they ask me for help. I had to leave messages for two, but Bill Meyers in Dallas answered on the second ring.

'Howdy,' Meyers said.

I'm serious. He actually answered the phone that way.

'Bill, it's Dresden.'

'Harry,' he said politely. Bill was always polite with me. He saw me do something scary once. 'Speak of the devil and he appears.'

'Is that why my nose was itching?' I asked.

'Likely,' Bill drawled. 'I was gonna give you a call in the morning.'

'Yeah? What's up?'

'Rumors,' Bill said. 'I spotted two Wardens coming out of the local entrance to the Ways, but when I asked them what was up, they stonewalled me. I figured you might know what was going on.'

'Darn,' I said. 'I called to ask *you*.'

He snorted. 'Well, we're a fine bunch of wise men, aren't we?'

'As far as the Council is concerned, the US Wardens are a bunch of mushrooms.'

'Eh?'

'Kept in the dark and fed on bullshit.'

'I hear that,' Meyers said. 'What do you want me to do?'

'Keep an ear to the ground,' I told him. 'Captain Luccio will tell us sooner or later. I'll call you as soon as I learn anything. You do the same.'

'Gotcha,' he said.

We hung up, and I frowned at the phone for a moment.

The Council hadn't talked to me about Morgan. They hadn't talked to any of the Wardens in my command about him, either.

I looked up at Mister and said, 'It's almost like they want to keep me in the dark. Like maybe someone thinks I might be involved, somehow.'

Which made sense. The Merlin wasn't going to be asking me to Christmas dinner anytime soon. He didn't trust me. He might have given the order to keep me fenced out. That wouldn't hit me as a surprise.

But if that was true, then it meant that Anastasia Luccio,

captain of the Wardens, was going along with it. She and I had been dating for a while, now. Granted, she had a couple of centuries on me, but a run-in with a body-switching psychopath several years before had trapped her in the body of a coed, and she didn't look a day over twenty-five. We got along well. We made each other laugh. And we occasionally had wild-monkey sex to our mutual, intense satisfaction.

I would never have figured Anastasia to play a game like that with me.

I got on the phone to Ramirez in LA, the other regional commander in the United States, to see if he'd heard anything, but just got his answering service.

At this rate, I was going to have to go to the spirit world for answers – and that was risky in more ways than one, not the least of which was the very real possibility that I might get eaten by the same entity I called up to question.

But I was running a little low on options.

I pulled back the rug that lay over the trapdoor leading down to my lab, and was about to go down and prepare my summoning circle when the phone rang.

'I'm meeting Justine in half an hour,' my brother told me.

'Okay,' I said. 'Come get me.'

8

Chicago's club scene is wide and diverse. You want to listen to extemporaneous jazz? We got that. You want a traditional Irish pub? A Turkish-style coffeehouse? Belly dancers? Japanese garden party? Swing dancing? Ballroom dancing? Beat poetry? You're covered.

You don't have to look much harder to find all sorts of other clubs – the kind that Ma and Pa Tourist don't take the kids to. Gay clubs, lesbian clubs, strip clubs, leather clubs, and more subtle flavors within the genre.

And then there's Zero.

I stood with Thomas outside what looked like a fire-exit door at the bottom of a stairway, a story below street level in the side of a downtown building. A red neon oval had been installed on the door, and it glowed with a sullen, lurid heat. The thump of a bass beat vibrated almost subaudibly up through the ground.

'Is this what I think it is?' I asked him.

Thomas, now dressed in a tight-fitting white T-shirt and old blue jeans, glanced at me and arched one dark eyebrow. 'Depends on if you think it's Zero or not.'

Zero's one of those clubs that most people only hear rumors about. It moves around the city from time to time, but it's always as exclusive as a popular nightspot in a metropolis can possibly be. I've been a PI in Chicago for better than a decade. I'd heard of Zero, but that was it.

It was where the rich and beautiful (and rich) people of Chicago went to indulge themselves.

'You know somebody here?' I asked. 'Because they aren't going to let us—'

Thomas popped a key into the lock, turned it, and opened the door for me.

'In,' I finished. A wash of heat and smoke heavy with legally questionable substances pushed gently against my chest. I could hear the *whump-whump-whump* of techno dance music somewhere behind the red-lit smoke.

'It's a family business,' Thomas explained. He put the keys back in his pocket, an odd expression on his face. 'I met Justine at Zero.'

'There any more of the other side of the family in there?' I asked him. White Court vampires were the least physically dangerous of any of the various vamps running around – and the most scary. Creatures of seduction, they fed upon the emotions and life energy of those they preyed upon. Their victims became addicted to the act, and would willingly offer themselves up over and over, until eventually there was nothing left to give. The poor suckers in thrall to a White Court vampire were virtually slaves. Tangling with them in any sense of the word was a bad idea.

Thomas shook his head. 'I doubt it. Or Justine wouldn't have chosen to meet us here.'

Unless she'd been forced to do so, I thought to myself. I didn't say anything. I like to stay cozy with my paranoia, not pass her around to my friends and family.

'After you,' Thomas said, and then he calmly stripped his shirt off.

I eyed him.

'The club has an image they strive to maintain,' he said. He might have been just a little bit smug, the bastard. His abs look like they were added in with CGI. My abs just look like I can't afford to feed myself very well.

'Oh,' I said. 'Do I need to take my shirt off, too?'

'You're wearing a black leather coat. That's wardrobe enough.'

'Small favors,' I muttered. Then I went through the door.

We walked down a hallway that got darker, louder, and more illicitly aromatic as we went. It ended at a black curtain, and I pushed it aside to reveal a few more feet of hallway, a door, and two politely formidable-looking men in dark suits standing in front of it.

One of them lifted a hand and told me, 'I'm sorry, sir, but this is a private—'

Thomas stepped up next to me and fixed the man with a steady grey gaze.

He lowered his hand, and when he spoke, it sounded rough, as if his mouth had gone dry. 'Excuse me, sir. I didn't realize he was with you.'

Thomas kept staring.

The bouncer turned to the door, unlocked it with a key of its own, and opened the door. 'Will you be in need of a table, sir? Drinks?'

Thomas's unblinking gaze finally shifted from the guard, as if the man had somehow vanished as a matter of any consequence. My brother walked by him without saying anything at all.

The bouncer gave me a weak smile and said, 'Sorry about that, sir. Enjoy your evening at Zero, sir.'

'Thanks,' I said, and followed my brother into a scene

that split the difference between a Dionysian bacchanal and a Fellini flick.

There was no white light inside Zero. Most of it was red, punctuated in places with pools of blue and plenty of black lights scattered everywhere so that even where shadows were thickest, some colors jumped out in disquieting luminescence. Cigarette smoke hung in a pall over the large room, a distance-distorting haze under the black lights.

We had entered on a kind of balcony that overlooked the dance floor below. Music pounded, the bass beat so loud that I could feel it in my lower stomach. Lights flashed and swayed in synchronicity. The floor was crowded with sweating, moving bodies dressed in a broad spectrum of clothing, from full leather coverings including a whole-head hood, at one extreme, to one girl clad in a few strips of electrical tape on the other. There was a bar down by the dance floor, and tables scattered around its outskirts under a thirty-foot-high ceiling. A few cages hung about eight feet over the dance floor, each containing a young man or woman in provocative clothing.

Stairways and catwalks led up to about a dozen platforms that thrust out from the walls, where patrons could sit and overlook the scene below while gaining a measure of privacy for themselves. Most of the platforms were furnished with couches and chaise longues rather than tables and chairs. There were more exotic bits of furniture up on the platforms, as well: the giant X shape of a St Andrew's cross, which was currently supporting the bound form of a young man, his wrists and ankles secured to the cross, his face to the wood, his hair falling down over his naked back. Another platform had a shiny brass pole in its center, and a pair of girls danced around it, in the middle of a circle of men and women sprawled over the couches and loungers.

Everywhere I looked, people were doing things that would have gotten them arrested anywhere else. Couples, threesomes, foursomes, and nineteensomes were fully engaged in sexual activity on some of the private platforms. From where I stood, I could see two different tables where lines of white powder waited to be inhaled. A syringe disposal was on the wall next to every trash can, marked with a bright biohazard symbol. People were being beaten with whips and riding crops. People were bound up with elaborate arrangements of ropes, as well as with more prosaic handcuffs. Piercings and tattoos were everywhere. Screams and cries occasionally found their way through the music, agony, ecstasy, joy, or rage all indistinguishable from one another.

The lights flashed constantly, changing and shifting, and every beat of the music created a dozen new frozen montages of sybaritic abandon.

The music, the light, the sweat, the smoke, the booze, the drugs – it all combined into a wet, desperate miasma that was full of needs that could never be sated.

That's why the place was called Zero, I realized. Zero limits. Zero inhibitions. Zero restraint. It was a place of perfect, focused abandon, of indulgence, and it was intriguing and hideous, nauseating and viscerally *hungry*.

Zero fulfillment.

I felt a shudder run through me. This was the world as created by the White Court. This is what they would make of it, if they were given the chance. Planet Zero.

I glanced aside at Thomas and saw him staring around

the club. His eyes had changed hue, from their usual grey to a paler, brighter silver, actual flecks of metallic color in his eyes. His eyes tracked over a pair of young women who were passing by us, dressed in black lingerie under long leather coats, and holding hands with their fingers intertwined. The women both turned their eyes toward him as if they'd heard him call their names, and stared for a second, their steps slowing and faltering.

Thomas dragged his eyes away, and let that inhuman stillness fill him again. The women blinked a few times, then continued on their way, their expressions vaguely puzzled.

'Hey,' I yelled through the music. 'You all right?'

He nodded once, and then twitched his chin up at the highest platform in the building, on the far side of the dance floor. 'Up there.'

I nodded, and Thomas took the lead. We negotiated the maze of catwalks and stairs. They had been purposely designed to be just barely too narrow for two people to pass one another without touching, as I found out when Thomas and I passed a girl in leather shorts and a bustier, both of which strained to match themselves to a body whose curves were made ripe and inviting by the red light's primitive rhythm. She slid by Thomas, her eyes locked on his chest, as if she was about to lean over and bite him.

He ignored her, but then the girl reached me – and I take up more room than Thomas. I felt her hip brush me, and she arched her back as I stepped past her, turned sideways. Her breasts pressed against my sternum, pliant, resilient warmth, and her lips were parted, her eyes too bright. Her hand brushed over my thigh, a touch that could have been accidental but wasn't, and my body was suddenly demanding that I stop for a moment and see where this would lead.

You can't trust your body when it tells you stuff like that. It doesn't understand about things like actual affection, interaction, pregnancy, STDs. It just *wants*. I tried not to pay any attention to it – but there were other people on the catwalks, and evidently there was no such thing as a less than gorgeous woman inside Zero's walls. Most of them seemed perfectly happy to make sure I knew it as they went by.

So did some of the men, for that matter, but that was less of an issue, as far as my focus went.

It probably didn't help matters that we were walking by things that I hadn't ever seen before, not even in movies. There was this one girl doing a thing with her tongue and an ice cube that—

Look, just trust me on this one. It was distracting as hell.

Thomas was walking faster as we approached the stairway leading up to the highest platform, and he took the last steps three at a time. I followed along behind him, scanning around me steadily, trying to be on the lookout for potential bad guys. This had the side effect of me getting to ogle more pretty girls than I'd ever seen in one place at one time. But it was professional ogling. One of them could have been concealing—

Well, actually, I was sort of shocked at what one of them *was* concealing.

I made it up the last stairway just in time to see Thomas throw himself into a woman's arms.

Justine wasn't particularly tall, for a girl, or at least she hadn't been before she'd put on the boots with the five-inch heels. She looked like I remembered her last – a gorgeous face that still fell into the girl-next-door category, with a heart-melting smile. Her hair was silver-white, and was being held in a tight bun up high on the back of her head with a pair of white chopsticks.

Of course, the last time I'd seen her, she hadn't been dressed in a formfitting white rubber cat suit that included gloves over her fingers. It emphasized absolutely everything and did it well.

Thomas fell to his knees and wrapped his arms around her waist, drawing her to him. She twined her rubber-covered arms around his neck and clung tightly. Both of them closed their eyes, and just stood there for a long minute, embracing without moving, just holding each other close.

It was an alien act in that place.

I turned away, leaned on the platform's safety railing, and stared down at the club, trying to give my brother and the woman he loved a moment of privacy. Justine hadn't worn the cover-everything suit for the sake of fashion. The touch of honest love, real and selfless love, was anathema to the White Court. Thomas had told me about White Court vampires who had been badly burned by the touch of some wedding rings, or the brush of a sweetheart's rose. But most dangerous of all to them was the touch of someone who was loved and who loved in return.

I'd seen Thomas give himself a second-degree burn on his lips and mouth the last time he'd kissed Justine.

They hadn't been together since the night she had laid down her life to save his, offering herself up to his hunger so that he could survive the evening. Thomas, in turn, had refused to devour her, denying his own darker nature. It had nearly killed her anyway, turning her hair white literally overnight. It had taken her years to recover her mind, after a long-term addiction to being fed upon by an incubus, but she'd done it. She was currently an assistant to Thomas's older sister, Lara, and positioned to find out all kinds of juicy details about the White Court. Being protected by love meant that the vamps couldn't feed on Justine, which Lara thought ideal in a personal assistant.

It also meant that my brother couldn't touch the woman he loved. If he'd been like most of the White Court, only interested in feeding his hunger, he'd have been able to have her all he wanted. Instead . . .

Sometimes irony is a lot like a big old kick in the balls.

I stared down at the dance floor for a while, not so much ogling as simply taking in the light and motion as a whole, until I saw them part in my peripheral vision. Then I turned and walked over to join them, as Justine gestured for us to sit on a pair of couches that had been moved to face each other.

Thomas sat down in a corner of the couch, and Justine pressed up close against him, careful to keep what little of her was exposed from touching his skin. I settled down across from them, leaning my elbows forward onto my knees.

I smiled at Justine and nodded to her. The floor and half-wall railing of the platform must have been made from sound-absorbing material. The roar of the club was much reduced up here. 'Justine. You look like the Michelin Man's wet dream.'

She laughed, pink touching her cheeks. 'Well. The club has a look we try to maintain. How are you, Harry?'

'Half buzzed on this smoke, and floundering,' I said. 'Thomas told me you had some information.'

Justine nodded seriously, and picked up a manila file folder from the couch beside her. 'Word is out about a hunt for a renegade Warden,' she said. 'There weren't a lot of details, but I was able to turn up this.'

She slid the folder over to me, and I opened it. The first page was a printout of a Web site of some kind. 'What the hell is Craigslist?'

'It's a site on the Internet,' Justine said. 'It's sort of like a giant classified ads section, only you can get to it from anywhere in the world. People use it to advertise goods they want to buy or sell.'

'Goods,' Thomas put in, 'and services. Help wanted, with veiled language for the less-legal things. A lot of shady deals happen there because it's relatively easy to do so anonymously. Escorts, mercenaries, you name it.'

There was an ad printed on it:

WANTED FOR PERMANENT POSITION,
DONALD MORGAN, 5MIL FINDER'S FEE,
CONSIDERATIONS.
lostwardenfound@yahoo.com.

'Hell's bells,' I cursed quietly.

I passed the page to Thomas. 'A wanted poster,' he said.

I nodded. 'And not dead or alive, either. They just want him dead.'

Every supernatural hitter on the bloody planet was going to be coming after Morgan. Not so much for the money, probably, as for the favors that the ad promised. They carry a hell of a lot more weight than cash in the world of the weird. The five million was just there to provide scope, a sense of scale for the favors that would come with it.

'Every button man in the world and his brother,' I muttered. 'This just keeps getting better and better.'

'Why would your people do that?' Justine asked.

'They wouldn't,' I said.

Thomas frowned. 'How do you know?'

'Because the Council solves things in-house,' I said. Which was true. They had their own assassin for jobs like this, when he was needed. I grimaced. 'Besides, even if they did put out a hit, they sure as hell wouldn't use the Internet to do it.'

Thomas nodded, fingers idly stroking Justine's rubberized shoulder. 'Then who did?'

'Who indeed,' I said. 'Is there any way to find out who put this here? Or who this e-mail thingy belongs to?'

Justine shook her head. 'Not with any confidence.'

'Then we'll have to make contact ourselves,' Thomas said. 'Maybe we can draw them out.'

I scratched my chin, thinking. 'If they've got a lick of sense, they won't show themselves to anyone who isn't established in the field. But it's worth a try.' I sighed. 'I've got to move him.'

'Why?' Thomas asked.

I tapped the page with my finger. 'When the hard cases start coming out of the woodwork, things are going to get messy, and old people live upstairs from me.'

Thomas frowned and nodded. 'Where?'

I began to answer when the tempo of the beat suddenly changed below, and a wave of frenzied cries rolled up, deafening despite any soundproofing. A second after that, an odd frisson crawled across my nerves, and I felt my heart pound a little more quickly, and the earlier demands my body had been making returned in a rush.

Across from me, Justine shivered and her eyes slid almost completely closed. She took a deep breath, and her nipples tightened against the rubber cat suit. Her hips shifted in a small, unconscious movement, brushing against Thomas's thigh.

My brother's eyes flashed from light grey to cold, hard silver for a second, before he narrowed them and rose, carefully disentangling himself from Justine. He turned to face the dance floor, his shoulders tense.

I followed his example. 'What is it?'

'Trouble,' he said, and looked over his shoulder at me. 'Family's come to visit.'

9

Thomas stared hard at the floor below, and then nodded once, as if in recognition. 'Harry,' he said in a steady, quiet voice, 'stay out of this.'

'Stay out of what?' I asked.

He turned to look at me, his expression inhumanly remote. 'It's family business. It won't involve you. The House has given orders that wizards are not to be molested without clearance. If you don't get involved, I won't have to worry about you.'

'What?' I said. 'Thomas . . .'

'Just let me handle it,' he said, his voice hard.

I was going to answer him when the vampire entered the room.

It was one of those sensations you have trouble remembering afterward – like the last moments of the dream you have just before waking. You know that once you're outside the dream, you're going to forget – and you can't believe you could lose something so significant, so undeniably tangible.

I turned to look the second she entered – just like everyone else in the room.

She wore white, of course. A white dress, a simple shift made of some kind of glistening silken fabric, which fell to the top of her thighs. She was at least six feet tall, more so in the partially transparent shoes she wore. Her skin was pale and perfect, her hair dark and shining with highlights that changed color in the beat of the strobe lighting of the club. Her face was perfect beauty that remained unmarred by the obvious arrogance in her expression, and her body could have been used on recruiting posters for wet dreams.

She descended to the dance floor and crossed to the stairways and catwalks with a predator's easy motion, each stride making her hips roll and shoulders sway, somehow in time to the music, and far more graceful than the efforts of the sweating dancers, more sensual than the frantic lovers.

At the foot of the first stairway, she came to a young man in leather pants and the scraps of a shirt that looked like it had been torn to pieces by ardent admirers. Without hesitation, she pushed him up against the railing beside the stairway and pressed her body up against his.

She twined her arms slowly around his neck and kissed him. A kiss, and that was all – but apparently no one told the young man that. From his reaction, you'd have thought that she'd mounted him then and there. Her lips were sealed to his, their tongues lashing one another, for maybe a minute. Then she turned away with that same precise grace, and began walking up the stairs – slowly, so that every shift and change of muscle in her perfectly formed legs danced in mesmerizing ripples beneath her soft white skin.

The young man simply melted onto the floor, muscles twitching, his eyes closed. I didn't think he was actually aware that she had left.

The woman had every eye in the building and she knew it.

It wasn't an enormous event, the way she took the

attention of everyone there. It wasn't a single large simultaneous, significant motion when everyone turned to look. There was no sudden silence, no deepening stillness. That would have been bad enough.

Her influence was a lot scarier than that.

It was simply a *fact*, like gravity, that everyone's attention should be directed to her. Every person there, men and women alike, glanced up, or tracked her movement obliquely with their eyes, or paused for half a beat in their . . . conversations. For most of them it was an entirely unconscious act. They had no idea that their minds had already been ensnared.

And as I realized that, I realized that mine was in danger, too.

It was a real effort to close my eyes and remind myself of where I was. I could feel the succubus's aura, like the silken brush of cobwebs against my eyelashes, something tingling and delicious and fluttering that swayed up my legs and through my groin on its way to my brain.

It was only a promise, a whisper to the flesh – but it was a *good* whisper. I had to make an effort to wall it away from my thoughts, until suddenly reason reasserted itself, and that fluttering haze froze and cracked and blew away under the chill wind of sensible fear.

When I opened my eyes, the woman was stalking toward us along that last catwalk, slithering nearer in her thin white dress as she mounted the last few stairs. She paused there, letting us look at her, knowing what effect she was having. Even on guard against it, I could feel the subtle sweetness of her presence calling out to me, whispering that I should relax and let my eyes run over her for a while.

She turned her cornflower blue eyes to me for a moment,

and her mouth parted, spreading slowly into a smile that shrunk my pants about three sizes in as many seconds.

'Cousin Thomas,' she purred. 'Still noble and starving, I see.'

'Madeline,' Thomas replied, a small smile showing white, perfect teeth. 'Still undisciplined and blatant, I see.'

Madeline Raith's mouth and eyes reacted in completely different ways to my half brother's remark. Her smile widened into a beauty-pageant expression, wide and immobile, but her eyes narrowed and went completely white, the pale blue vanishing from her irises. She looked from Thomas to Justine.

'Lara's little pet mortal,' Madeline said. 'I wondered where you were running off to. Now I find you meeting with your old flame and . . .' Her eyes slid to me. 'The enemy.'

'Don't be ridiculous,' Justine replied. Though her voice was calm, her cheeks were bright pink, her eyes dilated. 'I came to go over the books, the way I do every week.'

'But this time you wore perfume,' Madeline said. 'And a rather provocative ensemble, not that you don't do it justice, darling. I find it' – her tongue touched her upper lip – 'interesting.'

'Madeline,' Thomas said, in a tone of exaggerated patience, 'please go away.'

'I have every right to be here,' she murmured. It didn't seem right that she should be able to keep her voice so maddeningly soft and sensual over the beat of the club's music. She turned to me and took a few steps my way, with her full attention on me.

I suddenly felt like a teenager – a little bit afraid, a whole lot excited, and filled with so many hormones demanding so many inexplicable things that I nearly lost the ability to focus my eyes.

She stopped just out of the reach of my hand. 'Don't mind my cousin's horrible manners. The infamous Harry Dresden hardly needs an introduction.' She looked me up and down and twined a finger through a tendril of dark hair. 'How could I come to Chicago so many times without meeting you?'

'But I've seen you,' I said. My voice was a little rough, but it worked.

'Oh?' she asked, the sexy smile widening. 'Are you the sort who likes to watch, Harry?'

'You betcha,' I said. 'And that time, I was watching *Who Framed Roger Rabbit?*'

Her smile faltered a fraction.

'You *are* Jessica Rabbit, right?' I asked. 'All slinky and overblown and obvious?'

The smile vanished.

'Because I know I've seen you somewhere, and gosh, I'll be embarrassed if it turns out that you were the evil princess from *Buck Rogers* instead.'

'What?' she said. 'Buck what?'

I gave her my best forced smile. 'Hey, don't get me wrong. You do that ensemble justice. But you're trying too hard.' I leaned a little closer and fake-whispered, 'Lara does more for me just sitting in a chair than you did with your whole entrance.'

Madeline Raith became as still and cold as a statue of a furious goddess, and the air temperature around us dropped several degrees.

I suddenly sensed Thomas's presence beside me, and found my brother had leaned back against the railing on his elbows, his hands loose and relaxed. He was standing just a tiny bit closer to Madeline than I was.

'Madeline,' he said in the precise same tone he'd used a moment before, 'go away before I beat you to death with my bare hands.'

Madeline jerked her head back as if Thomas had slapped her. 'What?'

'You heard me,' he said calmly. 'It isn't quite cricket as family squabbles go, I know, but I'm tired, I don't give a fuck what you or anyone else in the House thinks of me, and I don't respect you enough to play games with you, even if I was in the mood.'

'How *dare* you?' Madeline snarled. 'How *dare* you threaten me? Lara will have the skin flayed from your body for this.'

'Oh?' Thomas gave her a wintry smile. 'After what you projected at the wizard, he'd be well within his rights to burn you right down to your overpriced shoes.'

'I never—'

'And despite the orders handed down from the King,' Thomas said, shaking his head. 'Lara's getting tired of cleaning up after you, Mad. She'd probably buy me a new set of steak knives if I found a way to make her life a bit less trying.'

Madeline laughed. It reminded me of glass breaking. 'And do you think she loves you any better, cousin mine? You refuse to appear with the House at meetings of the Court, and spend your time among the kine, grooming them and bringing shame upon your family. At least tell me you are planning to take the beasts to some sort of auction.'

'You aren't capable of understanding why I do what I do,' Thomas said.

'Who would *want* to?' she retorted. 'You're as much a degenerate as any of those fools in Skavis and Malvora.'

Thomas's mouth ticked at the corner, but that was all the reaction he gave her. 'Go away, Madeline. Last warning.'

'Two members of the oldest bloodlines in Raith murdering each other?' Madeline said, sneering. 'The White King could not tolerate such a divisive act and you know it.' She turned away from Thomas and walked toward Justine. 'You're bluffing,' she said over her shoulder. 'Besides. We haven't heard from our little pink rose yet.'

Her voice sank to a throaty purr, and Justine quivered in place, seemingly unable to move as Madeline approached.

'Pretty Justine.' Madeline put a hand on Justine's shoulder and slid a single fingertip down the slope of one breast. 'I don't generally enjoy does as much as some, darling, but even I find the thought of taking you delicious.'

'You c-can't touch me,' Justine stammered. She was breathing faster.

'Not yet,' Madeline said. 'But there's not enough will left in your pretty little head to control yourself for long.' Madeline stepped closer, sliding her hand along Justine's waist. 'Some night, perhaps I'll come to you with some beautiful young buck and whisper pretty things to you until you're mad to be taken. And after he has made use of you, little doe, I'll take you in one big bite.' She licked her lips. 'I'll take you whole and make you scream how much you love it as it happen—'

Thomas broke a chair over Madeline's head.

It was particularly impressive, given that all the chairs on the balcony were made of metal.

It happened fast, during an eye blink. One instant he

was standing beside me, tightening with anger, and the next there were popped rivets zinging everywhere and Madeline had been crushed to the floor of the balcony.

The air went cold. Thomas dropped the ruined chair. Madeline bounced up from the floor and threw a blow at Thomas's jaw. He hunched and twisted, a boxer's defense, and took it on the shoulder with a grunt of pain. Then he seized her ankle and slammed her in a half circle, smashing a 36-24-36 dent into the drywall.

Madeline cried out and her limbs went loose. Thomas swung her in another arc that brought her crashing down onto the low coffee table between the couches. She lay there and let out a single choked gasp, her eyes unfocused. Without pausing, my brother snatched both chopsticks from Justine's hair, letting the white-silver locks tumble down her back.

Then, in two sharp, swift motions, he slammed the chopsticks through Madeline's wrists and into the table beneath them, pinning her like a butterfly to a card.

'You're right of course,' he snarled. 'Lara couldn't ignore one member of the family murdering another. It would make the King look weak.' His hand closed over Madeline's face, and he pulled her head up toward his, making her arms strain at a painful angle. 'I was bluffing.'

He shoved her back down against the table. 'Of course,' he said, 'you're family. Families don't murder one another.' He looked up at Justine and said, 'They share.'

She met his eyes. A very small, very hard smile graced Justine's features.

'You wanted to taste her,' Thomas said, his fingers twining with Justine's rubber-clad ones. 'Well, Madeline. Be my guest.'

Justine leaned over and kissed Madeline Raith's forehead, her silken silver hair falling to veil them both.

The vampire screamed.

The sound was lost in the pounding rhythm and flashing lights.

Justine lifted her head a few seconds later, and swept her hair slowly down the length of Madeline's form. The vampire writhed and screamed again, while Thomas held her pinned to the table. Wherever Justine's hair glided over exposed fleshed, the skin sizzled and burned, blackening in some places, forming blisters and welts in others. She left a trail of ruin down one of Madeline's legs and then rose together with Thomas, two bodies making one motion.

Madeline Raith's face was a ruin of burn marks, and the imprint of Justine's soft mouth was a perfect black brand on pale flesh in the center of her forehead. She lay on the table, still pinned by the chopsticks, and quivered in jerking little motions, gasping and breathless with the pain.

Thomas and Justine walked, hand in hand, to the stairs leading down from our platform. I followed them.

They passed beneath an air-conditioning outlet, and a few strands of Justine's hair blew against Thomas's naked arm and chest. Small bright lines of scarlet appeared. Thomas didn't flinch.

I walked over to them and passed Justine a pair of pencils, taken from my coat pocket. She took them with a nod of thanks, and quickly bound up her hair again. I looked over my shoulder as she did.

Madeline Raith lay helpless and gasping – but her white eyes burned with hate.

Thomas took his T-shirt from where he'd stowed it on a belt loop, and put it back on. Then he slid his arms around Justine again and pulled her against his chest, holding her close.

'Will you be all right?' he asked.

Justine nodded, her eyes closed. 'I'll call the House. Lara will send someone for her.'

'You leave her there and it's going to make trouble,' I told him.

He shrugged. 'I couldn't get away with killing her. But our House has rather stern views on poaching.' Something hard and hot entered his eyes. 'Justine is mine. Madeline had to be shown that. She deserved it.'

Justine clung a little bit tighter to him. He returned the gesture.

We all started down the stairs together, and I was glad to be leaving Zero.

'Still,' I said. 'Seeing her like that, I feel like maybe somebody went too far. I feel a little bit bad for her.'

Thomas arched an eyebrow and glanced back at me. 'You do?'

'Yeah,' I said. I pursed my lips thoughtfully. 'Maybe I shouldn't have said that Jessica Rabbit thing.'

10

The hot summer night outside Zero felt ten degrees cooler and a million times cleaner than what we'd left behind us. Thomas turned sharply to the right and walked until he'd found a spot of shadow between streetlights, and leaned one shoulder against the wall of the building. He bowed his head, and stayed that way for a minute, then two.

I waited. I didn't need to ask my brother what was wrong. The display of strength and power he'd used on Madeline had cost him energy – energy that other vampires gained by feeding on victims, as Madeline had done to that poor sap inside. He wasn't upset by what had happened in Zero. He was hungry.

Thomas's struggle against his own hunger was complicated, difficult, and maybe impossible to sustain. That never stopped him from trying, though. The rest of the Raith family thought he was insane.

But I got it.

He walked back over to me a minute later, his cool features distant and untouchable as Antarctic mountains.

He fell into pace beside me as we began walking down the street toward the lot where he'd parked his car.

'Ask you a question?' I said.

He nodded.

'The White Court only get burned when they try to feed on someone touched by true love, right?'

'It isn't as simple as that,' Thomas said quietly. 'It's got to do with how much control the hunger has over you when you touch.'

I grunted. 'But when they feed, the hunger's in control.'

Thomas nodded slowly.

'So why'd Madeline try to feed on Justine? She had to know it would hurt her.'

'Same reason I do,' Thomas said. 'She can't help it. It's reflex.'

I frowned. 'I don't get it.'

He was quiet long enough to make me think he wasn't going to say anything, before he finally spoke. 'Justine and I were together for years. And she . . . means a lot to me. When I'm near her, I can't think about anything else but her. And when I touch her, everything in me wants to be nearer to her.'

'Including your hunger,' I said quietly.

He nodded. 'We agree on that point, my demon and I. So I can't touch Justine without it being . . . close to the surface, I suppose you could call it.'

'And it gets burned,' I said.

He nodded. 'Madeline is the other end of the spectrum. She thinks she should get to feed on anyone she wants, anywhere, anytime. She doesn't see other people. She just sees food. Her hunger controls her completely.' He smiled a bitter little smile. 'So for her it's reflex, just like for me.'

'You're different. For her it's everyone,' I said, 'not only Justine.'

He shrugged. 'I don't care about everyone. I care about Justine.'

'You're different,' I said.

Thomas turned to face me, his expression rigid and cold. 'Shut up, Harry.'

'But—'

His voice dropped to a low snarl. 'Shut. Up.'

It was a little scary.

He stared hard at me for a while longer, then shook his head and exhaled slowly. 'I'll get the car. Wait here.'

'Sure,' I said.

He walked away on silent feet, his hands in his pockets, his head bowed. Every woman he passed, and some of the men, turned their heads to watch him go by. He ignored them.

I got a lot of looks, too, but that was because I was standing on a sidewalk near a lot of Chicago's night spots on a hot summer night wearing a long leather coat and carrying a quarterstaff carved with mystic runes. Thomas's looks had all been subtitled: *Yum*. My looks all said: *Weirdo*.

Tough to believe I was coming out ahead on that one.

While I waited, my instincts nagged me again, a hairs-on-the-back-of-my-neck certainty that someone was focused on me. My instincts had been on a streak, so I paid attention to them, quietly preparing my shield bracelet as I turned my head in a slow, casual look up and down the street. I didn't spot anybody, but my vision sort of flickered as it passed over an alley across the street. I focused on that point intently for a moment, concentrating, and was able to make out a vaguely human shape there.

Then the flicker was abruptly replaced with the form of Anastasia Luccio, who raised a hand and beckoned me.

Yikes.

I jaywalked over to her, timing my crossing in between the occasional passing car, and we took several steps back into the alley.

'Evening, Stacy,' I said.

She turned to me and, in a single motion, drew a curved saber from a sheath at her hip and produced a gun in her other hand. The tip of the blade menaced my face, and I had to jerk my head back, which put me off balance, and I wound up with my shoulders pressed up against a wall.

Anastasia arched an eyebrow, her soft mouth set in a hard line. 'I hope for your sake that you are the true Harry Dresden, only using that abomination of a nickname to make sure that I was the true Anastasia' – she emphasized the word slightly – 'Luccio.'

'Well, yes, Anastasia,' I said, being careful not to move. 'And by your reaction, I can tell that it really is you.'

She dropped the sword's point and lowered the gun. The tension faded from her body, and she put her hardware away. 'Well, of course it's me. Who else would it be?'

I shook my head. 'I've had a bad shapeshifter night.'

She arched an eyebrow. Anastasia Luccio was the captain of the Wardens of the White Council. She had a couple of centuries of experience.

'I've had those,' she said, and put a hand on my arm. 'Are you all right?'

We stepped into each other and hugged. I hadn't realized how stiffly I'd been holding myself until I exhaled and relaxed a little. She felt slender and warm and strong in my arms. 'So far I'm not dead,' I said. 'I take it you used a tracking spell to run me down – since you don't seem to be worried about whether or not I'm me.'

She lifted her face to mine and planted a soft kiss on

my mouth. 'Honestly, Harry,' she said, smiling. 'Who would pretend to be *you*?'

'Someone who wanted to be kissed in dark alleys by seductive older women, apparently.'

Her smile widened for a second, and then faded. 'I thought I was going to have to break down the door and come in after you. What were you doing in that White Court cesspit?'

I didn't think I'd done anything to cause it, but we stepped out of each other's arms. 'Looking for information,' I said quietly. 'Something's up. And someone's cut me out of the loop.'

Anastasia pressed her lips together and looked away. Her expression was closed, touched with anger. 'Yes. Orders.'

'Orders,' I said. 'From the Merlin, I guess.'

'From Ebenezar McCoy, actually.'

I grunted in surprise. McCoy had been my mentor when I was young. I respected him.

'I get it,' I said. 'He was afraid that if I heard Morgan was on the run, I'd hat up and dish out some payback.'

She glanced up at me, and then across the street at Zero. She shrugged, without quite looking me in the face. 'God knows you have enough cause to do so.'

'You agreed with him,' I said.

She looked up at me, her eyes a little wider. 'If I did, then why am I standing here?'

I frowned at her and scratched my head. 'Okay. You've got me on that one.'

'Besides,' she said. 'I was worried about you.'

'Worried?'

She nodded. 'Morgan's done something that is hiding

him from even the Senior Council's abilities. I was afraid
that he might come here.'

Poker face don't fail me now. 'That's crazy,' I said. 'Why
would he do that?'

She squared her shoulders and faced me steadily. 'Maybe
because he's innocent.'

'And?'

'There are a number of people who have sought permission from the Senior Council to investigate and interrogate
you under the presumption that you were the traitor who has
been feeding information to the Red Court.' She looked away
again. 'Morgan has been one of the most overt agitators.'

I took a deep breath. 'You're saying that Morgan knows
he isn't the traitor. And he thinks it's me.'

'And he might be moving toward you, in an attempt
to prove his own innocence or, failing that . . .'

'Kill me,' I said, quietly. 'If he's going to go down, you
think he might have decided to take out the real traitor
before he gets the axe.'

And suddenly I had to wonder if Morgan had shown
up at my door for the reasons he'd given me. Anastasia
had been Morgan's mentor, when he was an apprentice.
She'd known the man for the vast majority of his life, literally for generations.

What if her judgment of him was better than mine?

Sure, Morgan wasn't in any shape to kill me personally –
but he wouldn't need to. All he had to do is call the Wardens
and tell them where he was. A lot of people in the Council
didn't like me much. I'd go down with Morgan, for giving
aid and comfort to a traitor.

I suddenly felt naive and vulnerable and maybe a little
stupid.

'He was already in custody,' I said. 'How did he get away?'

Luccio smiled faintly. 'We aren't sure. He thought of something we didn't. And he put three Wardens in the hospital when he left.'

'But you don't think he's guilty.'

'I . . .' She frowned for a moment and then said, 'I refuse to let fear turn me against a man I know and trust. But it doesn't matter what I think. There's enough evidence to kill him.'

'What evidence?' I asked.

'Other than finding him standing over LaFortier's corpse with a literal bloody knife in his hand?'

'Yeah,' I said. 'Other than that.'

She raked her fingers back through her curly hair. 'The information the Red Court has obtained was exclusive to a very small pool of suspects, of which he was one. We have telephone records of him in frequent contact with a known operative of the Red Court. We also tracked down an offshore account belonging to him, in which several million dollars had recently been deposited.'

I snorted derisively. 'Yeah, that's him. Morgan the mercenary, nothing but dollar signs in his eyes.'

'I know,' she said. 'That's what I mean about fear clouding people's judgment. We all know that the Red Court is going to come after us again. We know that if we don't eliminate the traitor, their first blow could be fatal. The Merlin is desperate.'

'Join the club,' I muttered. I rubbed at my eyes and sighed.

She touched my arm again. 'I thought you had a right to know,' she said. 'I'm sorry I wasn't able to get here sooner.'

I covered her hand with mine and pressed gently. 'Yeah,' I said. 'Thanks.'

'You look awful.'

'You sweet talker, you.'

She lifted her hand to touch my face. 'I've got a few hours before I need to be back on duty. I was thinking a bottle of wine and a massage might be in order.'

I only barely kept from groaning in pleasure at the very thought of one of Anastasia's massages. What she didn't know about inflicting merciless pleasure on a man's aching body hadn't been invented. But I sure as hell couldn't have her back over to the apartment. If she found out about Morgan, and if he truly intended to betray me, it would be frighteningly easy for her head to wind up on the floor next to Morgan's and mine.

'I can't,' I told her. 'I've got to go to the hospital.'

She frowned. 'What happened?'

'A skinwalker picked up my trail earlier tonight, when I was at Billy Borden's place. Kirby's dead. Andi's in the hospital.'

She sucked in a breath, wincing in empathy. '*Dio*, Harry. I'm so sorry.'

I shrugged. I watched my vision blur, and realized that I wasn't only making an excuse to keep her away from my place. Kirby and I hadn't been blood brothers or anything – but he was a friend, a regular part of my life. Emphasis on the *was*.

'Is there anything I can do?' she asked.

I shook my head. Then I said, 'Actually, yeah.'

'Very well.'

'Find out whatever you can about skinwalkers. I'm going to kill this one.'

'All right,' she said.

'Meanwhile,' I said, 'is there anything I can do for you?'

'For me?' She shook her head. 'But . . . Morgan could use whatever help he can get.'

'Yeah,' I said. 'Like I'm gonna help Morgan.'

She lifted her hands. 'I know. I know. But there's not much I can do. Everyone knows he was my apprentice. They're watching me. If I try to help him openly, they'll suspend me as captain of the Wardens, at best.'

'Don't you just love it when justice can't be bothered with petty concerns like fact?'

'Harry,' she said. 'What if he's innocent?'

I shrugged. 'The way I was all those years? I'm too busy admiring the karma to lend a hand to the bastard.' Out on the street, Thomas's Jag cruised by the end of the alley, then pulled up to the curb and stopped.

I glanced at the car and said, 'There's my ride.'

Anastasia arched an eyebrow at Thomas and his car. 'The vampire?'

'He owed me a favor.'

'Mmmm,' Anastasia said. Her look at Thomas did not say *yum*. She looked more like someone who was trying to judge by how much she would need to lead a moving target. 'You're sure?'

I nodded. 'The White King told him to play nice. He will.'

'Until he doesn't,' she said.

'Walkers can't be choosers,' I said.

'The *Beetle* died again?'

'Uh-huh.'

'Why don't you get a different car?' she asked.

'Because the *Blue Beetle* is *my* car.'

Anastasia smiled faintly up at me. 'I wonder how you make something like that so endearing.'

'It's my natural good looks,' I said. 'I could make athlete's foot endearing, if I really had to.'

She rolled her eyes, but was still smiling. 'I'll head back to Edinburgh and help coordinate the search. If there's anything I can do . . .'

I nodded. 'Thank you.'

She put her hands on my cheeks. 'I'm sorry about your friends. When this is over, we'll find some quiet spot and relax.'

I turned my head to one side and kissed the pulse in her wrist, then gently clasped her hands with mine. 'Look, I'm not making any promises. But if I see something that might help Morgan, I'll let you know.'

'Thank you,' she said quietly.

She stood up on her toes and kissed me goodbye. Then she turned and vanished into the shadows farther down the alley.

I waited until she was gone to turn around and join my brother in the white Jag.

'Damn, that girl is fit,' Thomas drawled. 'Where to?'

'Stop looking,' I said. 'My place.'

If Morgan was going to give me the shaft, I might as well find out now.

11

Thomas stopped his Jag in front of the boardinghouse where my apartment was and said, 'I'll have my cell phone on me. Try to call me before things start exploding.'

'Maybe this time it'll be different. Maybe I'll work everything out through reason, diplomacy, dialogue, and mutual cooperation.'

Thomas eyed me.

I tried to look wounded. 'It could happen.'

He reached into his jeans pocket, pulled out a plain white business card with a phone number on it, and passed it to me. 'Use this number. It's to a clone.'

I looked at him blankly.

'It's a supersecret sneaky phone,' he clarified. 'No one knows I have it, and if someone traces your calls and goes looking for me, they'll find someone else.'

'Oh,' I said. 'Right.'

'You sure you don't want to just load Morgan up and go?'

I shook my head. 'Not until I give him the score. He sees me coming in with a vampire in tow, he's going to flip out. As in try to kill us both.' I got out of the Jag, glanced at the house, and shook my head. 'You stay alive for a dozen decades doing what Morgan does, paranoia becomes reflex.'

Thomas grimaced. 'Yeah. Give me an hour or so to get what you need. Call me when you've got him ready to go.'

I glanced at the number, committed it to memory,

and pocketed the card. 'Thanks. I'll pay you back for the gear.'

He rolled his eyes. 'Shut up, Harry.'

I snorted out a breath, and nodded my head in thanks. We rapped knuckles, and he pulled out onto the street and cruised out into the Chicago night.

I took a slow look around the familiar shapes of dark buildings where only a few lights still burned. I'd lived in this neighborhood for years. You'd think I'd be confident about spotting anything out of the ordinary fairly quickly. But, call me crazy, there were just too many players moving in this game, with God only knew what kinds of abilities to draw upon.

I didn't spot anyone out there getting set to kill me to get to Morgan. But that didn't mean that they weren't there.

'If that's not paranoid reflex,' I muttered, 'I don't know what is.'

I shivered and walked down the steps to my apartment. I disarmed the wards, and reminded myself, again, that I really needed to do something about the deep divots in the steel security door. The last thing I needed was for old Mrs Spunkelcrief, my near-deaf landlady, to start asking me why my door looked like it had been shot a dozen times. I mean, I could always tell her, 'because it has been', but that isn't the sort of conversation one has with one's landlady if one wants to keep one's home.

I opened the bullet-dented door, went inside, turned toward the bedroom door, and was faced with a bizarre tableau.

Morgan was off the bed, sitting on the floor with his back to it, his wounded leg stretched out in front of him.

He looked awful, but his eyes were narrowed and glittered with suspicion.

Sprawled in the bedroom doorway was my apprentice, Molly Carpenter.

Molly was a tall young woman with a bunch of really well-arranged curves and shoulder-length hair that was, this month, dyed a brilliant shade of sapphire. She was wearing cutoff blue jeans and a white tank top, and her blue eyes looked exasperated.

She was sprawling on the floor because Mouse was more or less lying on top of her. He wasn't letting his full weight rest on her, because it probably would have smothered her, but it seemed obvious that she was not able to move.

'Harry!' Molly said. She started to say something else, but Mouse leaned into her a little, and suddenly all she could do was gasp for air.

'Dresden!' Morgan growled at about the same time. He shifted his weight, as if to get up.

Mouse turned his head to Morgan and gave him a steady look, his lips peeling back from his fangs.

Morgan settled down.

'Hooboy,' I sighed, and pushed the door shut, leaving the room in complete darkness. I locked the door, put the wards back up, and then muttered, *'Flickum bicus.'* I waved my hand as I spoke, and sent a minor effort of will out into the room, and half a dozen candles flickered to life.

Mouse turned to me and gave me what I could have sworn was a reproachful look. Then he got up off of Molly, padded into the alcove that served as my kitchen, and deliberately yawned at me before flopping down on the floor to sleep. The meaning was clear: *now it's your problem.*

'Ah,' I said, glancing from Mouse to my apprentice to my guest. 'Um. What happened here, exactly?'

'The warlock tried to sneak up on me while I slept,' Morgan spat.

Molly quickly stood up and scowled at Morgan, her hands clenched into fists. 'Oh, that's ridiculous.'

'Then explain what you're doing here this late at night,' Morgan said. 'What possible reason could you have to show up here, now?'

'I'm making concentration-supporting potions,' she said from between clenched teeth, in a tone that suggested she'd repeated herself about a hundred times already. 'The jasmine has to go in at night. Tell him, Harry.'

Crap. In all the excitement, I'd forgotten that the grasshopper was scheduled to show up and pull an all-nighter. 'Um,' I said. 'What I meant to ask was, how is it that Mouse came to be sitting on you both?'

'The warlock summoned up her will and prepared to attack me,' Morgan said frostily. 'The dog intervened.'

Molly rolled her eyes and glared at him. 'Oh, *please*. You are *such* an asshole.'

The air in the room seemed to tighten a little, as power gathered around the young woman.

'Molly,' I said gently.

She glanced over at me, scowling. 'What?'

I cleared my throat and gestured at her with one hand.

She blinked for a second, then seemed to catch on. She closed her eyes, took a deep breath, and exhaled it slowly. As she did, the ominous sense of stormy energy faded. Molly ducked her head a little, her cheeks flushing. 'Sorry. But it wasn't like that.'

Morgan snorted.

I ignored him. 'Go on,' I told Molly. 'Talk.'

'He just . . . I just got so angry,' Molly said. 'He made me so upset. I couldn't help it.' She gestured to Mouse. 'And then he just . . . just flattened me. And he wouldn't let me up, and he wouldn't let Morgan move, either.'

'Seems to me that the dog had better sense than you,' I said. I glanced up at Morgan. 'Either of you. You're supposed to stay still. You wanna kill yourself?'

'It was a reaction to her approach,' Morgan said calmly. 'I survived it.'

I shook my head. 'And you,' I said to Molly. 'How many months have we spent working on your emotional control?'

'I know, I know,' she said. 'It's never good to use magic in anger. I know, Harry.'

'You'd better know it,' I said quietly. 'If it's so easy to get a rise out of you that one bitter old washed-up Warden can blow your O-ring, the first reactionary goomba to come along looking for an excuse to take you out is going to put you in a casket, claim it was self-defense, and get away with it.'

Morgan bared his teeth in an expression only remotely resembling a smile. 'You'd know all about that, Dresden, wouldn't you?'

'You son of a bitch!' Molly snarled and whirled toward Morgan, seizing a candlestick and hefting it like a club. The candle on it tumbled to the floor.

Morgan sat perfectly still with that same gruesome smile on his face, never flinching.

I lurched forward and grabbed Molly's arm on her backswing, an instant before she would have brought the heavy candlestick crashing down on Morgan's skull. Molly was strong for a woman, and I had to make a pretty serious effort to hold her back, my fingers digging into her wrist, while I snagged her around the waist with my other arm and bodily hauled her away from Morgan.

'No!' I demanded. 'Dammit, Molly, no!' I actually had to lift her feet off the ground to turn her away from the bedroom. I tightened my grip on her wrist and said, 'Drop the candlestick, Molly. Now.'

She let out a sound full of anger and laced with a little pain, and the heavy candlestick dropped to the floor, making a dull thud as it hit the rug-covered concrete. The air around her was alive with power, buzzing against my skin like a thousand tiny sparks of static electricity in a dry winter. 'He can't talk to you like that,' Molly snarled.

'*Think,*' I told her, my voice hard but measured. 'Remember the lessons. They're just words, Molly. Look for the thought behind them. He set you up for this reaction. You're *allowing* him to make you embarrass me.'

Molly opened her mouth on an angry retort, then forced her mouth closed and turned her face away from me. She remained rigidly tense, and after a fuming half minute, she said, her voice more calm, 'I'm sorry.'

'Don't be sorry,' I replied as gently as I could. 'Be disciplined. You can't afford to let them rattle you. Not ever.'

She took another deep breath, exhaled, and then I felt her begin to ease down, relaxing her mental grasp on the power she'd instinctively prepared. 'Okay,' she said. 'Okay, Harry.'

I let her go slowly. She began to rub at her right wrist with her other hand. I winced a little on her behalf. I thought I'd left bruises on her skin.

'Do me a favor,' I said. 'Take Mouse and grab the mail.'

'I'm fine. I don't need—' she began. Then she stopped herself, shook her head, and looked at Mouse.

The big dog heaved himself up, walked over to the basket next to the door, grasped his leather lead in his jaws, and dragged it out. Then he looked up at Molly, his head cocked to one side, his tail wagging hopefully.

Molly let out a rueful little laugh and knelt down to hug the big dog. She clipped his lead onto his collar, and the two of them left.

I turned and eyed the candle. It had spilled hot wax onto a genuine Navajo rug on the floor, but it hadn't set anything on fire. I bent down and picked up the candle, then started trying to clean up the spilled wax as best I could.

'Why?' I asked in a hard voice.

'It's one way to take a measure of a man,' he said. 'Looking at his students.'

'You didn't look,' I said. 'You needled her until she broke.'

'She's a self-proclaimed warlock, Dresden,' he replied. 'Guilty of one of the most hideous and self-destructive crimes a wizard can commit. Is there some reason she *shouldn't* be tested?'

'What you did was cruel,' I said.

'Was it?' Morgan asked. 'There are others she is going to meet, one day, who will be even less gracious. Are you preparing her to deal with those people?'

I glared at him.

His gaze never wavered. 'You aren't doing her any favors by going easy on her, Dresden,' he said, more quietly. 'You aren't preparing her for exams. She doesn't receive a bad mark if she fails.'

I was quiet for a minute. Then I asked, 'Did you learn shields as an apprentice?'

'Of course. One of my earliest lessons.'

'How did your master teach you?'

'She threw stones at me,' he said.

I grunted, without looking at him.

'Pain is an excellent motivator,' he said. 'And it teaches one to control one's emotions at the same time.' He tilted his head. 'Why do you ask?'

'No reason,' I told him. 'She could have broken your head open, you know.'

He gave me that same unsettling smile. 'You wouldn't have let her.'

Molly came back into the apartment, carrying a handful of mail, including one of those stupid Circuit City fliers that they just won't stop sending me. She shut the door, put the wards back up, and took Mouse's lead off. The big dog went over to the kitchen and flopped down.

Molly put the mail on the coffee table, gave Morgan a level pensive look, and then nodded at him. 'So . . . what's he doing here, boss?'

I stared at Molly for a moment, and then at Morgan. 'What do you think?' I asked him.

He shrugged a shoulder. 'She already knows enough to implicate her. Besides, Dresden – if you go down with me, there's no one left to take responsibility for her. Her sentence will not remain suspended.'

I ground my teeth together. Molly had made a couple of bad choices a few years back, and violated one of the Laws of Magic in doing so. The White Council takes a harsh view of such things – their reactions start with beheadings, and become progressively less tolerant. I'd staked my own life on the belief that Molly wasn't rotten to the core, and that I could rehabilitate her. When I did it, I'd known that I was risking my own well-being.

If Molly backslid, I'd bear the responsibility for it, and get a death sentence about twenty seconds after she did.

I hadn't really considered that it would also work the other way around.

Say for a minute that it was Morgan's intention to get caught and take me down with him. It also meant that Molly would take a fall. He'd get rid of both of the Council's former warlocks with the same move. Two birds, one stone.

Well, crap.

'Okay,' I sighed. 'I guess you're in.'

'I am?' Molly looked at me with widening eyes. 'Um. In what?'

I told her.

12

'I don't like it,' Morgan growled, as I pushed the wheel-chair over the gravel toward the street and the van Thomas had rented.

'Gee. There's a shock,' I said. Morgan was a lot to push around, even with the help of the chair. 'You upset with how I operate.'

'He's a vampire,' Morgan said. 'He can't be trusted.'

'I can hear you,' Thomas said from the driver's seat of the van.

'I know that, vampire,' Morgan said, without raising his voice. He eyed me again.

'He owes me a favor,' I said, 'from that coup attempt in the White Court.'

Morgan glowered at me. 'You're lying,' he said.

'For all you know it's true.'

'No, it isn't,' he said flatly. 'You're lying to me.'

'Well, yes.'

He looked from me to the van. 'You trust him.'

'To a degree,' I said.

'Idiot,' he said, though he sounded like his heart wasn't in it. 'Even when a White Court vampire is sincere, you can't trust it. Sooner or later, its demon takes control. And then you're nothing but food. It's what they are.'

I felt a little surge of anger and clubbed it down before it could make my mouth start moving. 'You came to me, remember? You don't like how I'm helping you, feel free to roll yourself right out of my life.'

Morgan gave me a disgusted look, folded his arms – and shut his mouth.

Thomas turned on the hazard lights as the van idled on the street; then he came around and opened up the side door. He turned to Morgan and picked up the wheelchair the wounded Warden sat in with about as much effort as I'd use to move a sack of groceries from the cart into my car's trunk. Thomas put the wheelchair carefully into the van, while Morgan held the IV bag steady on its little metal pole clamped to the chair's arm.

I had to give Morgan a grudging moment of admiration. He was one tough son of a bitch. Obviously in agony, obviously exhausted, obviously operating in the shambles of his own shattered pride, he was still stubborn enough to be paranoid and annoying. If he wasn't aiming it all at me, I probably would have admired him even more.

Thomas slid the door shut on Morgan, rolled his eyes at me, and got back into the driver's seat.

Molly came hurrying up, carrying a pair of backpacks, holding one end of Mouse's leash. I held out my hand, and she tossed me the black nylon pack. It was my trouble kit. Among other things, it contained food, water, a medical kit, survival blankets, chemical light sticks, duct tape, two changes of clothing, a multitool, two hundred dollars in cash, my passport, and a couple of favorite paperbacks. I always kept the trouble kit ready and available, in case I need to move out in a hurry. It had everything I would need to survive about ninety percent of the planet's environments for at least a couple of days.

Molly, acting on her own initiative, had begun putting

her own trouble kit together the same day she'd learned about mine. Except that her backpack was pink.

'You sure about this?' I asked her, pitching my voice low enough that Morgan wouldn't hear.

She nodded. 'He can't stay there alone. You can't stay with him. Neither can Thomas.'

I grunted. 'Do I need to search your bag for candlesticks?'

She gave me a chagrined shake of her head.

'Don't feel too bad, kid,' I told her. 'He had a couple of hours to work you up to that. And he's the guy who nearly cut your head off, during that mess around SplatterCon.'

'It wasn't that,' she said quietly. 'It's what he said to you. What he's done to you.'

I put my hand on her arm and squeezed gently.

She smiled faintly at me. 'I've never . . . never really felt . . . hate before. Not like that.'

'Your emotions got the better of you. That's all.'

'But it isn't,' she insisted, folding her arms against her stomach, her shoulders hunching a little. 'Harry, I've seen you all but kill yourself to help people who were in trouble. But for Morgan, that doesn't matter. You're just this . . . this *thing* that did something wrong once, and you'll never, ever be anything else.'

Aha.

'Kid,' I said quietly, 'maybe you should think about who you were really angry with back there.'

'What do you mean?'

I shrugged. 'I mean there's a reason you snapped when he started in on me. Maybe the fact that he was being Morgan just happened to be coincidental.'

She blinked her eyes several times, but not fast enough to stop one tear.

'You did a bad thing once,' I said. 'It doesn't make you a monster.'

Two more tears fell. 'What if it does?' She wiped at her cheeks with a brusque frustrated motion. 'What if it *does*, Harry?'

I nodded. 'Because if Morgan's right, and I'm just a ticking timebomb, and I'm trying to rehabilitate *you*, you haven't got a chance in hell. I get it.'

She pressed her lips together, and it made her words sound stiff. 'Just before Mouse knocked me down, I wanted to . . . to do things to Morgan. To his mind. To *make* him act differently. I was so angry, and it felt *right*.'

'Feeling something and acting on it are two different things.'

She shook her head. 'But who would want to do that, Harry? What kind of monster would *feel* that?'

I slung the pack over one shoulder so that I could put my hands on either side of her face and turn her eyes to mine. Her tears made them very blue.

'The human kind. Molly, you are a good person. Don't let anyone take that away from you. Not even yourself.'

She didn't even try to stop the tears. Her lip quivered. Her eyes were wide and her cheeks were fever-warm under my fingers. 'A-are you sure?'

'Yes.'

She bowed her head, and her shoulders shook. I leaned down to rest my forehead against hers. We stayed that way for a minute. 'You're okay,' I told her quietly. 'You aren't a monster. You're gonna be all right, grasshopper.'

A series of sharp, rapping sounds interrupted us. I looked

over my shoulder and found Morgan glowering at me. He held up a pocket watch – an honest-to-God gold pocket watch – and jabbed a forefinger at it impatiently.

'Jerk,' Molly mumbled, sniffling. 'Big fat, grumpy jerk.'

'Yes. But he has a point. Tick-tock.'

She swiped a hand at her nose and collected herself. 'Okay,' she said. 'Let's go.'

The storage rental facility was located a couple of blocks from Deerfield Square in a fairly upscale suburban neighborhood north of Chicago proper. Most of the buildings nearby were residential, and it was tough to go more than a quarter of an hour without spotting a patrol car.

I'd picked it as the spot for my bolt hole for one reason: shady characters would stand out against the upper-middle-class background like mustard stains under a black light.

Granted, it would probably work even better if I wasn't *one* of them.

I used my key at the security gate, and Thomas pulled the van around to my unit, a storage unit the size of a two-car garage. I unlocked the steel door and rolled it up while Thomas got Morgan out of the van. Molly followed, and when I beckoned, she wheeled Morgan into the storage space. Mouse got down out of the van and followed us. I rolled the door back down, and called wizard light to the amulet I held up in my right hand, until its blue-white glow filled the unit.

The interior of the place was mostly empty. There was a camp cot, complete with sleeping bag and pillow, placed more or less in the middle of the room, along with a footlocker I had filled with food, bottled water, candles, and supplies. A second footlocker sat next to the first one, and was filled with hardware and magical gear – a backup blasting rod, and all manner of useful little items one could use to accomplish a surprisingly broad spectrum of thaumaturgic workings. A camp toilet with a couple of jugs of cleaning liquid sat on the opposite side of the cot.

The floor, the walls, and the ceiling were covered in sigils, runes, and magical formulae. They weren't proper wards, like the ones I had on my home, but they worked on the same principles. Without a threshold to build them upon, no single one of the formulae was particularly powerful – but there were *lots* of them. They began to gleam with a silvery glow in the light coming from my amulet.

'Wow,' Molly said, staring slowly around her. 'What is this place, Harry?'

'Bolt hole I set up last year, in case I needed someplace quiet where I wouldn't get much company.'

Morgan was looking, too, though his face was pale and drawn with pain. He swept his eyes around and said, 'What's the mix?'

'Concealment and avoidance, mostly,' I replied. 'Plus a Faraday cage.'

Morgan nodded, glancing around. 'It looks adequate.'

'What's that mean?' Molly asked me. 'A Faraday what?'

'It's what they call it when you shield equipment from electromagnetic pulses,' I told her. 'You build a cage of conductive material around the thing you want to protect, and if a pulse sweeps over it, the energy is channeled into the earth.'

'Like a lightning rod,' Molly said.

'Pretty much,' I said. 'Only instead of electricity, this is built to stop hostile magic.'

'Once,' Morgan corrected me primly.

I grunted. 'Without a threshold to work with, there's only so much you can do. The idea is to protect you from a surprise assault long enough for you to go out the back door and run.'

Molly glanced at the back of the storage unit and said, 'There's no door there, Harry. That's a wall. It's kind of the opposite of a door.'

Morgan nodded his head at the back corner of the space, where a large rectangular area on the floor was clear of any runes or other markings. 'There,' he said. 'Where's it come out?'

'About three long steps from one of the marked trails the Council has right of passage on in Unseelie territory,' I said. I nodded at a cardboard box sitting in the rectangle. 'It's cold there. There're a couple of coats in the box.'

'A passage to the Nevernever,' Molly breathed. 'I hadn't thought of that.'

'Hopefully whoever was coming after me wouldn't, either,' I said.

Morgan eyed me. 'One can't help noting,' he said, 'that this place seems ideally suited to hiding and sheltering a fugitive from the Wardens.'

'Hunh,' I said. 'Now that you mention it, yeah. Yeah it *does* seem kind of friendly to that sort of purpose.' I gave Morgan an innocent look. 'Just an odd coincidence, I'm sure, since I happen to *be* one of those paranoid lunatics, myself.'

Morgan glowered.

'You came to me for a reason, Chuckles,' I said. 'Besides. I wasn't thinking about the Wardens nearly so much as I was . . .' I shook my head and shut my mouth.

'As who, Harry?' Molly asked.

'I don't know who they are,' I said. 'But they've been involved in several things lately. The Darkhallow, Arctis Tor, the White Court coup. They're way too handy with magic. I've been calling them the Black Council.'

'There is no Black Council,' Morgan snapped, with the speed that could only have been born of reflex.

Molly and I traded a look.

Morgan let out an impatient breath. 'Any actions that may have been taken are the work of isolated renegades,' he said. 'There is no organized conspiracy against the White Council.'

'Uh-*huh*,' I said. 'Gosh, I'd have thought you'd be right on board with the conspiracy thing.'

'The Council is *not* divided,' he said, his voice as hard and cold as I had ever heard it. 'Because the moment we turn upon one another, we're finished. There *is* no Black Council, Dresden.'

I lifted both eyebrows. 'From my perspective, the Council's been turning on me for most of my life,' I said. 'And I'm a member. I have a robe and everything.'

'*You*,' Morgan spat, 'are . . .' He almost seemed to be choking on something before he blew out a breath and finished, '. . . vastly irritating.'

I beamed at him. 'That's the Merlin's line, isn't it?' I said. 'There is no conspiracy against the Council.'

'It is the position of the *entire* Senior Council,' Morgan shot back.

'Okay, smart guy,' I said. 'Explain what happened to you.'

He glowered again, only with more purple.

I nodded sagely, then turned to Molly. 'This place should protect you from most tracking spells,' I said. 'And the avoidance wards should keep anyone from wandering by or asking any questions.'

Morgan made a growling noise.

'Suggestions, not compulsions,' I said, rolling my eyes. 'They're in common usage and you know it.'

'What do I do if someone does come?' she asked.

'Veil and run,' I said.

She shook her head. 'I don't know how to open a way to the Nevernever, Harry. You haven't shown me yet.'

'I can show her,' Morgan said.

Both of us stopped and blinked at him.

He was very still for a second and then said, 'I can do it. If she watches, maybe she'll learn something.' He glared at me. 'But doors open both ways, Dresden. What if something comes *in* through it?'

Mouse went over to the open space and settled down about six inches away from it. He sighed once, shifted his weight a bit, and went to sleep again, though his ears twitched at every noise.

I went to the first footlocker and opened it, took out a boxed fruit drink, and passed it to him. 'Your blood sugar's getting low. It's making you grumpy. But if you do get an unexpected visitor from the other side . . .' I went to the second locker, opened it, and drew out a pump-action shotgun, its barrel cut to well below the minimum legal length. I checked it, and passed the weapon to Molly. 'It's loaded with a mix of steel shot and rock salt. Between that and Mouse, it should discourage anything that comes through.'

'Right,' Molly said. She checked the weapon's chamber and then worked the pump, chambering a shell. She double-checked the safety, and then nodded at me.

'You taught her guns,' Morgan said. 'But not how to open passages to the Nevernever.'

'There's enough trouble right here in the real world,' I said.

Morgan grunted. 'True enough. Where are you going?'

'Only one place I can go.'

He nodded. 'Edinburgh.'

I turned toward the door and opened it. I looked from Morgan with his juice box to Molly with her shotgun. 'You two play nice.'

13

Wizards and technology don't get on so well, and that makes travel sort of complicated. Some wizards seemed to be more of a bad influence on technology than others, and if any of them were harder on machinery than me, I hadn't met them yet. I'd been on a jet a couple of times and had one bad experience – just one. After the plane's computers and guidance system went bad, and we had to make an emergency landing on a tiny commercial airfield, I wasn't eager to repeat the experience.

Buses were better, especially if you sat toward the back, but even they had problems. I hadn't been on a bus trip longer than three or four hundred miles without winding up broken down next to the highway in the middle of nowhere. Cars could work out, especially if they were fairly old models – the fewer electronics involved, the better. Even those machines, though, tended to provide you with chronic problems. I'd never owned a car that ran more than maybe nine days in ten – and most of them were worse than that.

Trains and ships were the ideal, especially if you could keep yourself a good way from the engines. Most wizards, when they traveled, stuck with ships and trains. Either that or they cheated – like I was about to do.

Back at the beginning of the war with the Vampire Courts, the White Council, with the help of a certain wizard private investigator from Chicago who shall remain nameless, negotiated the use of Ways through the near reaches of the Nevernever controlled by the Unseelie Court. The Nevernever, the world of ghosts and spirits and fantastic beings of every description, exists alongside our own mortal reality – but it isn't the same shape. That meant that in places, the mortal world touched upon the Nevernever at two points that could be very close together, while in the mortal realm, they were very far apart. In short, use of the Ways meant that anyone who could open a path between worlds could use a major shortcut.

In this case, it meant I could make the trip from Chicago, Illinois, to Edinburgh, Scotland, in about half an hour.

The closest entry point to where I wanted to go in the Nevernever was a dark alley behind a building that had once been used for meat packing. A lot of things had died in that building, not all of them cleanly and not all of them cows. There's a dark sense of finality to the place, a sort of ephemeral quality of dread that hangs so lightly on the air that the unobservant might not notice it at all. In the middle of the alley, a concrete staircase led down to a door that was held shut with both boards and chains – talk about overkill.

I walked down the steps to the bottom of the stairs, closed my eyes for a moment, and extended my other-worldly senses, not toward the door, but toward the section of concrete beside it. I could feel the thinness of the world there, where energy pulsed and hummed just beneath the seemingly rigid surface of reality.

It was a hot night in Chicago, but it wouldn't be on the Ways. I wore a long-sleeved shirt and jeans, and a couple of pairs of socks beneath my hiking shoes. My heavy leather duster had me sweating. I gathered up my will, reached out my hand, and with a whisper of '*Aparturum,*' I opened a Way between worlds.

Honestly, it sounds quite a bit more dramatic than it looks. The surface of the concrete wall rippled with a quick flickering of color and began to put out a soft glow. I took a deep breath, gripped my staff in both hands, and stepped directly forward into the concrete.

My flesh passed through what should have been stone, and I emerged in a dark wood that lay covered in frost and a thin layer of snow. At least this time the ground in Chicago had been more or less level with the ground in the Nevernever. Last time, I'd had a three-inch drop I hadn't expected, and I'd fallen on my ass into the snow. No harm done, I suppose, but this part of the Nevernever was just chock-full of things you did *not* want to think you were clumsy or vulnerable.

I took my bearings with a quick look around. The woods were the same, all three times I'd been through them. A hillside sank down ahead of me, and climbed steadily into the night behind me. At the top of the small mountain I stood upon, I was told, was a narrow and bitterly cold pass that led into the interior of the Unseelie Mountains, to Mab's stronghold of Arctis Tor. Below me, the land sank into foothills and then into plains, where Mab's authority ended and that of Titania the Summer Queen began.

I stood at a crossroads – which was only sensible, since I'd arrived from Chicago, one of the great crossroads of the world. One trail led upslope and down. The other crossed it at almost perfect right angles, and ran along the face of the hillside. I took a left, following the face of the hillside in a counterclockwise direction, also known as widdershins, in the parlance of the locals. The trail ran between frozen trees, their branches bowed beneath their burden of frost and snow.

I moved quickly, but not quickly enough to slip and blow out an ankle or brain myself on a low-hanging branch. The White Council had Mab's permission to move through the woods, but they were by no means safe.

I found that out for myself about fifteen minutes into my walk, when snow suddenly fell softly from the trees all around, and silent black shapes descended to encircle me. It happened quickly, and in perfect silence – maybe a dozen spiders the size of ponies alit upon the frozen ground or clung to the trunks and branches of the surrounding trees. They were smooth-surfaced, sharp-edged creatures, like orbweavers, long-limbed and graceful and deadly-looking. They moved with an almost delicate precision, their bodies of a color of grey and blue and white that blended flawlessly with the snowy night.

The spider who had come down onto the trail directly in front of me raised its two forelegs in warning, and revealed fangs longer than my forearm, dripping with milky-white venom.

'Halt, man-thing,' said the creature.

That was actually scarier than the mere appearance of economy-sized arachnids. Between its fangs, I could see a mouth moving – a mouth that looked disturbingly human. Its multiple eyes gleamed like beads of obsidian. Its voice was a chirping, buzzing thing. 'Halt, he whose blood will warm us. Halt, intruder upon the Wood of the Winter Queen.'

I stopped and looked around the circle of spiders. None of them seemed to be particularly larger or smaller than the others. If I had to fight my way clear, there wasn't any obvious weak link to exploit. 'Greetings,' I said, as I did. 'I am no intruder, honored hunters. I am a Wizard of the White Council, and I and my folk have the Queen's permission to tread these paths.'

The air around me shivered with chitters and hisses and clicks.

'Man-things speak often with false tongues,' said the lead spider, its forelimbs thrashing the air in agitation.

I held up my staff. 'I guess they always have one of these, too, huh?'

The spider hissed, and venom bubbled from the tips of its fangs. 'Many a man-thing bears such a long stick, mortal.'

'Careful, legs,' I said. 'I'm on speaking terms with Queen Mab herself. I don't think you want to play it like this.'

The spider's legs shifted in an undulating motion, and the spider rippled two or three feet closer to me. The other spiders all shifted, too, moving a bit nearer. I didn't like that, not even a little. If one of them jumped, they'd be all over me – and there were just too many of the damn big things to defend myself against them effectively.

The spider laughed, the sound hollow and mocking. 'Mortals do not speak to the Queen and live to tell the tale.'

'It lies,' hissed the other spiders, the phrase a low buzzing around me. 'And its blood is warm.'

I eyed all those enormous fangs and had an acutely uncomfortable flashback to Morgan driving his straw through the top of that damn juice box.

The spider in front of me flowed a little to the left and a little to the right, the graceful motion intended to distract me from the fact that it had gotten about a foot closer to me. 'Man-thing, how are we to know what you truly are?'

In my professional opinion, you rarely get handed a straight line that good.

I thrust the tip of my staff forward, along with my gathered will, focusing it into an area the size of my own clenched fist as I shouted, '*Forzare!*'

An invisible force hammered into the lead spider, right in its disturbing mouth. It lifted the huge beast off all eight of its feet, drove it fifteen feet backward through the air, and ended at the trunk of an enormous old oak. The spider smacked into it like an enormous water bottle, making a hideous splattering sound upon impact. It bounced off the tree and landed on the frozen ground, its legs all quivering and jerking spasmodically. Maybe three hundred pounds of snow shaken loose by the impact came plummeting down from the oak tree's branches and half buried the body.

Everything went still and silent.

I narrowed my eyes and swept my gaze around the circle of monstrous arachnids. I said nothing.

The spider nearest its dead companion shifted its weight warily from leg to leg. Then, in a much quieter voice, it trilled, 'Let the wizard pass.'

'Damn right let him pass,' I muttered under my breath. Then I strode forward as though I intended to smash anything else that got in my way.

The spiders scattered. I kept walking without slowing, breaking stride, or looking back. They didn't know how fast my heart was beating or how my legs were trembling with fear. And as long as they didn't, I would be just fine.

After a hundred yards or so, I did look back – only to

see the spiders gathered over the body of their dead companion. They were wrapping it up in silk, their fangs twitching and jerking hungrily. I shuddered and my stomach twisted onto itself.

One thing you can count on when visiting the Nevernever: you don't ever get bored.

I turned off the forest path onto a foot trail at a tree whose trunk had been carved with a pentacle. The trees turned into evergreens and crowded close to the trail. Things moved out of sight among the trees making small scuttling noises, and I could barely hear high-pitched whispers and sibilant voices coming from the forest around me. Creepy, but par for the course.

The path led up to a clearing in the woods. Centered in the clearing was a mound of earth about a dozen yards across and almost as high, thick with stones and vines. Massive slabs of rock formed the posts and lintel of a black doorway. A lone figure in a grey cloak stood beside the doorway, a lean and fit-looking young man with cheekbones sharp enough to slice bread and eyes of cobalt blue. Beneath the grey cloak, he wore an expensive dark blue cashmere suit, with a cream-colored shirt and a metallic copper-colored tie. A black bowler topped off the ensemble, and instead of a staff or a blasting rod, he bore a silver-headed walking cane in his right hand.

He was also holding the cane at full extension, pointed directly at me with narrowed, serious eyes as I came down the trail.

I stopped and waved a hand. 'Easy there, Steed.'

The young man lowered the cane, and his face blossomed into a smile that made him look maybe ten years younger. 'Ah,' he said. 'Not too obvious a look, one hopes?'

'It's a classic,' I said. 'How you doing, Chandler?'

'I am freezing off my well-tailored ass,' Chandler said cheerily, in an elegant accent straight from Oxford. 'But I endure thanks to excellent breeding, a background in preparatory academies, and metric tons of British fortitude.' Those intense blue eyes took a second look at me, and though his expression never changed, his voice gained a touch of concern. 'How are you, Harry?'

'Been a long night,' I said, walking forward. 'Aren't there supposed to be five of you watching the door?'

'Five of *me* guarding the door? Are you mad? The sheer power of the concentrated fashion sense would obliterate visitors on sight.'

I burst out in a short laugh. 'You must use your powers only for good?'

'Precisely, and I shall.' He tilted his head thoughtfully. 'I can't remember the last time I saw you here.'

'I only visited once,' I said. 'And that was a few years ago, right after they drafted me.'

Chandler nodded soberly. 'What brings you out of Chicago?'

'I heard about Morgan.'

The young Warden's expression darkened. 'Yes,' he said quietly. 'It's . . . hard to believe. You're here to help find him?'

'I've found murderers before,' I said. 'I figure I can do it again.' I paused. For whatever reason, Chandler was almost always to be found working near the Senior Council. If anyone would know the scuttlebutt, he would. 'Who do you think I should talk to about it?'

'Wizard Liberty is coordinating the search,' he replied. 'Wizard Listens-to-Wind is investigating the scene of the murder. Ancient Mai is getting the word out to the rest of the Council to convene an emergency session.'

I nodded. 'What about Wizard McCoy?'

'Standing by with a strike team, when last I heard,' Chandler replied. 'He's one of the few who can reasonably expect to overpower Morgan.'

'Yeah,' I said. 'Morgan's a pain in the ass, all right.' I shivered and stamped my feet against the cold. 'I've got some information they're going to want. Where do I find them?'

Chandler considered. 'Ancient Mai should be in the Crystalline Hall, Wizard Liberty is in the Offices, Wizard McCoy should be somewhere near the War Room and Wizard Listens-to-Wind and the Merlin are in LaFortier's chambers.'

'How about the Gatekeeper?' I asked.

Chandler shrugged. 'Gatekeeping, I daresay. The only wizard I see less frequently than he is you.'

I nodded. 'Thanks, Chandler.' I faced him soberly and put a formal solemnity in my voice as I adhered to security protocols more than five centuries old. 'I seek entry to the Hidden Halls, O Warden. May I pass?'

He eyed me for a moment and gave me a slow, regal nod, his eyes twinkling. 'Be welcome to the seat of the White Council. Enter in peace and depart in peace.'

I nodded to him and walked forward through the archway.

I'd come in peace, sure. But if the killer was around and caught onto what I was doing, I wouldn't depart in peace.

Just in pieces.

14

The Hidden Halls of Edinburgh were the redoubt and fortress of the White Council of Wizardry from time immemorial. Well, actually, that last bit isn't true. It's been our headquarters for a little under five hundred years.

The White Council has existed since pre-Roman times, in one form or another, and its headquarters has shifted from time to time, and place to place. Alexandria, Carthage, Rome – we were in the Vatican in the early days of the Church, believe it or not – Constantinople and Madrid have all been home to the Council's leadership at one time or another – but since the end of the Middle Ages, they've been located in the tunnels and catacombs hewn from the unyielding stone of Scotland.

Edinburgh's tunnel network is even more extensive than those beneath the city of Chicago, and infinitely more stable and sturdy. The main headquarters of the complex is located deep beneath the Auld Rock itself – Edinburgh Castle, where kings and queens, lords and ladies, have defied, besieged, betrayed and slaughtered one another since pre-Christian times.

There's a reason a fortress has been there for as long as mankind can remember – it is one of the world's largest convergences of ley lines. Ley lines are the natural currents of magical energy running through the world. They are the most powerful means of employing magic known to man – and the lines that intersect in the earth deep below the Auld Rock represent a staggering amount of raw power waiting to be tapped by someone skilled or foolish enough.

I walked over a ley line about three steps after I entered the Hidden Halls, and I could feel its shuddering energy beneath my feet, rushing by like an enormous, silent subterranean river. I walked a bit faster for a few paces, irrationally nervous about being swept off of my feet by it, until I could only sense it as a dim and receding vibration in the ground.

I didn't need to call up a light. Crystals set in the walls glowed in a rainbow of gentle colors, bathing the whole place in soft, ambient illumination. The tunnel was ancient, worn, chilly, and damp. Water always seemed ready to condense into a half-frozen dew the instant it was given the opportunity by an exhaled breath or a warm body.

The tunnel was about as wide as my spread arms, and maybe eight feet high. The walls were lined with bas-relief carvings in the stone. Some of them were renditions of scenes of what I'd been told were the historical high points of the White Council. Since I didn't recognize anyone in the images, I didn't have much context for them, so they mostly just looked like the crudely drawn cast of thousands you see on the Bayeux Tapestry. The rest of the carvings were wards – seriously world-class heavyweight wards. I didn't know what they did, but I could sense the deadly power behind them, and I trod carefully as I passed deeper into the complex.

The entry tunnel from the Nevernever was more than a quarter of a mile long, sloping gently downward the whole way. There were metal gates every couple of hundred yards, each of them manned by a Warden backed up by a pair of Ancient Mai's temple-dog statues.

The things were three feet high at the shoulder, and looked like escapees from a Godzilla movie. Carved from stone, the blocky figures sat inert and immobile – but I knew that they could come to dangerous life at an instant's notice. I tried to think about what it might be like to be facing a pair of aggressive temple-dog statues in the relatively narrow hallway. I decided that I'd rather wrestle an oncoming subway locomotive. At least then it would be over quickly.

I exchanged polite greetings with the Wardens on guard until I passed the last checkpoint and entered the headquarters proper. Then I took a folded map from my duster pocket, squinted at it, and got my bearings. The layout of the tunnels was complex, and it would be easy to get lost.

Where to begin?

If the Gatekeeper had been around, I would have sought him out first. Rashid had been my supporter and ally on more than one occasion, God knew why. I wasn't on what anyone would call good terms with the Merlin. I barely knew Martha Liberty or Listens-to-Wind. I found Ancient Mai to be a very scary little person. That left Ebenezar.

I headed for the War Room.

It took me the better part of half an hour to get there. Like I said, the tunnel complex is enormous – and after the way the war had reduced the ranks of the Council, it seemed lonelier and emptier than ever. My footsteps echoed hollowly back from stone walls for minutes at a time, unaccompanied by any other sound.

I felt intensely uncomfortable as I paced the Hidden Halls. I think it was the smell that did it. When I'd been a young man, hauled before the Council to be tried as a violator of the First Law of Magic, they had brought me to Edinburgh. The musty, wet, mineral smell of the place had been almost all I knew while I had waited, hooded and bound, in a cell for a full day. I remember being horribly cold and tortured by the knots my muscles worked themselves into after so many hours tied hand and foot. I remember feeling more alone than ever in my life, while I awaited whatever was going to happen.

I had been scared. So scared. I was sixteen.

It was the same smell, and that scent had the power to animate the corpses of some of my darkest memories and bring them lurching back into the front of my thoughts. Psychological necromancy.

'Brains,' I moaned to myself, drawing the word out.

If you can't stop the bad thoughts from coming to visit, at least you can make fun of them while they're hanging around.

In a stroke of improbable logic, the War Room was located between the central chambers of the Senior Council and the barracks rooms of the Wardens, which included a small kitchen. The smell of baking bread cut through the musty dampness of the tunnel, and I felt my steps quickening.

I passed the barracks, which would doubtless be empty, for the most part. Most of the Wardens would be out hunting Morgan, as evidenced by the skeleton guard I'd seen at Chandler's post. I took the next left, nodded to the very young Warden on guard, opened a door, and passed into the War Room of the White Council.

It was a spacious vault, about a hundred feet square, but the heavy arches and pillars that supported the ceiling took away a lot of that room. Illuminating crystals glowed more brightly here, to make reading easier. Bulletin boards on rolling frames took up spaces between pillars, and were covered by maps and pins and tiny notes. Most of them had one or more chalkboards next to them, which were covered in diagrams, cryptic, brief notation, and cruder maps. Completely ordinary office furniture occupied the back half of the vault, broken up into cubicles.

Typewriters clacked and dinged. Men and women of the administrative staff, wizards all, moved back and forth through the room, speaking quietly, writing, typing, and filing. A row of counters on the front wall of the room supported coffeepots warmed by propane flames, and several well-worn couches and chairs rested nearby.

Half a dozen veteran Wardens lay sprawled on couches napping, sat in chairs reading books, or played chess with an old set upon a coffee table. Their staves and cloaks were all at hand, ready to be taken up at an instant's notice. They were dangerous, hard men and women, the Old Guard, survivors of the deadly days of the early Vampire War. I wouldn't have wanted to cross any of them.

Sitting in a chair slightly apart from them, staring at the flames crackling in a rough stone fireplace, sat my old mentor, Ebenezar McCoy. He held a cup of coffee in his thick, work-scarred fingers. A lot of the more senior wizards in the Council had a sense of propriety they took way too seriously, always dressed to the nines, always immaculate and proper. Ebenezar wore an old pair of denim overalls with a flannel shirt and leather work boots that could have been thirty or forty years old. His silver hair, what he had left of it, was in disarray, as if he'd just woken from a restless sleep. He was aging, even by wizard standards, but his shoulders were still wide, and the muscles in his forearms were taut and visible beneath age-spotted skin. He stared at the fire through wire-rimmed spectacles, his dark eyes unfocused, one foot slowly tapping the floor.

I leaned my staff against a handy wall, got myself a cup of coffee, and settled down in the chair beside Ebenezar's. I sipped coffee, let the warmth of the fire drive some of the wet chill out of my bones, and waited.

'They always have good coffee here,' Ebenezar said a few moments later.

'And they don't call it funny names,' I said. 'It's just coffee. Not frappalattegrandechino.'

Ebenezar snorted and sipped from his cup. 'Nice trip in?'

'Got tripped up by someone's thugs on the Winter trail.'

He grimaced. 'Aye. We've had our people harassed several times, the past few months. How are you, Hoss?'

'Uninformed, sir,' I said.

He eyed me obliquely. 'Mmmm. I did as I thought best, boy. I won't apologize for it.'

'Don't expect you to,' I said.

He nodded. 'What are you doing here?'

'What do you think?'

He shook his head. 'I won't take you on the strike team, Hoss.'

'You think I can't pull my weight?'

He turned his eyes to me. 'You have too much history with Morgan. This has got to be dispassionate, and you're just about the least dispassionate person I know.'

I grunted. 'You're sure it was Morgan who did LaFortier?'

His eyes returned to the fire. 'I would never have expected it. But too many things are in place.'

'No chance it's a frame?'

Ebenezar blinked and shot me a look. 'Why do you ask?'

'Because if the ass is finally getting his comeuppance, I want to make sure it's on the level,' I said.

He nodded a couple of times. Then he said, 'I don't see how it could have been done. It looks like a duck, walks like a duck, quacks like a duck, odds are it's a damn duck. Occam's razor, Hoss.'

'Someone could have gotten into his head,' I said.

'At his age?' Ebenezar asked. 'Ain't likely.'

I frowned. 'What do you mean?'

'As a mind grows older, it gets established,' he said, 'more set in its ways. Like a willow tree. Supple when it's young, but gets more brittle as it ages. Once you've been around a century or so, it generally ain't possible to bend a mind without breaking it.'

'Generally?'

'You can't push it that far,' Ebenezar said. 'Push a loyal man into betraying everything he believes in? You'd drive him insane before you forced him into that. Which means that Morgan made a choice.'

'If he did it.' I shook my head. 'I just keep asking myself who profits most if we axe Morgan ourselves.'

Ebenezar grimaced. 'It's ugly all the way around,' he said, 'but there it is. I reckon you 'gazed him, Hoss, but it ain't a lie detector. You know that, too.'

I fell silent for a while and sipped coffee. Then I asked, 'Just curious. Who holds the sword when you catch him? It's usually Morgan who does the head chopping.'

'Captain Luccio, I reckon,' Ebenezar said. 'Or someone she appoints. But she ain't the kind to foist something like that off on a subordinate.'

I got treated to the mental image of Anastasia

decapitating her old apprentice. Then of me, taking Molly's head. I shuddered. 'That sucks.'

Ebenezar kept staring at the fire, and his eyes seemed to sink into his head, as if he had aged twenty years right in front of me. 'Aye.'

The door to the War Room opened and a slender, reedy little wizard in a tan tweed suit entered, lugging a large portfolio. His short white hair was curled tightly against his head and his fingers were stained with ink. There was a pencil tucked behind one ear, and a fountain pen behind the other. He stopped and peered around the room for a moment, spotted Ebenezar, and bustled right on over.

'Pardon, Wizard McCoy,' he said. 'If you have a moment, I need you to sign off on a few papers.'

Ebenezar put his coffee on the floor and accepted a manila folder from the little guy, along with the fountain pen. 'What this time, Peabody?'

'First, power of attorney for the office in Jakarta to purchase the building for the new safe house,' Wizard Peabody said, opening the folder and turning a page. Ebenezar scanned it, then signed it. Peabody turned more pages. 'Very good. Then an approval on the revision of wages for Wardens – initial there, please, thank you. And the last one is approval for ensuring Wizard LaFortier's holdings are transferred to his heirs.'

'Only three?' Ebenezar asked.

'The others are eyes-only, sir.'

Ebenezar sighed. 'I'll drop by my office when I'm free to sign them.'

'Sooner is better, sir,' Peabody said. He blinked and seemed to notice me for the first time. 'Ah. Warden Dresden. What brings you here?'

'I thought I'd come see if someone wanted help taking Morgan down,' I drawled.

Peabody gulped. 'I . . . see.'

'Has Injun Joe found anything?' Ebenezar asked.

Peabody's voice became laced with diffident disapproval as he answered. 'Wizard Listens-to-Wind is deep in preparations for investigative divination, sir.'

'So, no,' I said.

Peabody sniffed. 'Not yet. Between him and the Merlin, I'm sure they'll turn up precisely how Warden Morgan managed to bypass Senior Council security.' He glanced at me and said, in a perfectly polite tone, 'They are both wizards of considerable experience and skill, after all.'

I glowered at Peabody, but I couldn't think of a good dig before he had accepted the papers and pen back from Ebenezar. Peabody nodded to him and said, 'Thank you, sir.'

Ebenezar nodded absently as he picked up his coffee cup, and Peabody bustled out again.

'Paper-pushing twit,' I muttered under my breath.

'Invaluable paper-pushing twit,' Ebenezar corrected me. 'What he does isn't dramatic, but his organizational skills have been a critical asset since the outbreak of the war.'

I snorted. 'Bureaucromancer.'

Ebenezar smiled faintly as he finished his cup, the first couple of fingertips of his right hand stained with blue ink. Then he rose and stretched, drawing several faint popping sounds from his joints. 'Can't fight a war without clerks, Hoss.'

I stared down at my half cup of coffee. 'Sir,' I said quietly. 'Speaking hypothetically. What if Morgan is innocent?'

He frowned down at me for a long moment. 'I thought you wanted a piece of him.'

'I've got this weird tic where I don't want to watch wrongly accused men beheaded.'

'Well, naturally you do. But, Hoss, you've got to underst—' Ebenezar froze abruptly and his eyes widened. They went distant with thought for a moment, and I could all but hear gears turning in his head.

His eyes snapped back to mine and he drew in a slow breath, speaking in a murmur. 'So that's it. You're sure?'

I nodded my head once.

'Hell's bells,' the old man sighed. 'You'd best start asking your questions a lot more careful than that, Hoss.' He lowered his chin and looked at me over the rims of his spectacles. 'Two heads fall as fast as one. You understand?'

I nodded slowly. 'Yeah.'

'Don't know what I can do for you,' he said. 'I've got my foot nailed to the floor here until Morgan's located.'

'Assuming it's not a duck,' I said, 'where do I start looking?'

He pursed his lips for a moment. Then he nodded slowly and said, 'Injun Joe.'

15

The Senior Council members, as it turned out, do not live like paupers.

After I passed through still more security checkpoints, the stone hallway yielded to a hall the size of a ballroom that looked like something out of Versailles. A white marble floor with swirls of gold in it was matched in color to elegant white marble columns. A waterfall fell from the far wall, into a pool around which grew a plethora of plants, from grass to roses to small trees, forming a surprisingly complex little garden. The faint sound of wind chimes drifted through the air, and the golden light that poured down from crystals in the ceiling was indistinguishable from sunlight. Birds sang in the garden, and I saw the quick, darting black shape of a nightingale slalom between the pillars and settle in one of the trees.

A number of expensive, comfortable-looking sets of furniture were spaced in and near the garden, like the sets you sometimes see at the pricier hotels. A small table against one wall was covered with an eclectic buffet of foods, everything from cold cuts to what looked like the sautéed tentacles of an octopus, and a wet bar stood next to it, ready to protect the Senior Council members from the looming threat of dehydration.

A balcony ran around the entire chamber, ten feet up, and doors opened onto the Senior Council members' private chambers. I paced through the enormous, grandiose space of the Ostentatiatory to a set of stairs that swept grandly up one wall. I looked around until I spotted which door had a pair of temple-dog statues standing guard along with a sleepy-looking young man in a Warden's cape and a walking cast. I walked around the balcony and waved a hand at him.

I was just about to speak when both temple-dog constructs abruptly moved, turning their heads toward me with a grating sound of stone sliding against stone.

I stopped in my tracks, and held my hands up a little. 'Nice doggy.'

The young Warden peered at me and said something in a language I didn't recognize. He looked like someone from eastern Asia, though I couldn't have guessed at his nation of origin. He stared at me for a second, and I recognized him abruptly as one of the young men on Ancient Mai's personal staff. The last time I'd seen him, he'd been frozen half to death, trying to bear a message to Queen Mab. Now a broken ankle had presumably kept him from joining the search for Morgan.

Some people are just born lucky, I guess.

'Good evening,' I said to him, in Latin, the official tongue of the White Council. 'How are you?'

Lucky stared at me for another moment before he said, 'We are in Scotland. It is morning, sir.'

Right. My half hour walk had taken me six time zones ahead. 'I need to speak with Wizard Listens-to-Wind.'

'He is occupied,' Lucky told me. 'He is not to be disturbed.'

'Wizard McCoy sent me to speak to him,' I countered. 'He felt it was important.'

Lucky narrowed his eyes until they were almost closed. Then he said, 'Wait here, please. Do not move.'

The temple dogs continued staring at me. Okay, I knew they weren't really *staring*. They were just rock. But for essentially mindless constructs, they had an intense gaze.

'That will not be a problem,' I told him.

He nodded and vanished through the door. I waited for ten uncomfortable minutes before he returned, touched each dog lightly on the head, and nodded to me. 'Go in.'

I took a wary step, watching the constructs, but they didn't react. I nodded and went on by them, trying not to look like a nervous cat as I passed from the Ostentatiatory into LaFortier's chambers.

The first room I came to was a study, or an office, or possibly a curio shop. There was a massive desk carved out of some kind of unstained wood, though use and age had darkened the front edge, the handles of the drawers, and the area immediately in front of the modern office chair. A blotter lay precisely centered on the desk, with a set of four matching pens laid in a neat row. Shelves groaned with books, drums, masks, pelts, old weaponry, and dozens of other tokens that looked as though they came from exotic lands. The wall spaces between the shelves were occupied by shields fronted with two crossed weapons – a Norman kite shield with crossed broadswords, a Zulu buffalo-hide shield with crossed assegais, a Persian round shield with a long spike in its center with crossed scimitars, and many others. I knew museums that would declare Mardi Gras in the galleries if they could get their hands on a collection half that rich and varied.

A door at the far end of the study led into what was

evidently a bedroom. I could see a dresser and the foot of a covered bed approximately the size of a railroad car.

I could also see red-black droplets of blood on the walls.

'Come on, Harry Dresden,' called a quiet, weathered voice from the bedroom. 'We're at a stopping point and waiting on you.'

I walked into the bedroom and found myself standing in a crime scene.

The stench hit me first. LaFortier had been dead for days, and the second I crossed the threshold into the room, the odor of decay and death flooded my nose and mouth. He lay on the floor near the bed. Blood was sprinkled everywhere. His throat gaped wide-open, and he was covered in a black-brown crust of dried blood. There were defensive wounds on his hands, miniature versions of the slash on his throat. There might have been stab wounds on his torso, under the mess, but I couldn't be sure.

I closed my eyes for a second, swallowed down my urge to throw up, and looked around the rest of the room.

A perfect circle of gold paint had been inscribed on the floor around the body, with white candles burning at five equidistant points. Incense burned at five more points halfway between the candles, and take it from me – the scent of sandalwood doesn't complement that of a rotting corpse. It just makes it more unpleasant.

I stood staring down at LaFortier. He had been a bald man, a little over average height, and cadaverously skinny. He didn't look skinny now. The corpse had begun to bloat. The front of his shirt was stretched tight against its buttons. His back was arched and his hands had locked into claws. His teeth were bared in a grimace.

'He died hard,' said the weathered voice, and 'Injun Joe'

Listens-to-Wind stepped out of a doorway that led to a bathroom, drying his hands on a towel. His long hair was grey-white, with a few threads of black in it. His leathery skin was the ruddy bronze of a Native American complexion exposed to plenty of sunshine, and his eyes were dark and glittering beneath white brows. He wore faded blue jeans, moccasin boots, and an old Aerosmith T-shirt. A fringed leather bag hung from a belt that ran slantwise across his body, and a smaller, similar bag hung from a thong around his neck. 'Hello, Harry Dresden.'

I bowed my head to him respectfully. Injun Joe was generally regarded as the most skilled healer on the White Council, and maybe in the world. He had earned doctoral degrees in medicine from twenty universities over the years, and he went back to school every decade or two to help him stay current with modern practice. 'Went down fighting,' I agreed, nodding to LaFortier.

Injun Joe studied the body for a moment, his eyes sad. Then he said, 'I'd rather go in my sleep, I think.' He glanced back at me. 'What about you?'

'I want to be stepped on by an elephant while having sex with identical triplet cheerleaders,' I said.

He gave me a grin that briefly stripped a century or two of care and worry from his face. 'I've known a lot of kids who wanted to live forever.' The smile faded as he looked back to the dead man. 'Maybe someday that will happen. But maybe not. Dying is part of being alive.'

There wasn't much I could say to that. I was quiet for a minute. 'What are you setting up here?'

'His death left a mark,' the old wizard replied. 'We're going to reassemble the psychic residue into an image.'

I arched an eyebrow. 'Is . . . that even possible?'

'Normally, no,' Injun Joe said. 'But this room is surrounded on all sides by wards. We know what they're all supposed to look like. That means we can extrapolate where the energy came from by what impact it had on the wards. It's also why we haven't moved the body.'

I thought about it for a minute. What Injun Joe was describing was possible, I decided, but only barely. It would be something like trying to assemble an image illuminated by a single flash of light by backtracking how the light in the flash had all bounced around the room. The amount of focus, concentration, and the sheer mental process that would be involved in imagining the spell that could reassemble that image were staggering.

'I thought this was open and shut already,' I said.

'The evidence is conclusive,' Injun Joe said.

'Then why are you bothering with this . . . this . . . thing?'

Injun Joe looked at me steadily and didn't say anything.

'The Merlin,' I said. 'He doesn't think Morgan did it.'

'Whether he did it or not,' Injun Joe said, 'Morgan was the Merlin's right hand. If he is tried and found guilty, the Merlin's influence, credibility, and power will wane.'

I shook my head. 'Gotta love politics.'

'Don't be a child,' Injun Joe said quietly. 'The current balance of power was largely established by the Merlin. If he is undone as the leader of the Council, it will cause chaos and instability across the supernatural world.'

I thought about that for a minute. Then I asked, 'You think he's going to try to fake something?'

Injun Joe didn't react for a moment, and then he shook his head slowly and firmly. 'I won't let him.'

'Why not?'

'Because LaFortier's death has changed everything.'

'Why?'

Injun Joe nodded toward the study. 'LaFortier was the member of the Council with the most contacts outside of the Western nations,' he said. 'Many, many members of the Council come from Asia, Africa, South America – most of them from small, less powerful nations. They feel that the White Council ignores their needs, their opinions. LaFortier was their ally, the only member of the Senior Council who they felt treated them fairly.'

I folded my arms. 'And the Merlin's right-hand man killed him.'

'Whether Morgan is guilty or not, they *think* he did it, possibly on the Merlin's orders,' Injun Joe said. 'If he is found innocent and set free, matters could turn ugly. Very ugly.'

My stomach turned again. 'Civil war.'

Injun Joe sighed and nodded.

Fantastic.

'Where do you stand?' I asked him.

'I would like to say that I stood with the truth,' he said, 'but I cannot. The Council could survive the loss of Morgan without falling to pieces, even if it means a period of chaos while things settle out.' He shook his head. 'A civil war would certainly destroy us.'

'So Morgan did it, and that's all there is to it,' I said quietly.

'If the White Council falls, who will stand between humanity and those who would prey upon it?' He shook his head, and his long braid gently bumped his back. 'I respect Morgan, but I cannot permit that to happen. He is one man balanced against mankind.'

'So it's going to be Morgan, when you're finished,' I said. 'No matter who it really is.'

Injun Joe bowed his head. 'I . . . doubt that it will work. Even with the Merlin's expertise.'

'What if it does? What if it shows you another killer? You start picking who lives and who dies, and to hell with the truth?'

Injun Joe turned his dark eyes to me, and his voice became quiet and harder than stone. 'Once, I watched the tribe I was expected to guide and protect be destroyed, Harry Dresden. I did so because my principles held that it was wrong for the Council or its members to involve itself in manipulating the politics of mortals. I watched and restrained myself, until it was too late for me to make a difference. When I did that, I chose who would live and who would die. My people died for my principles.' He shook his head. 'I will not make that mistake again.'

I looked away from him, and remained silent.

'If you would excuse me,' he said, and walked from the room.

Hell's bells.

I had been hoping to enlist Injun Joe's aid – but I hadn't counted on the additional political factors. I didn't think he'd try to stop me if he knew what I was up to, but he certainly wasn't going to help. The more I dug, the messier this thing kept getting. If Morgan was vindicated, doom. If he *wasn't* vindicated, doom.

Doom, doom, and doom.

Damn.

I couldn't even be angry at Injun Joe. I understood his position. Hell, if it was me on the Senior Council and

I was the one making the call, I wasn't completely confident that I wouldn't react the same way.

My headache started coming on again.

How the hell was I supposed to do the right thing if there *wasn't* a right thing?

16

I stared at LaFortier's corpse for a moment longer, shook my head, and then pulled one of those disposable cameras you can get from a vending machine out of my duster pocket. I walked around the room snapping pictures of the body, the blood splatters, and the broken bits of furniture. I ran through the entire role of film, making the most complete record of the scene that I could, and then pocketed the camera again and turned to leave LaFortier's chambers.

Back in the Ostentatiatory, I heard voices drifting up from below. I nodded pleasantly to Lucky, who gave me an inscrutable look, and walked to the balcony railing.

Listens-to-Wind and the Merlin were standing by the buffet table, speaking quietly. Peabody hovered in the background, carrying a different set of folders, ledgers, and pens.

I paused for a moment to Listen. It's a trick I picked up somewhere along the line – not really magic, per se, as much as it is turning my mental focus completely to my sense of hearing.

'. . . to find out the truth,' the Merlin was saying as he loaded up a plate with tiny sandwiches and wedges of cheese and fresh green grapes. 'Surely you have no objection to that.'

'I think the truth is already well established,' Listens-to-Wind replied quietly. 'We're just wasting time here. We should be focusing on controlling the fallout.'

The Merlin was a tall man, regal of bearing, with a long white beard and long white hair to go with it – every inch the wizard's wizard. He wore a blue robe and a silver circlet about his brow, and his staff was an elegant length of pure white wood, completely free of any marking. He paused in loading his plate and regarded Injun Joe with a level gaze. 'I'll take it under advisement.'

Injun Joe Listens-to-Wind sighed and held up his hands palms forward in a conciliatory gesture. 'We're ready to begin.'

'Let me get some food in me and I'll be right in.'

'Ahem,' Peabody said diffidently. 'Actually, Wizard Listens-to-Wind, if you could sign a few papers for me while the Merlin eats, it would be greatly appreciated. There are two files on your desk that need your approval and I have three . . .' He paused and began to juggle the load in his arms until he could peer into a folder. 'No four, four others here with me.'

Injun Joe sighed. 'Okay,' he said. 'Come on.' The two of them walked toward the stairs leading up to the balcony, turned the opposite way I had when they reached the top, and entered a chamber on the far side of the room.

I waited until they were gone to descend the staircase to the ground level.

The Merlin had seated himself in the nearest group of chairs and was eating his sandwiches. He froze for a second as he saw me, and then smoothly resumed his meal. Funny. I didn't like the Merlin much more than I would a case of flaming gonorrhea, but I had never seen him in this context before. I'd always seen him at the head of a convened Council, and as this remote and unapproachable figure of unyielding authority and power.

I'd never even considered the notion that he might eat sandwiches.

I was about to go on past him, but instead swerved and came to a stop standing over him.

He continued eating, apparently unconcerned, until he'd finished the sandwich. 'Come to gloat, have you, Dresden?' he asked.

'No,' I said quietly. 'I'm here to help you.'

He dropped the bit of cheese he'd been about to bite into. It fell to the floor, unnoticed, as his eyes narrowed, regarding me suspiciously. 'Excuse me?'

I bared my teeth in a cold little smile. 'I know. It's like having a cheese grater shoved against my gums, just saying it.'

He stared at me for a silent minute before taking in a slow breath, settling back into the chair, and regarding me with steady blue eyes. 'Why should I believe you would do any such thing?'

'Because your balls are in a vise and I'm the only one who can pull them out,' I said.

He arched an elegant silver eyebrow.

'Okay,' I said. 'That came out a little more homoerotic than I intended.'

'Indeed,' said the Merlin.

'But Morgan can't stay hidden forever and you know it. They'll find him. His trial will last about two seconds. Then he falls down and breaks his crown and your political career comes tumbling after.'

The Merlin seemed to consider that for a moment. Then he shrugged a shoulder. 'I think it's far more likely that you will work very, very hard to make sure he dies.'

'I like to think I work smarter, not harder,' I said.

'If I want him dead, all I need to do is stand around and applaud. It isn't as though I can make his case any worse.'

'Oh,' said the Merlin. 'I'm not so certain. You have vast talents in that particular venue.'

'He's already being hunted. Half the Council is howling for his blood. From what I hear, all the evidence is against him – and anything I find out about him is going to be tainted against him by our antagonistic past.' I shrugged. 'At this point, I can't do any more damage. So what have you got to lose?'

A small smile touched the corners of his mouth. 'Let's assume, for a moment, that I agree. What do you want from me?'

'A copy of his file,' I said. 'Everything you've found out about LaFortier's death, and how Morgan pulled it off. All of it.'

'And what do you intend to do with it?' the Merlin asked.

'I thought I'd use the information to find out who killed LaFortier,' I said.

'Just like that.'

I paused to think for a minute. 'Yeah. Pretty much.'

The Merlin took another bite of cheese and chewed it deliberately. 'If my own investigations yield fruit,' he said, 'I won't need your help.'

'The hell you won't,' I said. 'Everyone knows your interests are going to lie in protecting Morgan. Anything you turn up to clear him is going to be viewed with suspicion.'

'Whereas your antagonism with Morgan is well-known,' the Merlin mused. 'Anything you find in his favor will be viewed as the next best thing to divine testimony.'

He tilted his head and stared at me. 'Why would you do such a thing?'

'Maybe I don't think he did it.'

His eyebrows lifted in amusement that never quite became a smile. 'And the fact that the man who died was one of those whose hand was set against you when you were yourself held in suspicion has nothing to do with it.'

'Right,' I said, rolling my eyes. 'There you go. There's my self-centered, petty, vengeful motivation for wanting to help Morgan out. Because it serves that dead bastard LaFortier right.'

The Merlin considered me for another long moment, and then shook his head. 'There is a condition.'

'A condition,' I said. 'Before you will agree to let me help you get your ass out of the fire.'

He gave me a bleak smile. 'My ass is reasonably comfortable where it is. This is hardly my first crisis, Warden.'

'And yet you haven't told me to buzz off.'

He lifted a finger, a gesture reminiscent of a fencer's salute. 'Touché. I acknowledge that it is, technically, possible for you to prove useful.'

'Gosh, I'm glad I decided to be gracious and offer my aid. In fact, I'm feeling so gracious, I'm even willing to listen to your condition.'

He shook his head slowly. 'It simply isn't sufficient to prove that Morgan is innocent. The traitor within our ranks is real. He *must* be found. Someone must be held accountable for what happened to LaFortier – and not just for the sake of the Council's membership. Our enemies must know that there are consequences to such actions.'

I nodded. 'So not only prove Morgan innocent, but find

the guy who did it, too. Maybe I can set the whole thing to music and do a little dance while I'm at it.'

'I feel obligated to point out that you approached me, Dresden.' He gave me his brittle smile again. 'The situation must be dealt with cleanly and decisively if we are to avoid chaos.' He spread his hands. 'If you can't present that sort of resolution to the problem, then this conversation never happened.' His eyes hardened. 'And I will expect your discretion.'

'You'd hang your own man out to dry. Even though you know he's innocent.'

His eyes glittered with a sudden cold fire, and I had to work not to flinch. 'I will do whatever is necessary. Bear that in mind as you "help" me.'

A door opened upstairs, and in a few seconds Peabody began a precarious descent of the stairs, balancing his ledgers and folders as he did.

'Samuel,' the Merlin said, his eyes never leaving me. 'Be so good as to provide Warden Dresden with a complete copy of the file on LaFortier's murder.'

Peabody stopped before the Merlin, blinking. 'Ah. Yes, of course, sir. Right away.' He glanced at me. 'If you would come this way, Warden?'

'Dresden,' the Merlin said in a pleasant tone. 'If this is some sort of ruse, you would be well-advised to be sure I never learn of it. My patience with you wears thin.'

The Merlin was generally considered to be the most capable wizard on the planet. The simple words with their implied threat were almost chilling.

Almost.

'I'm sure you'll last long enough for me to help you out of this mess, Merlin.' I smiled at him and held up my hand, palm up, fingers spread, as if holding an orange in them. 'Balls,' I said. 'Vise. Come on, Peabody.'

Peabody blinked at me as I swept past him on the way to the door, his mouth opening and closing silently several times. Then he made a few vague, sputtering sounds and hurried to catch up with me.

I glanced back at the Merlin as I reached the door.

I could clearly see his cold, flat blue eyes burning with fury while he sat in apparent relaxation and calm. The fingers of his right hand twitched in a violent little spasm that did not seem to touch the rest of his body. For an instant, I had to wonder just how desperate he had to be to accept my help. I had to wonder how smart it was to goad him like that.

And I had to wonder if that apparent calm and restrained exterior was simply a masterful control of his emotions – or if, under the pressure, it had become some kind of quiet, deadly madness.

Damn Morgan, for showing up at my door.

And damn me, for being fool enough to open it.

17

Peabody went into an immaculate office lined with
shelves bearing books arranged with flawless precision,
grouped by height and color. Many of the shelves were
loaded with binders presumably full of files and documents, similarly organized, in a dazzling array of hues.
I guess it takes all kinds of colors to make a bureau-
cratic rainbow.

I started to follow him inside, but he turned on me
with a ferocious glare. 'My office is a bastion of order,
Warden Dresden. You have no place in it.'

I looked down at him for a second. 'If I was a sensitive
guy, that would hurt my feelings.'

He gave me a severe look over his spectacles and said,
as if he thought the words were deadly venom and might
kill me, 'You are an untidy person.'

I put my hand over my heart, grinning at him. 'Ow.'

The tips of his ears turned red. He turned around stiffly
and walked into the office. He opened a drawer and started
jerking binders out of it with more force than was strictly
necessary.

'I read your book, by the way,' I said.

He looked up at me and then back down. He slapped
a binder open.

'The one about the Erlking?' I said. 'The collected poems
and essays?'

He took a folder out of the binder, his back stiff.

'The Warden from Bremen said you got the German wrong on the title,' I continued. 'That must have been kind of embarrassing, huh? I mean, it's been published for like a hundred years or something. Must eat at you.'

'German,' said Peabody severely, 'is also untidy.' He walked over to me with the folder, a pad of paper, an inkwell, and a quill. 'Sign here.'

I reached out for the quill with my right hand, and seized the folder with my left. 'Sorry. No autographs.'

Peabody nearly dropped the inkwell, and scowled at me. 'Now see *here*, Warden Dresden—'

'Now, now, Simon,' I said, taking vengeance on behalf of the German-speaking peoples of the world. 'We wouldn't want to screw up anyone's plausible deniability, would we?'

'My given name is Samuel,' he said stiffly. 'You, Warden Dresden, may address me as Wizard Peabody.'

I opened the file and skimmed over it. It was modeled after modern police reports, including testimony, photographs, and on-site reports from investigating Wardens. The militant arm of the White Council, at least, seemed to be less behind the times than the rest of us dinosaurs. That was largely Anastasia's doing. 'Is this the whole file, Sam?'

He gritted his teeth. 'It is.'

I slapped it shut. 'Thanks.'

'That file is official property of the Senior Council,' Peabody protested, waving the paper and the ink. 'I must insist that you sign for it at once.'

'Stop!' I called. 'Stop, thief!' I put a hand to my ear, listened solemnly for a few seconds and shook my head. 'Never a Warden around when you need one, is there, Sam?'

Then I walked off and left the little wizard sputtering behind me.

I get vicious under pressure.

The trip back was quieter than the one in. No B-movie escapees tried to frighten me to death – though there were a few unidentifiable bits wrapped up in spider silk, hanging from the trees where I'd established the pecking order, apparently all that was left of the bug I'd smashed.

I came out of the Nevernever and back into the alley behind the old meatpacking plant without encountering anything worse than spooky ambience. Back in Chicago, it was the darkest hour of night, between three and four in the morning. My head was killing me, and between the psychic trauma the skinwalker had given me, the power I'd had to expend during the previous day, and a pair of winter wonderland hikes, I was bone-weary.

I walked another five blocks to the nearest hotel with a taxi stand, flagged down a cab, and returned to my apartment. When I first got into the business, I didn't think anything of sacrificing my sleeping time to the urgency of my cases. I wasn't a kid in my twenties anymore, though. I'd learned to pace myself. I wouldn't help anyone if I ran myself ragged and made a critical error because I was too tired to think straight.

Mister, my bobtailed grey tomcat, came flying out of the darkened apartment as I opened the door. He slammed his shoulder into my legs, startled me half to death, and nearly put me on my ass. He's the next best thing to thirty pounds of cat, and when he hits me with his shoulder block of greeting I know it.

I leaned down to grab him and prevent him from leaving,

and wearily let myself into the house. It felt a lot quieter and emptier without Mouse in it. Don't get me wrong: me and Mister were roommates for years before the pooch came along. But it had taken considerable adjustments for both of us to get used to sharing our tiny place with a monstrous, friendly dust mop, and the sudden lack of his presence was noticeable and uncomfortable.

But Mister idly sauntered over to Mouse's bowl, ate a piece of kibble, and then calmly turned the entire bowl over so that kibble rolled all over the floor of the kitchen alcove. Then he went to Mouse's usual spot on the floor and lay down, sprawling luxuriously. So maybe it was just me.

I sat down on the couch, made a call, left a message, and then found myself lacking sufficient ambition to walk all the way into my bedroom, strip the sheets Morgan had bloodied, and put fresh ones on before I slept.

So instead I just stretched out on the couch and closed my eyes. Sleep was instantaneous.

I didn't so much as stir until the front door opened, and Murphy came in, holding the amulet that let her in past my wards. It was morning, and cheerful summer sunlight was shining through my well windows.

'Harry,' she said. 'I got your message.'

Or at least, that's what I think she said. It took me a couple of tries to get my eyes open and sit up. 'Hang on,' I said. 'Hang on.' I shambled into the bathroom and sorted things out, then splashed some cold water on my face and came back into the living room. 'Right. I think I can sort of understand English now.'

She gave me a lopsided smile. 'You look like crap in the morning.'

'I always look like this before I put on my makeup,' I muttered.

'Why didn't you call my cell? I'd have shown up right away.'

'Needed sleep,' I said. 'Morning was good enough.'

'I figured.' Murphy drew a paper bag from behind her back. She put it down on the table.

I opened it. Coffee and donuts.

'Cop chicks are *so* hot,' I mumbled. I pushed Peabody's file across the table to her and started stuffing my face and guzzling.

Murphy went through it, frowning, and a few minutes later asked, 'What's this?'

'Warden case file,' I said. 'Which you are not looking at.'

'The worm has turned,' she said bemusedly. 'Why am I not looking at it?'

'Because it's everything the Council has about LaFortier's death,' I said. 'I'm hoping something in here will point me toward the real bad guy. Two heads are better than one.'

'Got it,' she said. She took a pen and a notepad from her hip pocket and set them down within easy reach. 'What should I be looking for?'

'Anything that stands out.'

She held up a page. 'Here's something,' she said in a dry tone. 'The vic was two hundred and seventy-nine years old when he died.'

I sighed. 'Just look for inconsistencies.'

'Ah,' she said wisely.

Then we both fell quiet and started reading the documents in the file.

Morgan had given it to me straight. A few days before,

a Warden on duty in Edinburgh heard a commotion in LaFortier's chambers. She summoned backup, and when they broke in, they found Morgan standing over LaFortier's still-warm corpse holding the murder weapon. He professed confusion and claimed he did not know what had happened. The weapon had been matched to LaFortier's wounds, and the blood had matched as well. Morgan was imprisoned and a rigorous investigation had turned up a hidden bank account that had just received a cash deposit of a hell of a lot of money. Once confronted with that fact, Morgan managed to escape, badly wounding three Wardens in the process.

'Can I ask you something?' Murphy said.

'Sure.'

'One of the things that make folks leery of pulling the trigger on a wizard is his death curse, right?'

'Uh-huh,' I said. 'If you're willing to kill yourself to do it, you can lay out some serious harm on your killer.'

She nodded. 'Is it an instantaneous kind of thing?'

I pursed my lips. 'Not really.'

'Then how long does it take? Minutes? Seconds?'

'About as long as it takes to pull a gun and plug somebody,' I said. 'Some would be quicker than others.'

'A second or three, then.'

'Yeah.'

'Did Morgan get blasted by LaFortier's death curse then?'

I lifted an eyebrow. 'Um. It's sort of hard to say. It isn't always an immediate effect.'

'Best guess?'

I sipped at the last of the coffee. 'LaFortier was a member of the Senior Council. You don't get there without some serious chops. A violent death curse from someone like that could turn a city block to glass. So if I had to guess, I'd say no. LaFortier didn't throw it.'

'Why not?'

I frowned some more.

'He had time enough,' Murphy said. 'There was obviously a struggle. The vic has defensive wounds all over his arms – and he bled to death. That doesn't take long, but it's plenty of time to do the curse thing.'

'For that matter,' I mused, 'why didn't either of them use magic? This was a strictly physical struggle.'

'Could their powers have canceled each other out?'

'Technically, I guess,' I said. 'But that sort of thing needs serious synchronization. It doesn't often happen by accident.'

'Well. That's something, then,' she said. 'Both men either chose not to use magic or else were *unable* to use magic. Ditto the curse. Either LaFortier chose not to use it, or he was incapable of using it. The question is, why?'

I nodded. 'Sound logic. So how does that help us get closer to the killer?'

She shrugged, unfazed. 'No clue.'

That's how investigation works, most of the time. Cops, detectives, and quixotic wizards hardly ever know which information is pertinent until we've actually got a pretty good handle on what's happening. All you can do is accumulate whatever data you can, and hope that it falls into a recognizable pattern.

'Good thought, but it doesn't help yet,' I said. 'What else have we got?'

Murphy shook her head. 'Nothing that I can see yet. But do you want a suggestion?'

'Sure.'

She held up the page with the details on the incriminating bank account. 'Follow the money.'

'The money?'

'Witnesses can be mistaken – or bought. Theories and deductions can throw you completely off target.' She tossed the page back onto the coffee table. 'But the money always tells you something. Assuming you can find it.'

I picked up the page and scanned it again. 'A foreign bank. Amsterdam. Can you get them to show you where the payment came from?'

'You're kidding,' Murphy said. 'It would take me days, weeks, maybe months to go through channels and get that kind of information from an American bank, if I could get it at all. From a foreign bank specializing in confidentiality? I've got a better chance of winning a slam-dunk contest against Michael Jordan.'

I grunted. I got the disposable camera out of my duster pocket and passed it over to Murphy. 'I snapped some shots of the scene – a lot more of them than are in the Wardens' file. I'd like to get your take on them.'

She took the camera and nodded. 'Okay. I can take them by a photo center and—'

My old rotary telephone rang, interrupting her. I held up a hand to her and answered it.

'Harry,' Thomas said, his voice tight. 'We need you here. Now.'

I felt my body thrum into a state of tension. 'What's happening?'

'*Hurry!*' my brother snapped. 'I can't take them on by m—'

The line went dead.

Oh, God.

I looked up at Murphy, who took one look at my face and rose to her feet, car keys in hand, already moving toward the door. 'Trouble?'

'Trouble.'

'Where?'

I rose, seizing my staff and blasting rod. 'Storage rental park off Deerfield Square.'

'I know it,' Murphy said. 'Let's go.'

18

The handy part about riding with a cop was that she has the cool toys to make it simpler to get places quickly, even on a busy Chicago morning. The car was still bouncing from sweeping into the street from the little parking lot next to my apartment when she slapped a whirling blue light on the roof and started a siren. That part was pretty neat.

The rest of the ride wasn't nearly as fun. Moving 'fast' through a crowded city is a relative term, and in Chicago it meant a lot of rapid acceleration and sudden braking. We went through half a dozen alleys, hopped one bad intersection by driving up over the curb through a parking lot, and swerved through traffic at such a rate that my freshly imbibed coffee and donuts started swirling and sloshing around in a distinctly unpleasant fashion.

'Kill the noise and light,' I said a couple of blocks from the storage park.

She did it, asking, 'Why?'

'Because whatever is there, there are several of them and Thomas didn't think he could handle them.' I drew my .44 out of my duster pocket and checked it. 'Nothing's on fire. So let's hope that nothing's gone down yet and we'll be all sneaky-like until we know what's happening.'

'Still with the revolvers,' Murphy said, shaking her head. She drove past the street leading to the storage units and went one block past it instead before she turned and parked. 'When are you going to get a serious gun?'

'Look,' I said, 'just because you've got twice as many bullets as me—'

'Three times as many,' Murphy said. 'The SIG holds twenty.'

'Twenty!? Look the point is that—'

'And it reloads a lot faster. You've just got some loose rounds at the bottom of your pocket, right? No speed loader?'

I stuck the gun back in my pocket and tried to make sure none of the bullets fell out as we got out of the car. 'That's not the point.'

Murphy shook her head. 'Damn, Dresden.'

'I know the revolver is going to work,' I said, starting toward the storage park. 'I've seen automatics jam before.'

'New ones?'

'Well, no . . .'

Murphy had placed her own gun in the pocket of her light sports jacket. 'It's a good thing you've got options. That's all I'm saying.'

'If a revolver was good enough for Indiana Jones,' I said, 'it's good enough for me.'

'He was a *fictional* character, Harry.' Her mouth curved up in a small smile. 'And he had a whip.'

I eyed her.

Her eyes sparkled. 'Do *you* have a whip, Dresden?'

I eyed her even more. 'Murphy . . . are you coming on to me?'

She laughed, her smile white and fierce, as we rounded a corner and found the white rental van where Thomas had left it, across the street from the storage park.

Two men in similar grey suits and grey fedoras were standing nonchalantly in the summer-morning sunshine on the sidewalk next to the van.

On second glance, they were wearing the exact same grey suit, and the exact same grey hat, in fact.

'Feds?' I asked Murphy quietly as we turned down the sidewalk.

'Even feds shop at different stores,' she said. 'I'm getting a weird vibe here, Harry.'

I turned my head and checked out the storage park through the ten-foot-high black metal fencing that surrounded it.

I saw another pair of men in grey suits going down one row of storage units. Two more pairs were on the next. And two more on the one after that.

'That makes twelve,' Murphy murmured to me. She hadn't even turned her head. Murphy has cop powers of observation. 'All in the same suit.'

'Yeah, they're from out of town,' I said. 'Lot of times when beings from the Nevernever want to blend in, they pick a look and go with it.' I thought about it for a couple of steps. 'The fact that they all picked the same look might mean they don't have much going for them in the way of individuality.'

'Meaning I'd only have to go on a date with one of them to know about the rest?' Murphy asked.

'Meaning that you need a sense of *self* to have a sense of *self-preservation*.'

Murphy exhaled slowly. 'That's just great.' She moved a hand toward her other pocket, where I knew she kept her cell. 'More manpower might help.'

'Might set them off, too,' I said. 'I'm just saying, if the

music starts, don't get soft and shoot somebody in the leg or something.'

'You've seen too many movies, Harry,' she said. 'If cops pull the trigger, it's because they intend to kill someone. We leave the trick shots to SWAT snipers and Indiana Jones.'

I looked at the booth beside the entrance to the storage park. There was normally an attendant there, during the day. But there was no one in the booth – or in sight on the street, for that matter.

'Where is your unit?' Murphy asked.

I waggled my eyebrows at her. 'Right where it's always been, dollface.'

She made a noise that sounded like someone about to throw up.

'First row past the middle,' I said. 'Down at the far end of the park.'

'We have to walk past those two jokers by the van to see it.'

'Yeah,' I said. 'But I don't think these suits have found it yet. They're still here, and still looking. If they had located Morgan, they'd be gone already.' As we approached, I noticed that the two tires next to the curb on the white rental van were flat. 'They're worried about a getaway.'

'Are you sure they aren't human?' Murphy asked.

'Um. Reasonably?'

She shook her head. 'Not good enough. Are they from the spirit world or not?'

'Might not be able to tell until we get closer,' I said. 'Might even need to touch one of them.'

She took a slow, deep breath. 'As soon as you're certain,' she said, 'tell me. Shake your head if you're sure they aren't human. Nod if you can't tell or if they are.'

We were less than twenty feet away from the van and there was no time to argue or ask questions. 'Okay.'

I took a few more steps and ran smack into a curtain of nauseating energy so thick and heavy that it made my hair stand on end – a dead giveaway of a hostile supernatural presence. I twitched my head in a quick shake, as the two men in grey suits spun around at precisely the same time at precisely the same speed to face me. Both of them opened their mouths.

Before any sound could come out, Murphy produced her sidearm and shot them both in the head.

Twice.

Double-tapping the target like that is a professional killer's policy. There's a small chance that a bullet to the head might strike a target at an oblique angle and carom off of the skull. It isn't a huge possibility – but a double tap drops the odds from 'very unlikely' to 'virtually impossible.'

Murphy was a cop and a competition shooter, and less than five feet away from her targets. She did the whole thing in one smooth move, the shots coming as a single pulsing hammer of sound.

The men in grey suits didn't have time to so much as register her presence, much less do anything to avoid their fate. Clear liquid exploded from the backs of their skulls, and both men dropped to the sidewalk like rag dolls, their bodies and outfits deforming like a snowman in the spring, leaving behind nothing but ectoplasm, the translucent, gooey gel that was the matter of the Nevernever.

'Hell's bells,' I choked, as my adrenaline spiked after the fact.

Murphy kept the gun on the two until it was obvious

that they weren't going to take up a second career as head-less horsemen. Then she looked up and down the street, her cold blue eyes scanning for more threats as she popped the almost-full clip from the SIG and slapped a fully loaded one back in.

She may look like somebody's favorite aunt, but Murph can play hardball.

A couple of seconds later, what sounded like the howls of a gang of rabid band saws filled the air. There were a lot more than twelve of them.

'Come on!' I shouted, and sprinted forward.

The grey suits weren't individualists. It wasn't unthinkable that they would possess some kind of shared conscious-ness. Whacking the lookouts had obviously both alerted and enraged the others, and I figured that they would respond the way any colony-consciousness does when one of its members gets attacked.

The grey suits were coming to kill us.

We couldn't afford to run, not when they were this close to Morgan and Molly, but if the grey suits caught us on the open street, we were hosed. Our only chance was to move forward, fast, to get into the storage park while *they* went screaming out of it, looking for us. If we were quick enough, we might have time to get to the storage unit, collect Morgan and company, and make a quick escape through the portal in the floor and into the Nevernever.

I pounded across the street and through the entrance, with Murphy on my heels. I threw myself forward as the howls grew louder, and made it into the center row just as maybe twenty or twenty-five grey suits came rushing out of the other rows. Some of them saw us and slammed on the brakes, throwing up gravel with their expensive shoes, putting up a new tone of howl. The others belatedly began to turn as well, and then we were all the way into the center row of storage units, still moving at a dead run.

The grey suits rushed after us, but Murphy and I had a good forty-yard lead, and they didn't appear to be superhumanly light on their feet. We were going to make it.

Then I remembered that the door to the storage bay was locked shut.

I fumbled for the key as I ran, trying to pull it out of the front pocket of my jeans so that it would be ready. I figured that if I didn't get the door unlocked and open on the first try, the grey suits would catch up to us and kill us both.

So naturally I dropped the damn key.

I cursed and slid to a stop, slipping on the gravel. I looked around wildly for the dropped key, horribly aware of the mob of grey suits rushing toward us, now in eerie silence.

'Harry!' Murphy said.

'I know!'

She appeared beside me in a shooting stance, aiming at the nearest grey suit. 'Harry!'

'I know!'

Metal gleamed amongst the gravel and I swooped down on it as Murphy opened fire with precise, measured shots, sending the nearest grey suit into a tumbling sprawl. The others just vaulted over him and kept coming.

I'd found the key, but it was already too late.

Neither of us was going to make it to the shelter of my hideaway.

19

'Stay close!' I shouted. I thrust the end of my staff into the gravel and dragged it through, drawing a line in the dust and stones. I swiftly inscribed a quick, rough circle maybe four feet across around Murphy and me, actually getting between her gun and the grey suits for a second.

'Dammit, Harry, get down!' she shouted.

I did so, reaching out to touch the line in the gravel, slamming a quick effort of will into the simple design. Murphy's gun barked twice. I felt the energy gather in the circle and coalesce in a rush, snapping into place in a sudden and invisible wall.

The nearest of the grey suits staggered, and then flung itself into a forward dive. Murphy flinched back, and I grabbed her, hard, before she could cross the circle and disrupt it.

The grey suit slammed into the circle as if striking a solid wall, rebounding from its surface in a flash of blue-white light that described a phantom cylinder in the air. An instant later, more of the grey suits did exactly the same thing, maybe twenty of them, each of them bouncing off the circle's field.

'Easy!' I said to Murphy, still holding her against me. 'Easy, easy!' I felt her relax a little, ceasing to struggle against being held in place. 'It's okay,' I said. 'As long as we don't break the circle, they can't get through.'

We were both shaking. Murphy took a pair of gulping

breaths. We just stood there for a moment, while the grey suits spread out around the circle, reaching out with their hands to find its edges. I had time to get a better look at them while they did.

They were all the same height and weight. Their features were unremarkable and similar, if not quite identical. They looked as if they could have all been from the same family. Their eyes were all the same color, an odd grey-green, and there was no expression, none whatsoever, on their faces.

One of them reached out as if to try to touch me, and his open hand flattened against the circle's field. As it did, a freaking *mouth* opened on his palm, parallel to his fingers. It was lined with serrated sharklike teeth, and a slithering, coiling purple-black tongue emerged to lash randomly against the circle, as if seeking a way through. Yellowish mucus dripped thickly from the tongue as it did.

'Okay,' Murphy said in a small, toneless voice. 'That is somewhat disturbing.'

'And it's gonna get better,' I muttered.

Sure enough, the other grey suits started doing the same thing. Within seconds, we were completely surrounded by eerie hand-mouths, writhing tongues, and dripping slime.

Murphy shook her head and sighed. 'Eckgh.'

'Tell me about it.'

'How long will this thing keep them off?'

'They're spirit beings,' I said. 'As long as the circle's here, they're staying outside it.'

'Couldn't they just scuff dirt on it or something?'

I shook my head. 'Breaking the circle isn't just a physical process. It's an act of choice, of will – and these things don't have that.'

Murphy frowned. 'Then why are they doing anything at all?'

I had to restrain myself from smacking my forehead with the heel of my hand. 'Because someone summoned them from the Nevernever,' I said. 'Their summoner, wherever he is, is giving them orders.'

'Could *he* break the circle?' Murphy asked.

'Yeah,' I said. 'Easily.'

'Which is an excellent note upon which to begin our conversation,' said a man's voice with a heavy cockney accent. 'Make a hole, lads.'

The suits on one side of the circle lowered their hands and stood back, revealing a blocky bulldog of a man in a cheap maroon suit. He was average height, but heavy and solid with muscle, and he wore a few too many extra beers around his middle. His features were blunt and rounded, like water-worn stone. His hair was graying and cut into the shortest buzz you could get without going bald, and his eyes were small and hard – and the exact same color as those of the grey suits, a distinctive grey-green.

'Ah, love,' said the man, grinning. 'I think it's quite fine to see couples who aren't afraid to express their affection for each other.'

I blinked at him, then down at Murphy, and realized I was still holding her loosely against me. By the expression on her face, Murph hadn't really taken note of the fact, either. She cleared her throat and took a small step back from me, being careful not to step on the circle in the gravel.

He nodded at us, still grinning. ''Allo, Dresden. Why not make this easy for all of us and tell me which unit Donald Morgan is hiding in?'

I suddenly realized that I recognized this jerk from the profile the Wardens had on him. 'Binder,' I said. 'That's what they call you, isn't it?'

Binder's smile widened and he bowed slightly at the waist. 'The same.'

Murphy frowned at Binder and said, 'Who is this asshole?'

'One of the guys the Wardens wish they could just erase,' I said.

'He's a wizard?'

'I do have some skills in that direction, love,' Binder said.

'He's a one-trick hack,' I said, looking directly at him. 'Got a talent for calling up things from the Nevernever and binding them to his will.'

'So, Binder,' Murphy said, nodding.

'Yeah. He's scum who sells his talent to the highest bidder, but he's careful not to break any of the Laws of Magic, so the Wardens haven't ever been able to take him down.'

'I know,' Binder said cheerfully. 'And that's why I am positively savoring the exquisite irony of me being the one to take down the famous Warden Donald Morgan. The self-righteous prig.'

'You haven't got him yet,' I said.

'Matter of time, my lad,' Binder said, winking. He stooped and picked up a single piece of gravel. He bounced it thoughtfully on his palm and eyed us. 'See, there's a bit of competition for this contract, and it's a fair bit of quid. So I'm willing to give you a chance to make my job easier in exchange for considerations.'

'What considerations?' I asked.

He held up the pebble between his thumb and fore-finger. 'I won't pitch this into your circle and break it. That way, my lads won't need to kill you both – and won't that be nice?'

Behind Binder, down at the end of the row of storage units, the dust stirred. Something unseen moved across the gravel. Given how my life had been going, odds were good that it couldn't be a good thing. Unless . . .

'Come on, Binder,' I said. 'Don't be a simp. What makes you think I won't ask the lady here to put a bullet through that empty spot in your head where your brain's supposed to go?'

'She does that, she lowers the circle, and my lads tear you apart,' Binder replied.

'That won't be your problem, by then,' I said.

Binder grinned at me. 'All of us go down in a blaze of gory, is it?'

Murphy calmly raised her gun and settled it on Binder's face.

Binder faced her, his grin never fading. 'Now, little lady. Don't you be doing nothing you'll regret. Without my, ah, personal guidance, my lads here will tear this good gentleman's throat out right quick. But they're consider-ably less, ah, professional with ladies.' His grin faded. 'And you, miss, do not want to know what they're like when they're not professional.'

Fingers and slimy tongues and fangs continued pressing against the outer edge of the circle's protective field.

Murphy didn't let it show on her face, but I saw her shudder.

'Decision time, miss,' Binder said. 'Either pull that trigger, right now, and live with what happens – or put it down like a proper lady and work through this politely.'

Murphy's eyes narrowed at his comments. 'For all I know, you're about to toss that rock at us. I think I'll keep the gun right where it is.'

'Bear something else in mind, Binder,' I said. 'I know that you think you can just have your pets step in front of you and throw the rock from behind a wall of them, but think about what happens to you if you kill me.'

'Your death curse, is it?' he asked. Binder raised his hands and flattened his palms against his cheek in mock horror. 'Oh no. A death curse. Whatever shall I do?'

I faced him with a chilly little smile. 'You'll spend the rest of your life unable to use magic, I think,' I said in a quiet, hopefully confident-sounding voice. 'When I die, I take away your power. Forever. No more summoning. No more binding.'

Binder's expression began to flatten out into neutrality.

'You ever had a job that you liked, Binder?' I asked him. 'I'm betting you haven't. I've read your file. You're the kind who likes to sleep late, spend a lot of money impressing people. Always buys room service, always with the champagne. And you like the women the money gets you.' I shook my head. 'How many bottles of champagne you think you'll be able to afford when a paper hat becomes part of your professional wear? You've got enough talent to live a nice, long life, man. As a nobody.'

He stared at me in silence for a second. 'You can't do that,' Binder said. 'Take away my talent. That isn't possible.'

'I'm a wizard of the White Council, Binder. Not some stupid hack who spent his life using his gift to hurt people. Do you think we go around advertising everything we can do? If you knew half the things I've done that you think are impossible, you'd already be running.'

Binder faced me, beads of sweat suddenly standing out on his jowls.

'So I'd think real careful before I threw that rock, Binder. Real careful.'

A police siren sounded, from fairly nearby.

I smiled, showing teeth. 'Hey, cops. This'll get interesting.'

'You?' he asked, incredulously. 'You'd bring the cops into a private matter?'

I pointed a finger sideways at Murphy, who produced her badge and tucked the back of its folder into her belt, so that the shield faced Binder.

'Already did,' Murphy said.

'Besides, the whole reason I picked this joint was how heavily the neighborhood was policed,' I said. 'One gunshot and nobody reports anything. Half a dozen and people get nervous.'

Binder's eyes narrowed, and he looked from us toward the front of the park.

'Tick-tock,' I said, applying the pressure as hard as I could. 'It's just a matter of time, my lad.'

Binder looked around him again, then shook his head and sighed. 'Balls. It's always messy when I have to deal with the cops. Idiots dying by the truckload. Buckets of blood.' He gestured at his men. 'Identical suspects fleeing in all directions. Everyone out chasing them, and more people dying when they manage to catch them.' He stared hard at me. 'How about it, wizard? Cop? Maybe you've got stones enough to take it when I threaten you. I can admire that.'

My stomach got a little sinking feeling. I had been counting out seconds, hoping that my nerves didn't make me rush. There should have been enough time by now.

'How about those policemen? You willing to have their deaths on your conscience?' He rolled his neck a little, like a prizefighter warming up. 'Because I'll tell you right now that they aren't going to stop me.'

I put my hand out and touched Murphy's wrist. She glanced aside at me, and then lowered the gun.

'That's better,' Binder said. There was no hint of jocularity in his manner now. 'All I want is the Warden. He's a dead man already, and you know it. What does it matter who takes him?'

Something stirred at the end of the row, behind Binder, and I started smiling.

'I've got no quarrel with you or with this town,' Binder continued. 'Tell me where he is, I'll leave peaceful, and Bob's your uncle.'

Murphy drew in a sharp breath.

'Okay,' I said. 'He's right behind you.'

Binder's smile, this time, was positively vulpine. 'Dresden. We have a bit of banter going between us. We're both here in a moment where neither of us wants to act rashly. And that's all good fun. It's one of the little things that makes a day more enjoyable.' His voice hardened. 'But don't do me the incredibly insulting disservice of assuming that I'm a bloody moron.'

'I'm not,' I told him. 'He's about forty feet behind you. In a wheelchair.'

Binder gave me a gimlet stare. Then he rolled his eyes and shot a brief glance over his shoulder – then did a double take as his mouth dropped open.

Morgan sat in his wheelchair about forty feet away from Binder, my shotgun in his hands. Mouse stood beside the chair, focused intently upon Binder and his minions, his body tensed and ready to spring forward.

'Hello, Binder,' Morgan said in a flat, merciless tone of voice. 'Now, Miss Carpenter.'

Molly appeared out of literally nowhere as she dropped the veil she'd been holding over herself since I'd first seen her moving at the beginning of the conversation with Binder. She was holding my spare blasting rod in her hand, its far end covered with pale dust from being dragged through the gravel. She knelt beside the long, lazy arc of the circle she'd drawn in the dust and touched her hand to it, frowning in concentration.

Circles of power are basic stuff, really. Practically anyone can make one if they know how to do it, and learning how to properly establish a circle is the first thing any apprentice is taught. Circles create boundaries that isolate the area inside from the magical energies of the world outside. That's why Binder's minions couldn't cross the plane of the circle I'd drawn on the ground – their bodies were made up of ectoplasm, held into a solid form by magical energy. The circle cut off that energy when they tried to cross it.

As it sprang to life at my apprentice's will, Molly's circle did the same thing as mine – only this time the grey suits were *inside* it. As the energy field rose up, it cut off the grey suits from the flow of energy they needed to maintain their solid forms.

And suddenly the next best thing to forty demonic thugs collapsed into splatters of transparent gook.

Binder let out a cry as it happened, spinning around desperately, mumbling some kind of incantation under his breath — but he should have saved himself the effort. If he wanted them back, he would have to get out of the isolating field of the enormous circle first, and then he would have to start from scratch.

'*Ow*, Binder,' I said in patently false empathy. 'Didn't see that one coming, did ya?'

'Ernest Armand Tinwhistle,' Morgan thundered in a tone of absolute authority, raising the shotgun to his shoulder. 'Surrender yourself or face destruction, you worthless little weasel.'

Binder's intense grey-green eyes went from Morgan to the two of us. Then he seemed to reach some kind of conclusion and charged us like a bull, his head down, his arms pumping.

Murphy's gun tracked to him, but with a curse she jerked the barrel up and away from Binder. He slammed a shoulder into her chest, knocking her down, even as I received a stiff arm in the belly.

I threw a leg at his as he went by, but I was off balance from the shove, and although I wound up on my ass, I forced him to stumble for a step or three. Murphy took the impact with fluid grace, tumbled onto her back, rolled smoothly over one shoulder, and came back up on her feet.

'Get them out of here,' she snarled as she spun and took off at a sprint after Binder.

Mouse came pounding up to my side, staring after Murphy with worried doggy eyes, then glancing at me.

'No,' I told him. 'Watch this.'

Binder was running as hard as he could, but I doubted he had been all that light on his feet when he was young, much less twenty years and forty pounds later. Murphy worked out practically every day.

She caught him about ten feet before the end of the row, timed her steps for a second, and then sharply kicked his rearmost leg just as he lifted it to take his next step. His foot got caught on the back of his own calf as a result, and he went down in a sprawl.

Binder came to his feet with an explosive snarl of rage and whirled on Murphy. He flung a handful of gravel at her face, and then waded in with heavy, looping punches.

Murph ducked her head down and kept the gravel out of her eyes, slipped aside from one punch, and then seized his wrist on the second. The two of them whirled in a brief half circle, Binder let out a yelp, and then his bald head slammed into the steel door of a storage unit. I had to give the guy credit for physical toughness. He rebounded from the door a little woozily, but drove an elbow back at Murphy's head.

Murphy caught that arm and continued the motion, using her own body as a fulcrum in a classic hip throw – except that Binder was facing in the opposite direction than usual for that technique.

You could hear his arm come out of its socket fifty feet away.

And *then* he hit the gravel face-first.

Binder got extra points for brains in my book, after that: he lay still and didn't put up a struggle as Murphy dragged his wrists behind his back and cuffed him.

I traded a glance with Mouse and said, wisely, 'Hard-core.'

The police sirens were getting louder. Murphy looked up at them, and then down the row at me. She made an exasperated shooing motion.

'Come on,' I said to Mouse. The two of us hurried down the row to Morgan's chair.

'I couldn't shoot him with this scatter pipe with the two of you standing there,' Morgan complained as I approached. 'Why didn't you do it?'

'That's why,' I said, nodding to the park entrance, where a patrol car was screeching to a halt, its blue bubbles flashing. 'They get all funny about corpses with gunshot wounds in them.' I turned to scowl at Molly. 'I told you to bug out at the first sign of danger.'

She took the handles of Morgan's wheelchair and we all started back toward the storage unit and its portal. 'We didn't know what was going on until we heard them all start shrieking,' she protested. 'And then Mouse went nuts, and started trying to dig his way through a metal door. I thought you might be in trouble. And you were.'

'That isn't the point,' I said. I glanced at the circle drawn in the gravel as we crossed it, breaking it and releasing its power. 'Whose idea was the circle?'

'Mine,' Morgan said calmly. 'Circle traps are a standard tactic for dealing with rogue summoners.'

'I'm sorry it took so long to draw,' Molly said. 'But I had to make it big enough to get them all.'

'Not a problem. He was happy to kill time running his mouth.' We all entered the storage bay, and I rolled the door closed behind us. 'You did good, grasshopper.'

Molly beamed.

I looked around us and said, 'Hey. Where's Thomas?'

'The vampire?' Morgan asked.

'I had him watching the outside of the park, just in case,' I said.

Morgan gave me a disgusted look and rolled himself forward toward the prepared portal into the Nevernever. 'The vampire goes missing just before a bounty hunter who couldn't possibly know my location turns up. And you're actually surprised, Dresden?'

'Thomas called me and told me there was trouble,' I said, my voice tight. 'If he hadn't, you'd have been drowning in grey suits by now.'

Molly chewed her lip worriedly and shook her head. 'Harry . . . I haven't seen him since he dropped us off.'

I glanced back toward the entrance of the park, clenching my teeth.

Where was he?

If he'd been able to do otherwise, Thomas would never have let Murphy and me fight alone against Binder's minions. He would have been right in there beside us. Except he hadn't been.

Why not? Had circumstances forced him to leave before I arrived? Or worse, had someone else involved in the current crisis decided to take measures against him? Psycho bitch Madeline came uncomfortably to mind. And the skinwalker had already demonstrated that it was happy to murder my allies instead of striking directly at me.

Or maybe he'd simply been overwhelmed by a crowd of grey-suited demons. Maybe his body was already cooling in some nook or cranny of the storage park. My mouth went dry at the thought.

Hell's bells.

What had happened to my brother?

Morgan spoke a quiet word and opened a shimmering rectangular portal in the floor. Molly walked over to it and stared down, impressed.

'Dresden,' Morgan said. 'We can't afford to become entangled with the local authorities.'

I wanted to scream at him, but he was right. More

sirens had closed in on the park. We had to leave. I grabbed the handles to Morgan's chair, started for the portal, and said, 'Let's go, people.'

Dammit, Thomas, I snarled to myself. *Where the hell are you?*

20

The portal in my hideaway opened three steps from the trail in the Nevernever, all right, but those three steps weren't handicapped-accessible. Molly and I each had to get under one of Morgan's arms and half carry him to the trail. I left Molly and Mouse with him, went back and got the wheelchair, and dragged it up the frozen slope to a path that was all but identical to the one I'd been on earlier.

We loaded Morgan into the wheelchair again. He was pale and shaking by the time we were finished. I laid a hand against his forehead. It was hot with fever.

Morgan jerked his head away from my fingers, scowling.

'What is it?' Molly asked. She had thought to grab both coats I'd had waiting, and had already put one of them on.

'He's burning up,' I said quietly. 'Butters said that could mean the wound had been infected.'

'I'm fine,' Morgan said, shivering.

Molly helped him into the second coat, looking around at the frozen, haunted wood with nervous eyes. 'Shouldn't we get him out of the cold, then?'

'Yeah,' I said, buttoning my duster shut. 'It's maybe ten minutes from here to the downtown portal.'

'Does the vampire know about that, too?' Morgan growled.

'What's that supposed to mean?'

'That you'd be walking into an obvious trap, Dresden.'

'All right, that's it,' I snapped. 'One more comment about Thomas and you're going body sledding.'

'*Thomas?*' Morgan's pale face turned a little darker as he raised his voice. 'How many corpses is it going to take to make you come to your senses, Dresden?'

Molly swallowed. 'Harry, um, excuse me.'

Both of us glared at her.

She flushed and avoided eye contact. 'Isn't this the Nevernever?'

'Yeah,' I said.

'Obviously,' Morgan said at the same time.

We faced each other again, all but snarling.

'Okay,' Molly said. 'Haven't you told me that it's sort of dangerous?' She took a deep breath and hurried her speech. 'I mean, you know. Isn't it sort of dumb to be standing here arguing in loud voices? All things considered?'

I suddenly felt somewhat foolish.

Morgan's glower waned. He bowed his head wearily, folding his arms across his belly.

'Yeah,' I said, reining in my own temper. 'Yeah, probably so.'

'Not least because anyone who comes through the Ways from Edinburgh to Chicago is going to walk right over us,' Morgan added.

Molly nodded. 'Which would be sort of . . . awkward?'

I snorted quietly. I nodded my head in the proper direction, and started pushing the wheelchair down the trail. 'This way.'

Molly followed, her eyes darting left and right at the sounds of movement in the faerie wood around us. Mouse fell into pace beside her, and she reached down to lay a hand on the dog's back as she walked, an entirely unconscious gesture.

We moved at a steady pace and in almost complete silence for maybe five minutes before I said, 'We need to know how they found out about you.'

'The vampire is the best explanation,' Morgan replied, his tone carefully neutral.

'I have information about him that you don't,' I said. 'Suppose it isn't him. How did they do it?'

Morgan pondered that for a time. 'Not with magic.'

'You certain?'

'Yes.'

He sounded like it.

'Your countermeasures are *that* good?' I asked.

'Yes.'

I thought about that for a minute. Then it dawned on me what Morgan had done to protect himself from supernatural discovery. 'You called in your marker. The silver oak leaf. The one Titan—' I forced myself to stop, glancing uneasily around the faerie forest. 'The one the Summer Queen awarded you.'

Morgan turned his head slightly to glance at me over his shoulder.

I whistled. I'd seen Queen Titania with my Sight once. The tableau of Titania and her counterpart, Mab, preparing to do battle with each other still ranked as the most humbling and awe-inspiring display of pure power I had ever witnessed. 'That's why you're so certain no one is going to find you. She's the one shielding you.'

'I admit,' Morgan said with another withering look, 'it's no donut.'

I scowled. 'How'd you know about that?'

'Titania's retainer told me. The entire Summer Court has been laughing about it for months.'

Molly made a choking sound behind me. I didn't turn around. It would just force her to put her hand over her mouth to hide the smile.

'How long did she give you?' I asked.

'Sundown tomorrow.'

Thirty-six hours, give or take. A few hours more than I'd believed I had, but not much. 'Do you have the oak leaf on you?'

'Of course,' he said.

'May I see it?'

Morgan shrugged and drew a leather cord from around his neck. A small leather pouch hung from the cord. He opened it, felt around inside, and came out with it – a small, exquisitely detailed replica of an oak leaf, backed with a simple pin. He held it out to me.

I took it and pitched it into the haunted wood.

Morgan actually *did* growl, this time. 'Why?'

'Because the Summer Queen bugged them. Last year, her goon squad was using mine to track me down all over Chicago.'

Morgan frowned at me, and glanced out toward where I had thrown it. Then he shook his head and rubbed tiredly at his eyes with one hand. 'Must be getting senile. Never even considered it.'

'I don't get it,' Molly said. 'Isn't he still protected, anyway?'

'He is,' I said. 'But that leaf isn't. So if the Summer Queen wants him found, or if someone realizes what she's doing and makes her a deal, she can keep her word to

Morgan to hide him, *and* give him away. All she has to do is make sure someone knows to look for the spell on the oak leaf.'

'The Sidhe are only bound to the letter of their agreements,' Morgan said, nodding. 'Which is why one avoids striking bargains with them unless there are no options.'

'So Binder could have been following the oak leaf?' Molly asked.

I shrugged. 'Maybe.'

'It is still entirely possible that the Summer Queen is dealing in good faith,' Morgan said.

I nodded. 'Which brings us back to the original question: how did Binder find you?'

'Well,' Molly said, 'not to mince words, but he didn't.'

'He would have found us in a matter of moments,' Morgan said.

'That's not what I mean,' she said. 'He knew you were in the storage park, but he didn't know which unit, exactly. I mean, wouldn't tracking magic have led him straight to you? And if Thomas sold you out, wouldn't he have told Binder exactly which storage bay we were in?'

Morgan started to reply, then frowned and shut his mouth. 'Hngh.'

I glanced over my shoulder at the grasshopper and gave her a nod of approval.

Molly beamed at me.

'Someone on the ground following us?' Morgan asked. 'A tailing car wouldn't have been able to enter the storage park without a key.'

I thought of how I'd been shadowed by the skinwalker the previous evening. 'If they're good enough, it would be possible,' I admitted. 'Not likely, but possible.'

'So?' Morgan said. 'Where does that leave us?'

'Baffled,' I said.

Morgan bared his teeth in a humorless smile. 'Where to next, then?'

'If I take you back to my place, they'll pick us up again,' I said. 'If someone's using strictly mortal methods of keeping track of our movements, they'll have someone watching it.'

Morgan looked back and up at me. 'I assume you aren't just going to push me in circles around Chicago while we wait for the Council to find us.'

'No,' I said. 'I'm taking you to my place.'

Morgan thought about that one for a second, then nodded sharply. 'Right.'

'Where the bad guys will see us and send someone else to kill us,' Molly said. 'No wonder I'm the apprentice; because I'm so ignorant that I can't see why that isn't a silly idea.'

'Watch and learn, grasshopper. Watch and learn.'

21

We left the trail again, and for the second time in a day I emerged from the Nevernever into the alley behind the old meatpacking plant. We made two stops and then walked until we could flag down another cab. The cabbie didn't seem to be overly thrilled with Mouse, or the wheel-chair, or how we filled up his car, but maybe he just didn't speak enough English to ably convey his enthusiasm. You never know.

'These really aren't good for you,' Molly said through a mouthful of donut, as we unloaded the cab.

'It's Morgan's fault. He started talking about donuts,' I said. 'And besides – you're eating them.'

'I have the metabolic rate of youth,' Molly said, smiling sweetly. 'You're the one who needs to start being health-conscious, O venerable mentor. I'll be invincible for another year or two at least.'

We wrestled Morgan into his chair, and I paid off the cabbie. We rolled Morgan over to the steps leading down to my apartment, and between the two of us managed to turn his chair around and get him down the stairs and into the apartment without dropping him. After that, I grabbed Mouse's lead, and the two of us went up to get the mail from my mailbox, and then ambled around to the boardinghouse's small backyard and the patch of sandy earth set aside for Mouse's use.

But instead of loitering around waiting for Mouse, I led him into the far corner of the backyard, which is a miniature jungle of old lilacs that hadn't been trimmed or pruned since Mr Spunkelcrief died. They were in bloom, and their scent filled the air. Bees buzzed busily about the bushy plants, and as I stepped closer to them, the corner of the building cut off the traffic sounds.

It was the only place on the property's exterior that was not readily visible from most of the rest of the buildings on the street.

I pressed past the outer branches of the lilacs and found a small and relatively open space in the middle. Then I waited. Within seconds, there was a buzzing sound, like the wings of a particularly large dragonfly, and then a tiny winged faerie darted through the lilacs to come to a halt in front of me.

He was simply enormous for a pixie, one of the Wee Folk, and stood no less than a towering twelve inches high. He looked like an athletically built youth dressed in an odd assortment of armor made from discarded objects and loose ends. He'd replaced his plastic bottle-cap helmet with one made of most of the shell of a hollowed-out golf ball. It was too large for his head, but that didn't seem to concern him. His cuirass had first seen service as a bottle of Pepto-Bismol, and hanging at his hip was what looked like the blade to a jigsaw, with one end wrapped in string to serve as a grip. Wings like those of a dragonfly buzzed in a translucent cloud of motion at his back.

The little faerie came to attention in midair, snapped off a crisp salute, and said, 'Mission accomplished, my lord of pizza!'

'That fast?' I asked. It hadn't been twenty minutes since I'd first summoned him, after we'd gotten donuts and before we'd gotten into the cab. 'Quick work, Toot-toot, even for you.'

The praise seemed to please the little guy immensely. He beamed and buzzed in a couple of quick circles. 'He's in the building across the street from this one, two buildings toward the lake.'

I grunted, thinking. If I was remembering right, that was another boardinghouse converted into apartments, like mine. 'The white one with green shutters?'

'Yes, that's where the rapscallion has made his lair!' His hand flashed to his waist and he drew his saw-toothed sword from its transparent plastic scabbard, scowling fiercely. 'Shall I slay him for you, my lord?'

I very carefully kept the smile off of my face. 'I don't know if things have escalated to that level just yet,' I said. 'How do you know this guy is watching my apartment?'

'Oh, oh! Don't tell me this one!' Toot jittered back and forth in place, bobbing in excitement. 'Because he has curtains on the windows so you can't see in, and then there's a big black plastic box with a really long nose poking through them and a glass eye on the end of the nose! And he looks at the back of it all the time, and when he sees someone going into your house, he pushes a button and the box beeps!'

'Camera, huh?' I asked. 'Yeah, that probably makes him our snoop.' I squinted up at the summer sunshine and adjusted the uncomfortably warm leather duster. I wasn't taking it off, though. There was too much hostility flying around for that. 'How many of your kin are about, Toot?'

'Hundreds!' Toot-toot declared, brandishing his sword. 'Thousands!'

I arched an eyebrow. 'You've been splitting the pizza a thousand ways?'

'Well, lord,' he amended. 'Several dozen, at any rate.'

The Wee Folk are a fractious, fickle bunch, but I've learned a couple of things about them that I'm not sure anyone else knows. First, that they're just about everywhere, and anywhere they aren't, they can usually *get*. They don't have much of an attention span, but for short, simple tasks, they are hell on wheels.

Second – they have a lust for pizza that is without equal in this world. I've been bribing the Wee Folk with pizza on a regular basis for years, and in return they've given me their (admittedly erratic) loyalty. They call me the Za-Lord, and the little fair folk who take my pizza also serve in the Za-Lord's Guard – which means, mostly, that the Wee Folk hang around my house hoping for extra pizza and protecting it from wee threats.

Toot-toot was their leader, and he and his folks had pulled off some very helpful tasks for me in the past. They had saved my life on more than one occasion. No one in the supernatural community ever expected everything of which they were capable. As a result, Toot and his kin are generally ignored. I tried to take that as a life lesson: never underestimate the little people.

This was a job that was right up Toot-toot's alley. Almost literally.

'Do you know which car is his?' I asked.

Toot threw back his head, Yul Brynner style. 'Of course! The blue one with *this* on the hood.' He threw his arms out and up at an angle and stood ramrod straight in a Y shape.

'Blue Mercedes, eh?' I asked. 'Okay. Here's what I want you to do. . . .'

Five minutes later, I walked back around the side of the house to the front opposite the street. Then I turned to face the house where the snoop was set up and put on my most ferocious scowl. I pointed directly at the curtained second-floor windows, then turned my hand over and crooked my finger, beckoning. Then I pointed to the ground right in front of me.

One of the curtains might have twitched. I gave it a slow count of five, and then started walking briskly toward the other boardinghouse, crossing the busy street in the process.

A young man in his twenties wearing khaki shorts and a green T-shirt came rushing out of the converted board-inghouse and ran toward a blue Mercedes parked on the street, an expensive camera hanging around his neck.

I kept walking, not changing my pace.

He rushed around to the driver's door, pointing some kind of handheld device at the car. Then he clawed at the door but it stayed closed. He shot another glance at me, and then tried to insert his key into the lock. Then he blinked and stared at his key as he pulled it back trailing streamers of a rubbery pink substance – bubble gum.

'I wouldn't bother,' I said as I got closer. 'Look at the tires.'

The young man glanced from me to his Mercedes and stared some more. All four tires were completely flat.

'Oh,' he said. He looked at his gum-covered key and sighed. 'Well. Shit.'

I stopped across the car from him and smiled faintly.

'Don't feel too bad about it, man. I've been doing this longer than you.'

He gave me a sour look. Then he held up his key. 'Bubble gum?'

'Coulda been superglue. Take it as a professional courtesy.' I nodded toward his car. 'Let's talk. Turn the air-conditioning on, for crying out loud.'

He eyed me for a moment and sighed. 'Yeah. Okay.'

We both got in the car. He scraped the gum off of his key and put it in the ignition, but when he turned it, nothing happened.

'Oh. Pop the hood,' I said.

He eyed me and did. I went around to the front of the car and reconnected the loose battery cable. I said, 'Okay,' and he started the engine smoothly.

Like I said, give Toot-toot and his kin the right job, and they are formidable as hell.

I got back in the car and said, 'You licensed?'

The young man shrugged and turned his AC up to 'deep freeze'. 'Yeah.'

I nodded. 'How long?'

'Not long.'

'Cop?'

'In Joliet,' he said.

'But not now.'

'Didn't fit.'

'Why are you watching my place?'

He shrugged. 'I got a mortgage.'

I nodded and held out my hand. 'Harry Dresden.'

He frowned at the name. 'You the one used to work for Nick Christian at Ragged Angel?'

'Yeah.'

'Nick has a good reputation.' He seemed to come to some kind of conclusion and took my hand with a certain amount of resignation. 'Vince Graver.'

'You got hired to snoop on me?'

He shrugged.

'You tail me last night?'

'You know the score, man,' Graver said. 'You take someone's money, you keep your mouth shut.'

I lifted my eyebrows. A lot of PIs wouldn't have the belly to be nearly so reticent, under the circumstances. It made me take a second look at him. Thin, built like someone who ran or rode a bicycle on his weekends. Clean-cut without being particularly memorable. Medium brown hair, medium height, medium brown eyes. The only exceptional thing about his appearance was that there was nothing exceptional about his appearance.

'You keep your mouth shut,' I agreed. 'Until people start getting hurt. Then it gets complicated.'

Graver frowned. 'Hurt?'

'There have been two attempts on my life in the past twenty-four hours,' I said. 'Do the math.'

He focused his eyes down the street, into the distance, and pursed his lips. 'Damn.'

'Damn?'

He nodded morosely. 'There go the rest of my fees and expenses.'

I arched an eyebrow at him. 'You're bailing on your client? Just like that?'

'"Accomplice" is an ugly word. So is "penitentiary".'

Smart kid. Smarter than I had been when I first got my PI license. 'I need to know who backed you.'

Graver thought about that one for a minute. Then he said, 'No.'

'Why not?'

'I make it a personal policy not to turn on clients or piss off people who are into murder.'

'You lost the work,' I said. 'What if I made it up to you?'

'Maybe you didn't read that part of the book. The "I" in PI stands for "investigator". Not "informer".'

'Maybe I call the cops. Maybe I tell them you're involved in the attacks.'

'Maybe you can't prove a damned thing.' Graver shook his head. 'You don't get ahead in this business if you can't keep your teeth together.'

I leaned back in my seat and crossed my arms, studying him for a moment. 'You're right,' I said. 'I can't make you. So I'm asking you. Please.'

He kept on staring out the windshield. 'Why they after you?'

'I'm protecting a client.'

'Old guy in the wheelchair.'

'Yeah.'

Graver squinted. 'He looks like a hard case.'

'You have no idea.'

We sat in the air-conditioning for a moment. Then he glanced at me and shook his head.

'You seem like a reasonable guy,' Graver said. 'Hope you don't get dead. Conversation over.'

I thought about pushing things, but I've been around long enough to recognize someone who was genuinely tough-minded when I see him. 'You got a business card?'

He reached into his shirt pocket and produced a plain

white business card with his name and a phone number. He passed it over to me. 'Why?'

'Sometimes I need a subcontractor.'

He lifted both eyebrows.

'One who knows how to keep his teeth together.' I nodded to him and got out of the car. I leaned down and looked in the door before I left. 'I know a mechanic. I'll give him a call and he'll come on out. He's got a compressor on his truck, and he can fill up your tires. I'll pay for it.'

Graver studied me with calm, intelligent eyes and then smiled a little. 'Thanks.'

I closed the door and thumped on the roof with my fist. Then I walked back to my apartment. Mouse, who had waited patiently in the yard, came shambling up to greet me as I stepped out of the street, and he walked alongside me as I went back to the apartment.

Morgan was lying on my bed again when I came back in. Molly was just finishing up changing his bandages. Mister watched the entire process from the back of the couch, his ears tilted forward, evidently fascinated.

Morgan nodded to me and rasped, 'Did you catch him?'

'Yeah,' I said. 'A local PI had been hired to keep track of me. But there was a problem.'

'What's that?'

I shrugged. 'He had integrity.'

Morgan inhaled through his nose and nodded. 'Pretty rare problem.'

'Yeah. Impressive young man. What are the odds?'

Molly looked back and forth between us. 'I don't understand.'

'He's quitting the job, but he won't tell us what we want to know about his client, because he doesn't think it would be right,' I said. 'He's not willing to sell the information, either.'

Molly frowned. 'Then how are we going to find out who is behind all of this?'

I shrugged. 'Not sure. But I told him I'd get someone to come by and put the air back in his tires. Excuse me.'

'Wait. He's still out there?'

'Yeah,' I said. 'Blue Mercedes.'

'And he's a young man.'

'Sure,' I said. 'A little older than you. Name's Vince Graver.'

Molly beamed. 'Well, then, I'll go get him to tell me.' She walked over to my icebox, opened it, pulled out a dark brown bottle of microbrewery beer, and walked toward the door.

'How you gonna do that?' I asked her.

'Trust me, Harry. I'll change his mind.'

'*No*,' Morgan said fiercely. He coughed a couple of times. 'No. I would rather be dead – do you hear me? Be *dead* than have you use black magic on my behalf.'

Molly set the beer down on the shelf by the door and blinked at Morgan. 'You're right,' she said to me. 'He *is* kind of a drama queen. Who said anything about magic?'

She pulled one arm into her T-shirt, and wriggled around a little. A few seconds later, she was tugging her bra out of the arm hole of her shirt. She dropped it on the shelf, picked up the bottle, and held it against each breast in turn. Then she turned to face me, took a deep breath, and arched her back a little. The tips of her breasts pressed quite noticeably against the rather strained fabric of her shirt.

'What do you think?' she asked, giving me a wicked smile.

I thought Vince was doomed.

'I think your mother would scream bloody murder,' I said.

Molly smirked. 'Call the mechanic. I'll just keep him company until the truck gets there.' She turned with a little extra hip action and left the apartment.

Morgan made a low, appreciative sound as the door closed.

I eyed him.

Morgan looked from the door to me. 'I'm not dead yet, Dresden.' He closed his eyes. 'Doesn't hurt to admire a woman's beauty once in a while.'

'Maybe. But that was just . . . just *wrong*.'

Morgan smiled, though it was strained with discomfort. 'She's right, though. Especially with a young man. A woman can make a man see everything in a different light.'

'Wrong,' I muttered. 'Just *wrong*.'

I went to call Mike the mechanic.

Molly came back about forty-five minutes later, beaming.

Morgan had been forced to take more pain medication and was tossing in a restless sleep. I closed the door carefully so that we wouldn't wake him.

'Well?' I asked.

'His car has really good air-conditioning,' Molly said smugly. 'He never had a chance.' Between two fingers, she held up a business card like the one I'd gotten.

I did the same thing with mine, mirroring her.

She flipped hers over, showing me a handwritten note on the other side. 'I'm worried about my job as your assistant.' She put the back of her hand against her forehead melodramatically. 'If something happens to you, whatever will I do? Wherever shall I go?'

'And?'

She held out the card to me. 'And Vince suggested that I might consider work as a paralegal. He even suggested a law firm. Smith Cohen Mackleroy.'

'His job-hunting suggestion, eh?' I asked.

She smirked. 'Well, obviously he couldn't just tell me who hired him. That would be wrong.'

'You are a cruel and devious young woman.' I took the card from her and read it. It said: Smith Cohen Mackleroy, listed a phone number, and had the name 'Evelyn Derek' printed under that.

I looked up to meet Molly's smiling eyes. Her grin widened. 'Damn, I'm good.'

'No argument here,' I told her. 'Now we have a name, a lead. One might even call it a clue.'

'Not only *that*,' Molly said. 'I have a date.'

'Good work, grasshopper,' I said, grinning as I rolled my eyes. 'Way to take one for the team.'

22

Smith Cohen and Mackleroy, as it turned out, was an upscale law firm in downtown Chicago. The building their offices occupied stood in the shadow of the Sears Tower, and must have had a fantastic view of the lake. Having plucked out the enemy's eyes, so to speak, I thought that I might have bought us some breathing space. Without Vince on our tail, I hoped that Morgan could get a few hours of rest in relative safety.

I'd figure out somewhere else to move him – just as soon as I leaned on Ms Evelyn Derek and found out to whom she reported Vince's findings.

I guess I looked sort of mussed and scraggly, because the building's security guard gave me a wary look as I entered solidly in the middle of lunch hour. I could practically see him deciding whether or not to stop me.

I gave him my friendliest smile – which my weariness and stress probably reduced to merely polite – and said, 'Excuse me, sir. I have an appointment with an attorney at Smith Cohen and Mackleroy. They're on the twenty-second floor, right?'

He relaxed, which was good. Beneath his suit, he looked like he had enough muscle to bounce me handily out the door. 'Twenty-four, sir.'

'Right, thanks.' I smiled at him and strode confidently past. Confidence is critical to convincing people that you really are supposed to be somewhere – especially when you aren't.

'Sir,' said the guard from behind me. 'I'd appreciate it if you left your club here.'

I paused and looked over my shoulder.

He had a gun. His hand wasn't exactly resting on it, but he'd tucked his thumb into his belt about half an inch away.

'It isn't a club,' I said calmly. 'It's a walking stick.'

'Six feet long.'

'It's traditional Ozark folk art.'

'With dents and nicks all over it.'

I thought about it for a second. 'I'm insecure?'

'Get a blanket.' He held out his hand.

I sighed and passed my staff over to him. 'Do I get a receipt?'

He took a notepad from his pocket and wrote on it. Then he passed it over to me. It read: *Received, one six-foot traditional Ozark walking club from Mr Smart-ass.*

'That's Doctor Smart-ass,' I said. 'I didn't spend eight years in insult college to be called Mister.'

He leaned the staff against the wall behind his desk and sat back down at his chair.

I went to the elevator and rode up. It was one of those express contraptions that goes fast enough to compress your spine and make your ears pop. It opened on the twenty-fourth floor facing a reception desk. The law office, apparently, took up the entire floor.

The receptionist was, inevitably, a young woman, and just as unavoidably attractive. She went with the solid-oak furnishings, the actual oil paintings, and the handcrafted furniture in the reception area, and the faint scent of lemon wood polish in the air – variations on a theme of beautiful practicality.

She looked up at me with a polite smile, her dark hair long and appealing, her shirt cut just low enough to make you notice, but not so low as to make you think less of her. I liked the smile. Maybe I didn't look like a beaten-up bum. Maybe on me it just looked ruggedly determined.

'I'm sorry, sir,' she said, 'but the addiction-counseling center is on twenty-six.'

Sigh.

'I'm actually here to see someone,' I said. 'Assuming that this is Smith Cohen and Mackleroy?'

She glanced rather pointedly – but still politely – at the front of her desk, where a plaque bore the firm's name in simple sans serif lettering. 'I see, sir. Who are you looking for?'

'Ms Evelyn Derek, please.'

'Do you have an appointment?'

'No,' I said. 'But she'll want to talk to me.'

The receptionist looked at me as though she had some kind of bitter, unpleasant taste in her mouth. I'd timed my arrival correctly, then. The young lady clearly would have been much more comfortable handing me off to a secretary, or executive assistant, or whatever you're supposed to call them now, and letting someone else decide if I was supposed to be there. And Ms Evelyn Derek's assistant was just as clearly out to lunch, which was the point of showing up during lunch hour. 'Who shall I say is here?'

I produced Vincent Graver's business card and passed it to her. 'Please tell her that Vince has acquired some un-expected information and that she needs to hear about it.'

She pushed a button, adjusted her headset, and dutifully passed on the message to whoever was on the other end. She listened and nodded. 'Straight back down the hall, sir, the second door on the left.'

I nodded to her and walked through the door behind her. The carpet got even thicker and the decor more expensive. A nook in the wall showcased a small rock fountain between a pair of two-thousand-dollar leather chairs. I shook my head as I walked through a hall that absolutely reeked of success, power, and the desire for everyone to know about it.

I bet they would have been seethingly jealous of the Ostentatiatory in Edinburgh.

I opened the second door on the left, went in, and closed it behind me, to find a secretary's desk, currently unoccupied, and an open door to what would doubtless be an executive office appropriate to the status of Evelyn Derek, attorney at law.

'Come in, Mr Graver,' said an impatient woman's voice from inside the office.

I walked in and shut the door behind me. The office was big, but not monstrous. She probably wasn't a full partner in the firm. The furnishings were sleek and ultramodern, with a lot of glass and space-age metal. There was only one small filing cabinet in the room, a shelf with a row of legal texts, a slender and fragile-looking laptop computer, and a framed sheepskin from somewhere expensive on the wall. She had a window, but it had been frosted over into bare translucency. The glass desk and sitting table and liquor cabinet all shone, without a smudge or a fingerprint to be seen anywhere. It had all the warmth of an operating theater.

The woman typing on the laptop might have come with the office as part of a complete set. She wore rimless glasses in front of the deepest green eyes I had ever seen. Her hair was raven black, and cut close to her head, showcasing her narrow, elegant features and the slender line of her neck. She wore a dark silk suit jacket with a matching skirt and a white blouse. She had long legs, ending in shoes that must have cost more than most mortgage payments, but she wore no rings, no earrings, and no necklace. There was something cold and reserved about her posture, and her fingers struck the keys at a rapid, decisive cadence, like a military drummer.

She said nothing for two full minutes, focusing intently on whatever she was typing. Obviously, she had something to prove to Vince for daring to intrude upon her day.

'I hope you don't think you can convince me to rehire you, Mr Graver,' she said, eventually, without looking up. 'What is it that you think is so important?'

Ah. Vince had quit already. He didn't let much grass grow under his feet, did he?

This woman was evidently used to being taken very seriously. I debated several answers and decided to start things off by annoying her.

I know. Me. Shocking, right?

I stood there treating her the same way she had treated me, saying nothing, until Evelyn Derek exhaled impatiently through her nose and turned a cool and disapproving stare toward me.

'Hi, cuddles,' I said.

I'll give the lady this much – she had a great poker face. The disapproval turned into a neutral mask.

She straightened slightly in her chair, though she looked more attentive than nervous, and put her palms flat on the desktop.

'You're going to leave smudges,' I said.

She stared at me for a few more seconds before she said, 'Get out of my office.'

'I don't see any Windex in here,' I mused, looking around.

'Did you hear me?' she said, her voice growing harder. 'Get. Out.'

I scratched my chin. 'Maybe it's in your secretary's desk. You want me to get it for you?'

Spots of color appeared on her cheeks. She reached for the phone on her desk.

I pointed a finger at it, sent out an effort of will, and hissed, '*Hexus.*'

Fouling up technology is a fairly simple thing for a wizard to do. But it isn't surgical in its precision. Sparks erupted from the phone, from her computer, from the overhead lights, and from something inside her coat pocket, accompanied by several sharp popping sounds.

Ms Derek let out a small shriek and tried to flinch in three directions at once. Her chair rolled backward without her, and she wound up sprawled on the floor behind her glass-topped desk in a most undignified manner. Her delicate-looking glasses hung from one ear, and her deep green eyes were wide, the whites showing all around them.

Purely for effect, I walked a couple of steps closer and stood looking down at her in silence for a long moment. There was not a sound in that room, and it was a lot darker in there without the lights.

I spoke very, very quietly. 'There are two shut doors

between you and the rest of this office – which is mostly empty anyway. You've got great carpets, solid-oak paneling, and a burbling water feature out in the hallway.' I smiled slightly. 'Nobody heard what just happened. Or they would have come running by now.'

She swallowed, and didn't move.

'I want you to tell me who had you hire a detective to snoop on me.'

She made a visible effort to gather herself together. 'I-I don't know what you're talking about.'

I shook my head, lifted my hand, and made a beckoning gesture at the liquor cabinet as I murmured, '*Forzare*,' and made a gentle effort of will. The door to the cabinet swung open. I picked a bottle of what looked like bourbon and repeated the gesture, causing it to flit from the opened cabinet across the room to my hand. I unscrewed the cap and took a swig. It tasted rich and burned my throat pleasantly on the way down.

Evelyn Derek stared at me in pure shock, her mouth open, her face whiter than rural Maine.

I looked at her steadily. 'Are you sure?'

'Oh, God,' she whispered.

'Evelyn,' I said in a chiding voice. 'Focus. You hired Vince Graver to follow me around and report on my movements. Someone told you to do that. Who was it?'

'M-my clients,' she stammered. 'Confidential.'

I felt bad scaring the poor woman. Her reaction to the use of magic had been typical of a straight who had never encountered the supernatural before – which meant that she probably had no idea of the nature of whoever she was protecting. She was terrified. I mean, I knew I wasn't going to hurt her.

But I was the only one in the room who did.

The thing about playing a bluff is that you have to play it all the way out, even when it gets uncomfortable.

'I really didn't want this to get ugly,' I said sadly.

I took a step closer and put the bottle down on the desk. Then I slowly, dramatically, raised my left hand. It had been badly burned several years before, and while my ability to recover from such things was more intense than other human beings, at least in the long term, my hand still wasn't pretty. It wasn't quite horror-movie special effects anymore, but the molten scars covering my fingers, wrist, and most of my palm were still startling and unpleasant, if you hadn't ever seen them before.

'No, wait,' Evelyn squeaked. She backed across the floor on her buttocks, pressed her back to the wall and lifted her hands. 'Don't.'

'You helped your client try to kill people, Evelyn,' I said in a calm voice. 'Tell me who.'

Her eyes widened even more. 'What? No. No, I didn't know anyone would get hurt.'

I stepped closer and snarled, 'Talk.'

'All right, all right!' she stammered. 'She—'

She stopped speaking as suddenly as if someone had begun strangling her.

I eased up on the intimidation throttle. 'Tell me,' I said, more quietly.

Evelyn Derek shook her head at me, fear and confusion stripping away the reserve I'd seen in her only moments before. She started shaking. I saw her open her mouth several times, but only small choked sounds emerged. Her eyes lost focus and started flicking randomly around the room like a trapped animal looking for an escape.

That wasn't normal. Not even a little. Someone like Evelyn Derek might panic, might be cowed, might be backed into a corner – but she would never be at a loss for words.

'Oh,' I said, mostly to myself. 'I *hate* this crap.'

I sighed, and walked around the desk to stand over the cowering lawyer. 'Hell, if I'd known that someone had . . .' I shook my head. She wasn't really listening very hard to me, and she'd started crying.

It was one of about a thousand possible reactions when someone's free will has been directly abrogated by some kind of psychic interdiction. I'd just created a situation in which every part of her logical, rational mind had been completely in favor of telling me who had hired her. Her emotions had been lined up right behind her reasoned thoughts, too.

Only I was betting that someone had gotten into her head. Someone had left something inside her that refused to let Ms Derek speak about her employer. Hell, she might not even *have* a conscious memory of who hired her – despite the fact that she wouldn't just hire some detective to spy on somebody for no reason.

Everyone always thinks that such obvious logical inconsistencies wouldn't hold up, that the mind would somehow tear free of the bonds placed upon it using those flaws. But the fact is that the human mind isn't a terribly logical or consistent place. Most people, given the choice to face a hideous or terrifying truth or to conveniently avoid it, choose the convenience and peace of normality. That doesn't make them strong or weak people, or good or bad people. It just makes them people.

It's our nature. There's plenty to distract us from the nastier truths of our lives, if we want to avoid them.

'Evelyn Derek,' I said in a firm, authoritative voice. 'Look at me.'

She flinched closer to the wall, shaking her head.

I knelt in front of her. Then I reached out to touch her chin, and gently lifted her face to mine. 'Evelyn Derek,' I said in a gentler voice. 'Look at me.'

The woman lifted her dark green eyes to mine and I held her gaze for the space of a long breath before the soulgaze began.

If the eyes are the windows to the soul, then wizards are the souls' voyeurs. When a wizard looks into another person's eyes, we get to see something of that person, a vision of the very core of their being. We each go through the experience a little differently, but it amounts to the same thing – a look into another person's eyes gives you an insight into the most vital portions of their character.

Evelyn Derek's deep green eyes almost seemed to expand around me, and then I found myself staring at a room that was, if anything, almost identical to the woman's office. The furniture was beautiful and minimalistic. Ms Derek, it seemed, was not the kind of person to overly burden her soul with the care and mementos most people collect over the course of a lifetime. She had devoted her life to her mind, to the order and discipline of her thoughts, and she had never left herself much room for personal entanglements.

But as I stared at the room, I saw Ms Derek herself. I would have expected her in her business clothing, or perhaps in student's attire. Instead, she was wearing . . .

Well. She was wearing very expensive, very minimalistic black lingerie. Stockings, garters, panties, and bra, all black. She wore them, ahem, very well. She was kneeling on the floor, her knees apart, her hands held behind the small of her back. She faced me with her lips parted, her breath coming in quickened pants. I was able to change my viewpoint slightly, as if walking around her, and those green eyes followed me, pupils wide with desire, her hips shifting in little yearning rolls with every tiny correction of her balance.

Her wrists were bound behind her back with a long, slender ribbon of white silk.

I caught a motion in the corner of my eye, and I snapped my gaze up, to see a slender, feminine form vanish into the corridors of Evelyn Derek's memory, showing me nothing more than a flash of pale skin—

—and a gleam of silver eyes.

Son of a bitch.

Someone had bound up Ms Derek's thoughts, all right, and woven those restraints together with her natural sexual desire, to give them permanence and strength. The method and the glimpses I'd seen of the perpetrator, flashes of memory that had managed to remain in her thoughts, perhaps, gave strong indicators as to who was responsible.

A vampire of the White Court.

And then there was a wrenching sensation and I was kneeling over Evelyn Derek. Her eyes were wide, her expression a mixture of terror and awe as she stared up at me.

Oh, yeah. That was the thing about a soulgaze. Whoever you look at gets a look back at you. They get to see you in just as much detail as you see them. I've never had anyone soulgaze me who didn't seem . . . disconcerted by the experience.

Evelyn Derek stared at me and whispered, 'Who are you?'

I said, 'Harry Dresden.'

She blinked slowly and said, her voice dazed, 'She ran from you.' Tears started forming in her eyes. 'What is happening to me?'

Magic that invades the thoughts of another human being is just about as black as it gets, a direct violation of the Laws of Magic that the Wardens uphold. But there are grey areas, like in any set of laws, and there are accepted customs as to what was or was not allowed in practice.

There wasn't much I could do for Evelyn. It would take a hand lighter and more skilled than mine to undo the harm that had been done to her mind, if it could be undone at all. But there was one thing I could do for her, a bit of grey magic that even the White Council acknowledged as an aid and a mercy, especially for those who had suffered the kind of psychic trauma Evelyn had.

I called up my will as gently as I could, and reached out with my right hand. I passed my fingertips gently over her eyes, causing her to close them, and as I passed my palm from her forehead down to her chin, I released that will with as much care as I possibly could, murmuring, '*Dorme, dormius,* Evelyn. *Dorme, dormius.*'

She let out a little whimpering sound of relief, and her body sagged to the floor in sudden and complete relaxation. She breathed in deeply once, exhaled, and then passed into simple and dreamless slumber.

I made her as comfortable as I could. With luck, when she woke, she would pass most of our confrontation off as a bad dream. Then I turned and left the law office behind me, quiet anger growing inside me with every step. I went by the security guard at the door as the anger started nudging over into fury. I slapped the receipt down on his desk, and with a gesture and a muttered word caused my staff to leap from where it leaned against the wall and into my hand.

The guard fell out of his chair, and I left without looking back.

The White Court was involved. They were trying to get Morgan killed – and *me* with him – and what's more, they were preying on people in *my* town, ripping into their psyches and inflicting harm that could blossom into madness given the right circumstances. There was a broad difference between their usual predation and what had been done to Evelyn Derek.

Someone was going to answer for it.

23

I got back to my apartment, shouldered open my door, and found a bizarre tableau.

Again.

Morgan lay on the floor about five feet from the bedroom door. He'd apparently seized my walking cane from the old popcorn tin by the door, where I keep things like Ozark folk art carved quarter staves, blasting rods, umbrellas, and so on. The cane is an old Victorian-style sword-cane. You twist the handle and pull, and you can draw a slender thirty-inch spring steel blade from the wooden cane. Morgan had. He lay on his side on the floor, his arm extended up at about a forty-five-degree angle, holding the sword.

Its tip rested against Molly's carotid artery, just under her left ear.

Molly, for her part, leaned back against one of my bookcases, her knees bent a little, her arms spread out to either side, as if she'd stumbled over something and flung out her hands to brace herself against the bookcase as she fell back.

To the left of the door, Mouse crouched with his fangs bared and resting lightly against Anastasia Luccio's throat. She lay on her back, and her gun lay on the rug-covered floor about two feet beyond the reach of her hand. She appeared to be quite relaxed, though I couldn't see much of her face from where I stood.

Mouse's deep brown eyes were focused steadily on Morgan. Morgan's steely gaze was locked on Mouse's jaws.

I stared at them aghast for a minute. No one moved. Except Mouse. When I looked at him, his tail wagged hopefully once or twice.

I blew out a heavy breath, set my staff aside, and plodded to the icebox, stepping over Anastasia's leg on the way. I opened it, considered the contents for a moment, and then pulled out a cold Coke. I opened it and took a long drink. Then I picked up a dry kitchen towel, went to the couch, and sat down.

'I would ask what the hell happened,' I said to the room at large. 'Except that the only one with any sense who witnessed it can't actually *talk*.' I eyed the dog and said, 'This had better be good.'

Mouse wagged his tail tentatively again.

'Okay,' I said. 'Let her go.'

Mouse opened his jaws and sat up and away from Anastasia at once. He immediately padded over to me, and leaned against me as his gaze flicked from Anastasia to Morgan and back.

'Morgan,' I said. 'Ease off the psycho throttle a little and put down the sword.'

'No,' Morgan said in a voice half strangled with fury. 'Not until this little witch is bound and wearing a gag and a blindfold.'

'Molly's already done duty as a beer-calendar model today,' I said. 'We're not dressing her up for a BDSM shoot next.' I put the Coke down and thought about it for a second. Threats weren't going to have any effect on Morgan, except to make him more determined. It was one of the charming side effects of having such a rigid old-school personality.

'Morgan,' I said quietly. 'You are a guest in my home.'

He flashed me a quick, guilty glance.

'You came to me for help and I'm doing my best. Hell, the kid has put herself into harm's way, trying to protect you. I've done everything for you that I would have for blood family, because you are my guest. There are monsters from whom I would expect better behavior, once they had accepted my hospitality. What's more, they'd give it to me.'

Morgan let out a pained sound. Then he turned his head sharply away from Molly and dropped the sword at the same time. The steel of the blade chimed as it bounced off the thin rug.

Morgan settled into a limp heap on the floor, and Molly sagged, lifting her hand and covering the vulnerable skin of her throat for a moment.

I waited until Anastasia sat up to toss her the towel I'd brought from the kitchen. She caught it, her expression neutral, and lifted it to begin drying her neck. Mouse is a great dog, but he has to work hard to control his slobber issues.

'So I take it things almost devolved into violence again,' I said to them. 'And Mouse had to get involved.'

'She just came walking in here,' Molly protested. 'She saw him.'

I blinked and looked at her. 'And you did . . . what, exactly?'

'She blinded me,' Anastasia said calmly. 'And then she hit me.' She lifted the towel and wiped at her nose. Some blood came away, though most of it stayed crusted and brown below one nostril. So they hadn't been in the standoff for long. Anastasia gave Molly a steady gaze and said, 'She hit me like a girl. For goodness' sake, child, have you had no combat training at all?'

'There's been a lot of material to cover,' I growled. 'Blinded you?'

'Not permanently,' Molly said, more sullenly now. She rubbed at the knuckles of her right hand with her left. 'I just . . . kind of veiled everything that wasn't her.'

'An unnecessarily complicated way to go about it,' Anastasia said primly.

'For you, maybe,' Molly said defensively. 'Besides, who was the one on the ground getting pounded?'

'Yes. You're forty pounds heavier than me,' Anastasia said calmly.

'Bitch, I know you didn't say just say that,' Molly bristled, stepping forward with her hands clenched.

Mouse sighed and heaved himself back to his feet.

Molly stopped, eyeing the big dog warily.

'Good dog,' I said, and scratched Mouse's ears.

He wagged his tail without taking his serious brown eyes from Molly.

'I had to stop her,' Molly said. 'She was going to report Morgan to the Wardens.'

'So you physically and magically assaulted her,' I said.

'What choice did I have?'

I eyed Morgan. 'And you staggered up out of the bed you're supposed to be staying in, grabbed the first pointy thing you could reach, and forced her off of Anastasia.'

Morgan eyed me wearily. 'Obviously.'

I sighed and looked at Anastasia. 'And you thought the only solution you had was to take them both down and sort everything out later, and Mouse stopped you.'

Anastasia sighed. 'There was a blade out, Harry. The situation had to be controlled.'

I eyed Mouse. 'And you wound up holding Anastasia hostage so Morgan wouldn't hurt Molly.'

Mouse ducked his head.

'I can't believe I'm about to say this,' I said. 'So think real careful about where this is coming from. Have you people ever considered *talking* when you've got a problem?'

That didn't please anybody, and they gave me looks with varying degrees of irritation mixed with chagrin.

Except for Mouse, who sighed and said something like, 'Uh-woof.'

'Sorry,' I told him at once. 'Four-footed nonvocalizing company excepted.'

'She was going to get the Wardens,' Molly said. 'If that happened before we proved who really killed LaFortier, all of us would be up the creek.'

'Actually,' Anastasia said, 'that's true.'

I turned my gaze to her. She rose and stretched, wincing slightly. 'I assumed,' she said quietly, 'that Morgan had recruited your apprentice to assist him in his escape scheme. And that they had done away with you.'

I made a small frustrated sound. 'Why the hell would you assume something like that?'

She narrowed her eyes as she stared at me. 'Why would Morgan flee to the home of the one wizard in the Council who had the most reason to dislike him?' she asked. 'I believe your words were: "that would be crazy".'

I winced. Ouch. 'Uh,' I said. 'Yeah. I . . .'

'You lied to me,' she said in a level tone. Most people probably wouldn't have noticed the undertone of anger and pain in her voice, or the almost imperceptible pause between each word. I could see bricks being mortared into place behind her eyes and I looked away from her.

The room was completely silent, until Morgan said, in a small and broken voice, 'What?'

I looked up at him. His hard sour face had gone gray. His expression was twisted up in shock and surprise, like that of a small child discovering the painful consequences of gravity for the first time.

'Ana,' he said, almost choking on the words. 'You . . . you think that I . . . How could you think that I would . . . ?'

He turned his face away. It couldn't have been a tear. Not from Morgan. He wouldn't shed tears if he had to execute his own mother.

But for a fraction of a second, something shone on one of his cheeks.

Anastasia rose and walked over to Morgan. She knelt down by him and put her hand on his head. 'Donald,' she said gently, 'we've been betrayed by those we trusted before. It wouldn't be the first time.'

'That was them,' he said unsteadily, not looking up. 'This is me.'

She stroked his hair once. 'I never thought you had done it of your own free will, Donald,' she whispered quietly. 'I thought someone had gotten into your mind. Held a hostage against your cooperation. Something.'

'Who could they have held hostage?' Morgan said in a bitter voice. 'There's no one. For that very reason. And you know it.'

She sighed and closed her eyes.

'You knew his wards,' Morgan went on. 'You've been through them before. Often. You opened them in under a second when you came in. You have a key to his apartment.'

She said nothing.

His voice turned heavy and hollow. 'You're involved. With Dresden.'

Anastasia blinked her eyes several times. 'Donald,' she began.

He looked up at her, his eyes empty of tears or pain or anything but weariness. 'Don't,' he said. 'Don't you dare.'

She met his eyes. I'd never seen such gentle pain on her face. 'You're running a fever. Donald, please. You should be in bed.'

He laid his head on the rug and closed his eyes. 'It doesn't matter.'

'Donald—'

'It doesn't matter,' he repeated dully.

Anastasia started crying in silence. She stayed next to Morgan, stroking her hand over his mottled silver-and-brown hair.

An hour later, Morgan was unconscious in bed again. Molly was down in the lab, pretending to work on potions with the trapdoor closed. I was sitting in the same spot with an empty can of Coke.

Anastasia came out of the bedroom and shut the door silently behind her. Then she leaned back against it. 'When I saw him,' she said, 'I thought he had come here to hurt you. That he had learned about the two of us and wanted to hurt you.'

'You,' I asked, 'and Morgan?'

She was quiet for a moment before she said, 'I never allowed it to happen. It wasn't fair to him.'

'But he wanted it anyway,' I said.

She nodded.

'Hell's bells,' I sighed.

She folded her arms over her stomach, never looking up. 'Was it any different with your apprentice, Harry?'

Molly hadn't always been the grasshopper she was today. When I'd first begun teaching her, she'd assumed that I would be teaching her all sorts of things that had nothing to do with magic and everything to do with her being naked. And that had been more than all right with her.

Just not with me.

'Not much,' I acknowledged. 'But he hasn't been your apprentice for a long, long time.'

'I have always been of the opinion that romantic involvement was a vulnerability I could not afford. Not in my position.'

'Not always,' I said, 'apparently.'

She exhaled slowly. 'It was a much easier opinion to hold in my previous body. It was older. Less prone to . . .'

'Life?' I suggested.

She shrugged. 'Desire. Loneliness. Joy. Pain.'

'Life,' I said.

'Perhaps.' She closed her eyes for a moment. 'When I was young, I reveled in love, Harry. In passion. In discovery and in new experiences and in life.' She gestured down at herself. 'I never realized how much of it I had forgotten until Corpsetaker left me like this.' She opened her pained eyes and looked at me. 'I didn't realize how much I missed it until you reminded me. And by then, Morgan wasn't . . . He was like I had been. Detached.'

'In other words,' I said, 'he'd made himself more like you. Patterned himself after you. And because he'd done that, after your change he wasn't capable of giving you what you wanted.'

She nodded.

I shook my head. 'A hundred years is a long time to carry a torch,' I said. 'That one must burn like hell.'

'I know. And I never wanted to hurt him. You must believe me.'

'Here's where you say, "The heart wants what the heart wants,"' I said.

'Trite,' she said, 'but true all the same.' She turned until her right shoulder leaned on the door, facing me. 'We should talk about where this leaves us.'

I toyed with the can of Coke. 'Before we can do that,' I said, 'we have to talk about Morgan and LaFortier.'

She exhaled slowly. 'Yes.'

'What do you intend to do?' I asked.

'He's wanted by the Council, Harry,' she said in a gentle voice. 'I don't know how he's managed to avoid being located by magical means, but sooner or later, in hours or days, he *will* be found. And when that happens, you and Molly will be implicated as well. You'll both die with him.' She took a deep breath. 'And if I don't go to the Council with what I know, I'll be right there beside you.'

'Yeah,' I said.

'You really think he's innocent?' she asked.

'Of LaFortier's murder,' I said. 'Yes.'

'Do you have proof?'

'I've found out enough to make me think I'm right. Not enough to clear him – yet.'

'If it wasn't Morgan,' she said quietly, 'then the traitor is still running around loose.'

'Yeah.'

'You're asking me to discard the pursuit of a suspect with strong evidence supporting his guilt in favor of chasing a damn ghost, Harry. Someone we've barely been able to prove exists, much less identify. Not only that, you're asking me to gamble your life, your apprentice's life, and my own against finding this ghost in time.'

'Yes. I am.'

She shook her head. 'Everything I've ever learned as a Warden tells me that it's far more likely that Morgan is guilty.'

'Which brings us back to the question,' I said. 'What are you going to do?'

Silence yawned.

She pushed off the door and came to sit down on the chair facing my seat on the couch.

'All right,' she said. 'Tell me everything.'

24

'This is not how diplomacy is done,' Anastasia said as we approached the Château Raith.

'You're in America now,' I said. 'Our idea of diplomacy is showing up with a gun in one hand and a sandwich in the other and asking which you'd prefer.'

Anastasia's mouth curved up at one corner. 'You brought a sandwich?'

'Who do I look like, Kissinger?'

I'd been to Château Raith before, but it had always been at night, or at least twilight. It was an enormous estate most of an hour away from Chicago proper, a holding of House Raith, the current ruling house of the White Court. The Château itself was surrounded by at least half a mile of old-growth forest that had been converted to an idyllic, even gardenlike, state, like you sometimes see on centuries-old European properties. Huge trees and smooth grass beneath them dominated, with the occasional, suspiciously symmetrical outgrowth of flowering plants, often located in the center of golden shafts of sunlight that came down through the green-shadowed trees at regular intervals.

The grounds were surrounded by a high fence, topped with razor wire that couldn't be readily seen from the outside. The fence was electrically charged, too, and the latest surveillance cameras – seemingly little more than glass beads with wires running out of them – monitored every inch of the exterior.

At night, it made for one extremely creepy piece of property. On a bright summer afternoon, it just looked . . . pretty. Very, very wealthy and very, very pretty. Like the Raiths themselves, the grounds were only scary when seen at the right time.

A polite security guard with the general bearing of ex-military had watched us get out of a cab, called ahead, and let us in with hardly a pause. We'd walked past the gate and up the drive through Little Sherwood until we reached the Château proper.

'How good are her people?' Anastasia asked.

'I'm sure you've read the file.'

'Yes,' she said, as we started up the steps. 'But I'd prefer your personal assessment.'

'Since Lara's taken over the hiring,' I said, 'they've improved significantly. I don't think they're fed upon to keep them under control anymore.'

'And you base that assessment on what?'

I shrugged. 'The before and after. The last batch of hired muscle was . . . just out of touch. Willing to die at a moment's notice, but not exactly the sharpest tacks in the box. Pretty and vacant. And pretty vacant.' I gestured back at the entrance. 'That guy back there had a newspaper nearby. And he was eating lunch when we showed up. Before, they just stood around like mannequins with muscle. I'm betting that most of them are ex-military. The hard-core kind, not the get-my-college-funded kind.'

'Officially,' she said, as we reached the top of the steps, 'they remain untested.'

'Or maybe Lara's just smart enough not to show them off until it's necessary to use them,' I said.

'Officially,' Anastasia said dryly, 'she remains untested.'

'You didn't see her killing super ghouls with a couple of knives the way I did during the White Court coup,' I said. I rapped on the door with my staff and adjusted the hang of my grey cloak. 'I know my word isn't exactly respected among the old guard Wardens, but take it from me. Lara Raith is one smart and scary bitch.'

Anastasia shook her head with a faint smile. 'And yet you're here to hold a gun to her head.'

'I'm hoping that if we apply some pressure, we'll get something out of her,' I said. 'I'm low on options. And I don't have time to be anything but direct.'

'Well,' she said, 'at least you're playing to your strengths.'

A square-jawed, flat-topped man in his thirties opened the door. He was wearing a casual beige sports suit accessorized by a gun in a shoulder holster and what was probably a Kevlar vest beneath his white tee. If that wasn't enough, he had some kind of dangerous-looking little machine gun hanging from a nylon strap over one shoulder.

'Sir,' he said with a polite nod. 'Ma'am. May I take your cloaks?'

'Thank you,' Anastasia said. 'But they're part of the uniform. If you could convey us directly to Ms Raith, that would be most helpful.'

The security man nodded his head. 'Before you accept the hospitality of the house, I would ask you both to give me your personal word that you are here in good faith and will offer no violence while you are a guest.'

Anastasia opened her mouth, as if she intended to readily agree, but I stepped slightly in front of her and said, 'Hell, no.'

The security man narrowed his eyes and looked a little less relaxed. 'Excuse me?'

'Go tell Lara that whether or not we rip this house to splinters and broken glass is still up for debate,' I said. 'Tell her there's already blood on the floor, and I think some of it is on her hands. Tell her if she wants a chance to clear the air, she talks to me. Tell her if she doesn't that it is answer enough, and that she accepts the consequences.'

The guard stared at me for several seconds. Then he said, 'You've got a real high opinion of yourself. Do you know what's around you? Do you have any idea where you're standing?'

'Yeah,' I said. 'Ground zero.'

More silence stretched, and he blinked before I did. 'I'll tell her. Wait here, please.'

I nodded to him, and he walked deeper into the house.

'Ground zero?' Anastasia muttered out of the corner of her mouth. 'A trifle melodramatic, don't you think?'

I answered her in a similar fashion. 'I was going to go with "three feet from where they'll find your body", but I figured that would have made it too personal. He's just doing his job.'

She shook her head. 'Is there some reason this can't be a civil visit?'

'Lara's at her most dangerous when everyone's being civil,' I said. 'She knows it. I don't want her feeling comfortable. It'll be easier to get answers out of her if she's worried about all hell breaking loose.'

'It might also be easier to question her if *we* aren't worried about it,' Anastasia pointed out. 'She does hold the advantage here. One notes that there is fairly fresh plaster on the walls on either side of us, for instance.'

I checked. She was right. 'So?'

'So, if I was the one preparing to defend this place, I think I might line the walls with antipersonnel mines wired to a simple charge and cover them in plaster until I needed them to remove a threat too dangerous to engage directly.'

I'd personally seen what an AP mine could do to human bodies. It wasn't pretty. Imagine what's left of a squirrel when it gets hit with large rounds from a heavy-gauge shotgun. There's not much there but scraps and stains. It's essentially the same when a human gets hit with a load of ball bearings the size of gumballs that spew from an AP mine. I glanced at either wall again. 'At least I was right,' I said. 'Ground zero.'

Anastasia smiled faintly. 'I just thought I'd mention the possibility. There's a fine line between audacity and idiocy.'

'And if she thinks she's in danger, Lara might just detonate them now,' I said. 'Preemptive self-defense.'

'Mmmm. Generally the favored method for dealing with practitioners. The customs of hospitality would have protected us from her as much as her from us.'

I thought about that for a second and then shook my head. 'If we were all calm and polite, she'd never give away anything. And she won't kill us. Not until she finds out what we know.'

She shrugged. 'You could be right. You've dealt with the smart, scary bitch more often than me.'

'I guess we'll know in a minute.'

A minute later, we were still there, and the security guy reappeared. 'This way, please,' he said.

We followed him through the wealthy splendor of the house. Hardwood floors. Custom carved woodworking.

Statues. Fountains. Suits of armor. Original paintings, one of them a van Gogh. Stained-glass windows. Household staff in formal uniform. I kept expecting to come across a flock of peacocks roaming the halls, or maybe a pet cheetah in a diamond-studded collar.

After a goodly hike, the guard led us to a wing of the house that had, apparently, been converted to corporate office space. There were half a dozen efficient-looking people working in cubicles. A phone with a digital ring tone chirruped in the background. Copiers wheezed. In the background, a radio played soft rock.

We went past the office, down a short hall past a break room that smelled of fresh coffee, and to the double doors at the end of the hallway. The guard held open one of the doors for us, and we went inside, to an outer office complete with a secretary's desk manned by a stunning young woman.

By Justine, in fact, her white hair held back in a tail, wearing a conservative grey pantsuit.

As we entered, she rose with a polite, impersonal smile that could have taken any number of competitive pageants. 'Sir, ma'am. If you'll come this way, please, Ms Raith is ready to see you.'

She went over to the door on the wall behind her desk, knocked once, and opened it enough to say, 'Ms Raith? The Wardens are here.' A very soft feminine voice answered her. Justine opened the door all the way and held it for us, smiling. 'Coffee, sir, ma'am? Another beverage?'

'No, thank you,' Anastasia said, as we entered. Justine shut the door carefully behind us.

Lara Raith's office had a few things in common with Evelyn Derek's. It had the same rich furnishings – though her style was more rich, dark hardwood than glass – the same clarity of function and purpose. The resemblance ended there. Lara's office was a working office. Mail was stacked neatly on a corner of the desk. Files and envelopes each had their own specific positions upon her desk and the worktable against one wall. A pen and ink set was in evidence on the desktop. Paperwork anarchy threatened the room, but order had been strongly imposed, guided by an obvious will.

Lara Raith, de facto ruler of the White Court, sat behind the desk. She wore a silk business suit of purest white, cut close to the flawless lines of her body. The cut of the suit elegantly displayed her figure, and contrasted sharply with the long blue-black hair, which hung in waves past her shoulders. Her features had the classically immortal beauty of Greek statues, balancing sheer beauty with strength, intelligence, and perception. Her eyes were a deep, warm grey, framed by thick sooty lashes, and just looking at her full soft mouth made my lips twitch and tingle as they demanded an introduction to Lara's.

'Warden Dresden,' she murmured, her voice soothing and musical. 'Warden Luccio. Please, be seated.'

I didn't need to check with Anastasia. Both of us just stood there, staff in hand, regarding her quietly.

She leaned back in her chair and a wicked little smile played over that mouth without ever getting as far as her eyes. 'I see. I'm being intimidated. Are you going to tell me why, or do I get three guesses?'

'Stop being cute, Lara,' I said. 'Your lawyer, Evelyn Derek, hired a private eye to tail me and report on my movements – and every time I turn around, something nasty has shown up to make a run at me.'

The smile remained in place. 'Lawyer?'

'I took a look at her head,' I said. 'And found the marks of the White Court all over it – including a compulsion not to reveal who she was working for.'

'And you think it was my doing?' she asked.

'In these parts?' I asked. 'Why not?'

'I'm hardly the only member of the White Court in the region, Dresden,' Lara said. 'And while I'm flattered that you think so highly of me, the others of my kind do not love me so well as to consult with me before every action they take.'

Anastasia stepped in. 'But they wouldn't engage the White Council in this sort of business without your approval.' She smiled. 'Such a thing would be seen as a challenge to your – to the authority of the White King.'

Lara studied Luccio for a while, grey eyes probing. 'Captain Luccio,' she said, 'I saw you dance in Naples.'

Anastasia frowned.

'It would have been . . . what? Two centuries ago, give or take a few decades?' Lara smiled. 'You were exquisitely gifted. Granted, that was before your . . . current condition.'

'Ms Raith,' Anastasia said, 'that is hardly germane to the subject at hand.'

'It could be,' Lara murmured. 'You and I attended the same party after your performance. I know the sort of appetites you indulged, back then.' Her lips curled into a hungry little smile, and it was suddenly all I could do to keep my knees from buckling in sheer, sudden, irrational sexual desire. 'Perhaps you'd care to revisit old times,' Lara purred.

And, as quickly as that, the desire was gone.

Anastasia took a slow, deep breath. 'I'm too old to be amused by such antics, Ms Raith,' she replied calmly. 'Just as I'm too intelligent to believe that you don't know something of what's been happening in Chicago.'

It took me a couple of seconds to pull my mind back from the places Lara had just sent it, but I managed. 'We know you're working with someone inside the Council,' I said quietly. 'I want you to tell us who it is. And I want you to release Thomas.'

Lara's eyes snapped to me on that last. 'Thomas?'

I leaned on my staff and watched her face closely. 'Thomas managed to warn me about the hit man Evelyn Derek had directed to me, but he disappeared before he could get involved. He's not answering either of his phones and no one at the salon has seen him, either.'

Lara's eyes went distant for a moment, and a frown line marred the perfection of her brow. 'Is that all you have, Dresden? A fading psychic impression that one of my kind manipulated this lawyer and the apparent disappearance of my little brother? Is that the basis of reasoning that brought you here?'

'At the moment,' I said. Now that I'd laid down a lot of truth, I threw in the little lie. 'But by the time we finish tracing the money back to its source, we'll know for certain that you're involved. And after that, there won't be any going back.'

Lara narrowed her eyes at that. 'You won't find anything,' she said in a firm cold tone. 'Because nothing of the sort is going on.'

Aha. That had touched a nerve. I applied pressure. 'Come on, Lara. You know and I know how you and your folk do business – from behind proxies and cat's-paws. You can't possibly expect me to believe you when you say that you don't have a hand in what's going on.'

Lara's eyes flickered in color, changing from deep grey to a far paler, more metallic shade, and she rose to her feet. 'Frankly, I don't care what you believe, Dresden. I have no idea what kind of evidence you think you've discovered, but I am not involved in *any* internal affairs of the White Council.' She lifted her chin as she sneered at us. 'Contrary to your own perceptions, the world is a great deal larger than the White Council of Wizardry. You aren't a vital body in today's world. You're a sad little collection of self-deluded has-beens whose self-righteous prattle has always taken second place to its hypocritical practice.'

Well. I couldn't argue with that, but the words made Anastasia's eyes narrow dangerously.

Lara leaned the heels of her hands on her desk and faced me, her words clipped and precise. 'You think you can simply walk into my home and issue commands and threats as it pleases you? The world is changing, Wardens. The Council isn't changing with it. It's only a matter of time before it collapses under its own obsolescent weight. This kind of high-handed arrogance will only—'

She broke off suddenly, turning toward the window, her head tilted slightly to one side.

I blinked and traded a glance with Anastasia.

An instant later, the lights went out.

Red emergency lights snapped on immediately, though they weren't needed in the office. A few seconds after that, a rapid, steady chiming sound filled the room, coming from speakers on the wall.

I looked down from the speaker to find Lara staring intently at me.

'What's happening?' I asked her.

Her eyes widened slightly. 'You don't know?'

'How the hell should *I* know?' I demanded, exasperated. 'It's your stupid alarm system!'

'Then this isn't your doing.' She gritted her teeth. 'Bloody *hell*.'

Her head whipped toward the window again and this time I heard it – the sound of a man screaming in high-pitched, shameless agony.

And then I felt it: a nauseating quiver of *wrongness* in the air, a hideous sense of the presence of something ancient and vile.

The skinwalker.

'We're under attack,' Lara snarled. 'Come with me.'

25

Justine knocked and entered the room, her eyes wide. 'Ms Raith?'

'Security status?' Lara asked in a calm voice.

'Unknown,' Justine said. She was breathing a little too fast. 'The alarm went off and I called Mr Jones, but the radios cut out.'

'Most of your electronics are probably gone. You've been hexed,' I said. 'It's a skinwalker.'

Lara turned and stared hard at me. 'Are you sure?'

Anastasia nodded and drew the sword from her hip. 'I feel it, too.'

Lara nodded. 'What can it do?'

'Everything I can, only better,' I said. 'And it's a shapeshifter. Very fast, very strong.'

'Can it be killed?'

'Yeah,' I said. 'But it's probably smarter to run.'

Lara narrowed her eyes. 'This thing has invaded my home and hurt my people. Like hell.' She turned, drove her fist with moderate force into a wooden wall panel and dislodged it completely. In the empty space behind the panel was a rack hung with a belt bearing two wavy-bladed swords and a machine pistol, like a baby Uzi. She kicked out of her expensive shoes, shrugged out of her coat, and began strapping on weapons. 'Justine, how many of the blood are in the house?'

'Four, counting you,' Justine replied immediately. 'Your sisters, Elisa and Natalia, and your cousin Madeline.'

She nodded. 'Wardens,' she said. 'If you would not mind delaying our argument for a time, I would take it as a personal favor.'

'Hell with that,' I said. 'This thing killed one of my friends.'

Lara glanced at the two of us. 'I propose a temporary alliance against this invader.'

'Concur,' Anastasia said sharply.

'Doesn't look like there's any way to get out of it,' I said.

Gunfire erupted somewhere in the halls – multiple automatic weapons all going off at the same time.

Then there were more screams.

'Justine,' I said, holding out my hand. 'Get behind me.'

The young woman hurried to comply, her expression strained but controlled.

Anastasia took up position on my right and Lara slid up next to me on the left. Her perfume was exquisite, and the surge of lust that hit me as I breathed it nearly had me turning to take a bite out of her, she smelled so good.

'It's fast and tough,' I said. 'And smart. But not invulnerable. We hit it from several directions at once and ran it off.'

A shotgun boomed, much closer to us than the earlier gunfire had been. It was immediately followed by the sounds of something heavy being slammed several times into the walls and floor.

The psychic stench of the skinwalker abruptly thickened and I said, 'Here it comes!'

By the time I got to 'it', the skinwalker was already through the door to the outer office, seemingly moving faster than the splinters that flew off the door when the creature shattered it. Covered in a veil, it was just a flickering blur in the air.

I brought my shield up, focused far forward, filling the doorway to Lara's office with invisible force. The skin-walker hit the barrier with all of its strength and speed. The shield held – barely – but so much energy had gone into the impact that wisps of smoke began curling up from the bracelet, and the skin on my wrist got singed. So much force surged into my shield that it physically drove me back across a foot of carpet.

As it hit, the energies of the skinwalker's veil came into conflict with those in my shield, each canceling out the other, and for a second the creature was visible as an immensely tall, lean, shaggy, vaguely humanoid *thing* with matted yellow hair and overlong forelimbs tipped in long, almost delicate claws.

As the shield fell, Anastasia pointed a finger at the thing and hissed a word, and a blindingly bright beam of light no thicker than a hair flashed out from her finger. It was fire magic not unlike my own, but infinitely more intense and focused and far more energy efficient. The beam swept past the skinwalker, intersecting with its upper left arm, and where it touched fur burned away and flesh boiled and bubbled and blackened.

The skinwalker flashed to one side of the doorway and vanished, leaving nothing behind but a view of the smoking pinprick hole in the expensive paneling of the outer office.

I pointed my staff at the door and Lara did the same thing with the gun.

For maybe ten seconds, everything was silent.

'Where is it?' Lara hissed.

'Gone?' Justine suggested. 'Maybe it got scared when Warden Luccio hurt it.'

'No, it didn't,' I said. 'It's smart. Right now it's looking for a better way to get to us.'

I looked around the office, trying to think like the enemy. 'Let's see,' I said. 'If *I* was a shapeshifting killing machine, how would I get in here?'

The options were limited. There was the door in front of us and the window behind us. I turned to face the window, still looking. Silence reigned, except for the sigh of the air-conditioning, billowing steadily into the office from the—

From the *vents*.

I turned and thrust my staff toward a large air vent, covered with the usual slatted steel contraption, drew forth my will, and screamed, '*Fulminos!*'

Blue-white lightning suddenly filled the air with flickering fire, while a spear of blinding heat and force crackled forth from my staff and slammed into the metal vent. The metal absorbed the electricity, and I knew it would carry it back through the vent itself – and into anything inside.

There was a weird, chirping scream and then the vent cover flew outward, followed by a python-shaped blur in the air. Even as it arced toward us, that shape flowed and changed into that of something low-slung, stocky, and viciously powerful, like maybe a badger or a wolverine.

It hit Anastasia high on the chest and slammed her to the floor.

And on the way down, I caught a flash of golden-yellow eyes dancing with sadistic glee.

I turned to kick the thing off of Anastasia, but Lara beat me to the metaphorical punch. She slammed the barrel of her machine pistol into its flank as if driving a beer tap into a wooden keg with her bare hands, and pulled the trigger on the way.

Fire and noise filled the room, and the skinwalker went bouncing to one side. It hit the ground once, twisted itself in midair and raked its claws across Justine's midsection. Using the reaction to control its momentum, it landed on its feet and hurled itself out of the room by way of the window behind Lara's desk.

Justine staggered and let out a small cry of pain.

Lara stared at the window for a second, her eyes wide, then breathed, 'Empty night.'

I turned to Anastasia but she waved me off with a grimace. It didn't look like she was bleeding. I turned to Justine and tried to assess her injuries. There were six horizontal lines sliced into the soft flesh of her abdomen, as neatly as if with a scalpel. Blood was welling readily from them — but I didn't think any of them had been deep enough to open the abdominal cavity or reach an artery.

I seized Lara's discarded coat, folded it hastily, and pressed it against Justine's belly. 'Hold it here,' I snapped to Justine. 'You've got to control the bleeding. Hold it here.'

Her teeth were bared in pain, but she nodded and grasped at the improvised pad with both hands as I helped her up.

Lara looked from Justine to the window, her eyes a little wide. 'Empty night,' she said again. 'I've never seen anything that fast.'

Given that I had once seen her cover ground in a dead sprint at maybe fifty miles an hour, I figured she knew what she was talking about. We were never going to get that thing to hold still long enough to kill it.

I went to the window, hoping to spot it, and found myself staring into an oncoming comet of purple flame, presumably courtesy of the skinwalker. I fell back, hurling my left arm and its shield bracelet in an instinctive gesture, and the fiery hammer of the explosion flung me supine to the floor.

That otherworldly shriek sounded again, mocking and full of spite, and then there was a crash from somewhere below us.

'It's back inside the house,' I said. I offered my hand to Anastasia to help her up. She took it, but as I began to pull, she clenched her teeth over a scream, and I eased her back onto the floor at once.

'Can't,' she panted, breathing hard. 'It's my collarbone.'

I spat out a curse. Of every kind of simple fracture there is, a fractured collarbone is one of the most agonizing and debilitating injuries you can get. She wasn't going to be doing any more fighting today. Hell, she wasn't going to be doing any more *standing*.

The floor beneath my feet abruptly exploded. I felt a steel cable wrap my ankle and pull, and then I was falling with a hideous stench filling my nose. I crashed down onto something that slowed my fall but gave way, and I went farther down still. The noise was hideous. Then the fall stopped abruptly, though I wasn't quite sure which way was up. About a hundred objects slammed into me all at the same time, pounding the wind out of my lungs.

I lay there stunned for a few seconds, struggling to remember how to breathe. The floor. The skinwalker had smashed its way up to me through the floor. It had pulled me down – but all the falling debris must have crashed through the floor the skinwalker had been standing on in turn.

I'd just fallen two stories amidst maybe a ton of debris, and managed to survive it. Talk about lucky.

And then, beneath my lower back, something moved.

The rubble shifted and a low growl began to reverberate up through it.

In a panic, I tried to force my dazed body to flee, but before I could figure out how it worked, a yellow-furred, too-long forearm exploded up out of the rubble. Quicker than you could say 'the late Harry Dresden', its long, clawed fingers closed with terrible strength on my throat and shut off my air.

26

Here's something a lot of people don't know: being choked unconscious *hurts*.

There's this horrible, crushing pain on your neck, followed by an almost instant surge of terrible pressure that feels like it's going to blow your head to tiny pieces from the inside. That's the blood that's being trapped in your brain. The pain surges and ebbs in time with your heartbeat, which is probably racing.

It doesn't matter if you're a waifish supermodel or a steroid-popping professional wrestler, because it isn't an issue of strength or willpower – it's simple physiology. If you're human and you need to breathe, you're going down. A properly applied choke will take you from feisty to unconscious in four or five seconds.

Of course, if the choker wants to make the victim hurt more, they can be sloppy about the choke, make it take longer.

I'll let you guess which the skinwalker preferred.

I struggled, but I might as well have saved myself the effort. I couldn't break the grip on my neck. The pile of rubble shifted and surged, and then the skinwalker sat up out of the wreckage, sloughing it off as easily as an arctic wolf emerging from a bed beneath the snow. The skin-walker's nightmarishly long arms hung below its knees, so as it began moving down the hallway, I was able to get my hands and knees underneath me, at least part of the time, preventing my neck from snapping under the strain of supporting my own weight.

I heard boots hitting hardwood. The skinwalker let out a chuckling little growl and casually slammed my head against the wall. Stars and fresh pain flooded my perceptions. Then I felt myself falling through the air and landing in a tumble of arms and legs that only seemed to be connected to me in the technical sense.

I lifted dazed eyes to see the security guy from the entrance hall come around the corner, that little machine gun held to his shoulder, his cheek resting against the stock so that the barrel pointed wherever his eyes were focused. When he saw the skinwalker, uncovered from its veil, he stopped in his tracks. To his credit, he couldn't have hesitated for more than a fraction of a second before he opened fire.

Bullets zipped down the hall, so close that I could have reached out a hand and touched them. The skinwalker flung itself to one side, a golden-furred blur, and rebounded off the wall toward the gunman, its form changing. Then it leapt into the air, flipping its body as it did, and suddenly a spider the size of a subcompact car was racing along the ceiling toward the security guy.

At that point, he impressed me again. He turned and ran, sprinting around a corner with the skinwalker coming hard behind.

'Now!' someone called, as the skinwalker reached the intersection of the two hallways, and a sudden howl of thunder filled the hallways with noise and light. Bullets ripped into the floor, the wall, and the ceiling, coming from some point out of sight around the corner, filling the air with splinters of shattered hardwood.

The skinwalker let out a deafening caterwaul of pain and boundless fury. The gunfire reached a thunderous, frantic crescendo.

Then men began screaming.

I tried to push myself to my feet, but someone had set the hallway on tumble dry, and I fell down again. I kept trying. Whoever had made the hall start acting like a Laundromat dryer had to run out of quarters eventually. By using the wall, I managed to make it to my knees.

I heard a soft sound behind me. I turned my head blearily toward the source of the noise and saw three pale, lithe forms drop silently from the floors above through the hole that the skinwalker had made. The first was Lara Raith. She'd torn her skirt up one side, almost all the way to her hip, and when she landed in a silent crouch, she looked cold and feral and dangerous with her sword in one hand and her machine pistol in the other.

The other two women were vampires as well, their pale skin shining with eerie beauty, their eyes glittering like polished silver coins – the sisters Justine had mentioned, I presumed. I guess I'd arrived in the middle of the night, vampire time, and gotten some people out of bed. The first sister wore nothing but weapons and silver body piercings, which gleamed on one eyebrow, one nostril, her lower lip, and her nipples. Her dark hair had been cropped close to her head except for where her bangs fell to veil one of her eyes, and she carried a pair of wavy-bladed swords like Lara's.

The second seemed to be taller and more muscular than the other two. She wore what looked like a man's shirt, closed with only a single button. Her long hair was a mess, still tousled from sleep, and she held an exotic-looking axe

in her hands, its blade honed along a concave edge instead
of the more conventional convex one.

Without any visible signal, they all started prowling
forward at the same time – and it *was* a prowl, an atavistic,
feline motion that carried what were very clearly predators forward in total silence. Lara paused when she reached
me, glanced over my injuries with cold silver eyes and
whispered, 'Stay down.'

No problem, I thought dully. *Down is easy.*

The screaming stopped with a last stuttering burst of
gunfire. The security guy came staggering around the
corner. Blood matted his hair and covered half of his face.
There was a long tear through his jacket on the left side.
His left arm hung uselessly, but he still gripped the handle
of his miniature assault weapon with his right. He wavered
and dropped to one knee as he spotted the three vampires.

Lara gestured with a hand, and the other two spread
out and moved forward, while she came to the side of the
wounded guard. 'What happened?'

'We hit it,' he said, his voice slurred. 'We hit it with
everything. Didn't even slow it down. They're dead. They're
all dead.'

'You're bleeding,' Lara said in a calm tone. 'Get behind
me. Defend the wizard.'

He nodded unsteadily. 'Yeah. Okay.'

Lara's guy had to be either incredibly lucky or really
good to have survived a close-quarters battle with the skinwalker. I stared dully at security guy for a second before
my impact-addled brain sent up a warning flag. Nobody
was that lucky.

'*Lara!*' I choked out.

Security guy turned in a blur of motion, sweeping

the machine gun at Lara's head like a club — but she had begun moving the instant she'd heard my warning and he missed knocking her head off her shoulders by a fraction of an inch. She flung herself to one side and rolled as security guy's other arm flashed out, lengthening and sprouting yellow fur and claws as it came. She avoided the worst of it, but the skinwalker's claws left a triple line of incisions down one shapely thigh, and they welled with blood a little too pale and pearly to be human.

The skinwalker followed her motion, surging forward, its body broadening and thickening into the form of something like a great bear with oversized jaws and vicious fangs. It overbore her by sheer mass, slapping and raking with its clawed paws, snapping with its steely jaws. I heard a bone break, heard Lara cry out in rage — and then the skinwalker flew straight up into the ceiling, its head and shoulders slamming into it with such force that it went cleanly through it, and out onto the floor above.

Lara had rolled to her back, and had launched the thing away from her with her legs. They were long and smoothly muscled and utterly desirable, even as she lowered them and rolled lightly to her feet, holding one arm tucked in close to her side. Her skin shone with cold, alien power, and her eyes had become spheres of pure white. She stared at the ceiling for a few seconds, slowly lifting and straightening her arm as she did.

Her forearm had received a compound fracture. I could see bone poking out through the flesh. But over the next few seconds, the flesh seemed to ripple and become more malleable. The bone withdrew, vanishing beneath the skin of her arm — even the hole that the bone had torn in the skin sealed slowly closed, and in ten seconds I couldn't even tell she'd been hurt.

She turned those empty white eyes to me and stared at me with an expression of focused naked hunger. For a second, I felt my body responding to her desire, even as woozy as I was, but that was quickly snuffed out by a surge of nausea. I turned my head and threw up onto the expensive floor while my head and neck screamed with pain.

When I looked up again, Lara had turned her head away from me. She picked up her fallen weapon – but the machine pistol had been bent into the shape of a comma by a blow from the skinwalker's sledgehammer paws. She discarded it, recovered her sword, and drew the matching weapon from her belt. She was breathing quickly – not in effort, but in raw excitement, and the tips of her breasts strained against her dirtied blouse. She licked her lips slowly and said, evidently for my benefit, 'I sometimes see Madeline's point.'

There was a feminine scream from somewhere close by, a challenge that was answered by a leonine roar that shook the hallway. The short-haired sister flew into the wall at the T intersection ahead, and collapsed like a rag doll. There were sounds of swift motion from around the corner, and a gasp.

Then silence.

A moment later, a blur came around the corner, dragging the axe-wielding sister's limp form by the hair. The veil faded as the skinwalker came closer, once more showing us its bestial, not-quite-human form. It stopped in front of us, maybe ten feet away. Then, quite casually, it lifted one of the unconscious vampire's hands to its fanged mouth and, never looking away from Lara, calmly nipped off a finger and swallowed it.

Lara narrowed her eyes, and her rich mouth split into a wide, hungry smile. 'Did you need a break before we continue?'

The skinwalker spoke, its voice weirdly modulated, as if several different creatures were approximating speech at the same time. 'Break?'

With the word, it calmly snapped the vampire girl's left arm in midhumerus.

Hell's bells.

'I am going to kill you,' Lara said calmly.

The skinwalker laughed. It was a hideous sound. 'Little phage. Even here at the center of your power, you could not stop me. Your warriors lay slain. Your fellow phages are fallen. Even the foolish pretenders to power visiting your house could not stop me.'

I'd gotten enough of my head back together to push myself to my feet. Lara never looked at me, but I could sense her attention on me nonetheless. I didn't have time to gather my will for a magical strike. The skinwalker would feel me doing it long before it became a fact.

Fortunately, I plan for such contingencies.

The eight silver rings I wore, one on each of my fingers, served a couple of purposes. The triple bands of silver were moderately heavy, and if I had to slug someone, they made a passably good imitation of brass knuckles. But their main purpose was to store back a little kinetic energy every time I moved one of my arms. It took a while to build up a charge, but when they were ready to go, I could release the force stored in each ring with instant precision. A blast from a single band of a ring could knock a big man off his feet and take the fight out of him in the process. There were three bands to each ring – which meant that I had a dozen times that much force ready to go on each hand.

I didn't bother to say anything to Lara. I just lifted my right fist and triggered every ring on it, unleashing a pile driver of kinetic energy at the skinwalker. Lara bounded forward at the same instant, swords spinning, ready to lay into the skinwalker when my strike threw it off balance and distracted it.

But the skinwalker lifted its left hand, fingers crooked into a familiar defensive gesture, and the wave of force that should have knocked it tail over teakettle bounced back from it like light from a mirror – and struck Lara full-on instead.

Lara let out a startled *whuff* as the equivalent force of a speeding car slammed into her, knocked her back, and flattened her against the mound of rubble still filling the hallway behind me.

The skinwalker's mouth split into a leering smile of its own, and its bestial voice purred, 'Break, little phage. Break.'

Lara gasped and lifted herself up with her arms. Her white eyes were fixed on the skinwalker, her lips twisted into a defiant snarl.

I stood there staring at the skinwalker. It was hard, and I had to use the wall to help me balance. Then I took a deep breath and stepped away from the wall, moving very carefully, until I stood between the skinwalker and Lara. I turned to face it squarely.

'Okay,' I said. 'Let's have it.'

'Have what, pretender?' the skinwalker growled.

'You aren't here to kill us,' I said. 'You could have done it by now.'

'Oh, so true,' it murmured, its eyes dancing with malicious pleasure.

'You don't have to gloat about it, prick,' I muttered under my breath. Then I addressed the skinwalker again. 'You must want to talk. So why don't you just say what you came to say?'

The skinwalker studied me, and idly nipped another finger from the unconscious vampire girl. It chewed slowly, with some truly unsettling snapping, popping sounds, and then swallowed. 'You will trade with me.'

I frowned. 'Trade?'

The skinwalker smiled again and tugged something from around its neck with one talon. Then it caught the object and tossed it to me. I caught it. It was a silver pentacle necklace, a twin to my own, if considerably less battered and worn.

It was Thomas's necklace.

My belly went cold.

'Trade,' the skinwalker said. 'Thomas of Raith. For the doomed warrior.'

I eyed the thing. So it wanted Morgan, too. 'Suppose I tell you to fuck off.'

'I will no longer be in a playful mood,' it purred. 'I will come for you. I will kill you. I will kill your blood, your friends, your beasts. I will kill the flowers in your home and the trees in your tiny fields. I will visit such death upon whatever is yours that your very name will be remembered only in curses and tales of terror.'

I believed the creature.

No reflexive comeback quip sprang from my lips. Given

what I'd seen of the skinwalker's power, I had to give that one a five-star rating on the threatometer.

'And to encourage you . . .' Its gaze shifted to Lara. 'If the wizard does not obey, I will unmake you as well. I will do it every bit as easily as I have done today. And it will bring me intense pleasure to do so.'

Lara stared at the skinwalker with pure white eyes, her expression locked into a snarl of hate.

'Do you understand me, little phage? You and that rotting bag of flesh you've attached yourself to?'

'I understand,' Lara spat.

The skinwalker's smile widened for an instant. 'If the doomed warrior is not delivered to me by sundown tomorrow, I will begin my hunt.'

'It might take more time than that,' I said.

'For your sake, pretender, pray it does not.' It idly flung the unconscious vampire away from it, to land in a heap atop the other sister. 'You may reach me through his speaking devices,' the skinwalker said.

Then it leapt lightly up through one of the holes in the ceiling, and was gone.

I slumped against the wall, almost falling.

'Thomas,' I whispered.

That nightmare had my brother.

27

Lara took charge of the aftermath.

A dozen security guards were dead, another dozen maimed and crippled. The walls in the hallway where the guards had sprung their ambush were so covered in blood that it looked like they had been painted red. At least a dozen more personnel hadn't been able to reach the battle before it was over, it had all happened so swiftly – which meant that there was someone available to help stabilize the wounded and clean up the bodies.

The skinwalker's hex had effectively destroyed every radio and cell phone in the Château, but the land lines, based on much older, simpler technology, were still up. Lara called in a small army of other employees, including the medical staff that the Raiths kept on retainer.

I sat with my back against the wall while all this happened, a little apart from the activity. It seemed appropriate. My head hurt. When scratching an itch, I noticed that there was a wide stripe of mostly dried blood covering my left ear and spreading down my neck. Must have been a scalp wound. They bleed like crazy.

After some indeterminately fuzzy length of time, I looked up to see Lara supervising the movement of her two wounded relatives. The two vampires were liberally smeared with their own blood, and both were senseless. When they were carried off in stretchers, the medics began helping wounded security guards, and Lara walked over to me.

She knelt down in front of me, her pale grey eyes concealing whatever thought was behind them. 'Can you stand, wizard?'

'Can,' I said. 'Don't want to.'

She lifted her chin slightly and looked down at me, one hand on her hip. 'What have you gotten my little brother involved in?'

'Wish I knew,' I said. 'I'm still trying to figure out where the bullets are coming from.'

She folded her arms. 'The doomed warrior. The skin-walker meant the fugitive Warden, I presume.'

'It's one way to interpret that.'

Lara studied me intently and suddenly smiled, showing neat white teeth. 'You have him. He came to you for help.'

'Why the hell would you think that?' I asked.

'Because people in hopeless situations come to you for help on a regular basis. And you help them. It's what you do.' She tapped her chin with one finger. 'Now, to decide what is more advantageous. To play along with the skin-walker's demands. Or to write Thomas off as a loss, take the Warden from you, and turn him into fresh political capital for those who are hunting him. There is a rather substantial reward for his capture or death.'

I eyed her dully. 'You're going to play along. You're hoping that you'll be able to act reluctant and get some concessions from me in exchange for your cooperation, but you're going to give it to me anyway.'

'And why should I do that?' Lara asked.

'Because after the coup attempt in the Deeps, Thomas is a White Court celebrity. If you let some big bad shag-nasty come along and kill him after it openly defies you in your own home, you look weak. We both know you can't live with that.'

'And by giving in to his demands, I avoid the appearance of weakness?' she asked skeptically. 'No, Dresden.'

'Damn right, no,' I said. 'You're going to play along, set Shagnasty up, and then take him out in the true, treacherous tradition of the White Court. You get Thomas back. You lay low a heavyweight. You gain status among your own folk.'

She narrowed her eyes at me, her expression giving me no hint to the direction of her thoughts. Then she said, 'And when that is done, what if I should take the Warden and turn him over to the White Council myself? It would be a formidable bargaining chip to bring to the table with your folk in the future.'

'Sure it would. But you won't do that.'

'Won't I?' Lara asked. 'What's stopping me?'

'I am.'

'I always enjoy dealing with a man possessing a well-developed sense of self-worth.'

It was my turn to show my teeth in a smile. 'Slugging matches aren't your style, Lara. If you play this situation right, it will further your reputation and influence. Why jeopardize that by throwing down with me?'

'Mmmm,' she said, her eyes wandering over me. She idly smoothed her skirt with one hand, instantly drawing my eyes to the pale length of thigh showing through the torn seam. Trickles of blood from her wounds slithered lovingly over smooth flesh. 'I wonder, occasionally, what it might be like to throw down with you, Dresden. To go to the mat. I wonder what might happen.'

I licked my lips and jerked my eyes away with an effort, incapable of speech.

'Do you know how to really control someone, Harry?' she asked, her voice a low purr.

I cleared my throat and rasped, 'How?'

Her pale grey eyes were huge and deep. 'Give them what they want. Give them what they need. Give them what no one else can give. If you can do that, they'll come back to you again and again.' She leaned down close and whispered in my ear, 'I know what I can give you, Harry. Shall I tell you?'

I swallowed and nodded, not daring to look at her.

'Surcease,' she breathed into my ear. 'I can make it stop hurting, wizard. I can take away the pains of the body. Of the mind. Of the heart. For a little time, I could give you something no one else can – freedom from your burdens of responsibility and conscience.' She leaned even closer, until I could feel the coolness of the air around her lips. 'Sweet Dresden. I could give you peace. Imagine closing your eyes with no worries, no pain, no fears, no regrets, no appetites, and no guilt. Only quiet and darkness and stillness and my flesh against yours.'

I shivered. I couldn't stop myself.

'I can give you that,' Lara said, her lips slinking into a smile. 'You wear your pain like a suit of armor. But one day, it will be too heavy to bear. And you'll remember this moment. And you'll know who can give you what you need.' She let out a small, sensual sigh. 'I don't require more food, Dresden. I have that in plenty. But a partner . . . You and I could do much together that we could not alone.'

'Sounds swell,' I croaked, barely able to get the words out. 'Maybe we'll start with getting Thomas back.'

She straightened her spine and leaned back from me, her beautiful pale face full of lust and hunger. She closed her eyes and stretched a little in place, the way cats sometimes will. It was a mind-numbing display of lithe femininity. She nodded slowly, then rose and regarded me with her usual cool detachment. 'You're right, of course. Business first. You want me to help you.'

'I want you to help yourself,' I said. 'We've both got the same problem.'

'And that would be?' she asked.

'Traitors within the organization,' I said. 'Inciting conflict and destabilizing the balance of power.'

She arched a raven black eyebrow. 'The Warden is innocent?'

'Only if I can find the guy who set him up.'

'You think there's a connection between your traitor and the skinwalker.'

'And another connection that led me here,' I said. 'One of your folk paid that lawyer and rewired her head.'

Lara's mouth twisted with distaste. 'If that's true, then someone was hideously gauche. One never leaves such obvious and overt blocks behind – and especially not in a contact only one layer removed. Such things call too much attention to themselves.'

'So,' I said. 'A White Court vampire who is gauche, overt, impatient. Oh, and who did not show up to defend the homestead when the skinwalker broke in. And who Thomas recently beat and humiliated in public.'

'Madeline,' Lara murmured.

'Madeline,' I said. 'I think whoever is pulling the strings on this operation is using her. I think we need to find her and follow the strings back to the puppeteer.'

'How?'

I reached into my duster pocket and took out the sheet

of paper with Morgan's supposed account on it, along with a photocopy of the huge deposit check. 'Find out who set up this account. Find out where the money came from.' I passed her the pages. 'After that, see if you can't find some way to track down where Thomas's cell phone is.'

'His cell phone?'

'Shagnasty said we could contact him by calling Thomas's phones. Isn't there some way that they can track where those things are?'

'It depends on a number of factors.'

'Well I'm betting the skinwalker doesn't have a subscription to *Popular Science*. He'll probably have some kind of countermeasure for a tracking spell, but he might not even realize that it's possible to physically trace the phone.'

'I'll see what I can find out,' she said. One of the medics approached us and stood back respectfully. Lara turned to the young man. 'Yes?'

He held up a clipboard. 'The triage report you wanted.'

She held out her hand. He passed her the clipboard as if he didn't want to move his feet too close to her. Lara scanned over the topmost page, and murmured, 'Hennesy and Callo both have broken backs?'

'It'll take an X-ray to confirm it,' the medic said nervously. 'But from what I was told, the, uh, the attacker just broke them over his knee and threw them down. They're paralyzed. Probably permanently.'

'And Wilson lost both eyes,' Lara murmured.

The medic avoided looking at her. 'Yes, ma'am.'

'Very well,' Lara said. 'Take Hennesy to Natalia's chambers. Callo will go to Elisa.'

'Yes, ma'am. Should I send Wilson to the infirmary?'

Lara stared at him with absolutely no expression on her

lovely face. Then she said, 'No, Andrew. I'll come for him in a moment.' She held out the clipboard, and the medic took it and hurried away.

I watched Lara for a moment and said, 'You're going to kill those men. When Elisa and Natalia wake up . . .'

'They will feed and their lives will be spared. Annoying as it may be to lose what I invested in those men, I can replace hired guns,' she said. 'I cannot so easily replace members of my family and my House. As their leader, it is my responsibility to provide adequate care and sustenance in times of need – particularly when loyalty to the House is what created that need.'

'They're your own men,' I said.

'That was before they became useless to the House,' she replied. 'They know too much of our internal affairs to be allowed to leave. Lives must be lost if my kin are to survive their injuries. Rather than inflict that upon one who can still be of use to us, I preserve lives by seeing to it that these men serve us one last time.'

'Yeah. You're a real humanitarian. A regular Mother Teresa.'

She turned that flat, empty gaze to me again. 'At what point did you forget that I am a vampire, Dresden? A monster. A habitually neat, polite, civil, and efficient monster.' Her eyes drifted down the hallway, to where a well-muscled young man was being helped to sit down, while a medic secured bandages over his eyes. Lara stared intently at him, the color of her eyes lightening to silver, and her lips parted slightly. 'I am what I am.'

I felt sick to my stomach. I pushed myself to my feet, and said, 'So am I.'

She glanced obliquely at me. 'Is that a threat, Dresden?'

I shook my head. 'Just a fact. One day I'm going to take you down.'

Her eyes went back to the wounded man, her lips shifting to one side in a smirk. 'One day,' she murmured. 'But not today.'

'No. Not today.'

'Is there anything else I can do for you, wizard mine?'

'Yeah,' I said.

She glanced at me and raised an eyebrow.

'I need a car.'

28

I sort of shambled up one floor and down a wing to the Château's infirmary, escorted there by a guard who was being very careful not to limp on a wounded leg. The skinwalker had smacked my bean against hardwood and knocked something loose. I felt fairly confident that if I jumped up and down and wiggled my head, my brain would slosh squishily around the inside of my skull.

Not that I was going to be doing any of those things. Walking was hard enough.

In the infirmary, I found a white-coated young woman tending to the wounded. She moved with the brisk professional manner of a doctor, and was just finishing seeing to Justine's injuries. The young woman was laid out on a bed, her midsection swathed in bandages, her eyes glazed with the distant, peaceful expression of someone on good drugs.

Anastasia sat on the bed next to Justine's, her back straight, her expression calm. Her right arm was bound up close against her body in a black cloth sling. She came to her feet as I entered the room. She looked a little pale and shaky, but she stood without leaning on her slender wooden staff. 'We're leaving now?'

'Yeah,' I said. I moved to her side to support her. 'You okay to walk?'

She leaned her staff toward me, stopping me from coming any closer, though she smiled slightly as she did.

'I'll bloody well walk out of here,' she said. And she said it in an atrocious Scottish accent.

I lifted both eyebrows at her in shock. 'You told me you fell asleep during *Highlander*.'

Her dark eyes sparkled. 'I always say that when I find myself at a vintage movie showing at a drive-in theater while in the company of a man two centuries younger than me.'

'And not because you didn't want to hurt my feelings with your professional opinion of the swordsmanship on display?'

'Young men can be so delicate,' she said, her dimples making a brief appearance.

'We should get you to a hospital,' I said, nodding at her sling.

She shook her head. 'The break is set back in place already. From here, all one can do is wear a sling and wait for it to stop hurting so badly.'

I grimaced. 'I've got some meds at my place.'

She smiled again, but this time I could see how much she was straining to keep up appearances. 'That would be lovely.'

'Harry,' said a soft voice.

I turned to face the wounded Justine, who looked at me with drowsy eyes. I turned to the bed and bent down to smile at her. 'Hey there.'

'We heard that thing talking,' she said. All the hard consonants in her words had blurred, rounded edges. 'We heard it talking to you and Lara.'

I glanced up at Anastasia, who gave me a short nod of her head.

'Yeah,' I said to Justine. I desperately did not want her

to say anything she ought not to be saying. 'I'll take care of it.'

Justine smiled at me, though she looked like she could hardly keep her eyes open. 'I know you will. He loves you, you know.'

I did *not* look up at Anastasia. 'Uh. Yeah.'

Justine took my hand in one of hers, her eyes reaching for mine. 'He always worried that he'd never be able to talk to you. That the world he came from was so different. That he wouldn't know enough about being human to relate. That he wouldn't know about being a br—'

'Brass-plated pain in my ass,' I said. 'He knows that plenty well.' I avoided her eyes. The last thing I needed was to endure another soulgaze now. 'Justine, you need to rest. I'll dig him up. Don't worry.'

She smiled again and her eyes closed all the way. 'You're like family to me, Harry. You always care.'

I bowed my head, embarrassed, and settled Justine's hands back on the bed, then tugged the thin hospital blankets up over her.

Anastasia watched me with thoughtful eyes as I did.

We walked back to the front of the house, and past the fairly fresh plaster that might have hidden ridiculously lethal booby traps, out over a front porch the size of a tennis court, and down several steps to the circular drive, where the car Lara had lent me was waiting.

I stopped so suddenly that Anastasia nearly walked into my back. She caught her balance with a hiss of discomfort, and then looked up and caught her breath. 'Oh, my.'

Nearly two tons of British steel and chrome sat idling in the drive. Its purring engine sounded like a sewing

machine. The white Rolls limo was an old model, something right out of a pulp-fiction adventure film, and it
was in gorgeous condition. Its panels shone, freshly waxed
and without blemish, and the chrome of its grill gleamed
sienna in the light of dusk over the Château.

I walked down to peer inside the Rolls. The passenger
seating in the back was larger than my freaking apartment. Or at least it looked that way. The interior was all
silver-grey and white leather and similarly colored woodwork, polished to a glowing sheen and accented with silver.
The carpet on the floor of the Rolls was thicker and more
luxurious than a well-kept lawn.

'Wow,' I said quietly.

Anastasia, standing beside me, breathed, 'That's a work
of bloody art.'

'Wow,' I said quietly.

'Look at the filigree.'

I nodded. 'Wow.'

Anastasia gave me a sidelong look. 'And there's plenty
of room in back.'

I blinked and looked at her.

Her expression was innocent and bland. 'All I'm
saying is that it *is* rather crowded in your apartment
right now. . . .'

'Anastasia,' I said. I felt my face getting a little warm.

The dimples reappeared. She was just teasing me, of
course. In her condition it would be some time before she
could engage in that kind of activity.

'What model is this?' she asked.

'Um,' I said. 'Well, it's a Rolls-Royce. It's . . . I think
it's from before World War Two. . . .'

'It's a Rolls-Royce Silver Wraith, of course,' said Lara's

voice from behind me. 'At this house? What else would it be?'

I looked over my shoulder, to see Lara Raith standing in the shadowy doorway of the house.

'You have special needs, obviously,' she said. 'So I provided you with an appropriate vintage. Nineteen thirty-nine.' She folded her arms, rather smugly, I thought, and said, 'Bring it back with a full tank.'

I tilted my head at her in a gesture that wasn't quite an affirmation, and muttered, as I opened the passenger-side door, 'The loan officer will have to run a check on my credit first. What's this thing get, about two gallons per mile?'

Anastasia slid into the car with a brief sound of discomfort. I winced and held out my hands in case she fell back, but she managed it without any other difficulty. I shut the door, and caught a glimpse of Lara taking a sudden step forward.

She focused sharply on Anastasia for a moment – and then upon me.

Lara's eyes flickered several shades paler as her ripe lips parted in dawning realization. A very slow smile crept over her mouth as she stared at me.

I turned away from her rather hurriedly, got into the Rolls, and got it moving. And I didn't look back again until the vampires' house was five miles behind us.

Anastasia let me get most of the way back to town before she looked at me and said, 'Harry?'

'Hmmm?' I asked. Driving the Rolls was like driving a tank. It had all kinds of momentum behind it, no power steering, and no power brakes. It was a vehicle that demanded that I pay my respects to the laws of physics and think a little bit further ahead than I otherwise might.

'Is there something you want to tell me?' she asked.

'Dammit,' I muttered.

She watched me with eyes much older than the face around them. 'You were hoping I didn't hear Justine.'

'Yeah.'

'But I did.'

I drove for another minute or two before asking, 'Are you sure?'

She considered that for a moment before she said, more gently, 'Are you sure there's nothing you want to tell me?'

'I have nothing to say to Captain Luccio,' I said. It came out harder than I had anticipated.

She reached out and put her left hand on my right, where it rested on the gearshift. 'What about to Anastasia?' she asked.

I felt my jaw tighten. It took me a moment to make it relax and ask, 'Do you have any family?'

'Yes,' she said. 'Technically.'

'Technically?'

'The men and women I grew up with, who I knew? They've been dead for generations. Their descendants are living all over Italy, in Greece, and there are a few in Algeria – but it isn't as though they invite their great-great-great-great-great-great-grandaunt to their Christmas celebrations. They're strangers.'

I frowned, thinking that over, and looked at her. 'Strangers.'

She nodded. 'Most people aren't willing to accept a radical fact like the life span of our kind, Harry. There are some families who have – Martha Liberty, for example, lives with one of her multiple-great-granddaughters and her children. But mostly, it ends badly when wizards try to stay too close to their kin.' She bowed her head, apparently studying her sling as she spoke. 'I look in on them every five or six years, without them knowing. Keep an eye out for any of the children who might develop a talent.'

'But you had a real family once,' I said.

She sighed and looked out the window. 'Oh, yes. It was a very long time ago.'

'I remember my father, a little. But I was raised an orphan.'

She winced. '*Dio*, Harry.' Her fingers squeezed mine. 'You never had anyone, did you?'

'And if I did find someone,' I said, feeling my throat constricting as I spoke, 'I would do anything necessary to protect him. Anything.'

Anastasia looked out the window, letting out a hiss of what sounded like anger. 'Margaret. You selfish bitch.'

I blinked and looked at her, and nearly got us both killed when a passing car cut me off and I almost couldn't stop the monster Rolls in time. 'You . . . you knew my mother?'

'All the Wardens knew her,' Anastasia said quietly.

'She was a Warden?'

Anastasia was silent for a moment before shaking her head. 'She was considered a threat to the Laws of Magic.'

'What does that mean?'

'It means that she made it a point to dance as close to the edge of breaking the Laws as she possibly could whenever she got the chance,' Anastasia replied. 'It took her all of a year after she was admitted to the Council to start agitating for change.'

I had to focus on the road. This was more than I had ever heard from anyone in the Council about the enigmatic figure who had given me life. My hands were sweating and my heart was thudding. 'What kind of change?'

'She was furious that "the Laws of Magic have nothing to do with right and wrong". She pointed out how wizards could use their abilities to bilk people out of their money, to intimidate and manipulate them, to steal wealth and property from others or destroy it outright, and that so long as the Laws were obeyed, the Council would do nothing whatsoever to stop them or discourage others from following their example. She wanted to reform the Council's laws to embrace concepts of justice as well as limiting the specific use of magic.'

I frowned. 'Wow. What a monster.'

She exhaled slowly. 'Can you imagine what would happen if she'd had her way?'

'I wouldn't have been unjustly persecuted by the Wardens for years?'

Anastasia's lips firmed into a line. 'Once a body of laws describing justice was applied to the Council, it would only be a short step to using that body to involve the Council in events happening in the outside world.'

'Gosh, yeah,' I said. 'You're right. A bunch of wizards trying to effect good in the world would be awful.'

'Whose good?' Anastasia asked calmly. 'No one is an unjust villain in his own mind, Harry. Even – perhaps even *especially* – those who are the worst of us. Some of the cruelest tyrants in history were motivated by noble ideals, or made choices that they would call "hard but necessary steps" for the good of their nation. We're all the hero of our own story.'

'Yeah. It was really hard to tell who the good guys and bad guys were in World War Two.'

She rolled her eyes. 'You've read the histories written by the victors of that war, Harry. As someone who lived through it, I can tell you that at the time of the war, there was a great deal less certainty. There were stories of atrocities in Germany, but for every one that was true, there were another five or six that weren't. How could one have told the difference between the true stories, the propaganda, and simple fabrications and myths created by the people of the nations Germany had attacked?'

'Might have been a bit easier if there'd been a wizard or three around to help,' I said.

She gave me an oblique look. 'Then by your argument, you would have had the White Council destroy the United States.'

'What?'

'Your government has drenched its hands in innocent blood as well,' she replied, still calm. 'Unless you think the Indian tribesmen whose lands were conquered were somehow the villains of the piece.'

I frowned over that one. 'We've gone sort of far afield from my mother.'

'Yes. And no. What she proposed would inevitably have drawn the Council into mortal conflicts, and therefore into mortal politics. Tell me the truth – if the Council, today, declared war upon America for its past crimes and current idiocy, would you obey the order to attack?'

'Hell, no,' I said. 'The US isn't a perfect place, but it's better than most people have managed to come up with. And all my stuff is there.'

She smiled faintly. 'Exactly. And since the Council is made up of members from all over the world, it would mean that no matter *where* we acted, we would almost certainly be faced with dissidence and desertion from those who felt their homelands wronged.' She shrugged – and grimaced in pain before arresting the motion. 'I myself would have issues if the Council acted against any of the lands where my family has settled. They may not remember me, but the reverse is not true.'

I thought about what she'd said for a long moment. 'What you're saying is that the Council would have to turn on some of its own.'

'And how many times would that happen before there *was* no Council?' she asked. 'Wars and feuds can live for generations even when there *isn't* a group of wizards involved. Settling the conflicts would have required even more involvement in mortal affairs.'

'You mean control,' I said quietly. 'You mean the Council seeking political power.'

She gave me a knowing look. 'One of the things that makes me respect you more than most young people is your appreciation for history. Precisely. And for gaining control over others, for gathering great power to oneself, there is no better tool than black magic.'

'Which is what the Laws of Magic cover already.'

She nodded. 'And so the Council limits itself. Any wizard is free to act in whatever manner he chooses with his power – provided he doesn't break any of the Laws. Without resorting to black magic, the amount of damage an individual can inflict on mortal society is limited. As harsh an experience as it has created for you, Harry, the Laws of Magic are not about justice. The White Council is not about justice. They are about restraining power.' She smiled faintly. 'And, occasionally, the Council manages to do some good by protecting mankind from supernatural threats.'

'And that's good enough for you?' I asked.

'It isn't perfect,' she admitted. 'But it's better than anything else we've come up with. And the things I've spent my lifetime building are there.'

'Touché,' I said.

'Thank you.'

I stroked her fingers with my thumb. 'So you're saying my mother was short-sighted.'

'She was a complex woman,' Anastasia said. 'Brilliant, erratic, passionate, committed, idealistic, talented, charming, insulting, bold, incautious, arrogant – and short-sighted, yes. Among a great many other qualities. She loved pointing out the areas of "grey" magic, as she called them, and constantly questioning their legitimacy.' She shrugged. 'The Senior Council tasked the Wardens to keep an eye on her. Which was damn near impossible.'

'Why?'

'The woman had a great many contacts among the Fey. That's why everyone called her Margaret LaFey. She knew more Ways through the Nevernever than anyone I've ever seen, before or since. She could be in Beijing at break-fast, Rome at lunch, and Seattle for supper and stop for coffee in Sydney and Capetown in between.' She sighed. 'Margaret vanished once, for four or five years. Everyone assumed that she'd finally run afoul of something in Faerie.

She never seemed able to restrain her tongue, even when she knew better.'

'I wonder what that's like.'

Anastasia gave me a rather worn sad smile. 'But she didn't spend all that time in Faerie, did she?'

I looked up at the rearview mirror, back toward Château Raith.

'And Thomas is the son of the White King himself.'

I didn't answer.

She exhaled heavily. 'You look so different from him. Except perhaps for something in the jaw. The shape of the eyes.'

I didn't say anything until we got to the apartment. The Rolls went together with the gravel lot like champagne and Cracker Jacks. I turned the engine off and listened to it click as it began to cool down. The sun was gone over the horizon by that time, and the lengthening shadows began to trigger streetlights.

'Are you going to tell anyone?' I asked quietly.

She looked out the window as she considered the question. Then she said, 'Not unless I think it relevant.'

I turned to look at her. 'You know what will happen if they know. They'll use him.'

She gazed straight out the front of the car. 'I know.'

I spoke quietly to put all the weight I could into each word I spoke next. 'Over. My. Dead. Body.'

Anastasia closed her eyes for a moment, and opened them again. Her expression never flickered. She took her hand slowly, reluctantly from mine and put it in her lap. Then she whispered, 'I pray to God it never comes to that.'

We sat in the car separately.

It seemed larger and colder, for some reason. The silence seemed deeper.

Luccio lifted her chin and looked at me. 'What will you do now?'

'What do you think?' I clenched my fists so that my knuckles popped, rolled my neck once, and opened the door. 'I'm going to find my brother.'

29

Two hours and half a dozen attempted tracking spells later, I snarled and slapped a stack of notepads off the corner of the table in my subbasement laboratory. They thwacked against the wall beneath Bob the Skull's shelf, and fell to the concrete floor.

'It was to be expected,' Bob the Skull said, very quietly. Orange lights like the flickers of distant campfires glittered in the eye sockets of the bleached human skull that sat on its own shelf high up on one wall of my lab, bracketed by the remains of dozens of melted candles and half a dozen paperback romances. 'The parent-to-child blood bond is much more sympathetic than that shared by half siblings.'

I glared at the skull and also kept my voice down. 'You just can't go a day without saying that you told me so.'

'I can't help it if you're wrong all the time yet continually ignore my advice, sahib. I'm just a humble servant.'

I couldn't scream at my nonmaterial assistant with other people in the apartment above me, so I consoled myself by snatching up a pencil from a nearby work shelf and flinging it at him. Its eraser end hit the skull between the eyes.

'Jealousy, thy name is Dresden,' Bob said with a pious sigh.

I paced up and down the length of my lab, burning off frustrated energy. It wasn't much of a walk. Five paces, turn, five paces, turn. It was a dank little concrete box of a room. Work benches lined three of the walls, and I had installed cheap wire shelving above them. The work benches and shelves were crowded with all manner of odds and ends, books, reagents, instruments, various bits of gear needed for alchemy, and scores of books and notebooks.

A long table in the middle of the room was currently covered by a canvas tarp, and the floor at the far end of the lab had a perfect circle of pure copper embedded in it. The remains of several differently structured tracking attempts were scattered on the floor around the circle, while the props and foci from the most recent failure were still inside it.

'One of them should have gotten me *something*,' I told Bob. 'Maybe not a full lock on Thomas's position – but a *tug* in the right direction, at least.'

'Unless he's dead,' Bob said, 'in which case you're just spinning your wheels.'

'He isn't dead,' I said quietly. 'Shagnasty wants to trade.'

'Uh-huh,' Bob scoffed. 'Because everyone knows how honorable the naagloshii are.'

'He's alive,' I said quietly. 'Or at least I'm going to proceed on that assumption.'

Bob somehow managed to look baffled. 'Why?'

Because you need your brother to be all right, whispered a quiet voice in my head. 'Because anything else isn't particularly useful toward resolving this situation,' I said aloud. 'Whoever is behind the curtains is using the skinwalker and probably Madeline Raith, too. So if I find Thomas, I find Shagnasty and Madeline, and I'll be able to start pulling threads until this entire mess unravels.'

'Yeah,' Bob said, drawing out the word. 'Do you think it'll take long to pull all those threads? Because the naagloshii is going to be doing something similar to your intestines.'

I made a growling sound in my throat. 'Yeah. I think I got its number.'

'Really?'

'I keep trying to punch Shagnasty out myself,' I said. 'But its defenses are too good – and it's fast as hell.'

'He's an immortal semidivine being,' Bob said. 'Of course he's good.'

I waved a hand. 'My point is that I've been trying to lay the beating on it myself. Next time I see it, I'm going to start throwing bindings on it, just to trip it up and slow it down, so whoever is with me can get a clean shot.'

'It might work . . .' Bob admitted.

'Thank you.'

'. . . if he's such an idiot that he only bothered to learn to defend himself from violent-energy attacks,' Bob continued, as if I hadn't spoken. 'Which I think is almost as likely as you getting one of those tracking spells to work. He'll know how to defend himself from bindings, Harry.'

I sighed. 'I've got gender issues.'

Bob blinked slowly. 'Uh. Wow. I'd love to say something to make that more embarrassing for you, boss, but I'm not sure how.'

'Not *my* . . . augh.' I threw another pencil. It missed Bob and bounced off the wall behind him. 'With the skin-walker. Is it actually a male? Do I call it a he?'

Bob rolled his eyelights. 'It's a semidivine immortal, Harry. It doesn't procreate. It has no need to recombine

DNA. That means that gender simply doesn't apply. That's something only you meat sacks worry about.'

'Then why is it that you stare at naked girls every chance you get,' I said, 'but not naked men?'

'It's an aesthetic choice,' Bob said loftily. 'As a gender, women exist on a plane far beyond men when it comes to the artistic appreciation of their external beauty.'

'And they have boobs,' I said.

'And they have *boobs*!' Bob agreed with a leer.

I sighed and rubbed at my temples, closing my eyes. 'You said the skinwalkers were semidivine?'

'You're using the English word, which doesn't really describe them very precisely. Most skinwalkers are just people – powerful, dangerous, and often psychotic people, but people. They're successors to the traditions and skills taught to avaricious mortals by the originals. The naagloshii.'

'Originals like Shagnasty,' I said.

'He's the real deal, all right,' Bob replied, his quiet voice growing more serious. 'According to some of the stories of the Navajo, the naagloshii were originally messengers for the Holy People, when they were first teaching humans the Blessing Way.'

'Messengers?' I said. 'Like angels?'

'Or like those guys on bikes in New York, maybe?' Bob said. 'Not all couriers are created identical, Mr Lowest-Common-Denominator. Anyway, the original messengers, the naagloshii, were supposed to go with the Holy People when they departed the mortal world. But some of them didn't. They stayed here, and their selfishness corrupted the power the Holy People gave them. Voila, Shagnasty.'

I grunted. Bob's information was anecdotal, which meant

it could well be distorted by time and by generations of retelling. There probably wasn't any way to know the objective truth of it – but a surprising amount of that kind of lore remained fundamentally sound in oral tradition societies like those of the American Southwest. 'When did this happen?'

'Tough to say,' Bob said. 'The traditional Navajo don't see time the way most mortals do, which makes them arguably smarter than the rest of you monkeys. But it's safe to assume prehistory. Several millennia.'

Yikes.

Thousands of years of survival meant thousands of years of accumulated experience. It meant that Shagnasty was smart and adaptable. The old skinwalker wouldn't still be around if it wasn't. I upgraded the creature, in my thoughts, from 'very tough' to 'damned near impossibly tough'.

But since it still had my brother, that didn't change anything.

'Don't suppose there's a silver bullet we can use?' I asked.

'No, boss,' Bob said quietly. 'Sorry.'

I grimaced, did a half-assed job of cleaning up the mess I'd made, and began to leave the lab. I paused before I left and said, 'Hey, Bob.'

'Yeah?'

'Any thoughts as to why, when LaFortier was being murdered by a wizard, no one threw any magic around?'

'People are morons?'

'It's damned peculiar,' I said.

'Irrationality isn't,' Bob said. 'Wizards just aren't all that stable to begin with.'

Given what I had done with my life lately, I could hardly argue with him. 'It means something,' I said.

'Yeah?' Bob asked. 'What?'

I shook my head. 'Tell you when I figure it out.'

I went back up into my living room through the trapdoor in its floor. The door was a thick one. Sound didn't readily travel up from the lab when it was closed. Luccio was loaded with narcotics and asleep on my couch, lying flat on her back with no pillow, and covered with a light blanket. Her face was slack, her mouth slightly open. It made her look vulnerable, and even younger than she already appeared. Molly sat in one of the recliners with several candles burning beside her. She was reading a paperback, carefully not opening the thing all the way to avoid creasing the spine. Pansy.

I went to the kitchen and made myself a sandwich. As I did, I reflected that I was getting really tired of sandwiches. Maybe I ought to learn to cook or something.

I stood there munching, and Molly came to join me.

'Hey,' she said in muted tones. 'How are you?'

She'd helped me bandage the fairly minor cut on my scalp when I had returned. Strips of white gauze bandage were wound around my head to form a lopsided, off-kilter halo. I felt like the fife player in Willard's iconic *Spirit of '76*.

'Still in one piece,' I replied. 'How are they?'

'Drugged and sleeping,' she said. 'Morgan's fever is up another half of a degree. The last bag of antibiotics is almost empty.'

I clenched my jaw. If I didn't get Morgan to a hospital soon, he was going to be just as dead as he would be if the Council or Shagnasty got hold of him.

'Should I get some ice onto him?' Molly asked anxiously.

'Not until the fever goes over one hundred and four, and stays there,' I said. 'That's when it begins to endanger him. Until then, it's doing what it's supposed to do and slowing the infection.' I finished the last bite of sandwich. 'Any calls?'

She produced a piece of notebook paper. 'Georgia called. Here's where Andi is. They're still with her.'

I took the paper with a grimace. If I hadn't let Morgan in my door half an eternity ago, he wouldn't have been in Chicago, Shagnasty wouldn't have been tailing me to find him, Andi wouldn't be hurt – and Kirby would still be alive. And I hadn't even tried to call and find out how she was. 'How is she?'

'They still aren't sure,' Molly said.

I nodded. 'Okay.'

'Did you find Thomas?'

I shook my head. 'Total bust.'

Mouse came shambling over. He sat down and looked up at me, his expression concerned.

She chewed on her lip. 'What are you going to do?'

'I . . .' My voice trailed off. I sighed. 'I have no idea.'

Mouse pawed at my leg and looked up at me. I bent over to scratch his ears, and instantly regretted it as someone tightened a vise on my temples. I straightened up again in a hurry, wincing, and entertained wild fantasies about lying down on the floor and sleeping for a week.

Molly watched me, her expression worried.

Right, Harry. You're still teaching your apprentice. Show her what a wizard should *do, not what* you *want* to do.

I looked at the paper. 'The answer isn't obvious, which means that I need to put some more thought into it. And while I'm doing that, I'll go look in on Andi.'

Molly nodded. 'What do I do?'

'Hold down the fort. Try to reach me at the hospital if anyone calls or if Morgan gets any worse.'

Molly nodded seriously. 'I can do that.'

I nodded and grabbed my gear and the key to the Rolls. Molly went to the door, ready to lock it behind me when I left. I started to do just that – and then paused. I turned to my apprentice. 'Hey.'

'Yeah?'

'Thank you.'

She blinked at me. 'Um. What did I do?'

'More than I asked of you. More than was good for you.' I leaned over and kissed her on the cheek. 'Thank you, Molly.'

She lifted her chin a little, smiling. 'Well,' she said. 'You're just so pathetic. How could I turn away?'

That made me laugh, if only for a second, and her smile blossomed into something radiant.

'You know the drill,' I said.

She nodded. 'Keep my eyes open, be supercareful, don't take any chances.'

I winked at her. 'You grow wiser, grasshopper.'

Molly started to say something, stopped, fidgeted for half a second, and then threw her arms around me in a big hug.

'Be careful,' she said. 'Okay?'

I hugged her back tight and gave the top of her head a light kiss. 'Hang in there, kid. We'll get this straightened out.'

'Okay,' she said. 'We will.'

Then I headed out into the Chicago night wondering how – or if – that was possible.

30

I don't like hospitals – but then, who does?

I don't like the clean, cool hallways. I don't like the stark fluorescent lights. I don't like the calm ring tones on the telephones. I don't like the pastel scrubs the nurses and attendants wear. I don't like the elevators, and I don't like the soothing colors on the walls, and I don't like the way everyone speaks in measured, quiet voices.

But mostly, I don't like the memories I've collected there.

Andi was still in intensive care. I wouldn't be able to go in to see her – neither would Billy and Georgia, if they hadn't arranged for power of attorney for medical matters, a few years back. It was long after standard visiting hours, but most hospital staffs stretch rules and look the other way for those whose loved ones are in ICU. The world has changed a lot over the centuries, but death watches are still respected.

Billy had come to me on the down low to set up power of attorney for me, in case he should be hospitalized without Georgia being nearby to handle matters. Though neither of us said so, we both knew why he really did it. The only reason Georgia wouldn't be there is if she was dead – and if Billy was in no shape to make decisions for himself, he didn't want to hang around and find out what his world would be like without her in it. He wanted someone he could trust to understand that.

Billy and Georgia are solid.

I'd spent some endless hours in Stroger's ICU waiting room, and it hadn't changed since I'd been there last. It was empty except for Georgia. She lay on the sofa, sleeping, still wearing her glasses. A book by what was presumably a prominent psychologist lay open on her stomach. She looked exhausted.

I bypassed the waiting room and went to the nurses' desk. A tired-looking woman in her thirties looked up at me with a frown. 'Sir,' she said, 'it's well after visiting hours.'

'I know,' I said. I took my notepad out of my pocket and scribbled a quick note on it. 'I'll go back to the waiting room. The next time you go past Miss Macklin's room, could you please give this to the gentleman sitting with her?'

The nurse relaxed a little, and gave me a tired smile. 'Certainly. It will just be a few minutes.'

'Thanks.'

I went back to the waiting room and settled into a chair. I closed my eyes, leaned my head back against the wall, and drowsed until I heard footsteps on tile.

Billy entered with a rolled-up blanket under his arm, glanced around the room, and nodded to me. Then he went immediately to Georgia. He took her glasses off, very gently, and picked up the book. Georgia never stirred. He put the book on the end table, and her glasses on top of it. Then he took the blanket from under his arm and covered her up. She murmured and stirred, but Billy shushed her quietly and stroked his hand over her hair. She sighed and shifted onto her side, then snuggled down under the blanket.

I reached up a hand and flicked the light switch beside my head. It left the room dim, if not really dark.

Billy smiled his thanks to me, and nodded toward the door. I got up and we walked out into the hallway together.

'Should have tried to call you sooner,' I said. 'I'm sorry.'

He shook his head. 'I know how it is, man. No apology needed.'

'Okay,' I said, without actually agreeing with him. 'How is she?'

'Not good,' he replied simply. 'There was internal bleeding. It took two rounds of surgery to get it stopped.' The blocky young man shoved his hands into the pockets of his jeans. 'They told us if she makes it through the night, she'll be out of the worst of it.'

'How are you holding up?'

He shook his head again. 'I don't know, man. I called Kirby's folks. I was his friend. I had to. The police had already contacted them, but it isn't the same.'

'No, it isn't.'

'They took it pretty hard. Kirby was an only child.'

I sighed. 'I'm sorry.'

He shrugged. 'Kirby knew the risks. He'd rather have died than stand by and do nothing.'

'Georgia?'

'I'd have lost it without her. Pillar of strength and calm,' Billy said. He glanced back toward the waiting room and a smile touched the corners of his eyes. 'She's good at setting things aside until there's time to deal with them. Once things have settled out, she'll be a wreck, and it'll be my turn to hold her up.'

Like I said.

Solid.

'The thing that did Kirby took Thomas Raith,' I said. 'The vampire you work with sometimes?'

'Yeah. As soon as I work out how to find it, I'm taking it down. The vampires are probably going to help – but I might need backup I can trust.'

Billy's eyes flickered with a sudden fire of rage and hunger. 'Yeah?'

I nodded. 'It's part of something bigger. I can't talk to you about everything that's going on. And I know Andi needs you here. I understand if you don't—'

Billy turned his eyes to me, those same dangerous fires smoldering. 'Harry, I'm not going to move forward blind anymore.'

'What do you mean?'

'I mean that for years, I've been willing to help you, even though you could barely ever tell me what was actually happening. You've played everything close to the chest. And I know you had your reasons for that.' He stopped walking and looked up at me calmly. 'Kirby's dead. Maybe Andi, too.'

My conscience wouldn't let me meet his gaze, even for an instant. 'I know.'

He nodded. 'So. If I'd had this conversation with you sooner, maybe they wouldn't be. Maybe if we'd had a better idea about what's actually going on in the world, it would have changed how we approached things. They follow my lead, Harry. I have a responsibility to make sure that I do everything in my power to make them aware and safe.'

'Yeah,' I said. 'I can see your point.'

'Then if you want my help, things are going to change. I'm not charging ahead blindfolded again. Not ever.'

'Billy,' I said quietly. 'This isn't stuff you can unlearn.

Right now, you're insulated from the worst of what goes on because you're ... I don't want to be insulting, but you're a bunch of amateurs without enough of a clue to be a real threat to anyone.'

His eyes darkened. 'Insulated from the worst?' he asked in a quiet, dangerous voice. 'Tell that to Kirby. Tell that to Andi.'

I took several steps away, pinched the bridge of my nose between thumb and forefinger, and closed my eyes, thinking. Billy had a point, of course. I'd been careful to control what information he and the Alphas had gotten from me, in an effort to protect them. And it had worked – for a while.

But now things were different. Kirby's death had seen to that.

'You're sure you don't want to back out?' I asked. 'Once you're part of the scene, you aren't getting out of it.' I clenched my jaw for a second. 'And believe it or not, Billy, yes. You *have* been insulated from the worst.'

'I'm not backing off on this one, Harry. I can't.' Out of the corner of my eye, I saw him fold his arms. 'You're the one who wants our help.'

I pointed a finger at him. 'I don't *want* it. I don't *want* to drag you into what's going on. I don't *want* you walking into more danger and getting hurt.' I sighed. 'But ... there's a lot at stake, and I think I might *need* you.'

'Okay, then,' Billy said. 'You know what it will cost.'

He stood facing me solidly, tired eyes steady, and I realized something I hadn't ever made into a tangible thought before: he wasn't a kid anymore. Not because he'd graduated, and not even because of how capable he was. He'd seen the worst – death, heartless and nasty, come to lay waste to everything it could. He knew in his heart of hearts, beyond a shadow of a doubt, that it could come for him, take him as easily as it had taken Kirby.

And he was making a choice to stand his ground.

Billy Borden, kid werewolf, was gone.

Will was choosing to stand with me.

I couldn't treat him like a child anymore. Will was ignorant of the supernatural world beyond the fairly minor threats that lurked around the University of Chicago. He and the other werewolves had been kids who learned one really neat magic trick, almost ten years before. I hadn't shared more with them, and the paranormal community in general is careful about what they say to strangers. He had, at best, only a vague idea of the scope of supernatural affairs in general, and he had not the first clue about how hot the water really was around me right now.

Will had picked his ground. I couldn't keep him in the dark and tell myself that I was protecting him.

I nodded to a few chairs sitting along the wall at a nearby intersection of hallways. 'Let's sit down. I don't have much time, and there's a lot to cover. I'll tell you everything when I get a chance, but for now all I can give you is a highlights reel.'

By the time I got done giving Will the CliffsNotes version of the supernatural world, I still hadn't come up with a plan. So, working on the theory that the proper answers just needed more time to cook, and that they could do so while I was on the move, I went back to my borrowed car and drove to the next place I should have visited sooner than I had.

Murphy used to have an office at the headquarters of

CPD's Special Investigations department. Then she'd blown off her professional duty as head of the department to cover me during a furball that went bad on an epic scale. She'd nearly lost her job altogether, but Murph was a third-generation cop from a cop clan. She'd managed to gain enough support to hang on to her badge, but she had been demoted to Detective Sergeant and had her seniority revoked – a dead end for her career.

Now her old office was occupied by John Stallings, and Murphy had a desk in the large room that housed SI. It wasn't a new desk, either. One leg was propped up with a small stack of triplicate report forms. It wasn't unusual in that room. SI was the bottom of the chute for cops who had earned the wrath of their superiors or, worse, had taken a misstep in the cutthroat world of Chicago city politics. The desks were all battered and old. The walls and floor were worn. The room obviously housed at least twice as many work desks as it had been meant to contain.

It was late. The place was quiet and mostly empty. Whoever was on the night shift must have been out on a call of some kind. Of the three cops in the room, I only knew one of them by name – Murphy's current partner, a blocky, mildly overweight man in his late fifties, with hair going steadily more silver in sharp contrast to the dark coffee tone of his skin.

'Rawlins,' I said.

He turned to me with a grunt and a polite nod. 'Evening.'

'What are you doing here this late?'

'Giving my wife ammunition for when she drags my ass to court to divorce me,' he said cheerfully. 'Glad you made it in.'

'Murph around?' I asked.

He grunted. 'Interrogation room two, with the British perp. Go on down.'

'Thanks, man.'

I went down the hall and around the corner. To my left was a security gate blocking the way to the building's holding cells. To the right was a short hallway containing four doors – two to the bathrooms, and two that led to the interrogation rooms. I went to the second room and knocked.

Murphy answered it, still wearing the same clothes she'd been in at the storage park. She looked tired and irritated. She grunted almost as well as Rawlins had, despite her complete lack of a Y-chromosome, and stepped out into the hall, shutting the door behind her.

She looked up and studied my head for a second. 'What the hell, Harry?'

'Got a visit from Shagnasty the Skinwalker when I went to talk to Lara Raith. Any trouble with Binder?'

She shook her head. 'I figured he'd have a hard time doing whatever he does if he can't get out of his chair or use his hands. I've been sitting with him, too, in case he tried to pull something.'

I lifted an eyebrow, impressed. There hadn't been time to advise her how to handle Binder safely, but she'd worked it out on her own. 'Yeah, that's a pretty solid method,' I said. 'What's he in for, officially?'

'Officially, I haven't charged him yet,' she said. 'If I need to stick him with something, I can cite trespassing, destruction of property, and assault on a police officer.' She shook her head. 'But we can't keep this close an eye on him forever. If I do press charges, it won't be long before he's under lighter security. I don't even want to think about what could happen if he got to turn those things loose inside a precinct house or prison.'

'Yeah,' I said, nodding. 'Long term, I don't think you can hold him.'

Her mouth twisted bitterly. 'Hate it when I have to let pricks like that walk.'

'Happen much?'

'All the time,' she said. 'Legal loopholes, incorrect procedures, crucial evidence declared inadmissible. A lot of perps who are guilty as hell walk out without so much as a reprimand.' She sighed and twitched her shoulders into something like a shrug. 'Ah, well. It's a messed-up world. Whatcha gonna do?'

'I hear that,' I said. 'Want to compare notes?'

'Sure,' she said. 'What did you get?'

I gave her the rundown of what had happened since I'd last seen her.

She grunted again when I finished. 'Isn't that sort of dangerous? Involving the vampires?'

'Yeah,' I said. 'But it's Thomas. I think Lara is probably sincere about getting him back. Besides. Why worry about smoking in bed when your building is already on fire?'

'Point,' she said. 'I got the photos. They don't tell me anything new. I ran those account numbers you gave me through the system to see if anything came up. Brick wall.'

'Dammit.'

'It was a long shot anyway,' she said.

'Binder give you anything?'

Her mouth scrunched up as if she wanted to spit out something that tasted terrible. 'No. He's a hard case. Career criminal. He's been grilled before.'

'Yeah,' I said. 'And he knows that you can't do anything but make him sit still for a little while. If he gives us anything on his employer, he'll lose his credibility with clients – assuming that he lives that long.'

She leaned her shoulders back against the wall. 'You say this Shagnasty thing has Thomas's cell phone?'

'Yeah. Think you can track it?'

'As part of what investigation?' she asked. 'I don't have the kind of freedom to act that I used to. If I wanted to get what amounts to a wiretap, I'd have to get approval from a judge, and I don't know any of them who would take "my friend the wizard's vampire brother was kidnapped by a demonic Navajo shapeshifter" as a valid justification for such a measure.'

'I hadn't really thought of it like that,' I said.

She shrugged. 'Honestly, I suspect Lara's resources and contacts are better than mine, given the time constraints.'

I couldn't quite suppress a growl of frustration. 'If she learns anything. If she's honest about what she learns.'

Murphy frowned, scrunching up her nose. 'Where was Thomas taken from?'

'I'm not certain, but I think he was at the storage park. His rental van was there, and he said something about not being able to handle all of them on his own.'

'Them? The grey suits?'

I nodded. 'Most likely. But since Thomas never pitched in during the fight, I figure Shagnasty probably snuck up on him and grabbed him while he was being distracted by Binder and his pets.'

'And you can't track him down with magic.'

'No,' I growled through clenched teeth. 'Shagnasty is countering it somehow.'

'How is that possible?'

I took a moment to assemble my thoughts. 'Tracking spells are like any kind of targeted thaumaturgy. You create a link, a channel to the target, and then pour energy into that channel. In the case of a tracking spell, you're basically just setting up a continuous trickle of energy, and then following it to the target – kind of like pouring water on a surface when you want to see which way is downhill.'

'Okay,' she said. 'I get that, mostly.'

'The way to stymie a tracking spell is to prevent that channel from ever being formed. If it never gets created, then it doesn't matter when the water gets poured. There's nothing to cause it to start flowing. And the way you prevent the channel from forming is to shield the target away from whatever focus you're using to create the link.'

'Like what?'

'Well, for example. If I had one of your hairs and wanted to use it as part of a tracking spell, you might beat it by shaving off your hair. If the hair in my spell doesn't match up to an end somewhere on your head, no link gets created. So, unless I had a hair that had been torn out from the roots, and fairly recently, you'd be hidden.'

'And that's the only way to beat a tracking spell?'

'Nah,' I said. 'A good circle of power could probably screen you off, if you took the time and money to give it serious juice. Theoretically, you could also cross into the Nevernever. Thaumaturgy originating on the earth doesn't cross into the spirit world very efficiently – and before you ask, yeah, I tried it from the Nevernever side, too. It was failed spell number three.'

Murphy frowned. 'What about Justine?' she asked. 'Justine was able to find him once before.'

I grimaced. 'She was able to give us a vague direction a few hours after Thomas had ripped most of the life out of her. It isn't the same this time.'

'Why not?'

'Because she wasn't sensing Thomas so much as the missing part of her own life force. They haven't been together like that in years. Thomas – digested, I guess you could say – all of that energy a long time ago.'

Murphy sighed. 'I've seen you do some neat stuff, Harry. But I guess magic doesn't fix everything.'

'Magic doesn't fix *anything*,' I said. 'That's what the person using it is for.' I rubbed at my tired eyes.

'Speaking of,' she said. 'Any thoughts as to why these wizards didn't seem to be using magic?'

'Not yet,' I said.

'Any thoughts as to the nature of our perpetrator?'

'A couple,' I said. 'There are all these disparate elements in play – Shagnasty, Binder, Madeline Raith. There is serious money moving around. And if we don't find this cockroach and drag him into the light, things are going to be bad for everyone. I don't know what that tells us about him.'

'That he's really smart,' Murphy said. 'Or really desperate.'

I arched an eyebrow. 'How do you figure?'

'If he's superbrilliant, it's possible that we haven't even seen the shape of his plan yet. All of this could be one big boondoggle to set us up for the real punch.'

'You don't sound like you think that's the case.'

She gave me a faint smile. 'Criminals aren't usually the crispiest crackers in the box. And you have to remember that even though we're flailing around looking for answers, the perp is in the same situation. He can't be sure where we are, what we know, or what we're doing next.'

'Fog of war,' I said thoughtfully.

She shrugged. 'I think it's a much more likely explanation than that our perp is some kind of James Bond super-genius villain slowly unfolding his terrible design. They've shown too much confusion for that.'

'Like what?'

'Shagnasty was following you a couple of nights ago, right?'

'Yeah.'

'Well, so was this PI you told me about. Why stick you with two tails? Maybe because the right hand didn't know what the left one was doing.'

'Hngh,' I agreed.

'From what you say, Shagnasty isn't exactly an errand boy.'

'No, it isn't.'

'But it's apparently coordinating with the perp, taking orders. It didn't absolutely need to deliver its demand in person. I think it's pretty obvious that it smashed its way into the Château to provide a distraction so that Madeline could make her getaway.'

I blinked. Once I'd alerted Lara to the probability of Madeline's treachery, she most certainly would have taken steps to detain her. Madeline must have known that. I tried to remember how long it had been between the time Luccio and I arrived, and when the naagloshii attacked.

Time enough for Madeline to hear about our presence, assume that the worst had happened, and make a phone call for help?

Maybe.

Murphy peered at me. 'I mean, it *is* obvious, right?'

'I got hit on the head, okay?'

She smirked at me.

'Hell's bells,' I muttered. 'Yes, it's obvious. But not necessarily stupid.'

'Not stupid, but I don't think it would be unfair to call it a desperation move. I think Shagnasty was the perp's ace in the hole. I think that when Morgan escaped, the perp figured out where he was headed, the pressure got to him, and he played his hole card. Only when Shagnasty found you, you weren't actually *with* Morgan. He got spooked when you and the werewolves nearly pinned him down, and ran off.'

'The perp grabs one of his other tools,' I said, nodding. 'Madeline. Tells her to find me and take me out, make me talk, whatever. Only Thomas beats her senseless instead.'

'Makes sense,' Murphy said.

'Doesn't mean that's how it happened.'

'Had to happen some way,' she said. 'Say we're in the right ballpark. What does that tell us?'

'Not much,' I said. 'Some very bad people are in motion. They're tough. The one guy we've managed to grab won't tell us a damned thing. The only thing we're *certain* we know is that we've got nothing.'

I was going to continue, but a thought hit me and I stopped talking.

I gave it a second to crystallize.

Then I started to smile.

Murphy tilted her head, watching, and prompted, 'We've got nothing?'

I looked from Murphy to the door to the interrogation room.

'Forget it,' she said. 'He isn't going to put us on to anyone.'

'Oh,' I drawled. 'I'm not so sure about that. . . .'

31

Murphy went back into the interrogation room.

Twenty minutes later, I came in and shut the door behind me. The room was simple and small. A table sat in the middle, with two chairs on each side. There was no long two-way mirror on the wall. Instead, a small security camera perched up high in one corner of the ceiling.

Binder sat on the far side of the table. His face had a couple of bruises on it, along with an assortment of small cuts with dark scabs. His odd green eyes were narrowed in annoyance. A foot-long hoagie sat on the table in front of him, its paper wrapper partially undone. He'd have been able to reach it easily – if he could have moved his arms. They were cuffed to the arms of the chair. A handcuff key rested centered on the edge of Murphy's side of the table, in front of her chair.

I had to suppress a smile.

'Bloody priceless,' Binder said to Murphy as I entered. 'Now you bring this wanker. It's police torture, is what it is. My solicitor will swallow you whole and spit out the bones.'

Murphy sat down at the table across from Binder, folded her hands, and sat in complete silence, spearing him with an unfriendly stare.

Binder sneered at her, and then at me, presumably so I wouldn't feel left out. 'Oh, I get this now,' he said. 'Good cop, bad cop, is it?' He looked at me. 'Stone-cold bitch here makes me sit for bloody hours in this chair to soften me up. Then you come in here, polite and sympathetic as you please, and I buckle under the stress, yeah?' He settled more comfortably into the chair, somehow conveying an insult with the motion. 'Fine, Dresden,' he said. 'Knock yourself out. Good cop me.'

I looked at him for a second.

Then I made a fist and slugged his smug face hard enough to knock him over backward in the chair.

He just lay there for a minute, on his side, blinking tears out of his eyes. Blood trickled from one nostril. One of his shoes had come off in the fall. I stood over him and glanced at my hand. It hurts to punch people in the face. Not as much as it hurts to *get* punched in the face, granted, but you know you've done it. My knuckles must have grazed his teeth. They'd lost a little skin.

'Don't give me this lawyer crap, Binder,' I said. 'We both know the cops can't hold you for long. But we also both know that you can't play the system against us, either. You aren't an upstanding member of the community. You're a hired gun, wanted for questioning in a dozen countries.'

He looked up at me with a snarl. 'Think you're a hard man, do you?'

I glanced at Murphy. 'Should I answer that one, or just kick him in the balls?'

'Seeing is believing,' Murphy said.

'True.' I turned to Binder and drew back my foot.

'Bloody hell!' Binder barked. 'There's a bloody camera watching your every move. You think you won't get dragged off for this?'

An intercom on the wall near the camera clicked and buzzed. 'He's got a point,' said Rawlins' voice. 'I can't see it all from here. Move him a couple of feet to the left and give me about thirty more seconds before you start on his nads. I'm making popcorn.'

'Sure,' I said, giving the camera a thumbs-up. Odds were good that it would fold if I was in the room for any length of time, but we'd made our point.

I sat down on the edge of the table, maybe a foot away from Binder and, quite deliberately, reached over to pick up the hoagie. I took a bite and chewed thoughtfully. 'Mmm,' I said. I glanced at Murphy. 'What kind of cheese is that?'

'Gouda.'

'Beef tastes great, too.'

'Teriyaki,' Murph said, still staring at Binder.

'I was really hungry,' I told her, my voice brimming with sincerity. 'I haven't eaten since, like, this morning. This is excellent.'

Binder muttered darkly under his breath. All I caught was '. . . buggering little bastard . . .'

I ate half the hoagie and put it back on the table. I licked a stray bit of sauce off of one finger and looked down at Binder. 'Okay, tough guy,' I said. 'The cops can't keep you. So that leaves the sergeant, here, with only a couple of options. Either they let you walk . . .'

Murphy made a quiet growling sound. It was almost as impressive as her grunt.

'She just hates that idea.' I got off the table and hunkered down beside Binder. 'Or,' I said, 'we do it the other way.'

He narrowed his eyes. 'You'll kill me – is that it?'

'Ain't no one gonna miss you,' I said.

'You're bluffing,' Binder snapped. 'She's a bloody cop.'

'Yeah,' I said. 'Think about that one for a minute. You

think a police detective couldn't work out a way to disappear you without anyone being the wiser?'

He looked back and forth between us, his cool mask not quite faltering. 'What do you want?'

'Your boss,' I said. 'Give me that and you walk.'

He stared at me for half a minute. Then he said, 'Set my chair up.'

I rolled my eyes and did it. He was heavy. 'Hell's bells, Binder. I get a hernia and the deal's off.'

He looked at Murphy and jiggled his wrists.

Murphy yawned.

'Bloody hell,' he snarled. 'Just one of them. I haven't eaten since yesterday.'

I snorted. 'Looks to me like you aren't in any immediate danger of starvation.'

'You want cooperation,' he spat, 'you're going to have to show me some. Give me the bloody sandwich.'

Murphy reached out, picked up the handcuff key, and tossed it to me. I unlocked his left wrist. Binder seized the sandwich and started chomping on it.

'All right,' I said, after a moment. 'Talk.'

'What?' he said through a mouthful of food. 'No soda?'

I swatted the last inch or two of hoagie out of his hand, scowling.

Binder watched me, unperturbed. He licked his fingers clean, picked a bit of lettuce out of his teeth, and ate it. 'All right then,' he said. 'You want the truth?'

'Yeah,' I said.

He leaned a bit toward me and jabbed a finger at me. 'The truth is that you ain't killing no one, biggun. You ain't and neither is the blond bird. And if you try to keep me, I'll bring down all manner of horrible things.'

He leaned back in his chair, openly wearing the smug smile again. 'So you might as well stop wasting my valuable time and cut me loose. *That's* the truth.'

I turned my head to Murphy, frowning.

She got up, walked around the table, and seized Binder by his close-cut head. It didn't provide much of a grip, but she used it to shove his head roughly down to the top of the table. Then she took the key back from me, undid the other set of cuffs, and released him.

'Get out,' she said quietly.

Binder stood up slowly, straightening his clothes. He leered at Murphy, winked, and said, 'I'm a professional. So there's nothing personal, love. Maybe next time we can skip business and give pleasure a go.'

'Maybe next time you'll get your neck broken resisting arrest,' Murphy said. 'Get out.'

Binder smirked at Murphy, then at me, and then sauntered out of the room.

'Well?' I asked her.

She turned and held out her hand. Several short hairs, some dark and some grey, clung to her fingers. 'Got it.'

I grinned at her, and took the hairs, depositing them in a white envelope I'd taken from Rawlins' desk. 'Give me about a minute and I'll have it up.'

'Hubba hubba,' Rawlins said through the intercom speaker. 'I like this channel.'

'This is a great way of chasing down the bad guy,' Murphy said half an hour later. She gave me a pointed look from her chair at her desk. 'Sit here and don't do anything.'

I sat in a chair next to her desk, my hand extended

palm down in front of me, holding a bit of leather thong that ended in a simple quartz crystal in a copper-wire setting. My arm was getting tired, and I had gripped it under my forearm with the other hand to support it. The crystal didn't hang like a plumb line. It leaned a bit to one side, as if being supported by a steady, silent puff of wind.

'Patience,' I said. 'Binder might not be a crispy cracker, but he's been in business for a couple of decades. He knows why you grabbed him by the hair. He's learned to shake off something like this.'

Murphy gave me an unamused look. She glanced at Rawlins, who sat at his desk. The desks were set up back-to-back, so that they faced each other.

'Don't look at me,' he said, without glancing up from his sudoku puzzle. 'I don't run as fast as I used to. I could get used to chasing down bad guys like this.'

The crystal abruptly dropped and began swinging back and forth freely.

'Ah!' I said. 'There, there, you see?' I let them look for a second and then lowered my arm. I rubbed my sore muscles for a moment. 'What did I tell you? He shook it off.'

'Oh, good,' Murphy said. 'Now we have no clue where he is.'

I put the crystal into my pocket and grabbed Murphy's desk phone. 'Yet,' I said. I punched in a number and found out that you had to dial nine to get out. I started over, added a nine to the beginning of the number, and it rang.

'Graver,' Vince said.

'It's Dresden,' I said. 'Tell me what he just did, like thirty seconds ago.'

'Be patient,' Vince said, and hung up on me.

I blinked at the phone.

Murphy looked at me for a second and then smiled. 'I just love it when I don't know part of the plan, and the guy who does is all smug and cryptic,' she said. 'Don't you?'

I glowered at her and put the phone down. 'He'll call back.'

'He who?'

'The PI who is following Binder,' I said. 'Guy named Vince Graver.'

Murphy's eyebrows went up. 'You're kidding.'

Rawlins began to chortle, still working on his puzzle.

'What?' I said, looking back and forth between them.

'He was a vice cop in Joliet a couple of years ago,' Murphy said. 'He found out that someone was beating up some of the call girls down there. He looked into it. Word came down to tell him to back off, but he went and caught a Chicago city councilman who liked to pound on his women for foreplay. What's-his-name.'

'Dornan,' Rawlins supplied.

'Right, Ricardo Dornan,' Murphy said.

'Huh,' I said. 'Took some guts.'

'Hell, yeah,' Rawlins said. 'And some stupid.'

'It's a fine line,' Murphy said. 'Anyway, he pissed off some people. Next thing he knows, he finds out he volunteered for a transfer to CPD.'

'Three guesses where,' Rawlins said.

'So he resigns,' Murphy said.

'Yeah,' Rawlins said. 'Without even giving us a chance to meet him.'

Murphy shook her head. 'Went into private practice. There's a guy who is a glutton for punishment.'

Rawlins grinned.

'He drives a Mercedes,' I said. 'Has his own house, too.'

Rawlins put his pencil down and they both looked up at me.

I shrugged. 'I'm just saying. He must be doing all right for himself.'

'Hngh,' Rawlins said. Then he picked up his pencil and went back to the puzzle. 'Ain't no justice.'

Murphy grunted with nigh-masculine skill.

A couple of minutes later, the phone rang, and Murphy answered it. She passed it to me.

'Your guy's a nut,' Vince said.

'I know that,' I told him. 'What's he doing?'

'Took a cab to a motel on the highway north of town,' Vince said. 'Stopped at a convenience store on the way. Then he goes to his room, shaves himself bald, comes out in his skivvies, and jumps in the damn river. Goes back inside, takes a shower—'

'How do you know that?' I asked.

'I broke into his room while he was doing it,' Vince said. 'Maybe you could save your questions until the end of the presentation.'

'Hard to imagine you not fitting in with the cops,' I said.

Vince ignored the comment. 'He takes a shower and calls another cab.'

'Tell me you followed the cab,' I said.

'Tell me your check cleared.'

'I'm good for it.'

'Yeah, I'm following the cab right now,' Vince said. 'But I don't need to. He's headed for the Hotel Sax.'

'Who are you, the Amazing Kreskin?'

'Listened in on the cabbie's CB,' he said. 'ETA, eighteen minutes.'

'Eighteen?' I asked.

'Usually found between seventeen and nineteen,' he said. 'I can't guarantee I can stay on him at the hotel, especially if he tumbles to the tail. Too many ways out.'

'I'll take it from there. Do not get close to him, man. You get an instinct he's looking in your direction, run for the hills. This guy's dangerous.'

'Yeah,' Vince said. 'Hell, I'm lucky I haven't wet my pants already.'

'I'm serious.'

'I know you are. It's cute. Seventeen minutes.'

'I'll be there.'

'With my check. I've got a two-day minimum. You know that, right?'

'Right, right,' I said. 'I'll be there.'

'What have we got?' Murphy asked as I put the phone down.

'Binder thinks he shook me,' I said. 'He's headed for a meeting at Hotel Sax.'

She stood up and grabbed her car keys. 'How do you know it's a meeting?'

'Because he's been made. If he was here alone, he'd be on his way out of town right now.' I nodded. 'He's running back to whoever hired him.'

'Who is that?' Murphy asked.

'Let's find out.'

32

The Hotel Sax is a pretty good example of its kind in the beating heart of downtown Chicago. It's located on Dearborn, just across the street from the House of Blues, and if you look up while standing outside of the place, it looks like someone slapped one of those fish-eye camera lenses on the sky. Buildings stretch up and up and up, at angles that seem geometrically impossible.

Many similar sections of Chicago have wider streets than you find in other metropolises, and it makes them feel slightly less claustrophobic, but outside of the Sax, the street was barely three narrow lanes across, curb to curb. As Murphy and I approached, looking up made me feel like an ant walking along the bottom of a crack in the sidewalk.

'It bugs you, doesn't it?' Murphy said.

We walked under a streetlight, our shadows briefly equal in length. 'What?'

'Those big things looming over you.'

'I wouldn't say it bothers me,' I said. 'I'm just . . . aware of them.'

She faced serenely ahead as we walked. 'Welcome to my life.'

I glanced down at her and snorted quietly.

We entered the lobby of the hotel, a place with a lot of glass and white paint with rich red accents. Given how late it was, it was no surprise only one member of the staff was visible: a young woman who stood behind one of the glass-fronted check-in counters. One guest reading a magazine sat in a nearby chair, and even though he was the only guy in the room, it took me a second glance to realize that he was Vince.

Vince set the magazine aside and ambled over to us. His unremarkable brown eyes scanned over Murphy. He nodded to her and offered me his hand.

I shook it, and offered a check to him with my left as we did. He took it, glanced at it noncommittally, and put it away in a pocket. 'He took an elevator to the twelfth floor,' Vince said. 'He's in room twelve thirty-three.'

I blinked at him. 'How the hell did you get that? Ride up with him?'

'Good way for me to get hurt. I stayed down here.' He shrugged. 'You said he was trouble.'

'He is. How'd you do it?'

He gave me a bland look. 'I'm good at this. You need to know which chair he's in, too?'

'No. That's close enough,' I said.

Vince looked at Murphy again, frowned, and then frowned at me. 'Jesus,' he said. 'You two look pretty serious.'

'Yeah,' I said. 'I told you, this guy's dangerous. He have anyone with him?'

'One person,' he said. 'A woman, I think.'

Murphy suddenly smiled.

'How the hell do you know that?' I asked him.

'Room service,' she said.

Vince smiled in faint approval at Murphy and nodded his head. 'Could have been someone else on twelve who ordered champagne and two glasses two minutes after he got off the elevator. But this late at night, I doubt it.'

Vince glanced at me. 'I'll take the bill I duked the steward out of my fee.'

'Appreciated,' I said.

He shrugged. 'That it?'

'Yeah. Thanks, Vince.'

'As long as the check clears,' he said, 'you're welcome.' He nodded to me, to Murphy, and walked out of the hotel.

Murphy eyed me, after Vince left, and smiled. 'The mighty Harry Dresden. Subcontracting detective work.'

'They're expecting me to be all magicky and stuff,' I said. 'And I gave them what they expected to see. Binder wouldn't have been looking for someone like Vince.'

'You're just annoyed because they pulled that trick on you,' Murphy said. 'And you're taking your vengeance.'

I sniffed. 'I like to think of it as symmetry.'

'That does make it sound nobler,' she said. 'We obviously can't just go up there and haul them off somewhere for questioning. What's the plan?'

'Get more information,' I said. 'I'm gonna listen in and see what they're chatting about.'

Murphy nodded, glancing around. 'Hotel security is going to have an issue with you lurking about the hallways. I'll go have a word with them.'

I nodded. 'I'll be on twelve.'

'Don't kick down any doors without someone to watch your back,' she warned me.

'No kicking at all,' I said. 'Not until I know enough to kick them where it's going to hurt.'

I went up to the twelfth floor, left the elevator, and pulled a can of Silly String out of my duster pocket. I shook it up as I walked down the hallway until I found room twelve thirty-three. Then, without preamble, I blasted a bit of the Silly String at the door. It slithered cheerfully through the air and stuck.

Then I turned and walked back down the hall until I found a door that opened onto a tiny room containing an ice dispenser and a couple of vending machines. I sat down, drew a quick circle around me on the tile floor with a dry-erase marker, and got to work.

I closed the circle with an effort of will, and it sprang up around me in a sudden invisible screen. It wasn't exactly a heavy-duty magical construct, but such a quick circle would still serve perfectly well to seal away external energies and allow me to gather my own and shape it for a specific purpose without interference. I took the Silly String and sprayed a bunch of it into the palm of my left hand so that it mounded up sort of like shaving cream. Then I set the can down, held the mound of Silly String out in front of me, closed my eyes, and gathered my will.

Working magic is all about creating connections. Earlier, I'd taken Binder's hairs to create a link back to him and used it for a tracking spell. I could have done any number of things with that connection, including some that were extremely nasty and dangerous. I'd seen it happen before, generally from the receiving end.

This time, I was creating a link between the Silly String in my hand, and the bit stuck to the door down the hall. They'd both come from the same can, and they'd been part of one distinct amount of liquid when they'd been canned. That meant I would be able to take advantage of that sameness and create a connection between them.

I focused my will on my desired outcome, gathered it all up together, and released it with a murmur of '*Finiculus sonitus.*' I reached out and smeared away a section of the circle I'd drawn, breaking it, and instantly began feeling a buzzing vibration in the palm of my left hand.

Then I tilted my head far to my right and slapped a bunch of Silly String into my left ear.

'Don't try this at home folks,' I muttered. 'I'm a professional.'

The first thing I heard was hectic-sounding, hyper-active music. A singer was screaming tunelessly and drums were pounding and someone was either playing electric guitars or slowly dipping partially laryngitic cats in boiling oil. None of the supposed musicians appeared to be paying attention to anything anyone else in the band was doing.

'Christ,' came Binder's accented voice. 'Not even you could dance to that tripe.'

There was a low-throated female laugh, and a slurred and very happy-sounding Madeline Raith replied, 'This music isn't about skill and precision, my sweet. It's about hunger and passion. And I could dance to it to make your eyes fall out.'

'I am not "your sweet",' Binder said, his voice annoyed. 'I am not your anything, ducks, excepting your contracted employee.'

'I'm not sure I'd emphasize that if I were you, Binder,' Madeline said. 'Since you've been a crushing disappoint-ment as a hireling.'

'I told you when I got started that if anyone from the White Council showed up, I couldn't make you any prom-ises,' he shot back, his voice annoyed. 'And lo and behold, what happens? That buggering lunatic Harry Dresden shows up with backup – and with the support of the local constabulary, to boot.'

'I'm getting so sick of this,' Madeline said. 'He's only one man.'

'One bloody member of the White bloody Council,' Binder countered. 'Bear in mind that someone like him can do everything I can do and considerable besides. And even people *on* the bloody Council are nervous about that one.'

'Well, I'm sick of him,' spat Madeline. 'Did you find out where he's got Morgan hidden?'

'Maybe you didn't hear, love, but I spent my day chained to a chair getting popped in the mouth.'

Madeline laughed, a cold, mocking sound. 'There are places you'd have to pay for that.'

'Not bloody likely.'

'Did you *find* Morgan?'

Binder growled. 'Dresden had him stashed in rental storage for a bit, but he hared off before the cops could pick him up. Probably took him into the Nevernever. They could be anywhere.'

'Not if Dresden is back in Chicago,' Madeline said. 'He'd never let himself be too far from Morgan.'

'So check his bloody apartment,' Binder said.

'Don't be an idiot,' Madeline said. 'That's the first place anyone would look. He's not a total moron.'

Yeah. I wasn't. Ahem.

Binder snickered. 'You're money, Raith. Money never really gets it.'

Madeline's voice turned waspish. 'What's that supposed to mean?'

'That not everyone has a bloody string of mansions around the world that they live in or extra cars that they never really drive or cash enough to not think twice about dropping two hundred bloody dollars on a bottle of forty-dollar room service champagne.'

'So?'

'So, Dresden's a bloody kid by Council standards. Lives in that crappy little hole. And pays for an office for his business, to boot. He ain't had a century or two of compounded interest to shore up his accounts, now, has he? And when he set himself up an emergency retreat, did he buy himself a furnished condo in another town? No. He rents out a cruddy little storage unit and stacks some camping gear inside.'

'All right,' Madeline said, her tone impatient. 'Suppose you're right. Suppose he's got Morgan at his apartment. He won't have left him unprotected.'

'Naturally not,' Binder replied. 'He'll have a bloody minefield of wards around the place. Might have some conjured guardians or some such as well.'

'Could you get through them?'

'Give me enough time and enough of my lads, and yeah,' he said. 'But it wouldn't be quick, quiet, or clean. There's a simpler way.'

'Which is?'

'Burn the bloody place down,' Binder said promptly. 'The apartment's got one door. If Morgan comes scurrying out, we bag him. If not, we collect his bones after the ashes cool. Identify him with dental records or something and claim the reward.'

I felt a little bit sick to my stomach. Binder was way too perceptive for my comfort level. The guy might not be overly smart, but he was more than a little cunning. His plan was pretty much exactly the best way to attack my apartment, defensive magicks notwithstanding. What's more, I knew he was capable of actually doing it. It would kill my elderly neighbors, the other residents of the building, but that wouldn't slow someone like Binder down for half of a second.

'No,' Madeline said after a tense moment of silence. 'I have my instructions. If we can't take him ourselves, we at least see to it that the Wardens find him.'

'The Wardens *have* found him,' Binder complained. '*Dresden's* a bloody Warden. Your boss should have paid up already.'

There was a quiet, deadly silence, and then Madeline purred, 'You've been modestly helpful to him in the past, Binder. But don't start thinking that you would survive telling him what he should or should not do. The moment you become more annoying than useful, you are a dead man.'

'No sin to want money,' Binder said sullenly. 'I did my part to get it.'

'No,' Madeline said. 'You lost a fight to one overgrown Boy Scout and one pint-sized mortal woman, got yourself locked up by the *police*, of all the ridiculous things, and missed your chance to earn the reward.' Sheets rustled, and soft footsteps whispered on the carpet. A moment later, a lighter flicked – Madeline smoked.

Binder spoke again, in a tone of voice that indicated he was changing the topic of conversation. 'You going to clean that up?'

'That's exactly why it's there,' Madeline said. She took a drag and said, 'Cleaning up. It's too bad you didn't get here five minutes sooner.'

'And why is that?'

'Because I probably would have waited to make the call.'

I felt myself leaning forward slightly and holding my breath.

'What call?' Binder said.

'To the Wardens, naturally,' Madeline said. 'I told them that Morgan was in town and that Dresden was sheltering him. They should be here within the hour.'

I felt my mouth drop open and my stomach did a cart-wheeling backflip with an integrated quadruple axle.

Oh, *crap*.

33

Murphy looked at the Rolls and said, 'You're kidding.'

We'd driven down to the Sax separately, and she hadn't seen the wheels I was using. I was parked closer to the hotel, so we were about to get into the Silver Wraith together.

'It's a loaner,' I said. 'Get in.'

'I am not a material girl,' she said, running a hand over the Rolls's fender. 'But . . . damn.'

'Can we focus, here?' I said. 'The world's coming to an end.'

Murphy shook her head and then got in the car with me. 'Well. At least you're going out in style.'

I got the Rolls moving. It got plenty of looks, even in the dead of night, and the other motorists out so late gave it a generous amount of room, as if intimidated by the Wraith's sheer artistry.

'Actually,' I said, 'I'm kind of finding the Rolls to be irrationally comforting.'

Murphy glanced aside at me. 'Why's that?'

'I know how I'm going to die, you know? One of these days, maybe real soon, I'm going to find out I've bitten off more than I can chew.' I swallowed. 'I mean, I just can't keep from sticking my nose in places people don't want it. And I always figured it would be the Council who punched my ticket, regardless of who believed what about me. Because there's a bunch of assholes there, and

I just can't let them wallow in their own bull and pretend it's an air of nobility.'

Murphy's expression became more sober. She listened in silence.

'Now the Council's coming. And they've got good reason to take me out. Or it looks like it to them, which is the same thing.' I swallowed again. My mouth felt dry. 'But . . . I somehow just have the feeling that when I go out . . . it *isn't* going to be in style.' I gestured at the Rolls with a vague sweep of one hand. 'This just isn't the car I drive to my death. You know?'

Murph's mouth tucked up at one corner, though most of the smile was in her eyes. She took my hand between hers and held it. Her hands felt very warm. Maybe mine were just cold. 'You're right, of course, Harry.'

'You think?'

'Definitely,' she said. 'This car just isn't you. You'll die in some badly painted, hideously recycled piece of junk that seems to keep on running despite the laws of physics that say it should be melted scrap by now.'

'Whew,' I said. 'I thought I might be the only one who thought that.'

Her fingers tightened on mine for a moment, and I clung back.

The Council was coming.

And there wasn't anything I could do to fight them.

Oh sure, maybe I could poke someone in the nose and run. But they would catch up to me sooner or later. There would be more of them than me, some of them every bit as strong as I was, and all of them dangerous. It might take a day or a week or a couple of weeks, but I had to sleep sooner or later. They'd wear me down.

And that pissed me off. My sheer helplessness in the face of this whole stupid mess was infuriating.

It wasn't as if I didn't have options. . . . Mab still held a job offer open to me, for example. And it was more than possible that Lara Raith might have the resources to shield me, or broker me a better deal than the Council was going to offer. When I thought of how *unfair* the whole thing was, I had more than a passing desire to grab whatever slender threads I could reach, until I could sort things out, later.

Put that way, it almost sounded reasonable. Noble, even. I would, after all, be protecting other wrongly persecuted victims of the Council who littered the theoretical landscape of the future. It didn't sound nearly so much like entering bargains that went against everything I believed so that I could forcibly impose my will over those who were against me.

I knew the truth. But just because it was true didn't make it any less tempting.

What the hell was I going to do? I had a hidey-hole planned out, but it had already been compromised. There was nowhere even a little bit safe I could take Morgan but my apartment, and the Wardens were *going* to find him there. And on top of all that, I still had no freaking clue as to the identity of our mysterious puppet master.

Maybe it was time to admit it.

This one was too big for me. It had been from the very start.

'Murph,' I said quietly. 'I don't know how I'm going to get out of this.'

Silence filled the beautiful old car.

'When's the last time you slept?' Murphy asked.

I had to take my hand back from hers to work the clutch. I gestured at my bandaged head. 'I can barely remember what day of the week it is. This morning, a couple hours, I think?'

She nodded judiciously. 'You know what your problem is?'

I eyed her and then started laughing. Or at least making an amused, wheezing sound. I couldn't help it.

'Problem, singular,' I choked out, finally. 'No, what?'

'You like to come off like you're the unpredictable chaos factor in any given situation, but at the end of the day you obsess about having everything ordered the way you want it.'

'Have you seen my lab?'

'Again with the inappropriately timed come-ons,' Murphy said. 'I'm serious, Harry.'

'I know some people who would really disagree with you. Like what's-his-face, Peabody.'

'He's Council?'

'Yeah. Says I have no place in his bastion of order.'

She smirked. 'The problem is that *your* bastion of order is sort of tough to coexist with.'

'I have no bastions. I am bastionless.'

'Hah,' Murphy said. 'You like the same car, the same apartment, the same restaurant. You like not needing to answer to anyone, and doing the jobs your conscience dictates you should do, without worrying about the broader issues they involve. You hang out, fairly happy without much in the way of material wealth and follow your instincts, and be damned to anyone who tells you otherwise. That's your order.'

I eyed her. 'Is there some other way it should be?'

She rolled her eyes. 'I rest my case.'

'And how is this my problem?'

'You've never really compromised your order for someone else's, which is why you drive the Wardens nuts. They have procedures, they have forms, they have reports – and you ignore them unless someone twists your arm to make you do it. Am I right?'

'Still don't see how that's a problem.'

She rolled down the passenger-side window and let one hand hang out. 'It's a problem because you never learned how to adjust inside someone else's order,' she said. 'If you had, you'd realize what an incredible force you have working on your side.'

'The A-Team?'

'Bureaucracy,' Murphy said.

'I would rather have the A-Team.'

'Listen and learn, maverick,' Murphy said. 'The Wardens are an organization, right?'

'Yeah.'

'Lots of members.'

'Almost three hundred and growing,' I said.

'Lots of members who all have many obligations, who live in different areas, who speak different languages, but who have to communicate and work together somehow?'

'Yeah.'

'Behold,' Murphy said. 'Bureaucracy. Organization to combat the entropy that naturally inhibits that kind of cooperative effort.'

'Is there going to be a quiz later, or . . . ?'

She ignored me. 'Bureaucracies share common traits – and I think you've got more time to move in than you realize. If you weren't tired and hurting and an obnoxious fly in the ointment to anyone's order but your own, you'd see that.'

I frowned. 'How so?'

'Do you think Madeline Raith called up the White Council on her home phone, identified herself, and just told them you were helping Morgan?' Murphy shook her head. '"Hello, I'm the enemy. Let me help you for no good reason."'

I sucked thoughtfully on my lower lip. 'The Wardens would probably assume that she was trying to divert their resources during a manpower-critical situation.'

Murphy nodded. 'And while they will look into it, they'll never really believe it, and it will go straight to the bottom of their priority list.'

'So she calls in an anonymous tip instead. So?'

'So how many tips do you think the Wardens have gotten?' Murphy asked. 'Cops go through the same thing. Some big flashy crime goes down and we have a dozen nuts claiming credit or convinced their neighbor did it, another dozen jerks who want to get their neighbor in trouble, and three times that many well-meaning people who have no clue whatsoever and think they're helping.'

I chewed on that thought for a moment. Murphy wasn't far off the mark. There were plenty of organizations and Lord only knew how many individuals who would want to stay on the Wardens' good side, or who would want to impress them, or who would simply want to have a real reason to interact with them. Murph was probably right. There probably *were* tips flooding in from all over the world.

'They'll check the tip out,' Murphy said. 'But I'm willing to bet you real money that, depending on their manpower issues, it won't happen until several hours after the tip actually makes it into the hands of the folks running the show – and with any luck, given the Council's issues with technology and communication, *that* will take a while as well.'

I mulled that one over for a minute. 'What are you saying?'

She put her hand on my arm and squeezed once. 'I'm saying don't give up yet. There's still a little time.'

I turned my head and studied Murphy's profile for a moment.

'Really?' I asked her quietly.

She nodded. 'Yeah.'

Like 'love', 'hope' is one of those ridiculously dispro-portional words that by all rights should be a lot longer.

I resettled my grip on the Rolls's steering wheel. 'Murph?'

'Mmm?'

'You're one hell of a dame.'

'Sexist pig,' she said. She smiled out the windshield. 'Don't make me hurt you.'

'Yeah,' I said. 'It wouldn't be ladylike.'

She shook her head as we neared my apartment. 'If you like,' she said, 'take him to my place. You can hide out there.'

I didn't actually smile, but her words made me feel like doing it. 'Not this time. The Wardens know where you live, remember? If they start looking hard at me . . .'

'. . . they'll check me out, too,' Murphy said. 'But you can't keep him at your place.'

'I know that. I also know that I can't drag anyone else into the middle of this clust— this mess.'

'There's got to be somewhere,' she said. 'Someplace quiet. And not well-known. And away from crowds.' She paused. 'And where you can protect him from tracking magic. And where you'd have the advantage, if it did come to a fight.'

I didn't say anything.

'Okay,' Murphy said. 'I guess maybe there aren't any places like that around here.'

I snapped my head up straight.

'Hell's bells!' I breathed. I felt a grin stretch my mouth. 'I think maybe there *is*!'

34

I came through my apartment door, took one look around the candle-lit place, and half shouted, 'Hell's bells! What is *wrong* with you people?'

Morgan sat slumped against the wall with the fireplace, and fresh spots of blood showed through his bandages. His eyes were only partly open. His hand lay on the floor beside him, limp, the fingers half curled. A tiny little semiautomatic pistol lay on the floor beneath his hand. It wasn't mine. I have no idea where he'd been hiding it.

Molly was on the floor in front of the sofa, with Mouse literally sitting on her back. She was heaving breaths in and out, making the big dog rise and settle slightly as she did.

Luccio lay where I'd left her on the couch, flat on her back, her eyes closed, obviously still unconscious. Mouse had one of his paws resting lightly on her sternum. Given the nature of her recent injury, it seemed obvious that he would need to exert minimal pressure on her to immobilize her with pain, should she awaken.

The air smelled of cordite. Mouse's fur, all down his left foreleg, was matted and caked with blood.

When I saw that, I rounded on Morgan in a fury, and if Murphy hadn't stepped forward and grabbed my arm with both hands, I would have started kicking his head flat against my wall. I settled for kicking the gun away instead. If I got a couple of his fingers, too, it didn't bother me much at the time.

Morgan watched me with dull, hardly conscious eyes.

'I swear,' I snarled. 'I swear to God, Morgan, if you don't explain yourself I'm going to strangle you dead with my own hands and drag your corpse back to Edinburgh by the balls.'

'Harry!' Murphy shouted, and I realized that she had positioned her entire body between me and Morgan and she was leaning against me like a soldier struggling to raise a flag.

Morgan bared his teeth, more rictus than smile. 'Your warlock,' he said, his voice dry and leathery, 'was trying to enter Captain Luccio's mind against her will.'

I surged forward, and Murphy pushed me back again. I weighed twice what she did, but she had good leverage and focus. 'And so you *shot* my *dog?*' I screamed.

'He interposed himself,' Morgan said. He coughed, weakly, and closed his eyes, his face turning greyer. 'Never meant . . . to hit . . .'

'I swear to God,' I snarled, 'that's it. That is *it*. Molly and I are going right to the wall for you, and this is how you repay us? I am pushing your paranoid ass out my door, leaving you there, and starting a pool on who comes for you first – the Black Council, the Wardens, or the goddamn buzzards.'

'H-Harry,' Molly said in a weak, nauseated, and . . . *shamed* voice barely more than a whisper.

I felt my anger abruptly drain away, to be replaced by a wave of denial and a slowly dawning sense of horror. I turned, slowly, to look at Molly.

'He was right,' she wheezed, not looking at me,

struggling to speak over the burden of Mouse's weight. I could hear the tears reflected in her voice as they began to fall. 'I'm sorry. I'm so sorry, Harry. He was right.'

I leaned my shoulders back against the wall and watched as Mouse looked at me with grave, pained eyes and stayed right where he was – both holding Molly down and shielding her body with his.

We got Morgan put back into bed, and then I went over to Mouse. 'Okay,' I said. 'Move.'

Only then did Mouse remove himself from Molly's back, limping heavily to one side. I knelt down by him and examined his leg. He flattened his ears and leaned away from me. I said firmly, 'Stop that. Hold still.'

Mouse sighed and looked miserable, but he let me poke at his leg. I found the wound, up near his shoulder, and a hard lump under the skin.

'Get up,' I said to Molly, my tone steady. 'Go to the lab. Get the medical kit under the table. Then get the little scissors and a fresh razor from the cabinet in my bathroom.'

She pushed herself up slowly.

'Move,' I said, my voice quiet and level and unyielding. She was obviously still recovering from being pinned to the floor. But she moved quicker, and staggered down to my lab.

Murphy knelt down next to me and ruffled Mouse's ears. He gave her a miserable look. She held up Morgan's gun. 'Twenty-five caliber,' she said. 'Big as he is, wouldn't have been easy to kill him with it, even on purpose.' She shook her head. 'Or Molly, for that matter.'

'Meaning what?' I asked her.

'Meaning maybe Morgan didn't intend the attack to be lethal. Maybe he used the smaller weapon for that reason.'

'He used the smaller weapon because it was the only one he had,' I said, my voice harsh. 'He'd have killed Molly if he could have.'

Murphy was quiet for a moment before she said, 'That's attempted murder.'

I glanced up at her for a second. Then I said, 'You want to arrest him.'

'It isn't an issue of what I want,' she said. 'I'm an officer of the law, Harry.'

I thought about that for a moment. 'The Council might – they *might* – respect it,' I said quietly. 'In fact, I'm certain they would. It would be the Merlin's call, and he'd love nothing better than to buy more time to work out how to get Morgan out of this mess.'

'But others wouldn't,' she said.

'Madeline and Shagnasty sure wouldn't,' I said. 'And if Morgan's in jail, there's no way to force Shagnasty into a confrontation where I have a chance to take Thomas back.' I looked at Mouse's wound. 'Or trade him.'

'You'd do that?' she asked.

'Morgan? For Thomas?' I shook my head. 'I . . . Hell's bells, it would make a mess. The Council would go berserk. But . . .'

But Thomas is my brother. I didn't say it. I didn't need to. Murphy nodded.

Molly reappeared with the things I'd sent her for, plus a bowl and a pair of needle-nose pliers. Smart girl. She poured rubbing alcohol into a bowl and started sterilizing the suture needle, the thread, the scalpel, and the pliers.

Her hands moved like they knew what they were doing without need for her to consciously direct them. That probably shouldn't have surprised me. Michael and Charity Carpenter's eldest daughter had probably been taught to deal with injuries since the time she was physically large enough to do so.

'Mouse,' I said. 'There's a bullet inside you. Do you know what that is? The thing that a gun shoots that hurts?'

Mouse looked at me uncertainly. He was shaking.

I put my hand on his head and spoke steadily. 'We've got to take it out of you or it could kill you. It's going to hurt, a lot. But I promise you that it won't take long and that you're going to be all right. I'll protect you. Okay?'

Mouse made a very soft noise that only the ungracious would have called a whine. He leaned his head against my hand, trembled, and then very slowly licked my hand, once.

I smiled at him and leaned my head against his for a second. 'It will be all right. Lie down, boy.'

Mouse did, stretching slowly, carefully out on his side, the wounded shoulder up.

'Here, Harry,' Molly said quietly, gesturing at the tools.

I looked at her, my face hard. 'You're doing it.'

She blinked at me. 'What? But what I did . . . I don't even—'

'I? I? Mouse just took a bullet for you, Miss Carpenter,' I said, my words precise. 'He wasn't thinking of himself when he did it. He was putting his life at risk to protect you. If you want to remain my apprentice, you will stop saying sentences that begin with "I" and repay his courage by easing his pain.'

Her face went white. 'Harry . . .'

I ignored her and moved around to kneel by Mouse's head, holding him down gently, stroking my hands over his thick fur.

My apprentice looked from me to Murphy, her expression uncertain. Sergeant Murphy stared back at her with calm cop eyes, and Molly averted her gaze hurriedly. She looked from her own hands to Mouse, and started crying.

Then she got up, went to the kitchen sink, and put a pot of water on the stove to boil. She washed her hands carefully, all the way to the elbow. Then she came back with the water, took a deep breath, and settled down beside the wounded dog, taking up the instruments.

She cut and shaved the area around the injury first, making Mouse flinch and quiver several times. I saw her cringe at each pained movement from the dog. But her hands stayed steady. She had to widen the tear in the dog's flesh with the scalpel. Mouse actually cried out when the knife cut him, and she closed her eyes tight for a long count of three before she went back to work. She slid the pliers into the shallow injury and pulled out the bullet. It was a tiny thing, smaller than the nail on the end of my pinky, a distorted, oblong bit of shiny metal. Mouse groaned as she tugged it free.

She cleaned the site of the wound again, using the boiled water and disinfectant. Mouse flinched and cried out when she did so – the most agonized sound I had ever heard him make.

'I'm sorry,' Molly said, blinking tears out of the way. 'I'm sorry.'

The injury was big enough to need a trio of stitches.

Molly did them as swiftly as she possibly could, drawing more shudders of pain from Mouse. Then she cleaned the site again and covered it with a small pad that she cut to the proper size, affixing it to the bare-shaved skin around the injury with medical tape.

'There,' she said quietly. She leaned down and buried her face in the thick ruff of fur around Mouse's throat. 'There. You'll be all right.'

Mouse moved very gingerly, moving his head to nudge against her hand. His tail thumped several times on the floor.

'Murph,' I said. 'Give us a minute?'

'Sure,' she said quietly. 'I need to make a call anyway.' She nodded to me and walked quietly to the apartment door – pointedly pausing to close the door from the living room to my small bedroom, shutting Morgan out of the conversation.

I sat with Mouse, stroking his head gently. 'Okay,' I said to Molly. 'What happened?'

She sat up and looked at me. She looked like she wanted to throw up. Her nose was running, now.

'I . . . it occurred to me, Harry, that . . . well, if the traitor wanted to really set the Council at one another's throats, the best way to do it would be to force one of them to do something unforgiveable. Like, maybe force Morgan to kill Wizard LaFortier.'

'Gee,' I said. 'That never once occurred to me, though I am older and wiser than you and have been doing this for most of your life, whereas you've been in the business for just under four years.'

She flushed. 'Yes. Well. Then I thought that the best way to use that sort of influence wouldn't be to use it on

Morgan,' she said. 'But on the people who would be after him.'

I lifted my eyebrows. 'Okay,' I said. 'At this point, I have to ask you if you know how difficult it is to manipulate the mind and will of anyone of significant age. Most wizards who are eighty or a hundred years old are generally considered more or less immune to that kind of gross manipulation.'

'I didn't know that,' Molly said humbly. 'But . . . what I'm talking about wouldn't be a severe alteration to anyone. It wouldn't be obvious,' she said. 'You wouldn't make someone turn into a raving lunatic and murderer. I mean, that's sort of noticeable. Instead, you make sure that you just . . . sort of nudge the people who are chasing after Morgan into being a little bit more like you want them to be.'

I narrowed my eyes. It was an interesting line of thought. 'Such as?'

'Well . . .' she said. 'If someone is naturally quick to anger and prone to fighting, you highlight that part of their personality. You give it more importance than it would have without intervention. If someone is prone to maneuvering politically to take advantage of a situation, you bring that to the forefront of their personality. If someone is nursing a grudge, you shine a spotlight on it in their thoughts, their emotions, to get them to act on it.'

I thought about that one for a second.

'It's how I'd do it,' Molly said quietly, lowering her eyes.

I looked at the young woman I'd been teaching. When I saw Molly, I always saw her smile, her sense of humor, her youth, and her joy. She was the daughter of a close friend. I knew her family and was often a guest in their home. I saw my apprentice, the effort she put into learning, her frustrations, and her triumphs.

I had never, until that very moment, thought of her as someone who might one day be a very, very scary individual.

I found myself smiling bitterly.

Who was I to throw stones?

'Maybe,' I said finally. 'It would be one hell of a difficult thing to prove.'

She nodded. 'But if it was going to be used, there's one person who would without doubt be a target.'

I glanced at Luccio. Her mouth was open slightly as she slept. She was drooling a little. It was ridiculous and adorable.

'Yeah,' Molly said. 'But she would never have let me look. You know she wouldn't have.'

'For good reason,' I said.

Molly's jaw tensed up for a second. 'I know.'

'So you thought you'd look while everyone was unconscious,' I said. 'When you wouldn't get caught.'

She shrugged her shoulders.

'You told yourself that you were doing the right thing,' I said. 'Just a peek, in and out.'

She closed her eyes. 'I was . . . Harry, what if she isn't being honest with you? What if all this time, she's been getting close to you because she doesn't trust you. What if she's just like Morgan – only a lot better at hiding it?'

'You don't know what you're talking about,' I said.

'No?' She met my eyes. 'Whose apprentice was he, Harry? Who *taught* him to be the way he is? Who did he idolize so much that he modeled himself after her?'

I just sat there for a second.

Molly pressed the issue. 'Do you honestly think that she *never* knew how Morgan treated you?'

I took a deep breath. Then I said, 'Yeah. I think that.'

She shook her head. 'You know better.'

'No,' I said. 'I don't.'

'You *should*,' she said fiercely. 'I couldn't take the chance that she would let you go down with Morgan. I had to know.'

I stared at her for a minute. Then I said, in a very quiet voice, 'I always know when I'm being tempted to do something very, very wrong. I start sentences with phrases like, "I would never, ever do this – *but*." Or "I know this is wrong *but*." It's the *but* that tips you off.'

'Harry,' Molly began.

'You broke one of the Laws of Magic, Molly. Willfully. Even though you knew it could cost you your life. Even though you knew that it could also cost mine.' I shook my head and looked away from her. 'Hell's bells, kid. I choose to trust Anastasia Luccio because that's what people *do*. You don't *ever* get to know for sure what someone thinks of you. What they really feel inside.'

'But I could—'

'No,' I said gently. 'Even psychomancy doesn't give you everything. We aren't meant to know what's going on in there. That's what talking is for. That's what trust is for.'

'Harry, I'm sorr—'

I lifted a hand. 'Don't apologize. Maybe I'm the one who let you down. Maybe I should have taught you better.' I petted Mouse's head gently, looking away from her. 'It doesn't matter at the moment. People have died because I've been trying to save Morgan's life. Thomas might still die. And now, if we *do* manage to save Morgan's crusty old ass, he's going to report that you've violated your parole. The Council will kill you. And me.'

She stared at me helplessly. 'I didn't mean to—'

'Get caught,' I said quietly. 'Jesus Christ, kid. I trusted you.'

She wept more heavily now. Her face was a mess. She bowed her head.

'If Morgan goes down for this,' I said, 'there's going to be trouble like you wouldn't believe. And even more people are going to die.' I stood up slowly. 'So. I'm going to do everything in my power to save him.'

She nodded without looking up.

'So you've got a choice to make, grasshopper. You can come with me, knowing the cost if we succeed. Or you can go.'

'Go?' she whispered.

'Go,' I said. 'Leave now. Run, for as long as you can. Hell, it looks a lot like I'm going to get myself killed anyway. Probably Morgan, too. In that case, things will go to hell, but the Wardens will be way too busy to chase you. You'll be able to ignore what's right all you want, do whatever you like – as long as you don't get caught.'

She pressed her arms against her stomach. She sounded like she was about to throw up, through the sobs.

I put a hand on her head and said, 'Or you can come with me. You can do something right. Something that has meaning.'

She looked up at me, her lovely young face discolored in anguish.

'Everyone dies, honey,' I said, very quietly. 'Everyone. There's no "if". There's only "when".' I let that sink in for a moment. '*When* you die, do you want to feel ashamed of what you've done with your life? Feel ashamed of what your life meant?'

She stared at my eyes for a minute and a half of silence broken only by the sound of her muted weeping. Then her head twitched in a single tiny shake.

'I promise that I'll be beside you,' I said. 'I can't promise anything else. Only that I'll stand beside you for as long as I can.'

'Okay,' she whispered. She leaned against me.

I put my hand on her hair for a minute. Then I said gently, 'We're out of time. The Wardens will know Morgan is in Chicago within a few hours at most. They might be on their way already.'

'Okay,' she said. 'Wh-what are we going to do?'

I took a deep breath. 'Among other things, I'm going to attempt a sanctum invocation,' I said.

Her eyes widened. 'But . . . you said that kind of thing was dangerous. That only a fool would take such a chance.'

'I agreed to help Donald freaking Morgan when he showed up at my door,' I sighed. 'I qualify.'

She wiped at her eyes and nose. 'What do I do?'

'Get my ritual box. Put it in the car Murphy's cuddling up with outside.'

'Okay,' Molly said. She turned away but then paused and looked back over her shoulder at me. 'Harry?'

'Yeah?'

'I know it was wrong, but . . .'

I looked at her sharply and frowned.

She shook her head and held up her hands. 'Hear me out. I know it was wrong, and I didn't get much of a look but . . . I swear to you. I think someone *has* tampered with Captain Luccio. I'd bet my life on it.'

I ignored the little chill that danced down my spine.

'Could be that you have,' I said quietly. 'And mine, too. Go get the box.'

Molly hurried to comply.

I waited until she was outside to look at Mouse. The big dog sat up, his eyes gravely concerned. He wasn't favoring his shoulder at all, and his movement was completely unimpaired.

Mouse got hit by the driver of a minivan once. He got back up, ran it down, and returned the favor. The Foo dog was very, very tough. I doubted he'd really needed the medical attention to recover, though I was also sure it would help speed things along. But I hadn't been completely certain the injury wasn't as serious as it looked.

In other words, the freaking dog had fooled Molly and me both.

'You were *acting*?' I said. 'To make it hit Molly harder?'

His tail wagged back and forth proudly.

'Damn,' I said, impressed. 'Maybe I should have named you Denzel.'

His jaws opened in a doggy grin.

'Earlier tonight,' I said, 'when I was trying to figure out how to find Thomas, you interrupted me. I didn't think about it before now, but you helped him track me down when Madrigal Raith was auctioning me off on eBay.'

His tail wagged harder.

'Could you find Thomas?'

'Woof,' he said, and his front paws bounced a couple of inches off the floor.

I nodded slowly, thinking. Then I said, 'I've got another mission for you. One that could be more important. You game?'

He shook his fur out and padded to the door. Then he stopped and looked back over his shoulder at me.

'Okay,' I told him, walking to the door myself. 'Listen up. Things are about to get sort of risky.'

35

I looked at Luccio's still-unconscious form. The stress of coordinating the search for Morgan for who knows how long before he showed up, coupled with the pains of her injuries and the sedative effect of the painkillers I'd given her, meant that she'd never stirred. Not when the gun went off, not when we'd been talking, and not when we'd all had to work together to get Morgan back up the stairs and out to the silver Rolls.

I made sure she was covered with a blanket. The moment I did, Mister descended from his perch atop one of my bookcases, and draped himself languidly over her lower legs, purring.

I scratched my cat's ears and said, 'Keep her company.'

He gave me an inscrutable look that said maybe he would and maybe he wouldn't. Mister was a cat, and cats generally considered it the obligation of the universe to provide shelter, sustenance, and amusement as required. I think Mister considered it beneath his dignity to plan for the future.

I got a pen and paper and wrote.

Anastasia,

I'm running out of time, and visitors are on the way. I'm going someplace where I might be able to create new options. You'll understand shortly.

I'm sorry I didn't bring you, too. In your condition, you'd be of limited assistance. I know you don't like it, but you also know that I'm right.

Help yourself to whatever you need. I hope that we'll talk soon.
Harry

I folded the note and left it on the coffee table, where she'd see it upon waking. Then I bent over, kissed her hair, and left her sleeping safe in my home.

I parked the Rolls in the lot next to the marina. If we hurried, we could still get there before the witching hour, which would be the best time to try the invocation. Granted, trying it while injured and weary with absolutely no preritual work was probably going to detract more than enough from the ritual to offset the premium timing, but I was beggared for time and therefore not spoiled for choice.

'Allow me to reiterate,' Murphy said, 'that I feel that this is a bad idea.'

'So noted,' I said. 'But will you do it?'

She stared out the Rolls's windshield at the vast expanse of Lake Michigan, a simple and enormous blackness against the lights of Chicago. 'Yes,' she said.

'If there was anything else you could do,' I said, 'I'd ask you to do it. I swear.'

'I know,' she said. 'It just pisses me off that there's nothing more I can add.'

'Well, if it makes you feel any better, you're going to be in danger, too. Someone might decide to come by and try to use you against me. And if word gets back to the Council about how much you know, they're going to blow a gasket.'

She smiled a bit. 'Yes, thank you. I feel less left out now that I know someone might kill me anyway.' She shifted, settling her gun's shoulder harness a little more comfortably. 'I am aware of my limits. That isn't the same thing as *liking* them.' She looked back at me. 'How are you going to reach the others?'

'I'd . . . really rather not say. The less you know—'

'The safer I am?'

'No, actually,' I said. 'The less you know, the safer *I* am. Don't forget that we might be dealing with people who can take information out of your head, whether you want to give it or not.'

Murphy folded her arms and shivered. 'I hate feeling helpless.'

'Yeah,' I said, 'me, too. How's he doing, Molly?'

'Still asleep,' Molly reported from the back of the limo. 'I don't think his fever is any higher, though.' She reached out and touched Morgan's forehead with the back of one hand.

Morgan's arm rose up and sharply slapped her arm away at the wrist, though he never changed the pace of his breathing or otherwise stirred. Christ. It was literally a reflex action. I shook my head and said, 'Let's move, people.'

Molly and I wrestled the wounded Warden into his wheelchair again. He roused enough to help a little, and sagged back into sleep as soon as he was seated. Molly slung the strap of my ritual box over her shoulder and started pushing Morgan across the parking lot to the marina docks. I grabbed a couple of heavy black nylon bags.

'And what do we have in there?' Murphy asked me.

'Party favors,' I said.

'You're having a party out there?'

I turned my eyes to the east and stared out over the lake. You couldn't see the island from Chicago, even on a clear day, but I knew it was there, a sullen and threatening presence. 'Yeah,' I said quietly. A real party. Practically everyone who'd wanted to kill me lately would be there.

Murphy shook her head. 'All of this over one man.'

'Over a hero of the Council,' I said quietly. 'Over the most feared man on the Wardens. Morgan nearly took out the Red King himself – a vampire maybe four thousand years old, surrounded by some disgustingly powerful retainers. If he hadn't bugged out, Morgan would have killed him.'

'You almost said something nice about him,' Murphy said.

'Not nice,' I said. 'But I can acknowledge who he is. Morgan has probably saved more lives than you could count, over the years. And he's killed innocents, too. I'm certain of it. He's been the Council's executioner for at least twenty or thirty years. He's obsessive and tactless and ruthless and prejudiced. He hates with a holy passion. He's a big, ugly, vicious attack dog.'

Murphy smiled faintly. 'But he's your attack dog.'

'He's our attack dog,' I echoed. 'He'd give his life without hesitation if he thought it was necessary.'

Murphy watched Molly pushing Morgan down the dock. 'God. It's got to be awful, to know that you're capable of disregarding life so completely. Someone else's, yours, doesn't really matter which. To know that you're so readily capable of taking everything away from a human being. That's got to eat away at him.'

'For so long there's not a lot left, maybe,' I said. 'I think you're right about the killer acting in desperation. This situation got way too confused and complicated for it to be a scheme. It's just . . . a big confluence of all kinds of chickens coming home to roost.'

'Maybe that will make it simpler to resolve.'

'World War One was kind of the same deal,' I said. 'But then, it was sort of hard to point a finger at any one person and say, "That guy did it." World War Two was simpler, that way.'

'You've been operating under the assumption that there is someone to blame,' Murphy said.

'Only if I can catch him.' I shook my head. 'If I can't . . . well.'

Murphy turned to me. She reached up with both hands, put them on the sides of my head, and pulled me down a little. Then she kissed my forehead and my mouth, neither quickly nor with passion. Then she let me go and looked up at me, her eyes worried and calm. 'You know that I love you, Harry. You're a good man. A good friend.'

I gave her a lopsided smile. 'Don't go all gushy on me, Murph.'

She shook her head. 'I'm serious. Don't get yourself killed. Kick whatsoever ass you need to in order to make that happen.' She looked down. 'My world would be a scarier place without you in it.'

I chewed my lip for a second, feeling very awkward. Then I said, 'I'd rather have you covering my back than anyone in the world, Karrin.' I cleared my throat. 'You might be the best friend I've ever had.'

She blinked quickly several times and shook her head. 'Okay. This is going somewhere awkward.'

'Maybe we should take it from "whatsoever ass",' I suggested.

She nodded. 'Find him. Kick his ass.'

'That is the plan,' I confirmed. Then I bent down and kissed her forehead and her mouth, gently, and leaned my forehead against hers. 'Love you, too,' I whispered.

Her voice tightened. 'You jerk. Good luck.'

'You, too,' I said. 'Keys are in the ignition.'

Then I straightened, hitched up the heavy bags, and stalked toward the docks. I didn't look at her as I walked away, and I didn't look back.

That way, we could both pretend that I hadn't seen her crying.

My brother owned an ancient battered commercial fishing boat. He told me it was a trawler. Or maybe he said troller. Or schooner. It was one of those – unless it wasn't. Apparently, nautical types get real specific and fussy about the fine distinctions that categorize the various vessels – but since I'm not nautical, I don't lose much sleep over the misuse of the proper term.

The boat is forty-two feet long and could have been a stunt double for Quint's fishing boat in *Jaws*. It desperately needed a paint job, as the white of its hull had long since faded to grey and smoke-smudged black. The only fresh paint on it was a row of letters on the bow that read *Water Beetle*.

Getting Morgan on board was a pain – literally, in his case. We got him settled onto the bed in the little cabin and brought all the gear aboard. After that, I climbed up onto the bridge, started the engines with my copy of the

Water Beetle's key, and immediately realized I hadn't cast off the lines. I had to go back down to the deck to untie us from the dock.

Look, I just told you – I'm not nautical.

Leaving the marina wasn't hard. Thomas had a spot that was very near the open waters of the lake. I almost forgot to flick on the lights, but got them clicked on before we got out of the marina and onto the open water. Then I checked the compass next to the boat's wheel, turned us a degree or two south of due east, and opened up the engine.

We started out over the blackness of the lake, the boat's engines making a rather subdued, throaty *lub lub dub lub* sound. The boat had originally been built for charter use in the open sea, and it had some muscle. The water was calm tonight, and the ride remained smooth as we rapidly built up speed.

I felt a little nervous about the trip. Over the past year, Thomas and I had gone out to the island several times so that I could explore the place. He'd been teaching me how to handle the boat, but this was my first solo voyage.

After a few minutes, Molly came partway up the short ladder to the bridge and stopped. 'Do I need to ask permission to come up there or something?'

'Why would you?' I asked.

She considered. 'It's what they do on *Star Trek*?'

'Good point,' I said. 'Permission granted, Ensign.'

'Aye aye,' she said, and came up to stand next to me. She frowned at the darkness to the east, and cast a wary glance back at the rapidly fading lights of the city. 'So.

We're going out to the weird island, the one with that big ley line running through it?'

'Yep,' I said.

'Where my dad got . . .'

I tried not to remember how badly Michael Carpenter had suffered when he had gone there with me. 'Crippled,' I said. 'Yeah.'

She frowned quietly. 'I heard him talking to my mom about the island. But when I tried to go look it up, I couldn't find it on any of the maps. Not even in the libraries.'

'Yeah,' I said. 'From what I hear, bad things happened to everyone who went out there. There used to be some kind of port facility for fishing and merchant traffic, big as a small town, but it was abandoned. Sometime in the nineteenth century, the city completely expunged the place from its records.'

'Why?'

'Didn't want anyone to go out there,' I said. 'If they merely passed a law, they knew that sooner or later some moron would go there out of sheer contrariness. So they pretty much unmade the place, at least officially.'

'And in more than a century, no one's ever seen it?'

'That dark ley line puts off a big field of energy,' I said. 'It makes people nervous. Not insane or anything, but it's enough to make them subconsciously avoid the place, if they aren't making a specific effort to get there. Plus, there are stone reefs around a big portion of the island, and people tend to swing wide around it.'

She frowned. 'Couldn't that be a problem for us?'

'I'm pretty sure I know where to get through them.'

'Pretty sure?'

'Pretty sure.'

Maybe she looked a little paler. 'Oh,' she said. 'Good. And we're going there why?'

'The sanctum invocation,' I said. 'The island has a kind of spirit to it, an awareness.'

'A *genius loci*,' she said.

I nodded approval. 'Exactly that. And fed by that ley line, it's a big, strong one. It doesn't much care for visitors, either. It's arranged to kill a bunch of them.'

Molly blinked. 'And you want to do a *sanctum invocation*? There?'

'Oh, hell no,' I said. 'I don't *want* to. But I've got to find some way to give myself an edge tomorrow, or it's all over but the crying.'

She shook her head slowly. Then she fell silent until we actually reached the island a little while later. It was dark, but I had enough moonlight and starlight to find the buoy Thomas and I had placed at the entry through the reef. I swung the *Water Beetle* through it, and began following the coastline of the island until I passed a second buoy and guided the boat into the small floating dock we'd constructed. I managed to get the vessel next to the dock without breaking anything, and hopped off with lines in hand to tie it off.

I looked up to find Molly holding my ritual box. She passed it to me and I nodded to her. 'If this works, it should take me an hour or so,' I told her. 'Stay with Morgan. If I'm not back by dawn, untie the boat, start the engine, and drive it back to the marina. It's not too different from a car, for what you'll be doing.'

She bit her lip and nodded. 'What then?' she asked.

'Get to your dad. Tell him I said that you need to disappear. He'll know what to do.'

'What about you?' she asked. 'What will you be doing?'

I slipped the strap to the ritual box over one shoulder, took up my staff, and started toward the interior of the island.

'Not much,' I said over my shoulder. 'I'll be dead.'

36

Grimm's fairy tales, a compilation of the most widely known scary stories of Western Europe, darn near always feature a forest as the setting. Monstrous and terrifying things live there. When the hero of a given story sets out, the forest is a place of danger, a stronghold of darkness — and there's a good reason for it.

It can be freaking frightening to be walking a forest in the dark. And if that isn't enough, it's dangerous, to boot.

You can't see much. There are sounds around you, from the sigh of wind in the trees to the rustle of brush caused by a moving animal. Invisible things touch you suddenly and without warning — tree branches, spiderwebs, leaves, brush. The ground shifts and changes constantly, forcing you to compensate with every step as the earth below you rises or dips suddenly. Stones trip up your feet. So do ground-hugging vines, thorns, branches, and roots. The dark conceals sinkholes, embankments, and the edges of rock shelves that might drop you six inches or six feet.

In stories, you read about characters running through a forest at night. It's a load of crap. Oh, maybe it's feasible in really ancient pine forests, where the ground is mostly clear, or in those vast oak forests where they love to shoot Robin Hood movies and adaptations of Shakespeare's work. But if you get into the thick native brush in the US, you're better off finding a big stick and breaking your own ankle than you are trying to sprint through it blind.

I made my way cautiously uphill, passing through the ramshackle, decaying old buildings of what had been a tiny town, just up the slope from the dock. The trees had reclaimed it long since, growing up through floors and out broken old windows.

There were deer on the island, though God knows how they got there. It's big enough to support quite a few of the beautiful animals. I'd found signs of foxes, raccoons, skunks, and wildcats, plus the usual complement of rabbits, squirrels, and groundhogs. There were a few wild goats there as well, probably descendants of escapees from the former human residents of the island.

I began to sense the hostile presence of the island before I'd gone twenty steps. It began as a low, sourceless anxiety, one I barely noticed against the backdrop of all the perfectly rational anxiety I was carrying. But as I continued up the hill, it got worse, maturing into a fluttery panic that made my heart beat faster and dried out my mouth.

I steeled myself against the psychic pressure, and continued at the same steady pace. If I let it get to me, if I wound up panicking and bolted, I could end up a victim of the normal threats of a forest at night. In fact, that was probably what the island had in mind, so to speak.

I gritted my teeth and continued, while my eyes slowly adjusted to the night, revealing the shapes of trees and rocks and brush, and making it a little easier to move safely.

It was a short hike to the mountain's summit. The final bit of hill was at an angle better than forty-five degrees, and the only way one could climb it safely was to use the old steps that had been carved into the rock face. They had felt weirdly familiar and comfortable the first time I went up them. That hadn't changed noticeably in sub-sequent visits. Even now, I could go up them in the dark, my legs and feet automatically adjusting to the slightly irregular spacing of the steps, without needing to consult my eyes.

Once at the top of the stairs, I found myself on a bald crown of a hilltop. A tower stood there, an old lighthouse made of stone. Well, about three-quarters of it stood there, anyway. Some of it had collapsed, and the stones had been cannibalized and used to construct a small cottage at the foot of the tower.

The silent presence of the island was stronger here, a brooding and dangerous thing that did not care for visitors.

I looked around the moonlit hilltop, nodded once, marched over to the flat area in front of the cottage and planted my ritual box firmly on the ground.

What I was about to attempt had its beginnings in ancient shamanic practice. A given tribe's shaman or wise one or spirit caller or whatever would set out into the wild near home and seek out a place of presence and power, such as this one. Depending on the culture involved, the practitioner would then invoke the spirit of the place and draw its full attention. The ritual that happened next wasn't quite an introduction, or a challenge, or a staking of a claim on the land, or a battle of wills, but it incor-porated elements of all of those things. If the ritual was successful, it would form a sort of partnership or peerage between the shaman and the *genius loci* in question.

If it wasn't successful, well . . . It's a bad thing to have the full attention of a dangerous spirit that can exert control over the environment around you. *This* spirit, bolstered by the dark energy of the ley line that ran beneath the tower, was more than capable of driving me insane or recycling me into food for its animals and trees.

'And yet here I am about to pop you in the nose,' I muttered. 'Am I daring or what?'

I set my staff down and opened the box.

First, the circle. Using a short whisk broom, I quickly cleared dirt and dust from the rock shelf beneath me in an area about three feet across. Then I used a wooden-armed chalk compass, like those used in geometry classrooms, to draw out a perfect circle on the stone in faintly luminescent, glow-in-the-dark chalk. The circle didn't have to be perfectly round in order to work, but it was a little bit more efficient, and I wanted every advantage I could get.

Next, I got five white candles out of the box, and checked a magnetic compass so that I could align them properly. The compass needle spun wildly and aimlessly. The turbulence of the nearby ley line must have been throwing it off. I put the thing away and sighted on the North Star, setting the candles out at the five points of a pentagram, its tip aligned with due north.

After that, I got out an old and genuine KA-BAR US Marine combat knife, along with a plain silver chalice and a silver former Salvation Army bell with a black wooden handle.

I double-checked each of the objects and the circle, then stepped a few feet away and undressed completely, losing my rings, bracelet, and all my other magical gear except for the silver pentacle amulet around my neck. I didn't have to do the ritual sky clad, but it reduced the chances of any of the enchantments on my gear causing interference by a small if significant amount.

All the while, the pressure from the island's awareness kept doubling and redoubling. My head started pounding, which was just lovely in combination with the fresh bumps on it. The hairs on the back of my neck stood up. Mosquitoes began to whine and buzz around me, and I shuddered to think of the places that were going to get bitten while I did this.

I went to the circle, checked everything again, got a box of matches out of the ritual box, and then knelt down in the circle. Yes, I could have lit them with a spell – but again, that would have left an energy signature on the candles that could potentially interfere. So I did it the old-fashioned way. As I struck the first match and leaned down to light the northernmost candle, a screech owl let out an absolutely alien-sounding cry from so nearby that I almost jumped out of my skin. I barely kept from losing my balance and smudging the circle.

'Cheap shot,' I muttered. Then I lit a fresh match and began again. I lit the five candles, then turned to face the north and reached out to gently touch the chalk circle. A mild effort of will closed it, and the psychic pressure I'd been feeling for the last half hour or more abruptly vanished.

I closed my eyes and began to regulate my breathing, relaxing my muscles group by group, focusing my thoughts on the task at hand. I felt my will begin to gather. Outside my circle, the owl shrieked again. A wildcat let out an earsplitting yowl. A pair of foxes set up a yipping, howling chorale in the brush.

I ignored them until I felt that I had gathered all the strength I could. Then I opened my eyes and picked up the bell. I rang it sharply once, and filled my voice with the power of my will. 'I am not some clueless mortal you can frighten away,' I said to the hilltop. 'I am magi, one of the Wise, and I am worthy of your respect.'

A wind came rushing up from the lake. The trees muttered and sighed with the force of it, a sound like angry surf, enormous and omnipresent.

I rang the bell again. 'Hear me!' I called. 'I am magi, one of the Wise, and I know your nature and your strength.'

The wind continued to rise around me, making the candles flicker. With an effort of will, I steadied their flames, and felt the temperature of my body drop a couple of degrees in reaction.

I set the bell down, took up the knife, and drew it along the knuckles of my left hand, opening a thin line in my flesh. Blood welled up immediately. I put the knife down, took up the chalice, and let my blood trickle into the cup.

And as it did, I used the one thing that made me think it was possible – just *possible* – to pull this thing off.

Soulfire.

During a case a little more than a year ago, an archangel had decided to invest in my future. Uriel had replaced the power I'd lost when I resisted the temptations offered me by one of the Fallen. The demon's Hellfire had been literal hell on wheels for destructive purposes. Soulfire was apparently the angelic equivalent of the same force, the flip side of the coin – fires of creation rather than those of destruction. I hadn't experimented with it much. Soulfire used my own life force as its source of energy. If I poured too much into any given working, it could kill me.

As the blood dripped down into the chalice, I reached out to the place in my mind where the archangel's gift resided, and poured soulfire into my blood. Silver-white sparks began to stream from the cuts and accompanied the blood down into the chalice, filling it with supernatural power far in excess of what my blood, a common source of magical energy, contained on its own.

I lifted the chalice in my right hand and the silver bell in my left. Droplets of blood and flickering sparks of soulfire fell on the silver, and when it rang again, the sound was piercing, the tone so perfect and pure that it could have shattered glass.

'Hear me!' I called, and my soulfire-enhanced voice rang out in a similar fashion, sharp and precise, strong and resonant. Small stones fell from a broken section of the tower wall. 'I am magi, one of the Wise! I make of my blood this gift to you, to honor your strength and to show my respect! Come forth!' I set the bell down and prepared to break the circle and release the spell. 'Come forth!' I bellowed, even louder. '*COME FORTH!*'

I simultaneously broke the circle, released my will, and poured out the scarlet and silver fire of my enhanced blood onto the stone of the hilltop.

Animals of the forest erupted into screams and howls. Birds exploded from their sleeping places to swarm in the skies above me. Half a dozen tree branches snapped all together in the rushing wind, the sounds crackling over the stony hilltop like rifle shots.

And, an instant later, a bolt of viridian lightning crashed down out of a completely clear sky and struck the ground in the center of the empty shell of the old lighthouse.

There was little enough in the lighthouse that could burn, but some brush and grasses grew there. Their light danced and flickered on the walls, if only for a few seconds – and then suddenly revealed an indistinct and solid shape inside.

I took a slow breath and rose to my feet, facing the lighthouse. It was a rare thing for such an entity to take material form, and I had thought it so unlikely to happen that I had scarcely bothered to plan for it.

The woods all around me rustled, and I darted my eyes left and right without moving.

Animals had appeared. Deer were the largest and most obvious, the stags' horns wicked in the moonlight. Foxes and raccoons were there, too, as well as rabbits and squirrels and all manner of woodland creatures, predator and prey alike. They were all staring at me with obvious awareness that was far more than they should have had, and all of them were eerily still.

I did my best not to think about what it might be like to be overrun and chewed to death by hundreds of small wild animals. I turned my eyes back to the tower, and waited.

The dark shape, indistinct in the heavy shadows, moved and came closer, until it looked like . . . something that was not quite human. Its shoulders were too wide, its stance too crooked, and it walked with a slow, limping gait, *drag-thump, drag-thump*. It was covered with what appeared to be a voluminous dark cloak – oh, and it was eleven or twelve feet tall.

Yikes.

Green eyes the same color as the bolt of unnatural lightning burned inside the darkness of the cloak's hood. They faced me and flashed brighter, once, and a gust of wind washed down onto me, almost taking me from my feet.

I gritted my teeth against it and endured, until a moment later it died away.

I looked at the dark shape for a moment, and then

nodded. 'Right,' I said. 'I get you.' I reached for my will, infused it with a meager portion of soulfire, and hurled my right hand forward, calling, *'Ventas servitas!'*

Wind festooned with ribbons of silver light rushed from my outstretched hand, crashing into the figure. It didn't move the thing – the entity was far too massive for that – but the wind cast the grey cloak back as sharply as a ship's flag caught in a gale, making the fabric snap and pop.

My evocation died away, and the entity's cloak settled down again. Once more, its eyes flashed, and the earth beneath my feet and slightly behind me erupted, solid rock splitting and cracking. Sharp shards flew up from the supernatural impact, and I instantly felt half a dozen hot, stinging cuts on my legs and back.

'Ow,' I muttered. 'At least they weren't in any tender spots, I guess.' Then again I summoned my will and soulfire, this time focusing on the earth near the entity. *'Geodas!'* I shouted, and the earth beneath the entity twisted and screamed, suddenly opening into a sinkhole.

The entity never moved. It just *stood* there on empty air, as if I hadn't literally pulled the ground out from under it.

The entity's eyes kindled to life again, but this time I had anticipated it. Flame gathered before it in a lance and rushed toward me, leaving a coating of sudden frost and ice on the ground beneath it as it came. But my own will had reached down into the ground below me, and found the water from the stream that fed the cottage's little well. I drew it up through the cracks the entity had created in the rock, taking advantage of the work it had done, with a shout of, *'Aquilevitas!'* A curtain of water rose up to meet the onrushing flame, and they consumed one another, leaving only darkness and a cloud of steam.

I lifted a hand and my soulfire-enhanced will and shouted, 'Fuego!' A column of silver-and-blue flame as thick as my chest roared across the ground and struck the entity hard in the center of its mass.

It rocked back at the impact. Not much. Maybe half an inch, though that column of fire would have blown apart a brick wall. But I *had* moved it that half an inch. There was no doubt about that.

Weariness was slowly seeping into my limbs as the entity stared at me. I forced myself to stand straight and face the being without blinking – and without looking weak.

'You want to keep it up?' I asked it aloud. 'I could do this all night.'

The entity stared at me. Then it walked closer. *Drag-thump. Drag-thump.*

I was not at all scared. Even a little. The only reason my mouth was so dry was all that fire that had been flying around.

It stopped five feet away, towering over me.

And I realized that it was waiting.

It was waiting for *me* to act.

My heart pounded harder as I bowed my head respect-fully. I don't know why I said what I did, exactly. I just know that my instincts screamed at me that it was the right thing to say, my voice infused with my will.

'I am Harry Dresden, and I give thee a name, honored spirit. From this day on, be thou called Demonreach.'

Its eyes flashed, burning more brightly, sending out

tendrils and streams of greenish fire in a nimbus around its head.

Then Demonreach mirrored my gesture, bowing its own head in reply. When it looked up, its head turned briefly toward the cottage. Then the wind rose again, and darkness fluttered over the hilltop.

When it passed, I was alone, the hilltop empty of entity and animal alike. I was also freezing.

I staggered toward my clothes and gathered them up, shaking so hard that I thought I might just collapse on the ground. As I rose with my gear in my arms, I saw a light flickering in the cottage.

I frowned and shambled over to it. The door, like the windows, had long since rotted away, and there was very little roof to speak of – but the cottage did have one thing in it that still functioned.

A fireplace.

A neat stack of fallen wood was burning in the fireplace, putting off a cheery warmth, its golden flames edged with flickers of green at their very edges.

I blinked at the fire for a moment, and then made my way over to it, reveling in the warmth as I dressed again. I glanced up, searching for that alien presence. I found it immediately, still there, still alien, still dangerous, though it no longer seemed determined to drive me away.

I slid will into my voice as I said, simply, 'Thank you.'

The gentle wind that sighed through the trees of Demonreach may have been a reply.

Or maybe not.

37

I didn't return to the dock by the same route I'd taken to the tower. There was a much shorter, easier way, down what looked like a sheer rock wall. It proved to have an ancient narrow gully worn into the stone, almost completely hidden by brush. The gully's floor had a thin layer of silt in it, leaving little room for plants to grow, and was as easy to traverse as a sidewalk, even in the dark. Following it brought me back to the island's shoreline in half the time it had taken to go up.

I didn't wonder how I'd known about the path until I stepped out of the woods and saw the dock again. I hadn't been that way before. I hadn't known it existed. Yet when I decided to take that trail, the knowledge had come to me as completely and immediately as if I had lived there for years: pure information.

I paused and looked around me. I knew not to walk directly to the dock from where I stood. There was a large hornets' nest in the earth at the base of a fallen tree, and I would risk arousing their anger if I accidentally crushed it while walking by. I also knew that a grumpy old skunk was trundling its way back to its den, thirty yards in the other direction, and that it would happily douse me with musk if I came anywhere close.

I glanced over my shoulder, back toward the tower, casting out my supernatural senses. The island's awareness continued being that same constant presence I'd felt ever since leaving the tower. I considered going back, taking the old stairs this time, to see what would happen, and immediately I understood that there was a cottonmouth that made its home in a large crack on the twenty-sixth step. If I delayed the trip until later in the morning, the snake would be out on the stones, sunbathing to build up its body heat for the day.

The dawn was approaching, and the sky had begun to lighten from black to blue. I could see the tower standing, lonely and wounded, but unbowed, a black shape against the sky. Demonreach began to awaken to the first trills of songbirds.

I walked down to the dock, thoughtfully, and walked out to where the *Water Beetle* was moored. 'Molly,' I called.

Feet pounded on the deck, and Molly burst up out of the ship's cabin. She flew across the distance between us, and nearly tackled me into the water on the far side of the dock with the enthusiasm of her hug. Molly, the daughter of two ferocious warriors, was no wilting violet. My ribs creaked.

'You came back,' she said. 'I was so worried. You came back.'

'Hey, hey. I need my rib cage, kid,' I said, but I hugged her in return for a quiet moment, before straightening.

'Did it work?' she asked.

'I'm not exactly sure. God, I need something to drink.' We both boarded the *Water Beetle*, and I went below and removed a can of Coke from a cabinet. It was warm, but it was liquid, and more important, it was Coke. I guzzled the can's contents and tossed it into the trash bin.

'How's Morgan?' I asked.

'Awake,' Morgan rumbled. 'Where are we?'

'Demonreach,' I said. 'It's an island in Lake Michigan.'

Morgan grunted without emphasis. 'Luccio told me about it.'

'Oh,' I said. 'Oh, good.'

'Miss Carpenter says you were attempting a sanctum invocation.'

'Yeah.'

Morgan grunted. 'You're here. It worked.'

'I think so,' I said. 'I'm not sure.'

'Why not?'

I shook my head. 'I thought that when a bond was formed with the land in question, it gave you access to its latent energy.'

'Yes.'

Which meant that my magic would be subsidized by the island, whenever I was here. I'd get a lot more bang for my buck, so to speak. 'I thought that was all it did.'

'Generally,' Morgan said. I saw him turn his head toward me in the dim cabin. 'Why? What else has happened?'

I took a deep breath and told him about the hidden trail, the hornets, and the skunk.

Morgan sat up in his bunk by the time I got to the end. He leaned forward intently. 'You're sure you aren't mistaken? Confrontations with a *genius loci* can leave odd aftereffects behind.'

'Hang on,' I said.

I went back to the woods where I knew the hornets were, and found their nest in short order. I retreated without crushing anything and went back to the boat.

'Yeah,' I said. 'I'm sure.'

Morgan sank back onto the bunk as if he was being slowly deflated. 'Merciful God,' he said. 'Intellectus.'

I felt my eyebrows go up. 'You're kidding.'

Molly muttered a couple of candles to light so that we could see each other clearly. 'Intell-whatsis?' she asked me.

'Intellectus,' I said. 'Um. It's a mode of existence for a very few rare and powerful supernatural beings – angels have it. I'm willing to bet old Mother Winter and Mother Summer have it. For beings with intellectus, all reality exists in one piece, one place, one moment, and they can look at the whole thing. They don't seek or acquire knowledge. They just *know* things. They see the entire picture.'

'I'm not sure I get that,' Molly said.

Morgan spoke. 'A being with intellectus does not understand, for example, how to derive a complex calculus equation – because it doesn't need the process. If you showed him a problem and an equation, he would simply understand it and skip straight to the answer without need to think through the logical stages of solving the problem.'

'It's *omniscient*?' Molly asked, her eyes wide.

Morgan shook his head. 'Not the same thing. The being with intellectus has to be focused on something via consideration in order to know it, whereas an omniscient being knows all things at all times.'

'Isn't that pretty close?' Molly asked.

'Intellectus wouldn't save you from an assassin's bullet if you didn't know someone wanted to kill you in the first place,' I said. 'To know it was coming, you'd first need to consider the question of whether or not an assassin might be lurking in a dark doorway or on top of a bell tower.'

Morgan grunted agreement. 'And since beings of intellectus so rarely understand broader ideas of cause and effect, they can be unlikely to realize that a given event might be an indicator of an upcoming assassination attempt.' He turned to me. 'Though that's a terrible metaphor, Dresden. Most beings like that are immortal. They'd be hard-pressed to notice bullets, much less feel threatened by them.'

'So,' Molly said, nodding, 'it might be able to know anything it wants to know — but it still has to ask the right questions. Which is always harder than people think it is.'

'Yeah,' I said. 'Exactly.'

'And now you've got this intellectus, too?'

I shook my head. 'It's Demonreach that has it. It stopped when I got out over the water.' I tapped my finger against my forehead. 'I've got nothing going on in here at the moment.'

I realized what I had said just as the last word left my mouth, and glanced at Morgan.

He lay on the bunk with his eyes closed. His mouth was turned up in small smile. 'Too easy.'

Molly fought not to grin.

Morgan pursed his lips thoughtfully. 'Can the entity feed you any other information, Dresden? The identities of those behind LaFortier's murder, for example.'

I almost hit myself in the head with the heel of my hand. I should have thought of that already. 'I'll let you know,' I said, and went back to the shore.

Demonreach sensed me at the same time as I perceived it, and the mutual sensation felt oddly like a hand wave of acknowledgment. I frowned thoughtfully and looked around the island, concentrating on the issue of LaFortier's killer.

Nothing sprang to mind. I tried half a dozen other things. Who was going to win the next World Series?

Could I get the *Blue Beetle* out of impound yet? How many books had Mister knocked off my shelves in my absence?

Zip.

So I thought about hornets' nests, and instantly felt certain that there were thirty-two of them spread around the hundred and fifty or so acres of the island, and that they were especially thick near the grove of apple trees on the island's northern side.

I went back to the boat and reported.

'Then it only exists upon the island itself,' Morgun rumbled, 'like any other *genius loci*. This one must be bloody ancient to have attained a state of intellectus, even if it is limited to its own shorelines.'

'Could be handy,' I noted.

Morgan didn't open his eyes but bared his teeth in a wolf's smile. 'Certainly. If your foes were considerate enough to come all the way out here to meet you.'

'Could be handy,' I repeated, firmly.

Morgan arched an eyebrow and gave me a sharp look.

'Come on, grasshopper,' I said to Molly. 'Cast off the lines. You're about to learn how to drive the boat.'

By the time we made it back to the marina, the sun had risen. I coached Molly through the steps of bringing the *Water Beetle* safely into dock, even though I wasn't exactly Horatio Hornblower myself. We managed to do it without breaking or sinking anything, which is what counts. I tied off the boat and went onto the dock. Molly followed me anxiously to the rail.

'No problem here, grasshopper. Take her out for about ten minutes in a random direction that you choose. Then turn off the engine and wait. I'll signal you when I'm ready for you to pick me up.'

'Are you sure we shouldn't stay together or something?' she asked anxiously.

I shook my head. 'Tracking spells can't home in too well over water,' I said. 'And you'll know if someone's coming for you from a mile away. Literally. Keep Morgan out there, and you should be as safe as anywhere.'

She frowned. 'What if he gets worse?'

'Use your noggin, kid. Do whatever you think is most likely to keep you both alive.' I started untying the line. 'I shouldn't be gone more than a couple of hours. If I don't show, the plan is the same as when I went up to the tower. Get yourself vanished.'

She swallowed. 'And Morgan?'

'Make him as comfortable as you can and leave him.'

She stared at me for a minute. 'Really?'

'If I get taken out, I don't think you'll be able to protect him,' I said, as matter-of-factly as I could. 'Or catch the real bad guy. So run like hell and let him look out for himself.'

I saw her think that over. Then she smiled slightly.

'It would really humiliate him if he found himself under the protection of a girl. An apprentice. And a possible warlock, to boot.'

I nodded. 'True.'

Molly pursed her lips thoughtfully. 'That might be worth staying for.'

'Kid,' I said, 'the smart thing for you to do if it all goes sour is to run.'

'Smart,' she said. 'But not right.'

I studied her soberly. 'You sure? Because there's a world of hurt waiting to fall.'

She nodded, her face pale. 'I'll try.'

And she would. I could see that in her eyes. She knew better than most exactly how dangerous such a thing would be for her, and it clearly terrified her. But she would try.

'Then if I'm taken off the board, see Murphy,' I said. 'She knows everything I do about the case. Listen to her. She's smart, and you can trust her.'

'All right,' she said.

I tossed the mooring lines back onboard. 'Get a move on.'

I started walking down the dock. Behind me, Molly called, 'Harry? What signal are you going to use?'

'You'll know it,' I called back.

I left the docks in search of the tool that could rip apart this tangled web of suspicion, murder, and lies.

I found it in the marina's parking lot.

A pay phone.

Lara answered on the second ring. 'Raith.'

'Dresden,' I said. 'What have you got for me?'

'Oh, to have straight lines like that more often,' she said, her tone wry. 'What makes you think I have anything for you?'

''Cause I've got something to trade.'

'Men generally seem to think that way. Most of them tend to overestimate the value of their wares.'

'Pheromone Lass,' I said, 'can we have the rest of this conversation above the waistline?'

She let out that rich, throaty laugh of hers, and my hormones sounded the charge. I ignored them. Stupid hormones.

'Very well,' she said. 'It should interest you to know

that the money deposited in Warden Morgan's account came from a dummy corporation called Windfall.'

'Dummy organization?' I asked. 'Who owns it?'

'I do,' she said calmly.

I blinked. 'Since you're sharing this information, I take it that it happened without your knowledge.'

'You are quite correct,' she said. 'A Mr Kevin Aramis is the corporation's manager. He is the only one, other than myself, with the authority to move that much money around.'

I thought furiously. Whoever aced LaFortier hadn't just intended the Council to implode. He or they had also gone to a lot of trouble to incite hostility with the White Court.

Hell's bells.

My imagination treated me to a prophetic nightmare. Morgan fights against the injustice of his frame. Hostilities erupt, creating strife between various factions of wizards. The Council eventually runs down the money trail, discovers Lara on the other end, and the Council seizes upon the opportunity to unify the factions again, thanks to a common enemy. Hostilities with the vampires start fresh. The Red Court sees the poorly coordinated Council exposing itself in battle with the White Court, and pounces, breaking the back of the Council. And after that, it would all be over but the heroic last stands.

Hell's bells, indeed.

'We're being played against one another,' I said.

'That was my conclusion as well.'

A couple more pieces clicked into place. 'Madeline,' I said. 'She got to this Aramis guy and coerced him into betraying you.'

'Yes,' Lara hissed. Barely suppressed, wholly inhuman

rage filled her level, controlled voice. 'When I catch up to her, I'm going to tear out her entrails with my bare hands.'

Which took care of my hormone problem. I shivered.

I'd seen Lara in action. I could never decide if it had been one of the most beautiful terrifying things I'd ever seen, or if it was one of the most terrifying beautiful things I'd ever seen.

'You might try looking at the Hotel Sax, room twelve thirty-three,' I said. 'If I'm right, you're going to find Mr Aramis's body there. Madeline's working for someone, a man. She didn't say anything that would help identify him. You should also know that she has hired the services of a mercenary named Binder. Not exactly a rocket scientist, but smart enough to be dangerous.'

Lara was silent for a second. Then she said, 'How did you learn this?'

'Shockingly, with magic.'

I heard her speaking to someone in the room with her. Then she got back on the phone and said, 'If Aramis is dead, Madeline has tied up the loose end in her plan. It will be impossible to provide credible evidence that I did not in fact pay for LaFortier's murder.'

'Yeah. That's why she did it.'

I heard her make a displeased sound, but it was still ladylike. 'What do we intend to do about this, Harry?'

'Do you have a nice dress?'

'Pardon?'

I found myself grinning maniacally. 'I'm throwing a party.'

Thomas's phone rang four times before the connection

opened. There was a moment of silence. Then Thomas spoke, his voice raw and ragged. 'Harry?'

My heart just about stopped beating to hear my brother's voice. 'Thomas. How's it going?'

'Oh,' he rasped, 'I'm just hanging around.'

I've seen Thomas in agony before. He sounded exactly like this.

The phone emitted random noises, and then the yowl-purring voice of the skinwalker came over the line. 'He is here. He is alive. For now. Give me the doomed warrior.'

'Okay,' I said.

There was a moment of silent consternation from the far end of the line.

'Bring him to me,' it said.

'Nah. That isn't going to happen.'

'What?'

'You're coming to me.'

'Do you wish me to end his life this instant?'

'Frankly, Shaggy, I don't give a damn,' I said, forcing boredom into my voice. 'It'd be nice to be able to return one of the vampires to his own, get myself a marker I can call in some day. But I don't need it.' I paused. 'You, on the other hand, need Thomas to be alive, if you expect me to trade Morgan for him. So this is how it's going to go down. At dusk, you will be contacted on this phone. You will be told where our meeting will take place. When you arrive, you will show me the vampire, alive and well, and when he is returned to me, you will take Morgan without contest.'

'I am *not* some mortal scum you can command, mageling,' Shagnasty seethed.

'No. You're immortal scum.'

'You blind, flesh-feeding *worm*,' Shagnasty snarled. 'Who are you to speak to me so?'

'The worm who's got what you need,' I said. 'Dusk. Keep the phone handy.'

I hung up on him.

My heart hammered against my chest and cold sweat broke out over my upper body. I felt myself shaking with terror for Thomas, with weariness, with reaction to the conversation with Shagnasty. I leaned my aching head against the earpiece of the phone and hoped that I hadn't just ended my brother's life.

One more call.

The White Council of Wizards uses telephone communications like everyone else, albeit with a lot more service calls. I gave headquarters a ring, gave them the countersign to their security challenge, and got patched through to one of the administrative assistants, an earnest young woman not quite finished with her apprenticeship.

'I need to get a message to every member of the Senior Council,' I told her.

'Very well, sir,' she said. 'What is the message?'

'Get this verbatim. Okay?'

'Yes, sir.'

I cleared my throat and spoke. 'Be advised that I have been sheltering Warden Donald Morgan from discovery and capture for the past two days. An informant has come to me with details of how Warden Morgan was framed for the murder of Senior Council Member LaFortier. Warden Morgan is innocent, and what's more, I can prove it.

'I am willing to meet with you tonight, on the uncharted island in Lake Michigan, east of Chicago at sundown. The informant will be present, and will produce testimony that will vindicate Warden Morgan and identify the true culprit of the crime.

'Let me be perfectly clear. I will *not* surrender Warden Morgan to the alleged justice of the Council. Come in peace and we will work things out. But should you come to me looking for a fight, be assured that I will oblige you.'

The assistant had started making choking sounds after the very first sentence.

'Then sign it "Harry Dresden",' I said.

'Um. Yes, sir. Sh-shall I read that back to you?'

'Please.'

She did. I'd heard sounds of movement in the background around her, but as she read aloud, all of those sounds died to silence. When she finished, she asked, in a rather small, squeaky voice, 'Do I have that down correctly, sir?'

Murmurs burst out in the background over the phone, excited and low.

'Yeah,' I told her. 'Perfect.'

38

I figured I had an hour, maybe, before someone was going to show up from Edinburgh. It was time enough to grab a cab and head to the hospital.

Back in the ICU, Will was sacked out in the waiting room and Georgia was the one sitting with Andi. A middle-aged couple who looked as if they hadn't slept much was in there with her. I knocked on the glass. Georgia said something to the couple and rose to come out into the hallway with me. She looked tired but alert, and had her long, rather frizzy hair pulled back into a ponytail.

'Harry,' she said, hugging me.

I returned the hug, cutting it off a little early. 'How is she?'

Georgia studied me for a second before she answered. 'In bad shape. The doctors don't seem to be willing to say whether or not she'll recover.'

'Better that way,' I said. 'If one of them said she'd be fine and then she wasn't . . .'

Georgia glanced at the couple sitting beside Andi's bed, holding each other's hands. 'I know. It would be cruel to offer false hope, but . . .'

'But you're still irrationally angry that the docs haven't saved her yet. You know better, but you're upset anyway.'

She nodded. 'Yes. Irrationality is not something I'm comfortable with.'

'It isn't irrational,' I said. 'It's human.'

She gave me a small smile. 'Will and I talked. And you're in a hurry.'

I nodded. 'I need you both, and right now.'

'I'll get him,' Georgia said.

We took Georgia's SUV back down to the marina and arrived with ten minutes to spare on my estimated time window. I definitely wanted to be out over open water by the time members of the Council started showing up. The water wouldn't be a perfect protection from incoming magic, but it would make it a lot harder for anyone to target me solidly, and it was a hell of a lot better than nothing.

'Okay,' I said. 'You guys wait here for a minute.'

Will frowned. 'Why?'

'I need to talk to someone who can be a little shy around strangers. One minute.' I hopped out of the SUV and walked down the rows of cars until I found two vans parked together. I slipped between them, put the fingers of one hand to my lips, and let out a sharp whistle.

There was a whirring sound and Toot-toot streaked down from overhead, came to a hover in front of me, drew his little sword, and saluted. 'Yes, my liege!'

'Toot, I have two missions for you.'

'At once, my lord!'

'No, I want you to do them one at a time.'

Toot lowered his sword, his expression crestfallen. 'Oh.'

'First, I want you to find the boat out on the lake that my apprentice is in. She's not more than a mile or two from shore.' I took off my silver pentacle amulet, wrapped the chain around it, and handed it to Toot-toot. 'Leave this where she will notice it right away.'

Toot accepted the amulet gravely, tucking it under one arm. 'It will be done.'

'Thank you.'

Toot-toot's chest swelled out, and he stood a little bit straighter.

'Second,' I told him. 'I need to know how many of the little folk you could convince to join the Guard for one night.'

He frowned and looked dubious. 'I don't know, Lord Harry. The pizza ration is already stretched as far as it can go.'

I waved a hand. 'The Guard's pay won't change. I'll order extra to pay for the new guys' service. Call them the Za-Lord's Militia. We only need them sometimes. How many do you think would agree to that?'

Toot buzzed in an excited circle. 'For *you*? Every sprite and pixie and dewdrop faerie within a hundred miles knows that you saved our kind from being imprisoned by the Lady of the Cold Eyes! There's not a one who didn't have comrade or kin languishing in durance vile!'

I blinked at him. 'Oh,' I said. 'Well. Tell them that there may be great danger. Tell them that if they wish to join the Militia, they must obey orders while they serve. And I will pay them one large pizza for every fourscore volunteers.'

'That's less than you pay the Guard, Harry,' Toot said smugly.

'Well, they're amateurs, not full-time veterans like you and your men, are they?'

'Yes, my lord!'

I looked at him seriously. 'If you can recruit a Militia and if they perform as asked, there's a promotion in it for you, Toot.'

His eyes widened. 'Does it come with cheese in the crust and extra toppings?'

'It isn't a pizza.' I said. 'It's a promotion. Get this work done, and from that time forward, you will be . . .' I paused dramatically. 'Major-General Toot-toot Minimus commanding the Za-Lord's Elite.'

Toot's body practically convulsed in a spasm of excitement. Had a giant yellow exclamation point suddenly appeared in the air over his head, I would not have been surprised. 'A *Major-General*?'

I couldn't resist. 'Yes, yes,' I said solemnly. 'A Major-General.'

He let out a whoop of glee and zipped up and down the little space between vans. 'What do you wish us to do when I have them, my lord!'

'I want you to play,' I said. 'Here's what we're going to do. . . .'

I rejoined Will and Georgia, and ten minutes later, the *Water Beetle* came chugging back toward the marina. The grasshopper got my brother's boat into dock with only a mildly violent impact. I secured lines quickly, and Will and Georgia jumped on. Almost before Will's feet were on the deck, I was already untying the lines and following them onto the boat. Molly, for her part, already had the engine in reverse.

'Now what?' she called down to me from the wheel atop the cabin.

'Use the compass on the dashboard. One to two degrees south of due east, and call me when you spot the island.'

'Aye aye!'

Will squinted at Molly and then at me. '"Aye aye"?'

I shook my head sadly. 'Landlubbers. I'm going to go shiver timbers or something. I haven't slept in a while.'

'Go ahead, Harry,' Georgia said. 'We'll wake you if anything happens.'

I nodded, shambled down to the second bunk, and passed out immediately.

Someone shook me two seconds later and I said, 'Go away.'

'Sorry, Harry,' Will said. 'We're here.'

I said several uncouth and thoughtless things, then manned up and opened my eyes, always the hardest part of waking up. I sat up, and Will retreated from the cramped cabin with a glance at Morgan's unconscious form. I sat there with my mouth feeling like it had been coated in Turtle Wax. It took me a second to identify a new sound.

Rain.

Raindrops pattered onto the deck of the boat and the roof of the cabin.

I shambled out onto the deck, unconcerned about the rain ruining my leather duster. One handy side effect of going through the painfully precise ritual of enchanting it to withstand physical force as if it had been plate steel was that the thing was rendered waterproof and stainproof as well – yet it still breathed. Let's see Berman's or Wilson's do *that*.

Sufficiently advanced technology, my ass.

I climbed up to the bridge, keeping an eye on the sky as I did. Lowering clouds of dark grey had covered the sky, and the rain looked to be a long, steady soaker – a rarity in a Chicago summer, which usually went for rough-and-tumble thunderstorms. The heat hadn't let up much, and as a result the air was thick and heavy enough to swim through.

I took the wheel from Molly, oriented myself by use of the compass and the island, now only a few minutes away, and yawned loudly. 'Well. This makes things less pleasant.'

'The rain?' Molly asked. She passed me my pentacle.

I slipped it back over my head and nodded. 'I'd planned on lying off the island until closer to dark.'

'Why?'

'Mostly because I just challenged the Senior Council to a brawl there at sundown,' I said.

Molly choked on her gum.

I ignored her. 'I didn't want to make it easy for them to slip up on me. Oh, and I've arranged to trade Thomas for Morgan with Shagnasty. He won't get word of where to go until later, though. I think otherwise he'd cheat and show up early. He looks like a shifty character.'

The pun went past Molly, or maybe she was just that good at ignoring it. 'You're trading Morgan for Thomas?'

'Nah. I just want to get Shagnasty out here with Thomas in one piece so that the White Court can take him down.'

Molly stared at me. 'The White Court, too?'

I nodded happily. 'They've got a stake in this as well.'

'Um,' she said. 'Why do you think the Senior Council will take you up on your challenge?'

'Because I told them I was going to be producing an informant who would give testimony about who really killed LaFortier.'

'Do you have someone like that?' Molly asked.

I beamed at her. 'No.'

She stared at me for a moment, clearly thinking. Then she said, 'But the killer doesn't know that.'

My smile widened. 'Why, no, Miss Carpenter. He doesn't. I made sure word got around headquarters of my challenge to the Senior Council. He's got no *choice* but to show up here if there's any chance at all that I might actually have found an informant ready to blow his identity – which, by the way, would also provide substantial proof of the existence of the Black Council.'

Her golden brows knitted. 'What if there's no chance of such an informant existing?'

I snorted. 'Kid, groups like these guys, the ones who maim and kill and scheme and betray – they do what they do because they love power. And when you get people who love power together, they're all holding out a gift in one hand while hiding a dagger behind their back in the other. They regard an exposed back as a justifiable provocation to stick the knife in. The chances that this group has no one in it who might believably have second thoughts and try to back out by bargaining with the Council for a personal profit are less than zero.'

Molly shook her head. 'So . . . he or she will call in the Black Council to help?'

I shook my head. 'I think this is happening because the killer slipped up and exposed himself to LaFortier. He had to take LaFortier out, but with all the security at Edinburgh, there was every chance something could go wrong and it did. Everything else he's done has smacked of desperation. I think that if the Black Council finds out that their mole has screwed up this thoroughly, they'd kill him themselves to keep the trail from leading back to them.' I stared at the glowering mass of Demonreach. 'His only chance is to tie off any loose ends that might lead back to him. He'll be here tonight, Molly. And he's *got* to win. He has nothing to lose.'

'But you're putting *everyone* together in a confined space, Harry,' Molly said. 'This is going to be a huge mess.'

'Pressure cooker, padawan,' I said, nodding. 'The perp is already desperate enough to be acting hastily and making mistakes. Especially the mistake of taking things a step too far and trying to incriminate the White Court in LaFortier's death as well.'

Molly stared out at the water thoughtfully. 'So you put him together in a confined space with two major groups of power who will want to kill him. His worst nightmare has got to be the wizards and the White Court being drawn into a *closer* alliance because of what he's done. And with as much power as they have, there's no way he's going to be able to fight them all.'

I smiled at her. 'Yeah. It *sucks* to feel helpless,' I said. 'Especially for a wizard, because we usually aren't. Or at least, we're usually able to convince ourselves that we aren't.'

'You think he'll crack,' she said.

'I think he'll be there. I think that with enough pressure, something is going to pop loose, somewhere. I think he'll try something stupid. Maybe a preemptive spell, something to take everyone down before they know a fight is on.'

'A sneak attack,' Molly said. 'Which won't be a sneak attack if you know where he is and what he's doing. Intellectus!'

I tapped my temple with a finger. 'Capital thinking, grasshopper.'

Thunder rumbled far away.

I sighed. 'Thomas can sail in bad weather, but I don't know how to do it intelligently. Something like this could turn ugly, fast. We're going to have to head into the dock and take our chances.'

I navigated. Sheesh, listen to me, 'navigated'. The boat had a steering wheel and a lever to make it go faster. It was about as complicated to make move as a bumper car. Granted, simple isn't the same thing as easy, but even so. The actual process of pointing the boat and making it go is not complicated enough to deserve to be called navigation.

I drove the *Water Beetle* around to the safe passage through the reef, and pulled her into the dock, much more smoothly this time. Will was waiting by the rail and ready. He hopped onto the dock and Georgia threw him the mooring lines.

'Don't step onto the land until I get a chance to get there, first!' I called to them. 'I want to, ah, sort of introduce you.'

Billy gave me an oblique look. 'Um. Okay, Harry.'

I climbed down from the bridge and was just about to hop to the dock when a tall, slender figure in a black robe, black cape, and black hood appeared from behind a veil, standing at the very end of the dock. He lifted his old rune-carved staff, muttered a word, and then brought it smashing down onto the wooden planks.

A disk of sparkling blue light washed out from the point of impact. I had time, barely, to draw in my will, cross my arms at the wrists, holding them against my chest, and slam will into both my shield bracelet and into strengthening my mental defenses.

Smears of deep blue, purple, and dark green appeared like puffs of smoke where the expanding ring struck Molly, Will, and Georgia, and the three of them simply collapsed, dropping into sprawling heaps on the dock and the deck of the boat. My vision darkened and for an instant I felt unbearably tired – but in a panic I forced more energy into my defenses, and the instant passed.

The robed figure stood staring at me for a few seconds. Then it spoke in a deep voice. 'Put the staff down, Dresden.' Swirling narcotic colors gathered around his staff, and he pointed it at me like a gun. 'It is over.'

39

The rain came down steadily. I risked a glance at the others. They were all down, but breathing. Molly's head, shoulders, and arms hung off the side of the boat. Wet, her sapphire-dyed hair looked like a much darker hue. Each rock of the boat made her hands swing. She was in danger of falling into the water.

I turned back to the cloaked figure and peered at him. Big billowy cloaks and robes are nicely dramatic, especially if you're facing into the wind – but under a calm, soaking rain they just look waterlogged. The outfit clung to the figure, looking rather miserable.

The rain also made the cloth look darker than it was. Looking closer, I could see faint hints of color in the cloth, which wasn't actually black. It was a purple so deep that it was close.

'Wizard Rashid?' I asked.

The Gatekeeper's staff never wavered as he faced me. He lifted a hand and drew back his hood. His face was long and sharp-featured and weathered like old leather. He wore a short beard that was shot through with silver, and his silver hair was short, stiff brush. One of his eyes was dark. The other had a pair of horrible old silver scars running through it, from his hairline down to his jaw. The injury had to have ruined his natural eye. It had been replaced with something that looked like a stainless-steel ball bearing. 'Indeed,' he said calmly.

'Should have seen it sooner. There aren't many wizards taller than me.'

'Lay aside your staff, Wizard Dresden. Before anyone else is hurt.'

'I can't do that,' I said.

'And I cannot permit you to openly challenge the White Council to battle.'

'No?' I asked, thrusting out my jaw. 'Why not?'

His deep, resonant voice sounded troubled. 'It is not yet your hour.'

I felt my eyebrows go up. 'Not *yet* . . . ?'

He shook his head. 'Places in time. This is not the time, or the place. What you are about to do will cost lives – among them your own. I wish you no harm, young wizard. But if you will not surrender, so be it.'

I narrowed my eyes at him. 'And if I don't do this, an innocent man is going to die. I don't want to fight you. But I'm not going to stand by and let the Black Council kill Morgan and dance off behind the curtains so that they can do it again in the future.'

He tilted his head slightly. 'Black Council?'

'Whatever you want to call them,' I said. 'The people the traitor is working for. The ones who keep trying to stir up trouble between the powers. Who keep changing things.'

The Gatekeeper's expression was unreadable. 'What things?'

'The weirdness we've been seeing. Mysterious figures handing out wolf belts to FBI agents. Red Court vampires showing up to fights with Outsiders on the roster. Faerie Queens getting idealistic and trying to overthrow the natural order of the Faerie Courts. The Unseelie standing by unresponsive when they are offered an enormous insult by the vampires trespassing on their territory. The attack on Arctis Tor. I can think of half a dozen other things to go with those, and those are just the things I've personally gotten involved with.' I made a broad gesture with one hand, back toward Chicago. 'The world is getting weirder and scarier, and we've been so busy beating on one another that we can't even see it. Someone's behind it.'

He watched me silently for a long moment. Then he said, 'Yes.'

I frowned at him, and then my lips parted as I realized what was going on. 'And you think I'm with them.'

He paused before speaking – but then, he damn near always did. 'Perhaps there is reason. Add to your list of upset balances such things as open warfare erupting between the Red Court and the White Council. A Seelie crown being passed from one young Queen to the next by bloody revolt, and not the will of Titania. Wardens consorting with White Court vampires on a regular basis. College students being taught magic sufficient to allow them to become werewolves. The Little Folk, Wyld fae, banding together and organizing. The most powerful artifacts of the Church vanishing from the world – and, as some signs indicate, being kept by a wizard who does not so much as pay lip service to the faith, much less believe.'

I scowled. 'Yeah, well. When you put it like *that*.'

He smiled faintly.

I held up my hand, palm out. 'I swear to you, by my magic, that I am not involved with those lunatics, except for trying to put out all these fires they keep starting. And if questionable things surround me, it's because that's the kind of thing that happens when you're as outclassed as I usually am. You have to find solutions where you can, not where convenient.'

The Gatekeeper pursed his lips thoughtfully, considering me.

'Look, can we agree to a short truce, to talk this out?' I said. 'And so that I can keep my apprentice from drowning?'

His gaze moved past me to Molly. He frowned and lowered his staff at once. 'Five minutes,' he said.

'Thanks,' I said. I turned around and got Molly hauled back onto the boat. She never stirred. Once she was safely snoozing on deck, I went down the dock to stand in front of the Gatekeeper. He watched me quietly, holding his staff in both hands, leaning on it gently. 'So,' I said. 'Where's the rest of the Senior Council?'

'On the way, I should think,' he said. 'They'll need to secure transportation to the island in Chicago and then find their way here.'

'But not you. You came through the Nevernever?'

He nodded, his eyes watching me carefully. 'I know a Way. I've been here before.'

'Yeah?' I shook my head. 'I thought about trying to find a Way out here, but I didn't want to chance it. This isn't exactly Mayberry. I doubt it hooks up to anything pleasant in the Nevernever.'

The Gatekeeper muttered something to himself in a language I didn't understand and shook his head. 'I cannot decide,' he said, 'whether you are the most magnificent liar I have ever encountered in my life – or if you truly are as ignorant as you appear.'

I looked at him for a minute. Then I hooked my thumb up at my ridiculous head bandage. 'Dude.'

He burst out into a laugh that was as rich and deep as his speaking voice, but . . . more, somehow. I'm not sure how to explain it. The sound of that laugh was filled with a warmth and a purity that almost made the air quiver around it, as if it had welled up from some untapped source of concentrated, unrestrained joy.

I think maybe it had been a while since Rashid had laughed.

'You,' he said, barely able to speak through it. 'Up in that tree. Covered with mud.'

I found myself grinning at him. 'Yeah. I remember.'

He shook his head and actually wiped tears away from his good eye. It took him another moment or two to compose himself, but when he spoke, his living eye sparkled, an echo of his laughter. 'You've endured more than most young people,' he said. 'And tasted more triumph than most, as well. It is a very encouraging sign that you can still laugh at yourself.'

'Well, gosh,' I said. 'I'm just so ignorant, I don't know what else to do.'

He stared at me intently. 'You don't know what this place is.'

'It's out of the way of innocent bystanders,' I said. 'And I know it better than most of the people who are on the way.'

He nodded, frowning. 'I suppose that is logical.'

'So?'

'Hmm?'

I sighed. Wizards. 'So? What *is* this place?'

He considered his words for a moment. 'What do you think it is, beyond the obvious physical and tactical terrain?'

'Well,' I said. 'I know there's a ley line that comes

through here. Very dark and dangerous energy. I know that there's a *genius loci* present and that it is real strong and isn't very friendly. I know that they tried to start up a small town here, linked with the shipping interests in the Great Lakes, but it went sour. Demonreach drove them away. Or insane, apparently.'

'Demonreach?' he asked.

'Couldn't find a name on the books,' I said. 'So I made up my own.'

'Demonreach,' the Gatekeeper mused. 'It's . . . certainly fitting.'

'So?'

He gave me a tight smile. 'It wouldn't help you for me to say anything more – except for this: one of your facts is incorrect. The ley line you speak of does not go *through* the island,' he said. 'This is where it wells up. The island is its *source*.'

'Ah,' I said. 'Wells up from what?'

'In my opinion, that is a very useful question.'

I narrowed my eyes. 'And you aren't going to give me anything else.'

He shrugged. 'We do have other matters to discuss.'

I glanced back at my unconscious friends. 'Yeah. We do.'

'I am willing to accept that your intentions are noble,' he said. 'But your actions could set into motion a catastrophic chain of events.'

I shrugged. 'I don't know about that,' I said. 'What I do know is that you don't kill a man for a crime he didn't commit. And when someone else tries to do it, you stop them.'

'And you think that this will stop them?' the Gatekeeper asked.

'I think it's my best shot.'

'You won't succeed,' he said. 'If you press ahead, it will end in violence. People will die, you amongst them.'

'You don't even know what I have in mind,' I said.

'You're laying a trap for the traitor,' he said. 'You're trying to force him to act and reveal himself.'

A lesser man might have felt less clever than he had a moment before. 'Oh.'

'And if I can work it out,' the Gatekeeper said, 'then so can the traitor.'

'Well, duh,' I said. 'But he'll show up anyway. He can't afford to do anything else.'

'And he'll come ready,' the Gatekeeper said. 'He'll choose his moment.'

'Let him. I've got other assets.'

Then he did something strange. He exhaled slowly, his living eye closing. The gleaming steel eye tracked back and forth, as if looking at something, though I could only tell it was moving because of the twitches of his other eyelid. A moment later, the Gatekeeper opened his eye and said, 'The chances that you'll survive it are minimal.'

'Yeah?' I asked him. I stepped around him and hopped off the dock and onto the island, immediately feeling the connection with Demonreach as I turned to face him. 'How about now?'

He frowned at me, and then repeated the little ritual.

Then he made a choking sound. 'Blood of the Prophet,' he swore, opening his eyes to stare at me. 'You . . . you've claimed *this* place as a sanctum?'

'Uh-huh.'

'*How?*'

'I punched it in the nose. Now we're friends,' I said.

The Gatekeeper shook his head slowly. 'Harry,' he said, his voice weary. 'Harry, you don't know what you've done.'

'I've given myself a fighting chance.'

'Yes. Today,' he replied. 'But there is always a price for knowledge. Always.'

His left eyelid twitched as he spoke, making the scars that framed the steel orb quiver.

'But it will be me paying the price,' I said. 'Not everyone else.'

'Yes,' he said quietly. We were both silent for several minutes, standing in the rain.

'Been longer than five minutes,' I said. 'How do you want it to be?'

The Gatekeeper shook his head. 'May I offer you two pieces of advice?'

I nodded.

'First,' he said, 'do not tap into the power of this place's well. You are years away from being able to handle such a thing without being altered by it.'

'I hadn't planned on touching it,' I said.

'Second,' he said, 'you must understand that regardless of the outcome of this confrontation, someone will die. Preferably, it would be the traitor – but if he is killed rather than captured, no one will be willing to accept your explanation of events, no matter how accurate it may be. Morgan will be executed. Odds are excellent that you will be as well.'

'I'm sure as hell not doing this for me.'

He nodded.

'Don't suppose you'd be willing to lend a hand?'

'I cannot set foot on the island,' he said.

'Why not?'

'Because this place holds a grudge,' he said.

I suddenly thought of the *drag-thump* limp of the island's manifest spirit.

Damn.

He turned to the dock behind him and flicked a hand at the air. A neat, perfectly circular portal to the Nevernever appeared without a whisper or flicker of wasted power. The Gatekeeper gave me a nod. 'Your friends will awaken in a moment. I will do what I can to help you.'

'Thank you,' I said.

He shook his head. 'Do not. It may be that true kindness would have been to kill you today.'

Then he stepped through the portal and was gone. It vanished an instant later. I stood there in the rain and watched the others begin to stir. Then I sighed and walked back to them, to help them up and explain what was going on.

We had to get moving. The day wasn't getting any younger, and there were a lot of things to do before nightfall.

40

We worked for three hours before I started dropping things, tripping on nice flat ground, and bumping into other people because I'd forgotten to keep an eye out for them.

'That's it, Harry,' Georgia said firmly. 'Your sleeping bag is in the cottage. Get some more sleep.'

'I'll be all right,' I said.

'Harry, if anything happens to you, we aren't going to have anyone we know looking out for us. You need to be able to focus. Go rest.'

It sounded awfully good, but my mouth opened on its own. 'We've still got to lay out the—'

Will had come up behind me in complete silence. He pulled my arm behind my back in a capable, strong grip, and twisted carefully. It didn't hurt, until he leaned gently into me and I had to move forward to keep the pressure off. 'You heard the lady,' he said. 'We can finish the rest of it on our own. We'll wake you up if anything happens.'

I snorted, twisted at the waist, bumping Will off balance with my hip, and broke the lock. Will could have broken my arm and kept hold of me, but instead he let go before it could happen. 'All right, all right,' I said. 'Going.'

I shambled into the cottage and collapsed onto a sleeping bag that lay on top of a foam camp pad.

Four hours later, when Will shook me awake, I was lying in the exact same position. Late-afternoon light slanted into the half-ruined cottage from the west. Morgan lay on his own pallet, made by stripping the foam mattress from the bunk on the *Water Beetle*. His eyes were closed, his breathing steady. Will must have carried him up from the boat.

'Okay,' I slurred. 'I'm up. I'm up.'

'Georgia has been patrolling the shoreline,' he said. 'She says there's a boat approaching.'

My heart began beating a little faster, and my stomach fluttered. I swallowed, closed my eyes for a moment, and imagined a tranquil tropical beach in an effort to calm my thoughts. But the beach kept getting overrun by shapeshifting zombie vampires with mouths on the palms of their hands.

'Well, that's useless,' I said in sleepy disgust. I got to my feet and gathered my things. 'Where's it coming from?'

'West.'

'He'll have to sail a third of the way around the island then, to get through the reefs,' I yawned. 'Where's Georgia?'

Claws scraped on hard-packed earth, and a large tawny wolf appeared in the doorway. She sat down and looked at me, her ears perked forward.

'Good work,' I told her. 'Molly?'

'Here, Harry,' she called, as she hurried into the cottage. She held a crystal of white quartz about two inches thick and a foot long in her hands.

'Get to work, grasshopper. Don't hesitate to use the crystal if things get dicey. And good luck to you.'

She nodded seriously and went to Morgan's side. She reached out and took his limp hand, frowned in mild concentration, and they both vanished behind one of her wonder veils. 'God be with you, Harry,' she said, her voice coming out of nowhere.

'Will,' I said. 'Get your game face on.' I turned to Will to find the young man gone and a burly dark-furred wolf sitting in his place next to a pile of loose clothes. 'Oh,' I said. 'Good.'

I checked my gear, my pockets, my shoelaces, and real-ized that I had crossed the line between making sure I was ready and trying to postpone the inevitable. I straightened my back, nodded once, and began to stride toward the cottage door. 'Let's go, people. Party time.'

It was getting darker over the enormous expanse of the lake. Twilight is a much different experience when you're far away from the lights of a city or town. Modern civilization bathes us in light throughout the hours of darkness – lighted billboards, streetlights, headlights, airplane lights, neon decorations, the interior lights of homes and businesses, floodlights that strobe across the sky. They're so much a part of our life that the darkness of night is barely a factor in our daily thinking anymore. We mock one another's lack of courage with accusations of being afraid of the dark, all the while industriously making our own lights brighter, more energy efficient, cheaper, and longer-lasting.

There's power in the night. There's terror in the dark-ness. Despite all our accumulated history, learning, and experience, we remember. We remember times when we were too small to reach the light switch on the wall, and when the darkness itself was enough to makes us cry out in fear.

Get a good ways out from civilization – say, miles and miles away on a lightless lake – and the darkness is there, waiting. Twilight means more than just time to call the children in from playing outside. Fading light means more than just the end of another day. Night is when terrible things emerge from their sleep and seek soft flesh and hot blood. Night is when unseen beings with no regard for what our people have built and no place in what we have deemed the natural order look in at our world from outside, and think dark and alien thoughts.

And sometimes, just sometimes, they do things.

I walked down the ancient hillsides of Demonreach and felt acutely aware of that fact; night wasn't falling, so much as sharpening its claws.

I walked out to the end of the floating dock alone. Billy and Georgia remained behind, in the woods. You would not believe how sneaky a wolf is capable of being until you've seen one in action. Wolves acting with human-level intelligence – and *exceptional* human intelligence at that – are all but invisible when they choose to be.

A boat was rounding the buoy that marked the opening in the reef. It was a white rental boat, like any number available to tourists in the area, a craft about twenty feet long and rigged for waterskiing. The wind had risen, coming in from the southwest, and the lake was getting choppier. The rental boat was wallowing a little, and bouncing irregularly against the waves, throwing up small shocks of spray.

I watched it come in over the last few hundred yards, until I could see who was on board. The boat was fairly new. Its engine made an odd, clattering noise, which served to identify the occupants. The White Council, it seemed, had arrived on time.

Ebenezar McCoy was at the wheel of the boat, his bald head shiny in the rain. Listens-to-Wind sat in the passenger seat, wearing a rain poncho, one hand gripping the side of the boat, the other holding on to the dashboard in front him. His weather-seamed face was grim.

In the center of the rear bench was a tiny figure in white silk embroidered with red flowers. Ancient Mai was Chinese, and looked as delicate and frail as an eggshell teacup. Her hair was pure white and long, held up with a number of jade combs. Though she was now old, even by the standards of the White Council, she was still possessed of a sizable portion of what would have been a haunting, ethereal beauty in her youth. Her expression was serene, her dark eyes piercing and merciless.

She frightened me.

Veteran Wardens sat on either side of Ancient Mai, dour in their grey cloaks, and three more were sitting or crouching elsewhere in the boat — all of them from the hard-bitten squad that had been on standby back in Edinburgh. They were all armed to the teeth, and their expressions meant business. Apparently Mai scared them at least as much as she did me: one of them was holding an umbrella for her.

I waited at the end of the dock, inviting Ebenezar by gesture to pull up on the side opposite the *Water Beetle*. He brought the boat in with considerably more skill than I had shown, killed the ailing engine while it was still moving, and got up to toss me a line. I caught it and secured the boat to the dock without taking my eyes off of anyone in the boat. No one spoke. Once the engine had fallen silent, the only sound was rain and wind.

'Evening,' I ventured, nodding to Ebenezar.

He was staring hard at me, frowning. I saw his eyes scan the shoreline and come back to me. 'Hoss,' he said.

He rose and stepped out onto the dock. One of the Wardens tossed him another line, and he secured the back end of the craft. Then he got off, walked up to me, and offered me his hand. I shook it.

'Rashid?' he whispered so low I could barely hear it over the rain.

'With us,' I replied as quietly, trying not to move my lips.

His head tipped me a tiny nod, and then he turned to beckon the others. Wardens and Senior Council members began clambering out of the boat. I walked down the dock beside Ebenezar, watching the Wardens over my shoulder. They were the sort of men and women who had no illusions about violence, magical or otherwise. If they decided that the best way to deal with me would be to shoot me in the back, they wouldn't hesitate.

I stepped off the dock and onto the island again, and immediately felt the presence of Demonreach. At the moment, the only persons on the island were those I had brought with me.

Ebenezar followed me, and I felt it the instant he stepped onto the shore. It wasn't as if someone had whispered in my ear. I simply *knew*, felt it, the way you know it when an ant is crawling across your arm. He stopped a step later, and I kept going until I was about ten feet away. I turned to face them as their group came down the dock to stand on the shore. I kept close track of them through the link with the island, making sure that there weren't any Wardens hiding behind veils so that they could sneak up behind me and start delivering rabbit punches.

Ebenezar, Ancient Mai, and Listens-to-Wind, his expression bearing a faintly greenish cast, stood side by side, facing me. The Wardens fanned out behind them, wary eyes watching every possible route of approach, including from the lake.

'Well, Wizard Dresden,' Ebenezar said. He leaned on his staff and regarded me blandly. 'We got your note.'

'I figured,' I said. 'Did you get as far as the part where I said if you wanted a fight, I would oblige you?'

The Wardens didn't actually bare their teeth and start snarling, but it was close.

'Aye, aye,' Ebenezar said. 'I thought it might be more profitable if we could talk about things first.'

'Indeed,' said Ancient Mai. Her voice was too smooth and too confident to match the tiny fragile person speaking in it. 'We can always kill you afterward.'

I didn't actually break out into rivulets of sweat, but it was close.

'Obviously, the disrespect you have offered the White Council merits some form of response,' she continued. 'Do not flatter yourself by thinking that we have come to you because we lack other options.'

Ebenezar gave Mai a mild look. 'At the same time,' he said, 'your reputation as an investigator is unrivaled within the Council. That, added to the nature of your relationship with the alleged murderer, is reason enough to hear what you have to say.'

'Wizard Dresden,' Listens-to-Wind said. 'You said you had proof of Morgan's innocence. You said you had a witness.'

'And more,' I replied.

'And where are they?'

'We need to wait a moment,' I said, 'until everyone arrives.'

Ancient Mai's eyes narrowed. The Wardens got even more alert, and spread out a bit, hands on their weaponry.

'What others, Hoss?' Ebenezar asked.

'Everyone directly involved in this plot,' I said. 'Warden Morgan wasn't the only one being set up as a patsy. When you manage to track down the source of the money found in Morgan's account, you'll find that it comes from a corporation owned by the White Court.'

Listens-to-Wind frowned. 'How do you know this?'

'I investigated,' I said. 'After further investigation, I concluded that the money had probably been moved without the knowledge of the White Court's leaders. The guilty party not only wished LaFortier dead, and Warden Morgan to take the blame for it, he also wanted to manipulate the Council into renewing hostilities with the Vampire Courts.'

The Wardens traded looks with one another when I said that. It was getting darker, and I had trouble making out their expressions. Listens-to-Wind's face became thoughtful, though. 'And there is proof of this?' he asked.

'I believe there will be,' I replied. 'But it might take time to find – longer than the duration of Morgan's unjust trial and undeserved execution, anyway.'

Ancient Mai suddenly smiled, an expression with all the joy and life of frozen porcelain. 'In other words,' she said, 'whatever measures being taken to veil Morgan from our tracking spells were near their limits, forcing you to seek this meeting.'

I had to work hard to keep from twitching. The only thing worse than scary is *smart* and scary.

Mai turned to Ebenezar. 'It seems obvious that Dresden was involved in this plot on some level, and if Dresden is here, Morgan is probably nearby. Arrest Dresden and resume attempting to track Morgan immediately. We can attend to the business in a proper and orderly fashion back at Edinburgh.'

Ebenezar eyed Mai and then looked at Listens-to-Wind.

The old medicine man stared at me for a time, and then reached up an ink-stained finger to pull back a few loose hairs that had been plastered to his face by the rain. He leaned on his staff and looked around the island for a long minute, his expression distant. 'No mention was made of other parties being present,' he said, finally. 'This is Council business, and no one else's. Adding representatives of the White Court to this . . . meeting could prove as disastrous as the war you claim to be trying to avoid, Wizard Dresden.'

Ebenezar's jaw tensed up. 'That's not the same thing as saying we should arrest him.'

Listens-to-Wind faced Ebenezar stolidly. 'If what he says is so, the truth will come out. We can postpone a trial so that if this evidence exists, it can be found.'

'You know as well as I do,' Ebenezar said, 'that the outcome of the trial is not going to be changed by the truth.'

Listen-to-Wind's voice became hard and rough, holding a deep and burning anger that I had never heard from the old man before. 'There is the world that should be,' he growled, 'and the world that *is*. We live in one.'

'And must create the other,' Ebenezar retorted, 'if it is ever to be.'

Listens-to-Wind looked down and shook his head. He looked very old and very tired. 'There are no good paths to choose, old friend,' he said quietly. 'All we can do is choose if many die, or a few.' He looked up at me, his face hard. 'I am sorry, Hoss Dresden. But I must agree. Arrest him.'

41

Demonreach allowed me to sense Billy and Georgia slinking closer, and to feel an uncertain sense of excitement that could have been tension or fear or anger coming from them. It had a much more vague idea of the emotions of the Wardens, but I could tell that they weren't eager to start a fight with me.

Which made me want to laugh. I mean, seriously. One on one, sure, maybe I could have been a handful for any of them. But there were *three* members of the Senior Council there, any one of which could have tied me in knots. And they had me outnumbered five to one, beyond that.

And then it hit me. They were dealing with something far more dangerous than me, Harry Dresden, whose battered old Volkswagen was currently in the city impound. They were dealing with the potential demonic dark lord nightmare warlock they'd been busy fearing since I turned sixteen. They were dealing with the wizard who had faced the Heirs of Kemmler riding a zombie dinosaur, and emerged victorious from a fight that had flattened Morgan and Captain Luccio before they had even reached it. They were dealing with the man who had dropped a challenge to the *entire* Senior Council, and who had then actually *showed*, apparently willing to fight – on the shores of an entirely too creepy island in the middle of a freshwater sea.

Granted, I technically was that person, but they had no

idea how close several of those calls had been. They didn't know the small details, the quirks of fate, or the assists from allies I probably didn't deserve that allowed me to shamble out of those clouds of insanity in more or less one piece.

They just knew that I was the one still standing – and that fact inspired a healthy and rational fear. More than that, they were afraid of what they *didn't* know I could do. And none of them knew that I would *so* much rather be back in my apartment, reading a good book and drinking a cold beer.

I didn't move when Listens-to-Wind made his statement. I just stood there, as if I wasn't much impressed. The Council had evidently sent the three Senior members as a kind of quorum, and I would think that the word of two of them would be enough to decide a course of action – but the oldest of the Wardens there, a large man with a big black beard whose name was Beorg, or Yorg, or Bjorn – definitely Scandinavian – turned to look at Ebenezar.

The wizard of the Ozarks stood looking at me, a small smile on his face. I recognized the smile. When I'd first gone to live with him, after I'd killed my foster father, we would go into town every week for supplies. A gang of teenage boys, bored, reacted to the presence of a new boy with typical adolescent thoughtlessness. One of them had tried to get me to fight him.

At the time, I remember being annoyed at the distraction from my day. Because I had just wiped out a major demon and a former Warden of the White Council in a pair of fair fights, local teenage bullies were really kind of beneath my notice. They were kids playing a game, and I had grown older very quickly. I could have killed them, all of them, without too much trouble, but the very idea was laughable. It would have been like using a flamethrower to clean cobwebs out of the house.

I'd stood there, just looking at them, while they tried to tease me into fighting. I hadn't moved, or said anything, or done anything. I just stood there in a wall of silence and stillness, until that silence had become heavier and heavier. They had eventually been pushed back by it, and I had simply walked past them.

And I was doing the same thing again, letting the silence fuel their uncertainty.

I met Ebenezar's gaze, and we both smiled faintly in acknowledgment of the memory.

'Well, gentlemen,' Ebenezar said, turning to face the Wardens. 'You've heard the will of the Council, such as it is. But you should be advised that since you'd be doing something foolish at the behest of someone acting foolish, I won't be assisting you.'

Mai's head snapped around to focus on Ebenezar. 'McCoy!'

Ebenezar bowed his head to her. 'Wizard Mai, I would advise you not to seek a quarrel with the young man. He's a fair hand in a fight.'

The old woman lifted her chin haughtily. 'He was not truly your apprentice. You kept watch over him for a mere two years.'

'And came to know him,' Ebenezar said. He turned to eye Listens-to-Wind. 'What did that raccoon pup you had think of him? You go on about what good judges of character young animals can be. Is he the sort of man who would involve himself in that kind of plot? You know the answer.'

Listens-to-Wind shook his head tiredly. 'It isn't about that and you know it.'

'If you do not assist us in subduing him,' Mai said, her voice crisp and thrumming with tension, 'it could be considered treason, Wizard McCoy.'

'I am assisting you,' Ebenezar said. 'By advising you to avoid conflict.' He paused and said, 'You might try asking him.'

'Excuse me?' Mai said.

'Asking him,' Ebenezar said. He hooked a thumb in one strap of his overalls. 'Ask him politely to come with you back to Edinburgh. Maybe he'd cooperate.'

'Don't bother, sir,' I said. 'I won't.'

'Ancient Mai,' rumbled Warden Bjork. 'If you would please return to the boat, we will see to this.'

I remained just as I'd been standing, and hoped that the others would be arriving soon. I didn't want to start up the dance music until everyone had taken the floor, but if the Wardens pressed me, I might need to.

'Ancient Mai,' Warden Yorgi repeated. 'Do you wish us to—'

He didn't get to finish the phrase before there was a deafening roar and a helicopter swept over the hillside behind us, flying about an inch and a half above the treetops. It soared past us and then banked around in a turn over the lake, only to return and hover thirty feet above the shoreline, maybe a hundred yards away.

In the movies, special forces guys come zipping down on lines. I've even been the guy on a line once, sort of, though I was more sack of meal than Navy SEAL. But when the people jumping off the helicopter are vampires, you don't bother with a lot of lines.

Or any lines. At all.

Three figures in white leapt from the hovering chopper, neatly flipped once on the way down, and landed together in a dancer's crouch. Then they all rose, the movement as beautiful, smooth, and coordinated as anything you'd see at the Cirque du Soleil.

Lara and her two sisters walked toward us, and they were good at it. Lara was wearing a white sundress that showed off her curves, with two black leather belts that crossed on her hips. A handgun in a holster hung from one of the belts. The other belt supported a sword, a genuine rapier whose worn handle looked as if it had seen actual use. Her long black hair was pulled up in a net, and the top of her head was covered in a white cloth, a very Gypsy sort of look. She wore a choker made of pure platinum, the metal seeming to hold its own glow, even in the failing light, and a single large bloodred ruby hung from it.

As she walked, it was impossible not to notice the gorgeously feminine curves of her body, the casual sway of her hips from side to side, each movement emphasizing the fact that she carried deadly weapons. And, since it was raining on her white dress, it was impossible not to notice a whole lot of other things about Lara – such as the fact that other than the weapons and her shoes, it was all she was wearing.

I concentrated on keeping my tongue from hanging down past my chin, and forced my eyes to look elsewhere.

Her sisters were wearing much different gear. Though they also wore white, they had both donned what looked like motorcycle leathers – not like archetypical American bikers, but more like the gear you see professional racing motorcyclists wearing. It looked very high-tech, and was obviously armored. In standard gear, the armor was heavy plastic, there to protect the rider in the event of a collision or a fall. I was willing to bet that it had been upgraded to something a lot stronger in the Raiths' gear. They, too, were equipped with sidearms of both the past and present. Their hair was tied up and back, and like Lara, their skin was pale, their eyes were wide and grey, their lips dark and inviting.

I watched the three Raith sisters come and thought to myself that if there was any justice in the universe, I would get to watch that in slow motion.

Alas.

Out of the corner of my eye, I saw Mai calmly lift a hand to Warden Berserkergang, motioning him to stand down. It didn't surprise me. Ancient Mai had very strong notions of proper behavior and how it ought to be followed. She would never condone observable division amongst members of the Council where outsiders could witness it.

Lara stopped twenty feet away, and her sisters stopped a couple of feet behind her. Their eyes were on the Wardens, who returned the vampires' stares with calm attention.

'Harry,' she said, her voice warm, as if we'd just run into one another at a soiree. 'You are a wicked, wicked man. You didn't tell me I'd have to share you with others tonight.'

'What can I say?' I asked, turning to face Lara. I smiled at her and bowed my head without taking my eyes off her. It was a more enjoyable paranoia than I'd observed for the Wardens, if no less wary. 'I used to be a trusting, gentle soul, but the rigors of the cruel world have made me cynical and cautious.'

Lara looked from the Wardens to me, her expression

speculative. Then she gave them a smile that could have melted plate steel and walked to me, somehow making a swagger look perfectly feminine. She extended both hands to me as she came.

I smiled in return, though mine was a lot stiffer and more artificial, and whispered, through my smiling teeth, 'You have got to be kidding.'

She cast her eyes down demurely, toning the smile down to a smirk, and breathed, 'Be nice to me, wizard mine, and I'll return the favor.'

I don't think I hesitated very long before I offered her my hands in return. We clasped them. Her fingers were silken-smooth and very cold. She smiled radiantly and inclined her head to me, a slow, graceful, formal gesture.

Then, faster than I could blink, much less move, she smacked me in the kisser.

She used her open hand, which prevented the blow from being a lethal one. Even so, it hit like a club. It knocked me several steps back, spinning me as I went, and I wound up caught in a drunken corkscrew that ended with my ass hitting the ground ten feet away.

'Once again you have *lied* to us,' Lara snarled. '*Used* us. I have had my fill of your deceits, wizard.'

I sat there with my mouth open, wondering if my jaw would start wobbling bonelessly in the rising breeze.

Fury radiated from her in a cold sphere, and every fiber of her body looked ready to do violence. She faced me with the members of the Council on her left, the darkness of the forest on her right. I focused on my shield bracelet, certain that there was every possibility that she might be about to draw her gun and plug me.

'If my brother is not returned to me whole this night,'

she continued, her voice cold and deadly, 'there will be blood between us and my honor will not be satisfied until one of us lies dead on the dueling ground.'

And then she winked at me with her right eye.

'Do you understand?' she demanded.

'Uh,' I said, trying to move my jaw. It was apparently whole. 'Yeah. Message received.'

'Arrogant child.' She spat on the ground in my direction. Then she turned and walked purposefully toward the Senior Council members. She stopped about ten feet from Ancient Mai, just before the Wardens standing behind her would have snapped and started hurling thunder and fury. She came to a graceful stance of attention, and then bowed, rather deeply, to Ancient Mai.

Mai's face revealed nothing. She returned the gesture, bowing less deeply.

'It is a pleasure to meet you in the flesh,' Lara said. 'You must be Ancient Mai.'

'Lara Raith,' Mai replied. 'I had not anticipated your presence at this meeting.'

'Nor I yours.' She gave me a rather disgusted glance. 'Courtesy, it seems, is a devalued commodity in this world.' She bowed again, to Ebenezar and Listens-to-Wind, and greeted them by name. 'Your reputations, gentlemen, precede you.'

Injun Joe nodded without speaking.

'Lady Raith,' Ebenezar said, calmly. 'Touch that boy again and the only things left for your kin to bury will be your five-hundred-dollar shoes.'

'Ai ya,' Ancient Mai said in a flat tone.

Lara paused at Ebenezar's statement. It didn't rattle her, precisely, but she gave Ebenezar another look and then inclined her head to him. 'Gentlemen, lady. Obviously we both have urgent concerns that must be addressed. Equally obviously, none of us anticipated the presence of the other, and a violent incident would benefit no one. On behalf of the White Court, I propose a formal agreement of nonaggression for the duration of this meeting.'

Ancient Mai gave Ebenezar a hard look, then lifted her chin slightly and turned away, somehow giving the impression that she had formally dismissed him from reality. 'Agreed,' she said. 'On behalf of the Council, I accept the proposal.'

I managed to stagger back to verticality. My wounded head felt like Lara had split it open, and I'd have a hand-shaped bruise on my cheek, but I wasn't going to sit there moaning about getting slapped by a girl. Granted, the girl was hundreds of years old and could change a fire truck's tires without using a jack, but there was a principle at work here. I got to my feet and then walked carefully over to stand beside Ebenezar, facing the vampires. One of the Wardens there made a little room for me, all his attention focused forward on Lara and her sisters.

Heh. They were much more comfortable with me when I was aimed at an enemy. I tried to keep a running portion of my awareness focused on Demonreach. I had done as much as I could in assembling this group. I was counting on my estimate of the killer to take it to the next level, and until he showed up, I had to keep stringing both Lara and the Council along.

The best way to do that, for the moment, was to keep quiet and let them talk.

'I suppose the first thing we must do is share knowledge,'

Lara said to Ancient Mai. 'Would you prefer it if I went first?'

Mai considered that for a moment and then bowed her head in a slight acknowledgment.

Lara proceeded without further ado. 'My brother, Thomas Raith, has been taken by a skinwalker, one of the ancient naagloshii. The skinwalker has offered an exchange. My brother for Warden Donald Morgan.'

Mai tilted her head to one side. 'How is Dresden involved in this matter?'

'He claims that he is attempting to establish Warden Morgan's innocence in some sort of matter internal to the Council. As a gesture of goodwill to the Council and to help keep the peace within Chicago, I have instructed my brother to offer reasonably low-risk aid and assistance to Dresden.' She glanced at me. 'He has abused my good intentions repeatedly. This time, he somehow involved my brother in his investigation, and Thomas was ambushed by the skinwalker.'

'And that is all?' Mai asked.

Lara glared at me again, and seemed to visibly force herself to take a moment to think. 'He claims that a third party was behind Warden Morgan's predicament, and attempting to set the Court against the Council. To my surprise, my own investigation did not immediately disprove his statements as lies. It seems possible that one of my financial managers may have been somehow coerced into embezzling the contents of a considerable account. Dresden claims the money was sent to an account that was made to appear to belong to Warden Morgan.'

Mai nodded. 'Was it?'

Lara shrugged elegantly. 'It is possible. My people are

working to find evidence that will establish what happened more precisely.'

Mai nodded and was still for several seconds before she said, 'Despite how carefully you have danced around the subject, you know exactly why we are here.'

Lara smiled very slightly.

'The tale Dresden tells us lacks the credibility of simplicity,' Mai continued. 'Despite how carefully you have danced around saying the actual words, it seems that you wish us to believe that the White Court was not involved in the matter of LaFortier's death. Thus, your story, too, lacks the credibility of simplicity.'

'In my experience, matters of state are rarely simple ones,' Lara responded.

Mai moved a hand, a tiny gesture that somehow conveyed acknowledgment. 'Yet given recent history, the actions of a known enemy seem a far more likely source for LaFortier's murder than those of some nameless, face-less third party.'

'Of course. You are, after all, wizards,' Lara said without a detectable trace of irony. 'You are the holders of great secrets. If such a group existed, you would surely know of it.'

'It is possible that I am unfairly judging your people in accusing them of plotting LaFortier's death,' Mai replied, her voice utterly tranquil. 'You are, after all, vampires, and well-known for your forthright and gentle natures.'

Lara inclined her head, smiling faintly. 'Regardless, we find ourselves here.'

'That seems incontrovertible.'

'I seek the safe return of my brother.'

Mai shook her head firmly, once. 'The White Council will not exchange one of our own.'

'It seems to me,' Lara said, 'that Warden Morgan is not in your company.'

'A transitory situation,' Mai said. She didn't look at me, but I felt sure that the steel in her voice was aimed in my direction.

'Then perhaps a cooperative effort,' Lara said. 'We need not allow the skinwalker to *take* the Warden.'

'Those who ally themselves with the White Court come to regret it,' Mai replied. 'The Council has no obligation to assist you or your brother.'

'Despite the recent efforts made on your behalf by my King and his Court?' Lara asked.

Mai faced her without blinking and said nothing more.

'He is my blood,' Lara said quietly. 'I will have him returned.'

'I appreciate your loyalty,' Mai said, in a tone that suggested she didn't. 'However, this matter of the skinwalker wishing an exchange is hardly germane to where we stand at the moment.'

'Actually,' I said. 'It kind of is, Ancient Mai. I had someone tell Shagnasty where to meet me tonight. Depending on how he crosses the water, he could be here any moment.'

Ebenezar blinked. Then he turned his face to me, his expression clearly asking whether or not I was out of my damned mind.

'Wile E. Coyote,' I said to him soberly. 'Suuuuuuper Genius.'

I saw him thinking and I recognized it when my old mentor got it, when he understood my plan. I could tell because he got that look on his face I've only seen when he knows things are about to go spectacularly wrong and he wants to be ready for it. He let his staff fall to rest against his chest and idly dug in a pocket, his eyes flicking across the woods around us.

I don't know where Mai's head was, or if she worked out anything at all. I had a feeling that she wouldn't. Since her thought processes would all have to start from given assumptions that were incorrect, she didn't have much of a chance of coming to a correct conclusion.

'All that means,' she said to me, 'is that it would be wise to finish our business here and retreat from this place.'

'Sadly, I am reaching a similar conclusion,' Lara said deliberately. 'Perhaps it is time for this meeting to adjourn.'

Behind her, one of her sisters shifted one hand very slightly.

Lightning flashed overhead, and thunder forced a pause into the conversation. The wind picked up again, and Listens-to-Wind suddenly lifted his head. His gaze snapped around to the north, and his eyes narrowed.

An instant later, I sensed a new presence on the island. More people had just touched down onto the far side of the bald hill where Demonreach Tower stood. There were twelve of them, and they began moving toward the hilltop at inhuman speed. White Court vampires, they had to be.

Seconds later, another pair of humanlike presences simply *appeared* in the woods four hundred yards away. And if that wasn't enough, two *more* people arrived on the northwest shore of the island.

Mai took immediate note of Injun Joe's expression and tilted her head, staring hard at Lara. 'What have you done?' she demanded.

'I have signaled my family,' Lara replied calmly. 'I did not come here to fight you, Ancient Mai. But I *will* recover my brother.'

I focused on the two smaller groups, both of them pairs of new presences, and found that their numbers were growing. On the beach, many, many more pairs of feet had begun beating the ground of Demonreach, thirty of them or more. In the forest nearby, a presence that the island had never before encountered appeared, followed by more and more and more of the same.

There was only one explanation for that – the new arrivals were calling forth muscle from the Nevernever. I was betting that the pair on the beach was Madeline and Binder, and that he had begun calling out his grey men the moment his feet hit the ground. The two who had simply appeared in the forest had to have taken a Way and emerged from the Nevernever onto the island directly. It was possible a second summoning like Binder's was under way, but I thought it far more likely that someone had gathered up support and brought it with them, through the Way.

Meanwhile, Mai and Lara were beginning to bare their claws.

'Is that a threat, vampire?' Mai said in a flat tone.

'I would prefer that you regard it as a truth,' Lara replied, her own tone losing the charm and conviviality it had contained in some measure throughout the conversation.

The Wardens behind me started getting nervous. I could feel it, both for myself and through Demonreach. I heard leather creak as hands were put to the grips of holstered guns and upon hilts of swords.

Lara, in response, rested her fingertips lightly upon her own weapons. Her two sisters did the same.

'Wait!' I snapped. 'Wait!'

Everyone turned to look at me. I must have looked like a raving madman, standing there with my eyes half focused, looking back and forth out of pure instinct and force of habit as the island's intellectus informed me of the rapidly transpiring events. The White Court reinforcements had bypassed the tower hill and were headed for the beach to support Lara – which was something, at least. Lara's helicopter hadn't dropped them up there specifically to look for Morgan. It must have come up low, from the north, using the terrain of the hilltop to mask the sound of its arrival.

I forced my attention back to the scene around me. 'Holy crap. I knew this would put the pressure on him. But this guy's gone to war.'

'What?' Listens-to-Wind asked. 'What are you talking about?'

'Don't start in on one another!' I snapped. 'Lara, we need to work together or we're all dead.'

She turned her head a little to one side, staring at me. 'Why?'

'Because better than a hundred – one hundred ten, now – beings have just arrived at different points of the island and they aren't here to cater the little mixer we've got going. There are only nine of us and fifteen of you. We're outnumbered five to one. *Six* to one, now.'

Mai stared at me. '*What?*'

Howls slithered into the air, muffled by the falling rain, but were made all the more eerie by the lack of direction to them. I recognized them at once – Binder's grey men. They were coming, moving with mindless purpose that cared nothing for the danger of a forest at night.

The second group was nearer. They'd stopped growing at a hundred and twenty-five, and were already on the move toward us. They weren't as fast as the grey men, but they were moving steadily and spreading out into an enormous curved line meant to sweep the forest and then encircle their quarry when they found it. Red light began to pour through the trees in their direction, casting eerie black shadows and turning the rain to blood.

I forced myself to think, to ask Demonreach the right questions. A second's consideration revealed that the two forces would converge on us at exactly the same time – they were working together.

The numbers disadvantage was too great. The Wardens might get some spells off, and the Senior Council members would probably leave mounds of corpses piled around them – but outnumbered six to one, on a dark night, when they would have trouble seeing their targets before they were within a few steps, they wouldn't prevail. The large group would hit them from one side, and the smaller one would come from the other, boxing us in.

Unless . . .

Unless we could get to one of the two groups first and eliminate it before its partner reached us and hit us from behind.

Outnumbered as hideously as we were, the smartest thing would have been to run like hell – but I knew that no one would. The Council still had to recover Morgan. Lara still had to recover Thomas. Neither of them enjoyed the advantage I did. To them, the danger was only a vague threat, some howls in the dark, and it would remain so until it was too *late* to run.

Which left us only one option.

We had to attack.

The grey men howled again, from much closer.

I gave Ebenezar a desperate glance and then stepped forward, lifting my staff. 'They've got us boxed in! Our only chance is to fight our way clear! Everyone, with me!'

Lara and her sisters stared at me in confusion. The Wardens did the same – but the fear in my voice and on my face was very real, and when one human being displays a fear response, those nearby it tend to find it psychologically contagious. The Wardens' eyes immediately went to Ancient Mai.

I started jogging, beckoning as I went, and Ebenezar immediately fell in with me. 'You heard the man!' Ebenezar roared. 'Wardens, let's move!'

At his bellow, the dam broke, and the Wardens surged forward to join us.

Lara stared at me for another half a second, and then cried, 'Go, go!' to her sisters. They began running with us, effortlessly keeping pace, their motion so graceful and light that it hardly seemed possible that they would leave footprints.

I looked over my shoulder as I slowly increased the pace. Ancient Mai had turned toward the hateful red glare coming from the forest to the south, facing it calmly. 'Wizard Listens-to-Wind, with me. Let us see if we can slow the progress of whatever is coming this way.'

Injun Joe went to her side, and the two of them stood there, gathering their will and muttering to each other.

I consulted Demonreach for the best route to follow toward the enemy, put my head down, and charged the demons that were coming to kill us, Wardens and vampires alike at my side.

42

Adrenaline does weird things to your head. You hear people talk about how everything slows down. That isn't the case. *Nothing* is happening slowly. It's just that you somehow seem to be able to fit a whole lot more thinking into the time and space that's there. It might *feel* like things have slowed down, but it's a transitory illusion.

For example, I had time to reflect upon the nature of adrenaline and time while sprinting through the woods at night. It didn't make me run any faster, though. Although if I wasn't actually moving my arms and legs faster than normal, then why was I twenty feet ahead of everyone else, the vampires included?

I heard someone curse in the dark behind me as they tripped over an exposed root. I didn't trip. It wasn't that I had become more graceful – I just knew where to put my feet. It was as if every step I took was over a path that I had walked so many times that it had become ingrained in my muscle memory. I knew when to duck out of the way of a low-hanging branch, when to bound forward at an angle to my last step in order to clear an old stump, exactly how much I needed to shorten a quick pair of steps so that I could leap a sinkhole by pushing off my stronger leg. Lara Raith herself was hard-pressed to keep pace with me, though she managed to close to within three or four yards, her pale skin all but glowing in the dark.

The whole time, I tried to keep track of the position of the enemy. It wasn't a simple matter. I didn't have a big map of the island in my head, with glowing dots marking their positions. I just *knew* where they were, as long as I concentrated on keeping track of them, but as the number of enemies continued to increase, it got harder to keep track.

The nearest of the hostile presences was about forty yards away when I lifted my fingers to my lips and let out a sharp whistle. 'Out there, in front of me!' I shouted. 'Now, Toot!'

It had been an enormous pain in the ass to wrap fireworks in plastic to waterproof them against the rain, and even more of a pain to make sure that a waterproof match was attached to each of the rockets, Roman candles, and miniature mortars. When I had Molly and Will scatter them around the woods in twenty separate positions, I'd gotten those 'Is he crazy?' looks from both of them.

After all, it isn't as if fireworks are heavy-duty weaponry, capable of inflicting grievous bodily harm and wholesale destruction. They're just loud and bright and distracting.

Which, under the circumstances, was more or less all I needed.

Toot-toot and half a dozen members of the Guard came streaking out of nowhere, miniature comets flashing through the vertical shadows of the trees. They went zipping ahead, alighting on low branches, and then tiny lights flickered as waterproof matches were set to fuses. A second later, a tiny shrill trumpet shrieked from somewhere ahead of us, and a dozen Roman candles began shooting balls of burning chemicals out into the darkness, illuminating the crouched running forms of at least ten of

Binder's grey men in their cheap suits, not fifty feet away. They froze at the sudden appearance of the flashing pyrotechnics, attempting to assess them as threats and determine where they were coming from.

Perfect.

I dropped to one knee, lifting my blasting rod, as the human-seeming demons shrieked at the sudden appearance of the bright lights. I trained it on the nearest hesitating grey man, slammed my will down through the wooden haft, and snarled, '*Fuego!*'

It was more difficult to do than it would have been if it hadn't been raining, but it was more than up to the task. A javelin of red-gold flame hissed through the rain, leaving a trail of white steam behind it. It touched the nearest of the grey men on one flank, and his cheap suit went up as readily as if it was lined with tar instead of rayon.

The grey man yawled and began thrashing furiously. The fire engulfed him, throwing out light for a good thirty yards in every direction, and illuminating his companions.

I dropped flat, and an instant later the forest behind me belched forth power and death.

Guns roared on full automatic fire. That would be the Raiths. Lara and her sisters' sidearms had been modified submachine guns, with an enlarged ammunition clip. Given the superhuman strength, perception, and coordination the vampires had at their disposal, they didn't suffer the same difficulties a human shooter would have faced, running at full speed in the dark, firing a weapon meant to be braced by a shooter's entire upper body in one hand – and their left hands at that. Bullets chewed into three different grey men, ten or eleven rounds each, all of them hitting between the neck and temple, blasting the demons back to ectoplasm.

Then it was the Wardens' turn.

Fire was the weapon of choice when it came to combat magic. Though it was taxing upon the will and physical stamina of the wizard, it got a lot of energy concentrated into a relatively small space. It illuminated darkness, something that was nearly always to a wizard's advantage – and it *hurt*. Every living thing had at least a healthy respect, if not an outright fear of fire. Even more to the point, fire was a purifying force in its nonphysical aspect. Dark magic could be consumed and destroyed by fire when used with that intent.

The Wardens used the zipping little fireballs from the Roman candles and my own improvised funeral pyre to target their own spells, and then the *real* fireworks started.

Each individual wizard has his own particular quirks when it comes to how he uses his power. There is no industrial standard for how fire is evoked into use in battle. One of the Wardens coming up behind me sent forth a stream of tiny stars that slewed through the night like machine-gun fire, effortlessly burning holes through trees, rocks, and grey men with equal disdain. Another sent a stream of fire up in a high arc, and it crashed down among several grey men, splashing and clinging to any moving thing it struck like napalm. Lances of scarlet and blue and green fire burned through the air, reminding me for a mad moment of a scene from a *Star Wars* movie. Steam hissed and snarled everywhere, as a swath of woodland forty yards across and half as deep vanished into light and fury.

Hell's bells. I mean, I'd seen Wardens at work before, but it had all been fairly precise, controlled work. This was pure destruction, wholesale, industrial-strength, and the heat of it was so intense that it sucked the air out of my lungs.

The grey men, though, weren't impressed. Either they weren't bright enough to attempt to preserve their own existence or they just didn't care. They scattered as they advanced, spreading out. Some of them rushed forward, low to the ground and half hidden by the brush. Others bounded into the trees and came leaping and swinging forward, branch by branch. Still more of them darted to the sides, out of the harsh glare of the fires, spreading out around us.

'Toot!' I screamed over the roaring chaos. 'Go after the flankers!'

A tiny trumpet added its own notes to the din, and the Pizza Patrol zipped out into the woods, two or three of the little faeries working together to carry fresh Roman candles. They gleefully kept on with the fireworks, sending the little sulfurous balls of flame chasing the grey men trying to slip around us through the shadows, marking their positions.

Lara let out a piercing call and came up to my side, gun in hand, snapping off snarling bursts every time a target presented itself. I pointed to either side and said, 'They're getting around us! We've got to stop them from taking Mai and Injun Joe from behind!'

Lara's eyes snapped left and right, and she said something to her sisters in ancient Etruscan, the tongue of the White Court. One of them went in either direction, vanishing into the dark.

A grey man came crashing out of the flame twenty feet away from me, blazing like a grease fire. He showed absolutely no concern for the flame. He just sprinted forward and leapt at me, hands spread wide. I made it up to my knees and braced one end of my quarterstaff against the ground, aiming the other at the grey man's center of mass. The staff struck it, but not squarely. It twisted to one side at the impact, bounced off the ground, took a fraction of a second to reorient itself on me—

And erupted into a cloud of ectoplasm as rounds from Lara's gun took its head apart.

The next attacker was already on the way, out in the darkness beyond the firelight. I came to my feet and on pure instinct snapped off another blast of fire at the empty air twenty feet beyond Lara and about ten feet up. There was nothing there as I released the blast, and I knew it, but as the fire hissed through the falling rain, it illuminated the form of a grey man in the midst of a spectacular leap that would have ended at the small of Lara's back. The blast struck him and hammered him to one side so that he came down like a burning jet, crashing across a dozen yards of ground before dissolving into flame-licked mounds of swiftly vanishing transparent jelly.

Lara didn't see the attacker until he'd tumbled past. 'Oh,' she said, her voice conversational. 'That was gentlemanly of you, Dresden.'

'I've been known to pull out chairs and open doors, too,' I said.

'How very unfashionable,' Lara said, her pale eyes gleaming. 'And endearing.'

Ebenezar stumped up to us, staff in hand, his eyes narrow and flickering all around us while Wardens continued to send blasts of power hammering into targets. Off in the woods behind us, submachine guns chattered.

Apparently Lara's sisters were still hunting the grey men who had gotten around us.

'We've got one Warden down,' Ebenezar said.

'How bad?'

'One of those things came out of a tree above her and tore her head off,' he said.

I tracked a slight motion in a nearby treetop and swiveled to point a finger. 'Sir, up there!'

Ebenezar grunted a word, reached out a hand, and made a sharp, pulling motion. The grey man who had been clambering toward us was seized by an unseen force, ripped out of the tree, and sent sailing on an arc that would land it in Lake Michigan a quarter of a mile from the nearest shore.

'Where is the second group?' Ebenezar asked.

I thought about it. 'They're at the dock, at the edge of the trees. They're closing on Mai and Injun Joe.' I glanced at Lara. 'I think the vampires have been holding them off.'

Ebenezar spat a curse. 'That summoner is still out there somewhere. His pets won't last long in this rain, but we can't afford to give him time to call up more. Can you find him?'

I checked. There was so much confusion and motion on the island that Demonreach had trouble distinguishing one being from another, but I had a solid if nonspecific idea of where Binder was. 'Yeah.' I sensed more movement and pointed behind us, to where a trio of grey men had managed to close on a pair of Wardens who were standing on either side of a still, red-spattered form on the ground. 'There!'

Ebenezar stopped talking to make another swift gesture, spoke a word, and one of the approaching grey men was suddenly and *literally* pounded flat by an invisible anvil. Ectoplasmic ichor flew everywhere. The two Wardens, warned by the magical strike and now facing even odds, made short work of the remaining two.

Ebenezar turned back to me and said, 'Shut down that summoner, Hoss. I'm taking the Wardens back to support Injun Joe and Mai. Let's go, vampire.'

'No,' Lara said. 'If Binder is nearby, then so is my sweet cousin Madeline. I'll stay with Dresden.'

Ebenezar didn't argue with her. He just snarled, made a fist, and lifted it up, and Lara let out a short, choking cry and rose up ten feet into the air, her arms and legs snapping down straight, locking her body into a rigid board.

I put a hand against his chest. 'Wait!'

He glanced at me from beneath shaggy grey brows.

'Let her down. She can come along.' Ebenezar had no way of knowing that I wasn't out there alone. Georgia and Will were lurking nearby, and could be at my side in a couple of seconds if necessary. Between the two of them, they had accounted for three grey men, too. I tried to put that knowledge behind a very slight emphasis in my tone and told him, 'I'll be fine.'

Ebenezar frowned at me, then shot a glance out at the woods and gave me a reluctant nod. He turned back to Lara and released her from the grip of his will. She didn't quite manage to fall gracefully, and landed in a sprawl that gave me a great look at her long, intriguingly lovely legs. The old man eyed her and said, 'You just remember what I told you, missy.'

She rose to her feet, her expression unreadable – but I knew her well enough to know that she was furious. My old mentor had just insulted her on multiple levels, not the least of which was pointing out to her exactly how easy it would be for him to make good on his previous threat. 'I'll remember,' she said, her tone frosty.

'Wardens!' Ebenezar said. 'On me!' The old man broke into a woodsman's lope, a shuffle-footed, loose-kneed gait that managed unpredictable terrain well and covered ground with deceptive speed. The four remaining Wardens fell into a wedge shape behind him and they moved out heading south, back toward the docks and the confrontation with whoever had come forth from the Nevernever with his own army.

Lara turned to me and nodded her head once, gesturing me to lead. I tried to fix Binder's presence firmly in mind, and was certain he was ahead of us and to the north, probably trying to circle widely around the scene of the battle with his minions. I started out through the woods again, pushing myself to move faster.

This time, Lara stayed close behind me. She mimicked my movements, down to the length of my stride, taking advantage of my instinctive knowledge of Demonreach.

'I have little interest in this mercenary,' she said to me as we ran. She wasn't even breathing hard. 'Do with him as you would. But Madeline is mine.'

'She might know something,' I said.

'I can't believe anyone with half a mind would entrust her with knowledge of any importance.'

'And I can't believe the treacherous bitch wouldn't steal every bit of information she could find to use against whoever she's working with,' I replied, glancing back.

Lara didn't dispute the statement, but her eyes hardened like silver mirrors, reflecting the dancing flames that were still burning here and there as we moved through the site of the battle and out the other side. 'Madeline has betrayed me, my House, and my Court. She is mine. I prefer you remained a living, breathing ally. You will not interfere.'

What do you say to something like that? I shut my mouth and concentrated on finding Binder.

It took us about five minutes to reach the piece of shoreline where Binder and his companion had come ashore. A pair of Jet Skis lay discarded on the beach. So that's how they'd done it. The tiny craft would have no problems at all skimming over the stone reefs surrounding the island, though they would have been hellish to ride in the rough water.

We swung past the discarded equipment and up a little ridgeline, running along a deer trail. I knew we were getting close, and suddenly Lara accelerated past me, supernaturally fleet of foot on the even ground.

I don't know what triggered the explosion. It might have been a tripwire stretched across the trail. It's possible that it was detonated manually, too. There was a flash of light, and something hit me in the chest hard enough to knock me down. An ugly asymmetrical shape was burned into my vision as I lay on my back, trying to sort out what had just happened.

Then my body tingled, and Madeline Raith appeared over me. I realized that she was straddling me. There was a fire burning somewhere close by, illuminating her. She was wearing a black surfer's wet suit with short arms and legs, unzipped past her navel. She held a mostly empty bottle of tequila in one hand. Her eyes were wide and shining with a disorienting riot of colors as she leaned down and kissed me on the forehead and . . .

And Hell's freaking bells.

The pleasure that surged through me from that simple touch was delicious to the point of pain. Every nerve ending in my entire body lit up, as though someone had run up the wattage on my pleasure centers, or injected their engines with nitrous. I felt my body arch up and shudder, a purely sexual reaction to a physical bliss that went far beyond sexuality. I stayed that way, locked into a quivering arch of ecstasy. It took maybe ten or fifteen seconds to subside.

From a *kiss* on the *forehead*.

God. No wonder people came back to the vampires for more.

I could barely register what was happening around me. So I only dimly noticed when Madeline produced a gun of her own, the other favorite model of those with more than human strength – a Desert Eagle.

'Good night, sweet wizard,' Madeline purred, her hips grinding a slow rhythm against mine. She drew the half-inch-wide mouth of the gun over my cheek as she took a slug of tequila and then rested the gun's barrel gently on the spot she'd just kissed. It felt obscenely good, like a caress on skin that has just been shaved smooth but hasn't yet been touched. I knew that she was about to kill me, but I couldn't stop thinking how *good* it felt. 'And flights of angels,' she panted, her breath coming faster, her eyes alight with excitement, 'sing thee to thy rest.'

43

I was still sorting things out after the titanic wallop the explosion had given the inside of my skull, when a dark-furred wolf emerged from the shadows of the night and slammed into Madeline Raith like a loaded armored car. I *heard* bones breaking under the impact, and she was ripped off me by the force of the dark wolf's rush.

Will didn't stop there. He'd already hammered her once, and he knew better than to try his strength infighting with a vampire, even if the members of the White Court were physically the weakest of the breed. He hit the ground and bounded away into the dark.

Madeline screamed in surprised rage, and her gun went off several times, but I'm not sure you could call it shooting. She was on her knees, firing that big old Desert Eagle with one delicate hand and holding the now-broken tequila bottle in the other when a sandy brown wolf swept by on silent paws and ripped at Madeline's weapon hand with her fangs. The rip went deep into the muscles and tendons of Madeline's forearm, an almost surgically precise attack. The gun tumbled from her fingers, and she whirled to swing the broken bottle at Georgia, but she was no more eager for a fair fight than Will had been, and by the time Madeline turned, Georgia was already bounding away – and Will, unnoticed, was on his way back in again.

Fangs flashed. Pale Raith blood flowed. The two wolves rushed back and forth in perfect rhythm, never giving the vampire a chance to pin one of them down. When Madeline finally realized how they were working her, she attempted to reverse herself suddenly the same instant Georgia began to retreat, to meet Will's rush squarely – but Will and Georgia had learned their trade from a real wolf, and they'd had eight years of what amounted to low-intensity but deadly earnest combat duty, defending several square blocks around the University from the depredations of both supernatural and mortal predators. They knew when the reverse was coming, and Georgia simply pirouetted on her paws and blindsided Madeline again.

The vampire screamed in frustrated rage. She was furious – and she was slowing down. The members of the White Court were flesh and blood beings. They bled. Bleed them enough, and they would die.

I forced myself to start using my head again, finally shaking off the effects of both Madeline's psychotically delicious kiss and the concussion of whatever had exploded. I realized that I was covered with small cuts and scratches, that I was otherwise fine, and that Binder was less than twenty feet away.

'Will, Georgia!' I screamed. 'Gun!'

The wolves leapt out of sight and vanished into the forest with barely a leaf disturbed by their movements, half a second before Binder came out of the woods, a semi-automatic assault shotgun pressed against his shoulder. The mercenary was dressed in a wet suit as well, though he'd put on a combat jacket and equipment harness over it, and wore combat boots on his feet.

Binder aimed the weapon after Will and Georgia and started rapidly hammering the woods with shells, more or less at random.

Everyone thinks that shotgun pellets spread out to some ridiculous degree, and that if you aim a shotgun at a garage door and pull the trigger, you'll be able to drive a car through the resulting hole. That isn't so, even when a shotgun has a very, very short barrel, which allows the load of pellets to spread out more. A longer-barreled weapon, like Binder's, will only spread the pellets out to about the size of my spread fingers at a hundred or a hundred and fifty yards. Odds were good that he hadn't hit a damned thing, and given his experience he probably knew it. He must have kept up the salvo to increase the intimidation factor and force the wolves to stay on the run.

In the heat and adrenaline of a battle, gunshots can be hard to count, but I knew he fired eight times. I knew because through Demonreach, I could feel the eight brass and plastic shell casings lying on the ground around him. He stood protectively over Madeline as he reached into his pockets, presumably to reload the weapon with fresh shells.

I didn't give him the chance. I pulled my .44 out of my duster pocket, sat up, and tried to stop wobbling. I sighted on his center mass and pulled the trigger.

The revolver roared, and Binder's left leg flew out from beneath him as if someone had hit it with a twenty-pound mallet. He let out a yelp of what sounded more like surprise than pain and hit the ground hard. In the odd little beat of heavy silence that came after the shot, I almost felt sorry for the guy. He'd had a tough couple of days. I heard him suck in a quick breath and clench his teeth over a howl of pain.

Madeline whirled toward me, her dark hair gone stringy and flat in the rain. Her eyes burned pure white, as the hunger, the demon inside her, fed her more and more of its power and asserted more and more control. Her wet suit had been torn open in several places, and paler-than-human blood smeared her paler-than-human flesh. She wasn't moving as well as she should have been, but she stalked toward me in a hunter's crouch, deliberate and steady.

My bells were still ringing hard, and I didn't think I had time or focus to pull together a spell. And besides, my gun was already right there. It seemed like it would be a waste not to use it.

I sighted on the spot where Madeline's heart should have been and shot her in the belly, which wasn't terrible marksmanship under the circumstances. She cried out and staggered to one knee. Then she looked up, her empty white eyes furious, and stood up, continuing toward me.

I shot again and missed, then repeated myself. I gripped the gun with both hands, clenching my teeth as I did, knowing I only had two more rounds. The next shot ripped a piece of meat the size of a racquetball out of one of her biceps, sending her down to one knee and drawing another scream.

Before she could start moving again, I aimed and fired the last round.

It hit her in the sternum, almost exactly between her wet suit-contoured breasts. She jerked, her breath exploding from her in a little huff of surprise. She swayed, her eyelids fluttering, and I thought she was about to fall.

But she didn't.

The vampire's empty white eyes focused on me, and her mouth spread into a maniac's sneer. She reached down and picked up her own fallen weapon. She had to do it left-handed. The right was covered in a sheet of blood and flopped limply.

Running low on options, I threw my empty gun at her face. She batted my revolver aside with the Desert Eagle.

'You,' Madeline said, her voice hollow and wheezing, 'are a bad case of herpes, wizard. You're inconvenient, embarrassing, no real threat, and you simply *will not* go away.'

'Bitch,' I replied, wittily. I still hadn't gotten my head back together. Everything's relative, right?

'Don't kill him,' Binder rasped.

Madeline shot him a look that could freeze vodka. 'What?'

Binder was sitting on the ground. His shotgun was farther away than he could reach. He must have tossed it there, because when he had fallen it was still in his hands. Binder had realized precisely how badly the fight had gone for his side, that he had been lamed and therefore probably could not escape, and he was making damned sure that he didn't look armed and dangerous. 'Death curse,' he said, breathing hard. 'He could level the island with it.'

I drew in my breath, lifted my chin, and tried to keep my eyes from slipping out of focus. 'Boom,' I said solemnly.

Madeline looked bad. One of the bullets might have opened an artery. It was hard to tell in the near-darkness. 'Perhaps you're right, Binder,' she said. 'If he was a better shot, I suppose I might be in trouble. As it is, I'm inconvenienced.' Her eyes widened slightly, and her tongue lashed quickly over her lips. 'And I need to feed if I'm to repair it.' She lowered the gun as if it had suddenly become too heavy to keep supporting. 'Don't worry, Binder,' she said. 'When he's screaming my name he won't be cursing anyone. And even if he tries it . . .' She shivered. 'I'll bet it will taste incredible.'

She came closer, all pale skin and mangled flesh, and my body suddenly went insane with lust. Stupid body. It had a lot more clout at the moment than it usually did, with my mind still reeling from the blast.

I aimed a punch at Madeline's face. She caught my hand as the weak blow came in, and kissed the inside of my wrist. Sweet silver lightning exploded up my arm and down my spine. Whatever was left of my brain went away, and the next thing I knew she was pressing her chest against mine, her mouth against mine, slowly, sensuously overbearing me.

And then a burned corpse came out of the woods.

That was all I could think of to describe it. Half the body was blacker than a hamburger that had fallen through the bars of a charcoal grill. The rest was red and purple and swollen with bruises and bloody blisters, with very, very occasional strips of pale white skin. A few wisps of dark hair were attached to her skull. I say her because technically the corpse was female, though that hardly mattered amongst all the burned and pulverized meat that smelled slightly of tequila.

The only things I really recognized were the cold silver eyes.

Lara Raith's eyes were bright with an insane rage and a terrible hunger as she snaked her bruised, swollen left arm around Madeline's windpipe, and tightened it with a horrible strength.

Madeline cried out as her head was jerked back sharply — and then she made no sound at all as the wind was trapped inside her lungs. The burned, blackened corpse that was Lara Raith dug one fire-ruined hip into Madeline's upper back, using Madeline's own spine as a fulcrum against her.

Lara spoke, and her voice was something straight from Hell. It was lower, smokier, but every bit as lovely as it ever was. 'Madeline,' she purred, 'I've wanted to do this with you since we were little girls.'

Lara's burned black right hand, withered, it seemed, down to bones and sinew, reached slowly, sensually around Madeline's straining abdomen. Slowly, very slowly, Lara sunk her fingertips into flesh, just beneath the floating rib on Madeline's left flank. Madeline's face contorted and she tried to scream.

Lara shuddered. Her shoulders twisted. And she ripped an open furrow as wide as her four fingers across Madeline's stomach, pale flesh parting, as wet red and grey *things* slithered out.

Lara's tongue emerged from her mouth, bright pink, and touched Madeline's earlobe. 'Listen to me,' she hissed. Her burned hand continued pulling things out of Madeline's body, a hideous intimacy. 'Listen to me.'

Power shuddered in those words. I felt an insane desire to rush toward Lara's ruined flesh and give her my ears, ripped off with my own fingers, if necessary.

Madeline shuddered, the strength gone out of her body. Her mouth continued trying to move, but her eyes went unfocused at the power in Lara's voice. 'For once in your life,' Lara continued, kissing Madeline's throat with her burned, broken lips, 'you are going to be useful.'

Madeline's eyes rolled back in her head, and her body sagged helplessly back against Lara.

My brain got back onto the clock. I pushed myself away from Lara and Madeline's nauseating, horribly compelling embrace. Binder was sitting with his hands over his ears, his eyes squeezed tightly shut. I grabbed him under the arms and hauled him away from the entwined Raiths, maybe fifty yards downhill, through some thick brush and around the bole of a large old hickory tree. Binder was obviously in pain as I pulled him – and he was pushing with his unwounded leg, doing his best to assist me.

'Bloody hell,' he panted, as I set him down. 'Bloody hell and brimstone.'

I staggered and sat down across from him, panting to get my breath back and to push the sight of Lara devouring Madeline out of my head. 'No kidding.'

'Some of the bloody fools I've known,' Binder said. 'Can't stop talking about how tragic they are. The poor lonely vampires. How they're just like us. Bloody idiots.'

'Yeah,' I said, my voice raw.

We sat there for a few seconds. From up the slope, there was a low, soft, and eager cry.

We shuddered and tried to look as if we hadn't heard anything.

Binder stared at me for a moment, and then said, 'Why?'

'Once Lara got going, she might not be able to stop. She'd have eaten you, too.'

'Too right,' Binder agreed fervently. 'But that ain't the question. Why?'

'Somebody has to be human.'

Binder looked at me as if I was speaking in a language he'd never been very good at, and hadn't heard in years. Then he looked sharply down and away. He nodded, without looking up, and said, 'Cheers, mate.'

'Fuck you,' I told him tiredly. 'How bad are you hit?'

'Broke the bone, I think,' he said. 'Didn't come out. Didn't hit anything too bad or I'd be gone by now.'

He'd already tied a strip of cloth tightly around the

wound. His wet suit was probably aiding it in acting as a pressure bandage.

'Who was Madeline working for?' I asked.

He shook his head. 'She didn't tell me.'

'Think,' I said. 'Think hard.'

'All I know,' he said, 'is that it was some bloke with a lot of money. I never talked to him. When she was on the phone with him, they spoke English. He wasn't a native speaker. Sounded like he'd learned it from a Continental.'

I frowned. Television has most people confident that they could identify the nationality of anyone speaking English, but in the real world, accents could be muddy as hell, especially when you learned from a non-native speaker. Try to imagine the results, for example, of a Polish man learning English from a German teaching at a Belgian university. The resulting accent would twist a linguist's brain into knots.

I eyed Binder. 'Can you get out of here on your own?'

He shivered. 'This place? I bloody well can.'

I nodded. Binder was responsible for the death of a Warden, but it wasn't as though it had been personal. I could bill that charge to Madeline Raith's corpse. 'Do business in my town or against the Council again and I'll kill you. Clear?'

'Crystal, mate. Crystal.'

I got up and started to go. I didn't have my staff, my blasting rod, or my gun. They were back up the hillside.

I'd come back for them later.

'Wait,' Binder said. He grunted and took off his belt, and I nearly kicked him in the head, thinking he was going for a weapon. Instead, he just offered the belt to me. It had a fairly normal-looking black fanny pack on it.

'What's that?' I asked him.

'Two more concussion grenades,' he said.

I put two and two together. My brain was back on the job. 'You'd rather not be holding the matches to the one that got Lara, eh?'

'Too right,' he said. I started to turn away and he touched my leg. He leaned toward me a bit and said, very quietly, 'Waterproof pocket inside has a phone in it. Boss lady had me hold it for her. It's powered off. Maybe the lady cop would find it interesting.'

I stared hard at him for a second, and an understanding passed between us. 'If this pans out,' I said, 'maybe I'll forget to mention to the Wardens that you survived.'

He nodded and sank back onto the ground. 'Never want to see you again, mate. Too right I don't.'

I snapped the belt closed and hung it across one shoulder, where I could get to the larger pouch in a hurry if I needed to. Then I got on to the next point of business – finding Will and Georgia.

They were both lying on the ground maybe sixty yards from where I'd last seen them. It looked like they'd been circling around the site of the battle with Madeline, planning on coming back in from the far side. I moved easily and soundlessly through the woods and found them on the ground, back in human form.

'Will,' I hissed quietly.

He lifted his head and looked around vaguely. 'Uh. What?'

'It's Harry,' I said, kneeling down next to him. I took off my pentacle amulet and willed a gentle light from it. 'Are you hurt?'

Georgia murmured in discomfort at the light. The two

of them were twined together rather intimately, actually, and I suddenly felt extremely, um, inappropriate. I shut off the light.

'Sorry,' he slurred. 'We were gonna come back, but it was . . . really nice out here. And confusing.'

'I lost track,' Georgia said. 'And fell over.'

Their pupils were dilated to the size of quarters, and I suddenly understood what had happened to them: Madeline's blood. They'd been inadvertently drugged while ripping at a succubus with their fangs. I'd heard stories about the blood of the White Court, but I hadn't been able to find any hard evidence, and it wasn't the sort of thing Thomas would ever talk about.

'Hell's bells,' I muttered, frustrated. Madeline seemed to have a habit of inflicting far more damage by coincidence than intention.

I heard a short, desperately pleasurable cry from nearby, in the direction where I knew Madeline and Lara were on the ground – then silence.

And Madeline wasn't on the island anymore.

I lifted a hand in the air and let out a soft whistle. There was a fluttering sound, and then a small faerie hovered in the air beside me, suppressing the light that usually gathered around them when they flew. I could hear its wings buzzing and sensed its position through the island's intellectus. It wasn't Toot-toot, but one of his subordinates. 'Put a guard around these two,' I said, indicating Will and Georgia. 'Hide them and try to lead off anyone who comes close.'

The little faerie let its wings blur with blue light twice in acknowledgment of the order and zipped off into the dark. A moment later, a double dozen of the

Militia were on the way, led by the member of the Guard.

Toot and company were generally reliable – within their limits. This was going to be pushing them. But I didn't have any other way of helping Will and Georgia at the moment, and the insanity was still in progress. Putting the Little Folk on guard duty might not be a foolproof protection, but it was the only one I had. I'd just have to hope for the best.

I reached out to Demonreach to find out about Ebenezar and the others, when a sense of fundamental *wrongness* twitched through my brain and sent runnels of fear and rage that did not belong to me oozing down my spine. I focused on the source of those feelings, and suddenly understood the island's outrage at the presence of a visitor it actively detested. It had come ashore on the far side of the island from Chicago, and was now moving swiftly through the trees, dragging a half-dead presence behind it.

My brother.

The naagloshii had come to Demonreach.

I stood there without allies, without most of my weapons, and grew sick with horror as the skinwalker bypassed the battle at the docks and moved in a straight line toward Demonreach Tower.

Toward Molly. Toward Donald Morgan. And it was moving fast.

I put my head down, found the fastest route up the hill, and broke out into a flat sprint, praying that I could beat the skinwalker to the tower.

44

As I ran, I tried to keep track of the battle between the White Council and the forces of the traitor who had brought them to the island. Whatever the enemy had brought with him, they weren't anything close to human-shaped, and they were all over the place. The Council's forces, together with the White Court, were arranged in a half circle at the shoreline, their backs protected by the lake. The attackers were stacked up at the tree line, where they would be able to hide, and they were probably making swift attacks at odd intervals. The two human-shaped presences who had arrived first were standing together in the forest, well back from the fight, and I felt a moment of severe frustration.

If I could only get word to the Wardens, to tell them where the traitor was, they might be able to launch an effective attack – but I was pretty sure it wasn't possible. If I used more of the Little Folk, I'd have to stop to whistle some of them up and dispatch them to the task, and it was always possible that they wouldn't find the right target to point out to the Council with their fireworks.

Then, too, a wizard would be a far different sort of threat to the Little Folk than a vampire or the grey men had been. A wizard, particularly one smart enough to remain hidden within the Council for years without betraying his treacherous goals, could swat Little Folk out of the air like insects, killing them by the score. Whether or not they thought they understood the risks, I wasn't going to send them into that.

But I had to figure out something. The fight wasn't going well for the home team: there was blood mixed heavily with the rain on the muddy ground in the center of their defensive position.

I gritted my teeth in frustration. I had to focus on my task, for my brother's sake. If I stopped moving now, if I tried to bail the Council and Lara's family out of their predicament, it could mean Thomas's life. Besides, if Ebenezar, Listens-to-Wind, and Ancient Mai couldn't hold off their attackers, it was pretty much a given that I wouldn't be able to do any better.

They would have to manage without me.

I didn't quite get up to the tower before the skinwalker, but it was damn near a tie. I guess being a nine-foot-tall shapeshifter with a nocturnal predator's senses and superhuman strength was enough to trump even my alliance with the island's spirit.

Taken as an omen for the rest of the evening, it was hardly encouraging, but if I did the smart thing every time matters got dangerous, the world would probably come to an end.

As it turned out, moving through the forest with perfect surety of where to put your feet is very nearly the same thing as moving in perfect silence. I reached the edge of the trees, and saw the skinwalker coming up the opposite side of the bald knoll. I froze in place, behind a screen of brush and shadows.

The wind had continued to rise and grow cooler, coming in from the northeast – which meant that it was at the skinwalker's back. It would warn the creature should anything attempt to come slipping up his back trail, but it offered me a small advantage: Shagnasty wouldn't be able to get my scent.

He came up the hill, all wiry limbs and stiff yellow fur that seemed entirely unaffected by what must have been a long swim or by the rain that was currently falling in intermittent splatters. The racing clouds overhead parted for a few seconds, revealing a moon most of the way toward being full, and a scythe of silver light swept briefly over the hilltop.

It showed me Thomas.

The naagloshii was dragging him by one ankle. His shirt was gone, and his upper body was covered in so many fine cuts and scratches that they looked like marked roads in a particularly detailed atlas. He'd been beaten, too. One eye was swollen up until it looked like someone had stuck half of a peach against the socket. There were dark bruises all over his throat, too – he'd been strangled, maybe repeatedly, maybe for fun.

His head, shoulders, and upper back dragged on the ground, and his arms followed limply along. When the naagloshii stopped walking, I saw his head move a little, maybe trying to spot some way to escape. His hair was still soaking wet and clinging to his head. I heard him let out a weak, wet cough.

He was alive. Beaten, tortured, half drowned in the icy water of Lake Michigan – but he was *alive*.

I felt my hands clench as a hot and hungry anger suddenly burned through me. I hadn't planned on trying to take the naagloshii alone. I'd wanted Lara and her people and every member of the Council present to be there, too. That had been part of the plan: establish a common interest by showing them that they had a common enemy. Then take the naagloshii on with overwhelming force and force it to flee, at the very least, so that we could recover Thomas. I just hadn't counted on the traitor showing up in such numerical strength.

Taking the naagloshii on alone would be a fool's mistake. Anger might make a man bolder than he would be otherwise. It was possible that I could use it to help fuel my magic, as well – but anger alone wouldn't give a man skill or strength that he didn't have already, and it wouldn't grant a mortal wizard undeniable power.

All it could do was get me killed if I let it control me. I swallowed down my outrage and forced myself to watch the naagloshii with cold, dispassionate eyes. Once I had a better opportunity, once I had spotted something that might give me a real chance at victory, I would strike, I promised my rage. I'd hit it with the best sucker punch of my life, backed by the ambient energy of Demonreach.

I focused my whole concentration on the skinwalker, and waited.

The skinwalker, I realized a moment later, was enormously powerful. I'd known that already, of course, but I hadn't been able to appreciate the threat it represented beyond the purely physical, even though I'd viewed it through my Sight.

(That memory welled up again, trying to club me unconscious as it had before. It was difficult, but I shoved it away and ignored it.)

Through Demonreach, I could appreciate its presence in a more tactile sense. The skinwalker was virtually its own ley line, its own well of power. It had so much metaphysical mass that the dark river of energy flowing up from beneath the tower was partially disrupted by its presence, in much the same way as the moon causes tidal shifts. The island reflected that disruption in many subtle ways. Animals fled from the naagloshii as they might from the scent of a forest fire. Insects fell silent. Even the trees themselves seemed to grow hushed and quiet, despite the cold wind that should have been causing their branches to creak, their leaves to whisper.

It paced up to the cottage, where Morgan and my apprentice were hiding, and something odd happened.

The stones of the cottage began to glimmer with streamers of fox fire. It wasn't a lot of light, only enough to be noticeable in the darkness, but as the naagloshii took another step forward, the fox fire brightened and resolved itself into symbols, written on each stone in gentle fire. I had no idea what script it was written in. I had never seen the symbols before.

The naagloshii stopped in its tracks, and another flicker of moonlight showed me that it had bared its teeth. It took another step forward, and the symbols brightened even more. It let out a low, snarling noise, and tried to take another step.

Suddenly, its wiry fur was plastered tight to the front of its body, and it seemed unable to take another step forward. It stood there with one leg lifted and let out a spitting curse in a language I did not know. Then it retreated several steps, snarling, and turned to the tower. It approached the ruined tower a bit more warily than it had the cottage, and once again those flowing sigils appeared upon the stones, somehow seeming to repulse the naagloshii before it could get closer than eight or ten feet to it.

It let out a frustrated sound, muttered something to itself, and flicked out a hand, sending unseen streamers of power fluttering toward the tower. The symbols only seemed to glow brighter for a moment, as if absorbing the magic that the skinwalker had presumably meant to disrupt them.

It cursed again, and then lifted Thomas idly, as though it planned on smashing its way through the stones using Thomas's skull. Then it glanced at my brother, cursed some more, and shook its head, muttering darkly to itself. It fell back from the tower, clearly frustrated, and just as clearly familiar with the symbols that allowed the stones to shed the power of a skinwalker as swiftly and as easily as they shed rainwater.

Demonreach's alien presence rarely seemed to convey anything understandable about itself – but for a few instants it did. As the skinwalker retreated, the island's spirit allowed itself a brief moment of smug satisfaction.

What the hell *was* that stuff?

Never mind. It didn't matter. Or, rather, it could wait for further investigation. The important thing was that the game had just changed.

I no longer had to get Thomas away from the skinwalker and then find a way to defeat it. All I had to do was get Thomas *away*. If I could grab my brother and drag him into the circle of the broken tower or into the sheltering walls of the cottage, it seemed as though we would be fine. If the very stones of the cottage repulsed the skinwalker's presence, then all we'd need to do is let Molly activate the crystal and wait the naagloshii out. Regardless of the outcome of this night's battle, the Council *would* win the day, eventually – and even the worst thing they might do to us would be a better fate than the skinwalker would mete out.

In an instant of rational clarity, I acknowledged to myself that there were about a million things that could go wrong with that plan. On the other hand, that plan had a significant advantage – there was at least *one* thing that could go *right*, which was exactly one more right thing than the previous 'take back my brother away and beat the skinwalker up' plan could produce if I tried it unassisted.

I might actually pull this one off.

'Wizard,' the skinwalker called. It faced the cottage and began walking in a slow circle around it. 'Wizard. Come forth. Give me the doomed warrior.'

I didn't answer him, naturally. I was busy changing position. If he kept pacing a circle around the cottage, he would walk between me and the empty doorway. If I timed it right, I might be able to unleash a kinetic blast that would rip Thomas out of its grip and throw him into the cottage.

Of course, it might also *fail* to rip Thomas out of the skinwalker's grip, in which case it might whiplash his limp body severely enough to break his neck. Or it might succeed and hit him hard enough to stop his heart or collapse a lung. And if my aim was off, I might be blasting Thomas out of the skinwalker's hands and into a stone wall. Given how badly off he looked at the moment, that might well kill him.

Of course, the skinwalker *would* kill him if I did nothing.

So. I would just have to be perfect.

I got into position and licked my lips nervously. It was harder to work with pure, raw kinetic energy, with force, than almost any other kind of magic. Unlike using fire or lightning, summoning up pure force required that everything in the spell had to come from the wizard's mind and will. Fire, once called, would behave exactly like fire unless you worked to make it otherwise. Ditto lightning. But raw will had no basis in the natural order, so the visualization of it had to be particularly vivid and intent in the mind of the wizard using it.

That was one reason I usually used my staff, or another article, to help focus my concentration when I worked with force. But my staff was several minutes away, and my kinetic energy rings, while powerful enough to handle the job, were essentially designed to send out lances of destructive energy — to hurt things. And I hadn't designed the magic that supported them with on-the-fly modifications in mind. I couldn't soften the blow, so to speak, if I worked with the rings. I could kill Thomas if I used them.

'Wizard!' the naagloshii growled. 'I grow weary of this! I have come to honor the exchange of prisoners! Do not force me to take what I want!'

Just a few more steps, and it would be in position.

My legs were shaking. My hands were shaking.

I stared at them in shock for a second, and realized that I was terrified. The mind specter of the skinwalker hammered at the doors of my thoughts and raked savagely at my concentration. I remembered the havoc it had wrought, the lives it had taken, and how easily it had avoided or overcome every threat that had been sent its way.

Anything less than a flawless execution of the spell could cost my brother his life. What if the skinwalker was good enough to sense it coming? What if I misjudged the amount of force I needed to use? What if I *missed*? I wasn't even using a tool to help me focus the power – and my control was a little shaky on the best of days.

What about the seconds after the spell? Even if I managed to do it right, it would leave me out in the open, with a vengeful and enraged naagloshii to keep me company. What would it do to me? The image of the half-cooked Lara ripping out Madeline's intestines burned in my thoughts. Somehow I knew that the naagloshii would do worse. A lot worse.

Then came the nastiest doubt of all: what if this had all been for nothing? What if the traitor escaped while I flailed around here? What if the politics of power meant that Morgan would pay the price for LaFortier's death despite everything?

God. I really wanted that cold beer and a good book.

'Don't screw this up,' I whispered to myself. 'Don't screw it up.'

The skinwalker passed in front of the empty cottage doorway.

And, a second later, he dragged Thomas into line between the doorway and me.

I lifted my right hand, focusing my will and aligning my thoughts, while the constantly shifting numbers and formulae of force calculation went spinning through my head.

I suddenly spread my fingers and called, *'Forzare!'*

Something approximately the same size and shape as the blade of a bulldozer went rushing across the ground between my brother and me, tearing up earth and gravel, root and plant. The unseen force dug into the earth an inch beneath Thomas, hammered into his unmoving form, and ripped him free of the naagloshii's grip. He went tumbling over ten feet of ground to the doorway – and struck his head savagely on the stone wall framing the door as he went through.

Had his head flopped about with a lethally rubbery fluidity after the impact? Had I just broken my brother's neck?

I let out a cry of agony and chagrin. At the same time, the skinwalker whirled to face me, crouched, and let out a furious roar that shook the air all around, sending drops of water that had beaded upon the leaves of the trees raining to the earth in a fresh shower. That roar held all the fury of a mortally offended, maniacal ego and promised a death that could only be described with the assistance of an encyclopedia of torments, a thesaurus, and a copy of *Gray's Anatomy*.

The naagloshii in my crystalline memory of the recent past and the one standing in front of me in the here-and-now both rushed at me, huge and unstoppable, determined to hit me from either side and rip me to shreds.

And suddenly I did not *care* that this creature was a foe on par with any number of nightmares I would never dare to trade blows with. I did not *care* that I was probably about to die.

I saw Kirby's still form in my head. I saw the small, broken figure of Andi in her hospital room. I saw my brother's wounds, remembered the agony the thing had caused me when I had seen it through my Sight. This creature had no place here. And if I was to die, I was not going to go out in a gibbering heap of terror. If I was to die, it wouldn't happen because I was half crippled with fear and Sight trauma.

If I was to die, it was going to be a bloody and spectacular mess.

'Bring it!' I screamed back at the naagloshii, my terror and rage making my voice sharp and high and rough. I cupped my right hand as if preparing to throw a baseball, drew up my will, and filled my palm with scarlet fire. I thrust out my left hand and ran my will through the shield bracelet hanging there, preparing a defense, and as I did I felt the power of the land beneath my feet, felt it spreading out around me, drawing in supportive energy. 'Bring it! Bring it, you dickless freak!'

The naagloshii's form shifted from something almost human to a shape that was more like that of a gorilla, its arms lengthening, its legs shortening. It rushed forward, bounding over the distance between us with terrifying speed, grace, and power, roaring as it came. It was also vanishing from sight, becoming one with the darkness as its veil closed around it, utterly invisible to the human eye.

But Demonreach knew where Shagnasty was. And so did I.

In some distant corner of my mind, where my common sense apparently had some kind of vacation home, my brain noted with dismay that I had broken into a sprint of my own. I don't remember making the decision, but I was charging out to meet the skinwalker, screaming out a challenge in reply. I ran, embracing a rage that was very nearly madness, filling the fire in my hand with more and more power that surged higher every time one of my feet hit the ground, until it was blazing as bright as an acetylene torch.

The naagloshi leapt at me, horrible eyes burning and visible from within the veil, its clawed arms reaching out.

I dropped into a baseball player's slide on my right hip,

and brought my shield up at an angle oblique to the skin-walker's motion. The creature hit the shield like a load of bricks and bounced up to continue in the same direction it had been leaping. The instant the naagloshii had rebounded, I dropped the shield, screaming, 'Andi!' and hurled a miniature sun up at the skinwalker's belly.

Fire erupted in an explosion that lifted the skinwalker another dozen feet into the air, tumbling it tail over teakettle – an expression that makes no goddamned sense whatsoever yet seemed oddly appropriate to the moment. My nose filled with the hideous scent of burning hair and scorched meat, and the naagloshii howled in savage ecstasy or agony as it came tumbling down, bounced hard a couple of times, and then rolled to its feet.

It came streaking toward me, its body shifting again behind its concealing veil, becoming something else, something more feline, maybe. It didn't matter to me. I reached out to the wind and rain and rumbling thunder around us and gathered a levy of lightning into my cupped hand. Then, instead of waiting for its charge, I turned my left hand over and triggered every charged energy ring I had left, unleashing their deadly force in a single salvo.

The naagloshii howled something in a tongue I didn't know, and the lances of force glanced off of his veil, leaving concentric rings of spreading color where they struck. A bare second later, I lifted my cupped hand and screamed, 'Thomas! *Fulminas!*'

Thunder loud enough to knock several stones loose from the tower shook the hilltop, and the blue-white flash of light was physically painful to the eyes. A thorny network of lightning leapt to the naagloshii, whose defenses had not yet recovered from deflecting the blasts of the force rings. The deadly-delicate tracery of lightning hammered into the exact center of its chest, stopping its charge in its tracks. Smaller strikes, spreading out from the main bolt like the branches of a tree, snapped into the rocky ground in half a dozen places, digging red-hot, skull-sized divots into the granite and flint.

Exhaustion hit me like a hammer, and stars swam in my vision. I had *never* thrown punches that hard before, and even with the assistance of Demonreach, the expenditure of energy needed to do so was literally staggering. I knew that if I pushed too hard, I'd collapse – but the skinwalker was still standing.

It stumbled to one side, its veil faltering for a second, its eyes wide with surprise. I could just see it going through the naagloshii's head: how in the world was I hitting him so accurately when it *knew* that its veil rendered it all but perfectly invisible?

For one quick fraction of a second, I saw fear in its eyes, and triumphant fury roared through my weary body.

The skinwalker recovered itself, changing again. With what looked like trivial effort, it reached down and ripped a section of rock shelf the size of a sidewalk paving stone from the rock. It flung the stone at me, three or four hundred pounds coming at me like a major-league fastball.

I dove to the side, slowed by exhaustion, but fast enough to get out of the way, and as I went, I gathered my will. This time the silver-white streamers of soulfire danced and glittered around my right hand. I lay on the ground, too tired to get back up, and ground my teeth in determination as it charged me for what would, one way or another, be the last time.

I didn't have the breath to scream, but I could snarl. 'And this,' I spat, 'is for Kirby, you son of a bitch.' I unleashed my will and screamed, *'Laqueus!'*

A cord of pure force, glittering and flashing with soul-fire, leapt out at the skinwalker. It attempted to deflect it, but it clearly hadn't been expecting me to turbocharge the spell. The naagloshii's defenses barely slowed it, and the cord whipped three times around its throat and tight-ened savagely.

The skinwalker's charge faltered and it staggered to one side, its veil falling to shreds by degrees. It started shifting form wildly, struggling to get loose of the supernatural garrote – and failing. The edges of my vision were blurry and darkening, but I kept my will on him, drawing the noose tighter and tighter.

It kicked and struggled wildly – and then changed tactics. It rolled up to a desperate crouch, extended a single talon, and swept it around in a circle, carving a furrow into the rock. It touched the circle with its will, and I felt it when the simple magical construct sprang up and cut off the noose spell from its source of power: me. The silver cord shimmered and vanished.

I lay there on the ground, barely able to lift my head. I looked toward the cottage and the safety it represented, standing only forty feet away. It might as well have been forty miles.

The naagloshii ran its talons along the fur at its throat and made a satisfied, growling noise. Then its eyes moved to me. Its mouth spread into a carnivorous smile. Then it stepped out of the circle and began to stalk nearer.

One bloody and spectacular mess, coming up.

45

The naagloshii walked over to me and stood there, smiling, as its inhuman features shifted and contorted, from something bestial back toward something almost human. It probably made it easier to talk.

'That was hardly pathetic at all,' it murmured. 'Who gifted you with the life fire, little mortal?'

'Doubt you know him,' I responded. It was an effort to speak, but I was used to meeting the rigorous demands of life as a reflexive smart-ass. 'He'd have taken you out.'

The skinwalker's smile widened. 'I find it astonishing that you could call forth the very fires of creation – and yet have no faith with which to employ them.'

'Hell's bells,' I muttered. 'I get sick of sadistic twits like you.'

It tilted its head. It dragged its claws idly across the stone, sharpening them. 'Oh?'

'You like seeing someone dangling on a hook,' I said. 'It gets you off. And once I'm dead, the fun's over. So you feel like you have to drag things out with a conversation.'

'Are you so eager to leave life, mortal?' the naagloshii purred.

'If the alternative is hanging around here with *you*, I sure as hell am,' I replied. 'Get it over with or buzz off.'

Its claws moved, pure, serpentine speed, and my face suddenly caught on fire. It hurt too much to scream.

I doubled up, clutching my hands at the right side of my face, and felt my teeth grinding together.

'As you wish,' the naagloshii said. It leaned closer. 'But let me leave you with this thought, little spirit caller. You think you've won a victory by taking the phage from my hands. But he was hanging meat for me for more than a day, and I left *nothing* behind. You don't have *words* for the things I did to him.' I could hear its smile widening. 'It is starving. Mad with hunger. And I smell a young female caller inside the hogan,' it purred. 'I was considering throwing the phage inside with her before you so kindly saved me the bother. Meditate upon *that* on your way to eternity.'

Even through the pain and the fear, my stomach twisted into frozen knots.

Oh, God.

Molly.

I couldn't see out of my right eye, and I couldn't feel anything but pain. I turned my head far to the right so that my left eye could focus on the naagloshii crouching over me, its long fingers, tipped with bloodied black claws, twitching in what was an almost sexual anticipation.

I didn't know if anyone had ever thrown a death curse backed by soulfire. I didn't know if using my own soul as fuel for a final conflagration would mean that it never went to wherever it is souls go once they're finished here. I just knew that no matter what happened, it wasn't going to hurt for much longer, and that I wanted to wipe that grin off the skinwalker's face before I went.

I wasn't sure how defiant you could look with a one-eyed stare, but I did my best, even as I prepared the blast that would burn the life from my body as I unleashed it.

Then there was a blur of light, and something darted past the naagloshii's back. It tensed and let out a snarl of surprise, whirling away from me to stare after the source of light. Its back, I saw, bore a long and shallow wound, straight across its hunched shoulders, as narrow and fine as if cut by a scalpel.

Or a box knife.

Toot-toot whirled about in midair, a bloodied utility knife clutched in one hand like a spear. He lifted a tiny trumpet to his lips and piped out a shrill challenge, the notes of a cavalry charge in high-pitched miniature. 'Avaunt, villain!' he cried in a shrill, strident tone. Then he darted at the skinwalker again.

The naagloshii roared and swept out a claw, but Toot evaded the blow and laid a nine-inch-long slice up the skinwalker's arm.

It whirled on the tiny faerie in a sudden fury, its form shifting, becoming more feline, though it kept the long forelimbs. It pursued Toot, claws snatching – but my miniature captain of the guard was always a hairsbreadth ahead.

'Toot!' I called, as loudly as I was able. 'Get out of there!'

The naagloshii spat out an acidic-sounding curse as Toot avoided its claws again, and slapped a hand at the air itself, hissing out words in an alien tongue. The wind rose in a sudden, spiteful little gale, and it hammered Toot's tiny body from the air. He crashed into a patch of blackberry bushes at the edge of the clearing, and the sphere of light around him winked out with a dreadfully sudden finality.

The naagloshii turned, kicking dirt back toward the fallen faerie with its hind legs. Then it stalked toward me again, seething in fury. I watched him come, knowing that there was nothing I could do.

At least I'd gotten Thomas away from the bastard.

The naagloshii's yellow eyes burned with hate as it closed the distance and lifted its claws.

'Hey,' said a quiet voice. 'Ugly.'

I turned and stared across the small clearing at the same time the skinwalker did.

I don't know how Injun Joe managed to get through the ring of attackers and to the summit of the hill, but he had. He stood there in moccasins, jeans, and a buck-skin shirt decorated with bone beads and bits of turquoise. His long silver hair hung in its customary braid, and the bone beads of his necklace gleamed pale in the night's gloom.

The naagloshii faced the medicine man without moving.

The hilltop was completely silent and still.

Then Listens-to-Wind smiled. He hunkered down and rubbed his hands in some mud and loose earth that lightly covered the rocky summit of the hill. He cupped his hands, raised them to just below his face, and inhaled through his nose, breathing in the scent of the earth. Then he rubbed his hands slowly together, the gesture somehow reminding me of a man preparing to undertake heavy routine labor.

He rose to his feet again, and said, calmly, 'Mother says you have no place here.'

The naagloshii bared its fangs. Its growl prowled around the hilltop like a beast unto itself.

Lightning flashed overhead with no accompanying rumble of thunder. It cast a harsh, eerily silent glare down on the skinwalker. Listens-to-Wind turned his face up to the skies and cocked his head slightly. 'Father says you are ugly,' he reported. He narrowed his eyes and straightened his shoulders, facing the naagloshii squarely as thunder rolled over the island, lending a monstrous growling undertone to the old man's voice. 'I give you this chance. Leave. Now.'

The skinwalker snarled. 'Old spirit caller. The failed guardian of a dead people. I do not fear you.'

'Maybe you should,' Listens-to-Wind said. 'The boy almost took you, and he doesn't even know the Diné, much less the Old Ways. Begone. Last chance.'

The naagloshii let out a warbling growl as its body changed, thickening, growing physically thicker, more powerful-looking. 'You are not a holy man. You do not follow the Blessing Way. You have no power over me.'

'Don't plan to bind or banish you, old ghost,' Injun Joe said. 'Just gonna kick your ass up between your ears.' He clenched his hands into fists and said, 'Let's go.'

The skinwalker let out a howl and hurled its arms forward. Twin bands of darkness cascaded forth, splintering into dozens and dozens of shadowy serpents that slithered through the night air in a writhing cloud, darting toward Listens-to-Wind. The medicine man didn't flinch. He lifted his arms to the sky, threw back his head, and sang in the wavering, high-pitched fashion of the native tribes. The rain, which had vanished almost entirely, came down again in an almost solid sheet of water that fell on maybe fifty square yards of hilltop, drenching the oncoming swarm of sorcery and melting it to nothing before it could become a threat.

Injun Joe looked back down again at the naagloshii. 'That the best you got?'

The naagloshii snarled more words in unknown tongues, and began flinging power with both arms. Balls of fire like the one I had seen at Château Raith were followed by crackling spheres of blue sparks and wobbling green spheres of what looked like Jell-O and smelled like sulfuric acid. It was an impressive display of evocation. Had a kitchen sink gone flying toward Listens-to-Wind, conjured from who knows where, it wouldn't have startled me. The naagloshii pulled out all the stops, hurling enough raw power at the small, weathered medicine man to scour the hilltop clean to the bedrock.

I have no idea how the old man countered it all, even though I watched him do it. Again he sang, and this time shuffled his feet in time with the music, bending his old body forward and back again, the motions obviously slowed and muted by his age but just as obviously part of a dance. He was wearing a band of bells on his ankles, and another on each wrist, and they jingled in time with his singing.

All of that power coming at him seemed unable to find a mark. Fire flashed by him as his feet shuffled and his body swayed without so much as singeing a hair. Crackling balls of lightning vanished a few feet in front of him, and resumed their course a few feet beyond him, apparently without crossing the space between. Globes of acid wobbled in flight and splattered over the earth, sizzling and sending up clouds of choking vapors, but not actually doing him any harm. The defense was elegant. Rather than trying to match force against force and power against power, the failure of the incoming sorcery to harm Listens-to-Wind seemed like part of the natural order, as if the world was a place in which such a thing was perfectly normal, reasonable, and expected.

But as the naagloshii hurled agony and death in a futile effort to overcome Listens-to-Wind's power, it was also striding forward, closing the distance between them, until it stood less than twenty feet from the old medicine man. Then its eyes glittered with a terrible joy, and with a roar it hurled itself physically upon the old man.

My heart leapt into my throat. Listens-to-Wind might not have come down on my side in this matter, but he had helped me more than once in the past, and was one of the few wizards to hold Ebenezar McCoy's respect. He was a decent man, and I didn't want to see him get hurt in my defense. I tried to cry out a warning, and as I did, I caught the look on his face as the naagloshii pounced.

Injun Joe was smiling a fierce, wolfish smile.

The naagloshii came down, its mouth stretching into a wolflike muzzle, extending claws on all four of its limbs as it prepared to savage the old man.

But Listens-to-Wind spoke a single word, his voice shaking the air with power, and then *his* form melted and shifted, changing as fluidly as if he'd been made of liquid mercury that until that moment had only been held in the shape of an old man by an effort of will. His form simply resolved itself into something different, as naturally and swiftly as taking a deep breath.

When the naagloshii came down, it didn't sink its claws into a leathery old wizard.

Instead, it found itself muzzle to muzzle with a brown bear the size of a minibus.

The bear let out a bone-shaking roar and surged forward, overwhelming the naagloshii with raw mass and muscle power. If you've ever seen a furious beast like that in action, you know that it isn't something that can be done justice in any kind of description. The volume of the roar, the surge of implacable muscle beneath heavy pelt, the flash of white fangs and glaring red-rimmed eyes combine into a whole that is far greater than the sum of its parts. It's terrifying, elemental, touching upon some ancient instinctual core inside every human alive that remembers that such things equal terror and death.

The naagloshii screamed, a weird and alien shriek, and raked furiously at the bear, but it had outsmarted itself. Its long, elegantly sharp claws, perfect for eviscerating soft-skinned humans, simply did not have the mass and power they needed to force their way through the bear's thick pelt and the hide beneath, much less the depth to cut through layers of fat and heavy muscle. It might as well have strapped plastic combs to its limbs, for all the good its claws did it.

The bear seized the skinwalker's skull in its vast jaws, and for a second, it looked like the fight was over. Then the naagloshii blurred, and where a vaguely simian creature had been an instant before, there was only a tiny flash of urine yellow fur, a long, lean creature like a ferret with oversized jaws. It wiggled free of the huge bear and evaded two slaps of its giant paws, letting out a defiant, mocking snarl as it slid free.

But Injun Joe wasn't done yet, either. The bear lifted itself into a ponderous leap, and came down to earth again as a coyote, lean and swift, that raced after the ferret nimbly, fangs bright. It rushed after the fleeing ferret – which suddenly turned, jaws opening wide, and then wider, and wider, until an alligator coated in sparse tufts of yellow fur turned to meet the onrushing canine, which found itself too close to turn aside.

The canine form melted as it shot toward the alligator's maw, and a dark-winged raven swept into the jaws and out the far side as they snapped shut. The raven turned its head and let out mocking caws of laughter as it flew away, circling around the clearing.

The alligator shuddered all over, and became a falcon, golden and swift, its head marked by tufts of yellowish fur that almost looked like the naagloshii's ears had in its near-human form. It hurtled forward with supernatural speed, vanishing behind a veil as it flew.

I heard the raven's wings beat overhead as it circled cautiously, looking for its enemy – and then was struck from behind by the falcon's claws. I watched in horror as the hooked beak descended to rip at the captured raven – and met the spiny, rock-hard back of a snapping turtle. A leathery head twisted and jaws that could cut through medium-gauge wire clamped onto the naagloshii-falcon's leg, and it let out another alien shriek of pain as the two went plummeting to the earth together.

But in the last few feet, the turtle shimmered into the form of a flying squirrel, limbs extended wide, and it converted some of its falling momentum into forward motion, dropping to a roll as it hit the ground. The falcon wasn't so skilled. It began to change into something else, but struck the stony earth heavily before it could finish resolving into a new form.

The squirrel whirled, bounded, and became a mountain lion in midleap, landing on the stunned, confused mass of feathers and fur that was the naagloshii. Fangs and claws tore, and black blood stained the ground to the sound of more horrible shrieks. The naagloshii coalesced into an eerie shape, four legs and batlike wings, with eyes and mouths everywhere. All the mouths were screaming, in half a dozen different voices, and it managed to tear its way free of the mountain lion's grip and go flapping and tumbling awkwardly across the ground. It staggered wildly and began to leap clumsily into the air, bat wings beating. It looked like an albatross without enough headwind, and the mountain lion was hard on its heels the whole way, claws lashing out to tear and rake.

The naagloshii disappeared into the darkness, its howls drifting up in its wake as it fled. It continued to scream in pain, almost sobbing, as it rushed down the slope toward the lake. Demonreach followed its departure with a surly sense of satisfaction, and I couldn't say that I blamed it.

The skinwalker fled the island. Its howls drifted on the night wind for a time, and then they were gone.

The mountain lion stared in the direction that the naagloshii had fled for long moments. Then he sat down, his head hanging, shivered, and became Injun Joe once more. The old man was sitting on the ground, supporting himself with both hands. He stood up slowly, and a bit stiffly, and one of his arms looked like it might be broken midway between wrist and elbow. He continued to look after his routed opponent, then snorted once and turned to walk carefully over to me.

'Wow,' I told him quietly.

He lifted his chin slightly. For a moment, pride and power shone in his dark eyes. Then he smiled tiredly at me, and was only a calm, tired-looking old man again. 'You claimed this place as a sanctum?' he asked.

I nodded. 'Last night.'

He looked at me, and couldn't seem to make up his

mind whether to laugh in my face or slap me upside the head. 'You don't get into trouble by halves, do you, son?'

'Apparently not,' I slurred. I spat blood from my mouth. There was a lot of that, at the moment. My face hadn't stopped hurting just because the naagloshii was gone.

Injun Joe knelt down beside me and examined my wounds in a professional manner. 'Not life-threatening,' he assured me. 'We need your help.'

'You're kidding,' I said. 'I'm tapped. I can't even walk.'

'All you need is your mind,' he said. 'There are trees around the battle below. Trees that are under strain. Can you feel them?'

He'd barely said the words when I felt them through my link to the island's spirit. There were fourteen trees, in fact, most of them old willows near the water. Their branches were bowed down, sagging beneath enormous burdens.

'Yeah,' I said. My voice sounded distant to me, and full of detached calm.

'The island can be most swiftly rid of the beings in them,' Injun Joe said. 'If it withdraws the water from the earth beneath those trees for a time.'

'So?' I said. 'How am I supposed to—'

I broke off in midsentence as I felt Demonreach respond. It seemed to seize upon Injun Joe's words, but then I understood that nothing of the sort had happened. Demonreach had understood Injun Joe only because it had understood the thoughts that those words created in my head. Communication by sound was a concept so inelegant and cumbersome and alien to the island's spirit that it could never have truly happened. But my thoughts – those it could grasp.

I could all but feel the soil shifting, settling slightly, as the island withdrew the water in the ground beneath those trees. It had the predictable side effect that I realized Injun Joe had been going for. Once the ground around the trees' roots had become arid, it began to leach water from the trees themselves, drawing it back out through the same capillary action that had brought it in. It flowed in from the outermost branches most quickly, leaving the structures behind it dry.

And brittle.

Tree branches began to break with enormous, popping cracks. A *lot* of branches broke, dozens, all within a few seconds, and it was like listening to packs of firecrackers going off. There was a sudden cacophony of thunder and gunfire that rose up from the docks below, and flashes of light that threw bizarre shadows against the clouds overhead.

I tried to focus on my other knowledge of the island, and I felt it – the surge in energy being released below, the increased flow of strange blood into the ground beneath the affected trees – blood that they drank thirstily, in their sudden drought conditions. The Wardens were moving forward, into the tree line. The vampires were racing ahead of them, their steps the light, swift stride of predators on the trail of wounded prey. Strange things were dying in the trees, amidst bursts of magic and flurries of gunfire.

A light rose over the island, a bright silver star that hung in the air for a long moment, like a flare.

Once he saw that, Injun Joe's shoulders sagged a little, and he let out a slow, relieved breath. 'Good. Good, that's done for them.' He shook his head and looked at me. 'You're a mess, boy. Do you have any supplies here?'

I tried to sit up and couldn't. 'The cottage,' I blurted. 'Molly. Thomas – the vampire.' I looked toward the bushes where one loyal little guardian had bought me precious seconds in the thick of the fight and started pushing my way to my feet. 'Toot.'

'Easy,' Listens-to-Wind said. 'Easy, *easy*, son. You can't just—'

The rest of what he had to say was drowned out by a vast roaring noise, and everything, all my thoughts and fears, stopped making any noise at all inside my head. It was just . . . quiet. Gorgeously quiet. And nothing hurt.

I had time to think to myself, *I could get to liking this.*

Then nothing.

46

I heard voices speaking somewhere nearby. My head was killing me, and my face felt tight and swollen. I could feel warmth on my right side, and smelled the scent of burning wood. A fire popped and crackled. The ground beneath me was hard but not cold. I was lying on blankets or something.

'. . . really no point to doing anything but waiting,' Ebenezar said. 'Sure, they're under a roof, but it's leaking. And if nothing else, morning should take care of it.'

'*Ai ya*,' Ancient Mai muttered. 'I'm sure we could counter it easily enough.'

'Not without risk,' Ebenezar said in a reasonable tone. 'Morgan isn't going anywhere. What's the harm in waiting for the shield to fall?'

'I do not care for this place,' Ancient Mai replied. 'Its feng shui is unpleasant. And if the child was no warlock, she would have lowered the shield by now.'

'No!' came Molly's voice. It sounded weirdly modulated, as if being filtered through fifty feet of a corrugated pipe and a kazoo. 'I'm not dropping the shield until Harry says it's okay.' After a brief pause she added, 'Uh, besides. I'm not sure how.'

A voice belonging to one of the Wardens said, 'Maybe we could tunnel beneath it.'

I exhaled slowly, licked my cracked lips, and said, 'Don't bother. It's a sphere.'

'Oh!' Molly said. 'Oh, thank God! Harry!'

I sat up slowly, and before I had moved more than an inch or two, Injun Joe was supporting me. 'Easy, son,' he said. 'Easy. You've lost some blood, and you got a knot on your head that would knock off a hat.'

I felt really dizzy while he said that, but I stayed up. He passed me a canteen and I drank, slowly and carefully, one swallow at a time. Then I opened my eyes and glanced around me.

We were all in the ruined cottage. I sat on the floor near the fireplace. Ebenezar sat on the hearth in front of the fireplace, his old wooden staff leaned up against one shoulder. Ancient Mai stood on the opposite side of the cottage from me, flanked by four Wardens.

Morgan lay on the bedroll where I'd left him, unconscious or asleep, and Molly sat cross-legged on the floor beside him, holding the quartz crystal in both hands. It shimmered with a calm white light that illuminated the interior of the cottage much more thoroughly than the fire did, and a perfectly circular dome of light the size of a small camping tent enclosed both Morgan and my apprentice in a bubble of defensive energy.

'Hey,' I said to Molly.

'Hey,' she said back.

'I guess it worked, huh?'

Her eyes widened. 'You didn't know if it would?'

'The design was sound,' I said. 'I'd just never had the chance to field-test it.'

'Oh,' Molly said. 'Um. It worked.'

I grunted. Then I looked up at Ebenezar. 'Sir.'

'Hoss,' he said. 'Glad you could join us.'

'We waste time,' Ancient Mai said. She looked at me

and said, 'Tell your apprentice to drop the shield at once.'

'In a minute.'

Her eyes narrowed, and the Wardens beside her looked a little more alert.

I ignored her and asked Molly, 'Where's Thomas?'

'With his family,' said a calm voice.

I looked over my shoulder to see Lara Raith standing in the doorway, a slender shape wrapped in one of the blankets from a bunk on the *Water Beetle*. She looked as pale and lovely as ever, though her hair had been burned down close to her scalp. Without it to frame her face, there was a greater sense of sharp, angular gauntness to her features, and her grey eyes seemed even larger and more distinct. 'Don't worry, Dresden. Your cat's-paw will live to be manipulated another day. My people are taking care of him.'

I tried to find something in her face that would tell me anything else about Thomas. It wasn't there. She just watched me coolly.

'There, vampire,' Ancient Mai said politely. 'You have seen him and spoken to him. What follows is Council business.'

Lara smiled faintly at Ancient Mai and turned to me. 'One more thing before I go, Harry. Do you mind if I borrow the blanket?'

'What if I do?' I asked.

She let it slip off of one pale shoulder. 'I'd give it back, of course.'

The image of the swollen, bruised, burned creature that had kissed Madeline Raith as it pulled out her entrails returned to my thoughts, vividly.

'Keep it,' I told her.

She smiled again, this time showing teeth, and bowed her head. Then she turned and left. I idly followed her progress down to the shore, where she walked out onto the floating dock and was gone.

I looked at Ebenezar. 'What happened?'

He grunted. 'Whoever came through the Nevernever opened a gate about a hundred yards back in the trees,' he said. 'And he brought about a hundred big old shaggy spiders with him.'

I blinked, and frowned. 'Spiders?'

Ebenezar nodded. 'Not conjured forms, either. They were the real thing, from Faerie, maybe. Gave us a real hard time. Some of them started webbing the trees while the others kept us busy, trying to trap us in.'

'Didn't want us getting behind them to whoever opened the gate,' Listens-to-Wind said.

'Didn't want anyone to see who it was, more likely,' I said. 'That was our perp. That was the killer.'

'Maybe,' Ebenezar said quietly, nodding. 'As soon as those trees and the webbing came down, we started pushing the spiders back. He ran. And once he was gone, the spiders scattered, too.'

'Dammit,' I said quietly.

'That's what all this was about,' Ebenezar said. 'There was no informant, no testimony.'

I nodded. 'I told you that to draw the real killer out. To force him to act. And he did. You saw it with your own eyes. That should be proof enough that Morgan is innocent.'

Ancient Mai shook her head. 'The only thing that proves is that someone else is willing to betray the Council and has something to hide. It doesn't mean that Morgan couldn't have killed LaFortier. At best, it suggests that he did not act alone.'

Ebenezar gave her a steady look. Then he said, 'So there *is* a conspiracy now – is what you're saying? What was that you were saying earlier about simplicity?'

Mai glanced away from him, and shrugged her shoulders. 'Dresden's theory is, admittedly, a simpler and more likely explanation.' She sighed. 'It is, however, insufficient to the situation.'

Ebenezar scowled. 'Someone's got to hang?'

Mai turned her eyes back to him and held steady. 'That is precisely correct. It is plausible that Morgan was involved. The hard evidence universally suggests that he is guilty. And the White Council will *not* show weakness in the face of this act. We cannot afford to allow LaFortier's death to pass without retribution.'

'Retribution,' Ebenezar said. 'Not justice.'

'Justice is not what keeps the various powers in this world from destroying the White Council and having their way with humanity,' Ancient Mai responded. 'Fear does that. Power does that. They must know that if they strike us, there will be deadly consequences. I am aware how reprehensible an act it would be to sentence an innocent man to death – and one who has repeatedly demonstrated his dedication to the well-being of the Council, to boot. But on the whole, it is less destructive and less irresponsible than allowing our enemies to perceive weakness.'

Ebenezar put his elbows on his knees and looked at his hands. He shook his head once, and then said nothing.

'Now,' Ancient Mai said, turning her focus back to me.

'You will instruct your apprentice to lower the shield, or I will tear it down.'

'Might want to take a few steps back before you do,' I said. 'If anything but the proper sequence takes it apart, it explodes. It'll take out the cottage. And the tower. And the top of the hill. The kid and Morgan should be fine, though.'

Molly made a choking sound.

'Hngh. Finally made that idea work, did you?' Ebenezar said.

I shrugged. 'After those zombies turned up and just hammered their way through my defenses, I wanted something that would give me some options.'

'How long did it take you to make?'

'Nights and weekends for three months,' I sighed. 'It was a real pain in the ass.'

'Sounds it,' Ebenezar agreed.

'Wizard McCoy,' Mai said sharply. 'I remind you that Dresden and his apprentice aided and abetted a fugitive from justice.'

From behind me, Listens-to-Wind said, 'Mai. That's enough.'

She turned her eyes to him and stared hard.

'Enough,' Listens-to-Wind repeated. 'The hour is dark enough without trying to paint more people with the same brush we're going to be forced to use on Morgan. One death is necessary. Adding two more innocents to the count would be callous, pointless, and evil. The Council will interpret Dresden's actions as ultimately to the support of the Laws of Magic and the White Council. And that will be the end of it.'

There was no expression on Mai's face – absolutely none.

I couldn't have told you a darn thing about what was going on behind that mask. She stared at the two older wizards for a time, then at me. 'The Merlin will not be pleased.'

'That is good,' Listens-to-Wind said. 'No one should be pleased with this day's outcome.'

'I'll take Morgan into custody, Mai,' Ebenezar said. 'Why don't you take the Wardens back to the city in the boat? It should give you less trouble without me and Injun Joe on it. We'll follow along in the other boat.'

'Your word,' Mai said, 'that you will bring Morgan to Edinburgh.'

'Bring him and bring him unharmed,' Ebenezar said. 'You have my word.'

She nodded her head once. 'Wardens.'

Then she walked calmly out. The four Wardens fell into step behind her.

I kept track of them once they were outside. They started down the path that would lead them back to the dock.

I looked up at Listens-to-Wind. 'I need your help with something.'

He nodded.

'There's a patch of blackberry bushes out there. One of the Little Folk tried to play guardian angel for me. The naaglosh—'

'Don't say the word,' Listens-to-Wind said calmly. 'It draws power from fear, and from spreading its reputation. Referring to them by name can only increase their power.'

I snorted. 'I saw you send it running. You think I'm giving it any fear?'

'Not at the moment,' Injun Joe said. 'But speaking the word doesn't accomplish anything good. Besides, it's a sloppy habit to get into.'

I grunted. I could accept that. He'd probably phrased things that way intentionally. Besides, of the two of us, which one had a better track record against naagloshii? I decided to not be an idiot and listen to the medicine man.

'The creature,' I said, 'knocked him out of the air. Maybe hurt or killed him.'

Injun Joe nodded. His broken arm had been splinted with a field dressing and wrapped in medical tape. The Wardens had probably brought their own gear. 'I saw the very end of your fight. Which is why I felt it appropriate to give the creature the same treatment.' He shook his head. 'It took a lion's courage for the little one to do what he did. I already went looking for him.'

I felt a little bit sick. 'Was he . . . ?'

Listens-to-Wind smiled faintly and shook his head. 'Knocked senseless for a while, and wounded by blackberry thorns, though his armor protected him from the worst of it.'

I found myself barking out a short little laugh of relief. 'That *armor*? You're kidding.'

He shook his head. 'Worst thing hurt was his pride, I think.' His dark eyes sparkled. 'Little guy like that, taking on something so far out of his weight class. That was a sight to see.'

Ebenezar snorted. 'Yeah. Wonder where the pixie learned that.'

I felt my cheeks coloring. 'I didn't want to do it. I had to.'

'You picked a good fight,' Listens-to-Wind said. 'Not a very smart fight. But that old ghost is as close to pure evil as you'll ever see. Good man always stands against that.'

'You had it on the run,' I said. 'You could have killed it.'

'Sure,' Listens-to-Wind said. 'Would have been a chase, and then more fight. Might have taken hours. Would have made the old ghost desperate. It would have started using innocents as shields, obstacles, distractions.' The old medicine man shrugged. 'Maybe I would have lost, too. And while it was going on, spiders would be eating fat old hillbillies and picking their fangs clean with their bones.'

Ebenezar snorted. 'Never would have happened. I don't much care for vampires, especially not those White Court weasels, but I'll say this much for them. They can fight, when they have a mind to. After the first rush, those bugs were a lot more careful.'

'Yeah,' I said. 'They didn't have much of a spine when they tried to stop me on the trail to Edinburgh.'

Both of the old wizards traded a look, and then Injun Joe turned back to me. 'You got jumped by spiders going through the Way?'

'Yeah,' I said. I thought about it and was surprised. Had it happened so recently? 'Two days ago, when I came to Edinburgh. I told you about it. The killer must have had some kind of watch put on the Chicago end of the Way, to get them into position in time to intercept me.' I let out a weary little snigger.

'What's so funny?' Ebenezar asked.

'Nothing,' I said. 'Just appreciating irony and getting punchy. I guess he didn't want me letting the Council know where Morgan was.'

'Sounds like a reasonable theory,' Injun Joe said. He looked at Ebenezar. 'Got to be somebody at Edinburgh. Cuts the suspect pool down even more.'

Ebenezar grunted agreement. 'But not much. We're

getting closer.' He exhaled. 'But it won't do Morgan any good.' He stood, and his knees popped a couple of times on the way. 'All right, Hoss,' he said quietly. 'I guess we can't put this off any longer.'

I folded my arms and looked at Ebenezar evenly.

The old man's face darkened. 'Hoss,' he said quietly, 'I hate this as much as you do. But as much as you don't like it, as much as I don't like it, Ancient Mai is right about this. The real killer will know that Morgan is innocent – but the other powers won't. They'll only see us doing business hard and quick, like always. Hell, it might even get the real killer enough confidence to slip up and make a mistake.'

'I told Morgan I'd help him,' I said. 'And I will.'

'Son,' Injun Joe said quietly, 'no one can help him now.'

I ground my teeth. 'Maybe. Maybe not. But I'm not giving him to you. And I'll fight you if you make me.'

Ebenezar looked at me and then shook his head, smiling sadly. 'You couldn't fight one of your little pixie friends right now, boy.'

I shrugged. 'I'll try. You can't have him.'

'Harry,' said a quiet voice, weirdly mutated by the shield.

I looked up to see Morgan lying quietly on his pallet, his eyes open and focused on me. 'It's all right,' he said.

I blinked at him. 'What?'

'It's all right,' he said quietly. 'I'll go with them.' His eyes turned to Ebenezar. 'I killed LaFortier. I deceived Dresden into believing my innocence. I'll give you a deposition.'

'Morgan,' I said sharply, 'what the hell are you doing?'

'My duty,' he replied. There was, I thought, a faint

note of pride in his voice, absent since he had appeared at my door. 'I've always known that it might call for me to give up my life to protect the Council. And so it has.'

I stared at the wounded man, my stomach churning. 'Morgan . . .'

'You did your best,' Morgan said quietly. 'Despite everything that has gone between us. You put yourself to the hazard again and again for my sake. It was a worthy effort. But it just wasn't to be. No shame in that.' He closed his eyes again. 'You'll learn, if you live long enough. You never win them all.'

'Dammit,' I sighed. I tried to put my face in my hands and had to flinch back as my right cheek touched my skin and began to burn with pain. I still couldn't see out of my right eye. 'Dammit, after all this. Dammit.'

The fire popped and crackled and no one said anything.

'He's in a lot of pain,' Listens-to-Wind said quietly, breaking the silence. 'At least I can make him more comfortable. And you need some more attention, too.' He put a hand on my shoulder. 'Take the shield down. Please.'

I didn't want to do it.

But this wasn't about me.

I showed Molly how to lower the shield.

We got Morgan settled into a bunk on the *Water Beetle* and prepared to leave. Molly, troubled and worried about me, had volunteered to stay with Morgan. Listens-to-Wind had offered to show her something of what he did with healing magic. I grabbed some painkillers while we were there, and felt like I could at least walk far enough to find Will and Georgia.

Demonreach showed me where they were sleeping, and I led Ebenezar through the woods toward them.

'How did Injun Joe know about me claiming this place as a sanctum?' I asked.

'Messenger arrived from Rashid,' Ebenezar said. 'He's more familiar with what you can do with that kind of bond. So he went up to find you and get you to take those trees out from under the bugs.'

I shook my head. 'I've never seen anyone do shapeshifting the way he did it.'

'Not many ever have,' Ebenezar said, with obvious pride in his old friend's skills in his voice. After a moment, he said, 'He's offered to teach you some, if you want to learn.'

'With my luck? I'd shift into a duck or something, and not be able to come back out of it.'

He snorted quietly, and then said, 'Not shifting. He knows more than any man alive about dealing with rage over injustice and being unfairly wronged. Don't get me wrong. I think it's admirable that you have those kinds of feelings, and choose to do something about them. But they can do terrible things to a man, too.' His face was distant for a moment, his eyes focused elsewhere. 'Terrible things. He's been there. I think if you spent some time with him, you'd benefit by it.'

'Aren't I a little old to be an apprentice?'

'Stop learning, start dying,' Ebenezar said, in the tone of a man quoting a bedrock-firm maxim. 'You're never too old to learn.'

'I've got responsibilities,' I said.

'I know.'

'I'll think about it.'

He nodded. Then he paused for a moment, considering

his next words. 'There's one thing about tonight that I can't figure out, Hoss,' my old mentor said. 'You went to all the trouble to get everyone here. To lure the killer here. I give you a perfect excuse to roam free behind the lines with no one looking over your shoulder so you can get the job done. But instead of slipping up through the weeds and taking down the killer – which would clear up this whole business – you go up the hill and throw down with something you know damn well you can't beat.'

'Yeah,' I said. 'I know.'

Ebenezar spread his hands. 'Why?'

I walked for several tired, heavy steps before answering. 'Thomas got into trouble helping me.'

'Thomas,' Ebenezar said. 'The vampire.'

I shrugged.

'He was more important to you than stopping the possible fragmentation of the White Council.'

'The creature was heading straight for the cottage. My apprentice and my client were both there – and he had Thomas, too.'

Ebenezar muttered something to himself. 'The girl had that crystal to protect herself with. Hell, son, if it went off as violently as you said it would, it might have killed the creature all by itself.' He shook his head. 'Normally, I think you've got a pretty solid head on your shoulders, Hoss. But that was a bad call.'

'Maybe,' I said quietly.

'No maybe about it,' he replied firmly.

'He's a friend.'

Ebenezar stopped in his tracks and faced me squarely. 'He's *not* your friend, Harry. You might be his, but he isn't yours. He's a vampire. When all's said and done, he'd eat you if he was hungry enough. It's what he is.' Ebenezar gestured at the woods around us. 'Hell's bells, boy. We found what was left of that Raith creature's cousin, after the battle. And I figure you *saw* what it did to its own blood.'

'Yeah,' I said, subdued.

'And that was her own *family*.' He shook his head. 'Friendship means nothing to those creatures. They're so good at the lie that sometimes maybe they even believe it themselves – but in the end, you don't make friends with food. I been around this world a while, Hoss, and let me tell you – it's their nature. Sooner or later it wins out.'

'Thomas is different,' I said.

He eyed me. 'Oh?' He shook his head and started walking again. 'Why don't you ask your apprentice exactly what made her drop the veil and use that shield, then?'

I started walking again.

I didn't answer.

We got back into Chicago in the witching hour.

Ancient Mai and the Wardens were waiting at the dock, to escort Ebenezar, Injun Joe, and Morgan to Edinburgh – 'in case of trouble'. They left within three minutes of me tying the *Water Beetle* to the dock.

I watched them go, and sipped water through a straw. Listens-to-Wind had cleaned my wounds and slapped several stitches onto my face, including a couple on my lower lip. He told me that I hadn't lost the eye, and smeared the entire thing with a paste that looked like guano and smelled like honey. Then he'd made me a shoo-in for first place in the International Walking Wounded

Idiot competition, by covering that side of my face and part of my scalp with another bandage that wrapped all the way around my head. Added to the one I needed for the damn lump the skinwalker had given me, I looked like the subject of recent brain surgery, only surlier.

Will and Georgia were sleeping it off under a spread sleeping bag on an inflatable mattress on the rear deck of the *Water Beetle*, when I walked down the dock, over to the parking lot, and up to a parked Mercedes.

Vince rolled down his window and squinted at me. 'Did you curse everyone who desecrated your tomb, or just the English-speaking guys?'

'You just lost your tip,' I told him. 'Did you get it?'

He passed me a manila envelope without comment. Then he leaned over and opened his passenger door, and Mouse hopped down from the passenger seat and came eagerly around the car to greet me, wagging his tail. I knelt down and gave the big beastie a hug.

'Your dog is weird,' Vince said.

Mouse was licking my face. 'Yeah. Whatcha gonna do?'

Vince grinned, and for just a second, he didn't look at all nondescript. He had the kind of smile that could change the climate of a room. I stood up and nodded to him. 'You know where to send the bill.'

'Yep,' he said, and drove away.

I went back down to the boat and poured some Coke into the now-empty water bottle. I sipped at it carefully so that I wouldn't break open one of the cuts and bleed some more. I was too tired to clean it up.

Molly fussed around the boat for a few minutes, making sure it was tied down, and then took two sets of spare shorts and T-shirts from the cabin's tiny closet and left them where Georgia and Will would find them. She finally wound up sitting down on the other bunk across the cabin from me.

'The shield,' I said quietly. 'When did you use it?'

She swallowed. 'The skinw – the creature threw Thomas into the cabin and he . . .' She shuddered. 'Harry. He'd changed. It wasn't . . . it wasn't *him*.' She licked her lips. 'He sat up and started sniffing the air like . . . like a hungry wolf or something. Looking around for me. And his body was . . .' She blushed. 'He was hard. And he did something and all of a sudden I wanted to just rip my clothes off. And I knew he wasn't in control. And I knew he would kill me. But . . . I wanted to anyway. It was so *intense*. . . .'

'So you popped the shield.'

She swallowed and nodded. 'I think if I'd waited much longer . . . I wouldn't have been able to think of it.' She looked up at me and back down. 'He was changed, Harry. It wasn't him anymore.'

I left nothing behind. You don't have words for the things I did to him.

Thomas.

I put the drink aside and folded my arms over my stomach. 'You did good, kid.'

She gave me a tired smile. An awkward silence fell. Molly seemed to search for something to say. 'They're . . . they're going to try Morgan tomorrow,' she said quietly. 'I heard Mai say so.'

'Yeah,' I said.

'They expect us to be there.'

'Oh,' I said, 'we will be.'

'Harry . . . we failed,' she said. She swallowed. 'An

innocent man is going to die. The killer is still loose. That entire battle took place and didn't accomplish anything.'

I looked up at her. Then, moving deliberately, I opened the manila envelope Vince had given me.

'What's that?' she asked.

'Surveillance photos,' I said quietly. 'Shot through a telephoto lens from a block away.'

She blinked at me. 'What?'

'I hired Vince to take some pictures,' I said. 'Well, technically Murphy hired him, because I was worried about my phone being bugged. But I'm getting the bill, so really, it was me.'

'Pictures? What pictures?'

'Of the Way to Chicago from Edinburgh,' I said. 'Where it opens up into that alley behind the old meatpacking factory. I had Vince take pictures of anyone coming out of it, right after I informed Edinburgh about the meeting on the island.'

Molly frowned. 'But . . . why?'

'Didn't give them time to think, kid,' I said. 'I was fairly sure the killer was in Edinburgh. So I made sure he or she had to come to Chicago. I made sure he didn't have time to get here by alternate means.'

I drew out the pictures and started flipping through them. Vince had done a crisp, professional job. You could have used them for portraits, much less identification. McCoy, Mai, Listens-to-Wind, Bjorn Bjorngunnarson, the other Wardens were all pictured, both in a wide shot, walking in a *Right Stuff* group, and in tight focus on each face. 'And I made sure Vince and Mouse were there to watch the only fast way into town from Scotland.'

While I did that, Molly puzzled through the logic. 'Then . . . that entire scenario on the island . . . the meeting, the fight . . . the entire *thing* was a ploy?'

'Wile E. Coyote,' I said wisely. 'Suuuuuper Genius.'

Molly shook her head. 'But . . . you didn't tell anyone?'

'Nobody. Had to look good,' I said. 'Didn't know who the traitor might be, so I couldn't afford to give anyone any warning.'

'Wow, Obi-Wan,' the grasshopper said. 'I'm . . . sort of impressed.'

'The smackdown-on-the-island plan might have worked,' I said. 'And I needed it to get a crack at the skin-walker on friendly ground. But lately I've started thinking that you don't ever plan on a single path to victory. You set things up so that you've got more than one way to win.

'What I really needed was a weapon I could use against the killer.' I stared at the last photo for a moment, and then flipped it over and showed it to her. 'And now,' I said, a snarl coming unbidden into my voice, 'I've got one.'

Molly looked at the picture blankly. 'Oh,' she said. 'Who's that?'

47

Morgan's trial was held the next day, but since Scotland was six hours ahead of Chicago, I wound up getting about three hours' worth of sleep sitting up in a chair. My head and face hurt too much when I lay all the way down.

When I got back to the apartment with Molly, Luccio was gone.

I had been pretty sure she would be.

I got up the next morning and took stock of myself in the mirror. What wasn't under a white bandage was mostly bruised. That was probably the concussion grenade. I was lucky. If I'd have been standing where Lara had been when Binder's grenade went off, the overpressure would probably have killed me. I was also lucky that we'd been outdoors, where there was nothing to contain and focus the blast. I didn't feel lucky, but I was.

It could have been a fragmentation grenade spitting out a lethal cloud of shrapnel – though at least my duster would probably have offered me some protection from that. Against the blast wave of an explosion, it didn't do jack. Having gained something like respect for Binder's know-how, when it came to mayhem, I realized that he may have been thinking exactly that when he picked his gear for the evening.

I couldn't shower without getting my stitches wet, so after changing my bandages, I took a birdbath in the sink. I wore a button-up shirt, since I would probably compress my brain if I tried to pull on a tee. I also grabbed my formal black Council robe with its blue stole and my Warden's cape. I did my best to put my hair in order, though only about a third of it was showing. And I shaved.

'Wow,' Molly said as I emerged. 'You're taking this pretty seriously.' She was sitting in a chair near the fireplace, running her fingers lightly down Mister's spine. She was one of the few people he deemed worthy to properly appreciate him in a tactile sense. Molly wore her brown apprentice's robe, and if her hair was bright blue, at least she had it pulled back in a no-nonsense style. She never wore a lot of makeup, these days, but today she was wearing none at all. She had made the very wise realization that the less attention she attracted from the Council, the better off she would be.

'Yup. Cab here yet?'

She shook her head and rose, displacing Mister. He accepted the situation, despite the indignity. 'Come on, Mouse,' she said. 'We'll give you a chance to go before we head out.'

The big dog happily followed her out the door.

I got on the phone and called Thomas's apartment. There was no answer.

I tried Lara's number, and Justine answered on the first ring. 'Ms Raith's phone.'

'This is Harry Dresden,' I said.

'Hello, Mr Dresden,' Justine replied, her tone businesslike and formal. She wasn't alone. 'How may I help you today?'

Now that the furor of the manhunt had blown over, my phone was probably safe to talk on. But only probably.

I emulated Justine's vocal mannerisms. 'I'm calling to inquire after the condition of Thomas.'

'He's here,' Justine said. 'He's resting comfortably, now.'

I'd seen what terrible shape Thomas was in. If he was resting comfortably, it was because he had fed, deeply and intently, with instinctive obsession.

In all probability, my brother had killed someone.

'I hope he'll recover quickly,' I said.

'His caretaker—'

That would be Justine.

'—is concerned about complications arising from his original condition.'

I was quiet for a moment. 'How bad is it?'

The businesslike meter of her voice changed, filling with raw anxiety. 'He's under sedation. There was no choice.'

My knuckles creaked as they tightened on the earpiece of the phone.

I left nothing behind. You don't have words for the things I did to him.

'I'd like to visit, if that can be arranged.'

She recovered, shifting back into personal assistant mode. 'I'll consult Ms Raith,' Justine said. 'It may not be practical for several days.'

'I see. Could you let me know as soon as possible, please?'

'Of course.'

'My number is—'

'We have that information, Mr Dresden. I'll be in touch soon.'

I thanked her and hung up. I bowed my head and found myself shaking with anger. If that thing had done my brother as much harm as it sounded like, I was going to find the naagloshii and rip him to gerbil-sized pieces if I had to blow up every cave in New Mexico to do it.

Molly appeared in the doorway. 'Harry? Cab's here.'

'Okay,' I said. 'Let's go spoil someone's day.'

I tried not to think too hard about the fact that Wile E. Coyote, Super Genius, pretty near always took a hideous beating at the hands of his foes, and finished the day by plunging off a two-mile-high cliff.

Well, then, Harry, I thought to myself, *you'll just have to remember not to repeat Wile E.'s mistake. If he would just keep going after he runs off the cliff, rather than looking down at his feet, everything would be fine.*

They held the trial in Edinburgh.

There wasn't much choice in that. Given the recent threats to the Senior Council and the unexpected intensity of the attack at Demonreach, they wanted the most secure environment they could get. The trial was supposed to be held in closed session, according to the traditions of how such things were done, but this one was too big. Better than five hundred wizards, a sizable minority of the whole Council, would be there. Most of them would be allies of LaFortier and their supporters, who were more than eager to See Justice Done, which is a much prettier thing to do than to Take Bloodthirsty Vengeance.

Molly, Mouse, and I took the Way, just as I had before. This time, when I reached the door, there was a double-sized complement of Wardens on duty, led by the big Scandinavian, all of them from the Old Guard. I got a communal hostile glare from them as I approached, with only a desultory effort to disguise it as indifference. I ignored it. I was used to it.

We went into the complex, past the guard stations – they were all fully manned, as well – and walked toward the Speaking Room. Maybe it said something about the mind-set of wizards in general that the place was called 'the Speaking Room' and not 'the Listening Room' or, in the more common vernacular, 'an auditorium'. It *was* an auditorium, though, rows of stone benches rising in a full circle around a fairly small circular stone stage, rather like the old Greek theaters. But before we got to the Speaking Room, I turned off down a side passage.

With difficulty, I got the Wardens on guard to allow me, Mouse, and Molly into the Ostentatiatory while one of them went to Ebenezar's room and asked him if he would see me. Molly had never been into the enormous room before, and stared around it with unabashed curiosity.

'This place is amazing,' she said. 'Is the food for the bigwigs only, or do you think they'd mind if I ate something?'

'Ancient Mai doesn't weigh much more than a bird,' I said. 'LaFortier's dead, and they haven't replaced him yet. I figure there's extra.'

She frowned. 'But is it supposed to be only for them?'

I shrugged. 'You're hungry. It's food. What do you think?'

'I think I don't want to make anyone angry at me. Angrier.'

The kid has better sense than I do, in some matters.

Ebenezar sent the Warden back to bring me up to his room at once, and he'd already told the man to make sure Molly was fed from the buffet table. I tried not to smile, at that. Ebenezar was of the opinion that apprentices were always hungry. Can't imagine who had ever given him that impression.

I looked around his receiving room, which was lined with bookshelves filled to groaning. Ebenezar was an eclectic reader. King, Heinlein, and Clancy were piled up on the same shelves as Hawking and Nietzsche. Multiple variants of the great religious texts of the world were shamelessly mixed with the writings of Julius Caesar and D. H. Lawrence. Hundreds of books were handmade and handwritten, including illuminated grimoires any museum worth the name would readily steal, given the chance. Books were crammed in both vertically and horizontally, and though the spines were mostly out, it seemed clear to me that it would take the patience of Job to find anything, unless one remembered where it had been most recently placed.

Only one shelf looked neat.

It was a row of plain leather-bound journals, all obviously of the same general design, but made with subtly different leathers, and subtly different dyes that had aged independently of one another into different textures and shades. The books got older and more cracked and weathered rapidly as they moved from right to left. The leftmost pair looked like they might be in danger of falling to dust. The rightmost journal looked new, and was sitting open. A pen held the pages down, maybe thirty pages in.

I glanced at the last visible page, where Ebenezar's writing flowed in a strong, blocky style.

. . . seems clear that he had no idea of the island's original purpose. I sometimes can't help but think that there is such a thing as fate – or at least a higher power of some sort, attempting to arrange

events in our favor despite everything we, in our ignorance, do to thwart it. The Merlin has demanded that we put the boy under surveillance at once. I think he's a damn fool.

Rashid says that warning him about the island would be pointless. He's a good judge of people, but I'm not so sure he's right this time. The boy's got a solid head on his shoulders, generally. And of all the wizards I know, he's among the three or four I'd be willing to see take up that particular mantle. I trust his judgment.

But then again, I trusted Maggie's, too.

Ebenezar's voice interrupted my reading. 'Hoss,' he said. 'How's your head?'

'Full of questions,' I replied. I closed the journal, and offered him the pen.

My old mentor's smile only touched his eyes as he took the pen from me: he'd intended me to see what he'd written. 'My journal,' he said. 'Well. The last three are. The ones before that were from my master.'

'Master, huh?'

'Didn't use to be a dirty word, Hoss. It meant teacher, guide, protector, professional, expert – as well as the negative things. But it's the nature of folks to remember the bad things and forget the good, I suppose.' He tapped the three books previous to his own. 'My master's writings.' He tapped the next four. '*His* master's writings, and so on, back to here.' He touched the first two books, very gently. 'Can't hardly read them no more, even if you can make it through the language.'

'Who wrote those two?'

'Merlin,' Ebenezar said simply. He reached past me to put his own journal back up in place. 'One of these days, Hoss, I think I'll need you to take care of these for me.'

I looked from the old man to the books. The journals and personal thoughts of master wizards for more than a thousand years? Ye gods and little fishes.

That would be one hell of a read.

'Maybe,' Ebenezar said, 'you'd have a thought or two of your own, someday, that you'd want to write down.'

'Always the optimist, sir.'

He smiled briefly. 'Well. What brings you here before you head to the trial?'

I passed him the manila envelope Vince had given me. He frowned at me, and then started looking through pictures. His frown deepened, until he got to the very last picture.

He stopped breathing, and I was sure that he understood the implication. Ebenezar's brain doesn't let much grass grow under its lobes.

'Stars and stones, Hoss,' Ebenezar said quietly. 'Thought ahead this time, didn't you?'

'Even a broken clock gets it right occasionally,' I said.

He put the papers back in the envelope and gave it back to me. 'Okay. How do you see this playing out?'

'At the trial. Right before the end. I want him thinking he's gotten away with it.'

Ebenezar snorted. 'You're going to make Ancient Mai and about five hundred former associates of LaFortier very angry.'

'Yeah. I hardly slept last night, I was so worried about 'em.'

He snorted.

'I've got a theory about something.'

'Oh?'

I told him.

Ebenezar's face darkened, sentence by sentence. He turned his hands palm up and looked down at them. They were broad, strong, seamed, and callused with work – and they were steady. There were scabs on one palm, where he had fallen to the ground during last night's melee. Ink stained some of his fingertips.

'I'll need to take some steps,' he said. 'You'd best get a move on.'

I nodded. 'See you there?'

He took his spectacles off and began to polish the lenses carefully with a handkerchief. 'Aye.'

The trial began less than an hour later.

I sat on a stone bench that was set over to one side of the stage floor, Molly at my side. We were to be witnesses. Mouse sat on the floor beside me. He was going to be a witness, too, though I was the only one who knew it. The seats were all filled. That was why the Council met at various locations out in the real world, rather than in Edinburgh all the time. There simply wasn't enough room.

Wardens formed a perimeter all the way around the stage, at the doors, and in the aisles that came down between the rows of benches. Everyone present was wearing his or her formal robes, all flowing black, with stoles of silk and satin in one of the various colors and patterns of trim that denoted status among the Council's members. Blue stoles for members, red for those with a century of service, a braided silver cord for acknowledged master alchemists, a gold-stitched caduceus for master healers, a copper chevron near the collar for those with a doctorate in a scholarly discipline (some of the wizards had so many of them that they had stretched the fabric of the stole), an embroidered white Seal of Solomon for master exorcists and so on.

I had a plain blue stole with no ornaments whatsoever, though I'd been toying with the idea of embroidering 'GED' on it in red, white, and blue thread. Molly was the only one in the room wearing a brown robe.

People were avoiding our gazes.

The White Council loved its ceremonies. Anastasia Luccio appeared in the doorway in her full regalia, plus the grey cloak of the Wardens. Her arm was still in a sling, but she carried the ceremonial staff of office of the Captain of the Wardens in one hand. She entered the room, and the murmuring buzz of the crowd fell silent. She slammed the end of the staff three times upon the floor, and the six members of the Senior Council entered in their dark robes and purple stoles, led by the Merlin. They proceeded to the center rear of the stage and stood solemnly. Peabody appeared, carrying a lap-sized writing desk, and sat down on the far end of the bench from Molly and me, to begin taking notes, his pen scratching.

I put my hand on Mouse's head and waited for the show to begin – because that's all this was. A show.

Two more Wardens appeared with a bound figure between them. Morgan was brought in and stood as all accused brought before the Council did – with his hands bound in front of him and a black hood over his head. He wasn't in any shape to be walking, the idiot, but he was managing to limp heavily along without being physically supported by either Warden. He must have been on a load of painkillers to manage it.

The Merlin, speaking in Latin, said, 'We have convened today on a matter of justice, to try one Donald Morgan, who stands accused of the premeditated murder of Senior Council Member Aleron LaFortier, conspiracy with the enemies of the White Council, and treason against the White Council. We will begin with a review of the evidence.'

They stacked things up against Morgan for a while, laying out all the damning evidence. They had a lot of it. Morgan, standing there with the murder weapon in his hand, over the still-warm corpse. The bank account with slightly less than six million dollars suddenly appearing in it. The fact that he had escaped detention and badly wounded three Wardens in the process, and subsequently committed sedition by misleading other wizards – Molly and I were just barely mentioned by name – into helping him hide from the Wardens.

'Donald Morgan,' the Merlin said, 'have you anything to say in your defense?'

That part was sort of unusual. The accused were very rarely given much of a chance to say anything.

It clouded issues so.

'I do not contest the charges,' Morgan said firmly through his black hood. 'I, and I alone, am responsible for LaFortier's death.'

The Merlin looked like he'd just found out that someone had cooked up his own puppy in the sausage at breakfast that morning. He nodded once. 'If there is no other evidence, then the Senior Council will now pass—'

I stood up.

The Merlin broke off and blinked at me. The room fell into a dead silence, except for the scratch of Peabody's pen. He paused to turn to a new page and pulled a second inkwell out of his pocket, placing it on the writing desk.

Anastasia stared at me with her lips pressed together, her eyes questioning. What the hell was I doing?

I winked at her, then walked out into the center of the stage and turned to face the Senior Council.

'Warden Dresden,' Ebenezar said, 'have you some new evidence to present for the Senior Council's consideration?'

'I do,' I said.

'Point of order,' Ancient Mai injected smoothly. 'Warden Dresden was not present at the murder or when the accused escaped custody. He can offer no direct testimony as to the truth or falsehood of those events.'

'Another point of order,' Listens-to-Wind said. 'Warden Dresden earns a living as a private investigator, and his propensity for ferreting out the truth in difficult circumstances is well established.'

Mai looked daggers at Injun Joe.

'Warden Dresden,' the Merlin said heavily. 'Your history of conflict with Warden Morgan acting in his role as a Warden of the White Council is well-known. You should be advised that any damning testimony you give will be leavened with the knowledge of your history of extreme, sometimes violent animosity.'

The Merlin wasn't the Merlin for nothing. He had instincts enough to sense that maybe the game wasn't over yet, after all, and he knew how to play to the crowd. He wasn't warning me, so much as making sure that the wizards present knew how much I didn't like Morgan, so that my support would be that much more convincing.

'I understand,' I said.

The Merlin nodded. 'Proceed.'

I beamed at him. 'I feel just like Hercule Poirot,' I said, in my reasonably functional Latin. 'Let me enjoy this for a second.' I took a deep breath and exhaled in satisfaction.

The Merlin had masterful self-control. His expression never changed – but his left eye twitched in a nervous tic. Score one for the cartoon coyote.

'I first became suspicious that Morgan was being framed . . . well, basically when I heard the ridiculous charge against him,' I said. 'I don't know if you know this man, but I do. He's hounded me for most of my life. If he'd been accused of lopping off the heads of baby bunny rabbits because someone accused them of being warlocks, I could buy that. But this man could no more betray the White Council than he could flap his arms and fly.

'Working from that point, I hypothesized that another person within the Council had killed LaFortier and set Morgan up to take the blame. So I began an independent investigation.' I gave the Senior Council and the watching crowd of wizards the rundown of the past few days, leaving out the overly sensitive and unimportant bits. 'My investigation culminated in the theory that the guilty individual was not only trying to fix the blame upon Morgan, but planting the seeds of a renewed outbreak of hostilities with the vampire White Court, by implicating them in the death.

'In an effort to manipulate this person into betraying himself,' I continued, 'I let it be known that a conspirator had come forward to confess their part in the scheme, and would address members of the White Council at a certain place and time in Chicago. Working on the theory that the true killer was a member of the Council – indeed, someone here at headquarters in Edinburgh – I hypothesized that he would have little choice but to come to Chicago through the Way from Edinburgh, and I had the exit of that Way placed under surveillance.' I held up the manila envelope. 'These are the photographs taken at the scene, of everyone who came through the Way during the next several hours.'

I opened the envelope and began passing the Senior Council the photos. They took them, looking at each in turn. Ebenezar calmly confirmed that the images of the Wardens exiting the Way together with himself, Mai, and Listens-to-Wind were accurate.

'Other than this group,' I said, 'I believe it is highly unlikely that anyone from Edinburgh should have randomly arrived at the Way in Chicago. Given that the group was indeed assaulted by creatures with the support of a wizard of Council-level skill at that meeting, I believe it is reasonable to state that the killer took the bait.' I turned, drawing out the last photo with a dramatic flourish worthy of Poirot, and held it up so that the crowd could see it while I said, 'So why don't you tell us what you were doing in the Chicago area last night . . . Wizard Peabody?'

If I'd had a keyboard player lurking nearby for a soap-opera organ sting, it would have been perfect.

Everyone on the Senior Council except Ebenezar and, for some reason, the Gatekeeper, turned to stare slack-jawed at Peabody.

The Senior Council's secretary sat perfectly still beneath his little lap desk. Then he said, 'I take it that you have proof more convincing than a simple visual image? Such things are easily manufactured.'

'In fact,' I said, 'I do. I had a witness who was close enough to smell you.'

On cue, Mouse stood up and turned toward Peabody.

His low growl filled the room like a big, gentle drum-roll.

'That's all you have?' Peabody asked. 'A photo? And a dog?'

Mai looked as if someone had hit her between the eyes with a sledgehammer. 'That,' she said, in a breathless tone, 'is a Foo dog.' She stared at me. 'Where did you *get* such a thing? And *why* were you allowed to keep it?'

'He sort of picked me,' I said.

The Merlin's eyes had brightened. 'Mai. The beast's identification is reliable?'

She stared at me in obvious confusion. 'Entirely. There are several other wizards present who could testify to the fact.'

'Yes,' rumbled a stocky, bald man with an Asian cast to his features.

'It's true,' said a middle-aged woman, with skin several tones darker than my own, maybe from India or Pakistan.

'Interesting,' the Merlin said, turning toward Peabody. There was something almost sharklike about his sudden focus.

'Working on the evidence Dresden found,' Ebenezar said, 'Warden Ramirez and I searched Peabody's chambers thoroughly not twenty minutes ago. A test of the inks he used to attain the signatures of the Senior Council for various authorizations revealed the presence of a number of chemical and alchemical substances that are known to have been used to assist psychic manipulation of their subjects. It is my belief that Peabody has been drugging the ink for the purpose of attempting greater mental influence over the decisions of members of the Senior Council, and that it is entirely possible that he has compromised the free will of younger members of the Council outright.'

Listens-to-Wind's mouth opened in sudden surprise and understanding. He looked down at his ink-stained fingertips, and then up at Peabody.

Peabody may not have seen the man turn into a grizzly, but he was bright enough to know that Injun Joe was getting set to adjust another relative ass-to-ears ratio. The little secretary took one look around the room, and then at my dog. The expression went out of his face.

'The end,' he said, calmly and clearly, 'is nigh.'

And then he flung his spare pot of ink onto the floor, shattering the glass.

Mouse let out a *whuff*ing bark of warning, and knocked Molly backward off of the bench as a dark cloud rose up away from the smashed bottle, swelling with supernatural speed, tendrils reaching out in all directions. One of them caught a Warden who had leapt forward, toward Peabody.

It encircled his chest and then closed. Everything the slender thread of mist touched turned instantly to a fine black ash, slicing through him as efficiently as an electric knife through deli meat. The two pieces of the former Warden fell to the floor with wet, heavy thumps.

I'd seen almost exactly the same thing happen once before, years ago.

'Get back!' I screamed. 'It's mordite!'

Then the lights went out, and the room exploded into screams and chaos.

48

The truly scary part wasn't that I was standing five feet away from a cloud of weapons-grade deathstone that would rip the very life force out of everything it touched. It wasn't that I had confronted someone who was probably a member of the Black Council, probably as deadly in a tussle as their members always seemed to be, and who was certainly fighting with his back to the wall and nothing to lose. It wasn't even the fact that the lights had all gone out, and that a battle to the death was about to ensue.

The *scary* part was that I was standing in a relatively small, enclosed space with nearly six *hundred* wizards of the White Council, men and women with the primordial powers of the universe at their beck and call – and that for the most part, only the Wardens among them had much experience in controlling violent magic in combat conditions. It was like standing in an industrial propane plant with five hundred chain-smoking pyromaniacs double-jonesing for a hit: it would only take one dummy to kill us all, and we had four hundred and ninety-nine to spare.

'No lights!' I screamed, backing up from where I'd last seen the cloud. 'No lights!'

But my voice was only one amongst hundreds, and dozens of wizards reacted in the way I – and Peabody – had known they would. They'd immediately called light.

It made them instant, easy targets.

Cloudy tendrils of concentrated death whipped out to strike at the source of any light, spearing directly through anyone who got in the way. I saw one elderly woman lose an arm at the elbow as the mordite-laden cloud sent a spear of darkness flying at a wizard seated two rows behind her. A dark-skinned man with gold dangling from each ear roughly pushed a younger woman who had called light to a crystal in her hand. The tendril missed the woman but struck him squarely, instantly dissolving a hole in his chest a foot across, and all but cut his corpse in half as it fell to the floor.

Screams rose, sounds of genuine pain and terror – sounds the human body and mind are designed to recognize and to which they have no choice but to react. It hit me as hard as the first time I'd ever heard it happen – the desire to be *away* from whatever was causing such fear, combined with the simultaneous engagement of adrenaline, the need to *act*, to help.

Calmly, said a voice from right beside my right ear – except that it couldn't have been there because bandages covered that side of my head completely, and it was physically impossible for a voice to come through that clearly.

Which meant that the voice was an illusion. It was in my head. Furthermore, I recognized the voice – it was Langtry's, the Merlin's.

Council members, get on the ground immediately, said the Merlin's calm, unshakable voice. *Assist anyone who is bleeding and do not attempt to use lights until the mistfiend is contained. Senior Council, I have already engaged the mistfiend and am preventing it from moving any farther away. Rashid, prevent it from moving forward and disintegrating me, if you please. Mai and Martha Liberty, take its right flank, McCoy and Listens-to-Wind its left. It's rather strong-willed, so let's not dawdle, and remember that we must also prevent it from moving upward.*

The entire length of that dialogue, though I could have sworn it was physically audible, was delivered in less than half a second – speech at the speed of thought. It came accompanied with a simplified image of the Speaking Room, as if it had been drawn on a mental chalkboard. I could clearly see the swirling outline of the mistfiend surrounded by short blocks, with each block labeled with the names of the Senior Council and drawn to represent a section of three-dimensional dome that would hem the cloudy terror in.

Hell's bells. The Merlin had, in the literal length of a second and a half, turned pure confusion into an ordered battle. I guess maybe you don't get to be the Merlin of the White Council by saving up frequent-flier miles. I'd just never *seen* him in motion before.

Warden Dresden, the Merlin said. Or thought. Or projected. *If you would be so good as to prevent Peabody from escaping. Warden Thorsen and his cadre are on the way to support you, but we need someone to hound Peabody and prevent him from further mischief. We do not yet know the extent of his psychic manipulations, so trust none of the younger Wardens.*

I love being a wizard. Every day is like Disneyland.

I ripped off my ridiculous stole, robe, and cloak as I turned toward the doorway. The frantic motions of panic made the two or three light sources that had not been instantly snuffed into independent stroboscopes. Running toward the room's exit was a surreal experience, but I was certain that Peabody had planned his steps before he'd begun to move, and he'd had plenty of time to sprint across the room in the darkness and leave the auditorium.

I tried to think like a wizard who had just been outed as Black Council and marked for capture, interrogation, and probable death. Given that I had been fairly sure it was going to happen to *me* over the past few days, I'd already given consideration to how to get out of Council HQ, and I figured Peabody had taken more time to plan than I had.

If I was him, I'd rip open a Way into the Nevernever and close it behind me. I'd find a good spot to get out, and then I'd make sure it was prepared to be as lethally hostile to pursuers as I could make it. The centuries upon centuries of wards placed upon the Edinburgh tunnels by generations of wizards, though, prevented any opening to the Nevernever from inside the security checkpoints, so Peabody would have to get through at least one Warden-manned security gate before he enacted his plan.

I had to stop him before he got that far.

I plunged through the doorway and noted that both Wardens on guard outside were of the younger generation who had risen to the ranks since the disastrous battle with the Red Court in Sicily. Both young men were standing blankly at attention, showing no reaction whatsoever to the furor in the Speaking Room.

A corner of a black formal robe snapped as its wearer rounded a corner in the hallway to my right, and I was off and running. I felt like hell, but for a refreshing change of pace, I had an advantage over an older, more experienced wizard – I was younger and in better shape.

Wizards might stay alive and vigorous for centuries, but their bodies still tend to lose physical ability if they do not take great pains to stay in training. Even then, they still don't have the raw capabilities of a young person –

and running at a dead sprint is as raw as physical activity gets.

I rounded the corner and caught a glimpse of Peabody, running up ahead of me. He turned another corner, and by the time I rounded that one, I had gained several steps on him. We blew through Administration and passed the Warden barracks, where three Wardens who were still freaking teenagers, the dangerous babies we'd hurried through military training for the war, emerged from the doors twenty feet ahead of Peabody.

'The end is nigh!' he snarled.

All three of them froze in their tracks, their expressions going blank, and Peabody went through the group, puffing, and knocked one of them down. I pushed harder, and he started glancing over his shoulder, his eyes wide.

He ducked around the next corner, and my instincts twigged to what he was about to try. I came around the corner and flung myself into a diving roll, and a spray of conjured liquid hissed as it went by overhead. It smacked against the wall behind me with a frantic chewing noise, like a thousand bottles of carbonated soda all shaken and simultaneously opened.

I hadn't had time to recharge my energy rings, and they were still on my dresser back home, but I didn't want Peabody to get comfortable taking shots at me over his shoulder. I lifted my right hand, snarled, '*Fuego!*' and sent a basketball-sized comet of fire flying down the hallway at him.

He spat out a few words and made a one-handed defensive gesture that reminded me of Doctor Strange, and my attacking spell splashed against something invisible a good three feet short of him. Even so, some of it wound up setting the hem of his formal robe on fire, and he frantically shucked out of it as he continued to flee.

I made up even more distance on him, and as he turned into one of the broad main hallways of the complex, I wasn't twenty feet away, and the first security checkpoint was right in front of us. Four Wardens, all of them young, manned the gate – which was to say that, since all the grown-ups, grandpas, and fussbudgets who might object were at the trial, they were sitting on the floor playing cards.

'Stop that man!' I shouted.

Peabody shrieked, obviously terrified, 'Dresden's gone warlock! He's trying to kill me!'

The young Wardens bounced to their feet with the reaction speed of youth. One of them reached for his staff, and another drew his gun. A third turned and made sure the gate was locked – and the fourth acted on pure instinct, whipping her hand around her head in a tight circle and making a throwing gesture as she shouted.

I brought up my shield in time to intercept an invisible bowling ball, but the impact hit the shield with enough force to stop me cold. My legs weren't ready for that, and I staggered, bouncing a shoulder off of one wall.

Peabody's eyes gleamed with triumph as I fell, and he snapped, 'The end is nigh!' freezing the young Wardens in place, as he'd done before. He ripped the key on its leather thong from around the neck of one of the Wardens, opened the gate, then turned with a dagger in his hand and sliced it along the thigh of the young woman who had clobbered me. She cried out and her leg began spurting blood in rhythm with her heart, a telltale sign of a severed artery.

I got back to my feet and hurled a club of raw force at Peabody, but he defeated it as he had the fireball, leapt through the gate, and ripped at the air, peeling open a passage between this world and the next.

He plunged through it.

'Son of a *bitch*,' I snarled. None of the young Wardens were moving, not even the wounded girl. If she didn't get help, she would bleed to death in minutes. 'Dammit!' I swore. 'Dammit, dammit, dammit!' I threw myself onto the girl, ripping the belt off of my jeans and praying that the wound was far enough down her leg for a tourniquet to do any good.

Footsteps hammered the floor, and Anastasia Luccio appeared, gun in her good hand, her face white with pain. She slid to a halt next to me, breathing hard, set the weapon on the floor, and said, 'I've got her. Go!'

On the other side of the security gate, the Way was beginning to close.

I rose and rushed it, diving forward. There was a flash of light, and the stone tunnel around me abruptly became a forest of dead trees that smelled strongly of mildew and stagnant water. Peabody was standing right in front of the Way as he tried to close it, and I hit him in a flying tackle before he could finish the job. He went over backward and we hit the ground hard.

For a stunned half second, neither of us moved, and then Peabody shifted his weight, and I caught the gleam of the bloodied dagger at the edge of my vision.

He thrust the point at my throat, but I got an arm in the way. He opened a vein. I grabbed at his wrist with my other hand, and he rolled, gaining the upper position and gripping the dagger with both hands, leaning against my one arm with all of his weight. Drops of my own blood fell onto my face as he forced the point slowly toward my eye.

I struggled to throw him off me, but he was stronger than he looked, and it was clear that he had more experience in close-quarters fighting than I did. I clubbed at him with my wounded arm, but he shrugged it off.

I felt my triceps giving way and watched the tip of the knife come closer. The breaking point was at hand and he knew it. He threw more effort into his attack, and the dagger's tip suddenly stung hot against my lower eyelid.

Then there was a huge noise, and Peabody went away. I remained still for a stunned moment, and then looked up.

Morgan lay on the ground just inside the still-open Way, Luccio's gun smoking in his hand, his wounded leg a mass of wet scarlet.

How he'd managed to run after us given his injury, I had no idea. Even with painkillers, it must have hurt like hell. He stared at Peabody's body with hard eyes. Then his hand started to shake, and he dropped the gun to the ground.

He followed it down with a groan.

I went to him, breathing hard. 'Morgan.' I turned him over and looked at his wound. It was soaked in blood, but it wasn't bleeding much anymore. His face was white. His lips looked grey.

He opened his eyes calmly. 'Got him.'

'Yeah,' I said. 'You got him.'

He smiled a little. 'That's twice I pulled your ass out of the fire.'

I choked out a little laugh. 'I know.'

'They'll blame me,' he said quietly. 'There's no confession from Peabody, and I'm a better candidate politically. Let them pin it on me. Don't fight it. I want it.'

I stared down at him. 'Why?'

He shook his head, smiling wearily.

I stared down at him for long seconds, and then I got it. Morgan had been lying to me from the very start. 'Because you already knew who killed LaFortier. She was there when you woke up in his chambers. You saw who did it. And you wanted to protect her.'

'Anastasia didn't do it,' Morgan said, his voice intense and low. 'She was a pawn. Asleep on her feet. She never even knew she was being used.' He shuddered. 'Should have thought of that. She got put in that younger body, made her mind vulnerable to influence again.'

'What happened?' I asked.

'Woke up, LaFortier was dead, and she had the knife. Took it from her, veiled her, and pushed her out the door,' Morgan said. 'Didn't have time to get both of us out.'

'So you took the blame thinking you'd sort things out in the aftermath. But you realized that the frame was too good for anyone to believe you when you tried to tell them what was up.' I shook my head. Morgan hadn't given a damn about his own life. He'd escaped when he realized that Anastasia had still been in danger, that he wouldn't be able to expose the real traitor alone.

'Dresden,' he said quietly.

'Yeah?'

'I didn't tell anyone about Molly. What she tried to do to Ana. I . . . I didn't tell.'

I stared at him, unable to speak.

His eyes became cloudy. 'Do you know why I didn't? Why I came to you?'

I shook my head.

'Because I knew,' he whispered. He lifted his right hand, and I gripped it hard. 'I knew that you knew how it felt to be an innocent man hounded by the Wardens.'

It was the closest he'd ever come to saying that he'd been wrong about me.

He died less than a minute later.

49

Thorsen kept me from bleeding to death from the cut Peabody had given me. The Swede and his backup squad had been faced with a long run to catch up, a lot of locked gates, and the confusion we'd left in our wake. They reached me about three minutes after Morgan died. They did their best to revive Morgan, but his body had taken enough torment and lost too much blood. They didn't even bother with Peabody. Morgan had double-tapped the traitor's head with Luccio's pistol.

They bundled me off to the infirmary, where Injun Joe and a crew of healers – some of whom had gone to medical school when the efficacy of *leeches* was still being debated – were caring for those wounded in the attack.

After that, things fell into place without requiring my participation.

The Senior Council managed to contain and banish the mordite-infused mistfiend, a rare and dangerous gaseous being from the far reaches of the Nevernever, before it had killed more than forty or fifty wizards. All things considered, it could have been a lot worse, but the fact that it had been the gathering of LaFortier's former political allies who had been subject to the attack occasioned an enormous outcry of suspicion, with the offended parties claiming that the Merlin had disregarded their safety, been negligent in his security precautions, etc., etc. The fact that the attack had occurred while unmasking LaFortier's true killer was brushed aside. There was political capital to be had.

Basically the entire supernatural world had heard about LaFortier's death, the ensuing manhunt for Morgan, and the dustup during his trial, though most of the details were kept quiet. Though there was never any sort of official statement made, word got out that Morgan had been conspiring with Peabody, and that both of them had been killed during their escape attempt.

It was a brutal and callous way for the Council to save face. The Merlin decided that it was ultimately less dangerous for the wizards of the world if everyone knew that the Council responded to LaFortier's murder with a statement of deadly strength and power – i.e., the immediate capture and execution of those responsible.

But I knew that whoever Peabody had been in bed with, the people who had *really* been responsible knew that the Council had killed an innocent man, and one of their largest military assets, at that, to get the job done.

Maybe the Merlin was right. Maybe it's better to look stupid but strong than it is to look smart but weak. I don't know. I'm not sure I want to believe that the world stage bears that strong a resemblance to high school.

The Council's investigators worked more slowly than Lara's had, but they got to the same information by following the money, eventually. The Council confronted the White Court with the information.

Lara sent them the heads of the persons responsible. Literally. Leave it to Lara to find a way to get one last bit of mileage out of Madeline and the business manager's corpses. She told the Council to keep the money, too, by way of apology. The next best thing to six million in cash buys a lot of oil to pour on troubled waters.

He might have wound up with his brains splattered all over a desolate little hellhole in the Nevernever, but Peabody had inflicted one hell of a lot of damage before he was through. A new age of White Council paranoia had begun.

The Merlin, the Gatekeeper, and Injun Joe investigated the extent of Peabody's psychic infiltration. In some ways, the worst of what he'd done was the easiest to handle. Damn near every Warden under the age of fifty had been programmed with that go-to-sleep trance command, and it had been done so smoothly and subtly that it was difficult to detect even when the master wizards were looking and knew where to find it.

Ebenezar told me later that some of the young Wardens had been loaded up with a lot more in the way of hostile psychic software, though it was impossible for one wizard to know exactly what another had done. Several of them, apparently, had been intended to become the supernatural equivalent of suicide bombers – the way Luccio had been. Repairing that kind of damage was difficult, unpredictable, and often painful to the victim. It was a long summer and autumn for a lot of the Wardens, and a mandatory psychic self-defense regimen was instituted within weeks.

It was tougher for the members of the Senior Council, in my opinion, all of whom had almost certainly been influenced in subtle ways. They had to go back over their decisions for the past several years, and wonder if they had been pushed into making a choice, if it had been their own action, or if the ambiguity of any given decision had been natural to the environment. The touch had been so light that it hadn't left any lasting tracks. For anyone with half a conscience, it would be a living nightmare, especially given the fact that they had been leading the Council in time of war.

I tried to imagine second-guessing myself on everything I'd done for the past eight years.

I wouldn't be one of those guys for the world.

I was in the infirmary for a week. I got visits from McCoy, Ramirez, and Molly. Mouse stayed at my bedside, and no one tried to move him. Listens-to-Wind was a regular presence, since he was pretty much my doctor. Several of the young Wardens I had helped train stopped by to have a word, though all of them were looking nervous.

Anastasia never visited, though Listens-to-Wind said she had come by and asked after me when I was asleep.

The Gatekeeper came to see me in the middle of the night. When I woke up, he had already created a kind of sonic shield around us that made sure we were speaking in privacy. It made our voices sound like our heads were covered with large tin pails.

'How are you feeling?' he asked quietly.

I gestured at my face, which was no longer bandaged. As Listens-to-Wind had promised, my eye was fine. I had two beautiful scars, though, one running down through my right eyebrow, skipping my eye, and continuing for an inch or so on my cheekbone, and another one that went squarely through the middle of my lower lip and on a slight angle down over my chin. 'Like Herr Harrison von Ford,' I said. 'Dueling scars and beauty marks. The girls will be lining up now.'

The quip didn't make him smile. He looked down at his hands, his expression serious. 'I've been working with the Wardens and administrative staff whose minds Peabody invaded.'

'I heard.'

'It appears,' he said, choosing his words carefully, 'that the psychic disruption to Anastasia Luccio was particularly severe. I was wondering if you might have any theories that might explain it.'

I stared across the darkened room quietly for a moment, then asked, 'Did the Merlin send you?'

'I am the only one who knows,' he said seriously. 'Or who will know.'

I thought about it for a moment before I said, 'Would my theory make any difference in how she gets treated?'

'Potentially. If it seems sound, it might give me the insight I need to heal her more quickly and safely.'

'Give me your word,' I said. I wasn't asking.

'You have it.'

'Before he died,' I said, 'Morgan told me that when he woke up in LaFortier's room, Luccio was holding the murder weapon.' I described the rest of what Morgan had told me of that night.

The Gatekeeper stared across the bed at the far wall, his face impassive. 'He was trying to protect her.'

'I guess he figured the Council might do some wacky thing like sentencing an innocent person to death.'

He closed his eyes for a moment, and then touched the fingertips of his right hand to his heart, his mouth, and his forehead. 'It explains some things.'

'Like what?'

He held up his hand. 'In a moment. I told you that the damage to Anastasia was quite extensive. Not because she had been persuaded to do violence – that much came easily to her. I believe her emotional attitudes had been forcibly altered.'

'Emotional attitudes,' I said quietly. 'You mean . . . her and me?'

'Yes.'

'Because she always believed in keeping her distance,' I said quietly. 'Until recently.'

'Yes,' he said.

'She . . . never cared about me.'

He shrugged his shoulders. 'There had to have been some kind of foundation upon which to build. It's entirely possible that she genuinely felt fond of you, and that something might have grown from it. But it was forced into place instead.'

'Who would do that?' I shook my head. 'No, that's obvious. *Why* would he do that?'

'To keep tabs on you, perhaps,' the Gatekeeper replied. 'Perhaps to have an asset in position to remove you, if it became necessary. You were, after all, virtually the only younger Warden who never gave Peabody an opportunity to exploit you, since you never came to headquarters. You're also probably the most talented and powerful of your generation. The other young Wardens like to associate with you, generally, so there was every chance you might notice something amiss. Taken as a whole, you were a threat to him.'

I felt a little sick. 'That's why she showed up in Chicago when she should have been back at headquarters helping with the manhunt.'

'Almost certainly,' he said. 'To give Peabody forewarning if you should get closer to his trail, and to locate Morgan so that Peabody could make him disappear. Morgan dead at the hands of White Council justice is one thing. Had

Peabody succeeded, killed Morgan, and gotten rid of the body, then as far as we knew the traitor would be at large in the world, and uncatchable. It would have been a continuous stone around our necks.'

'And a perfect cover for Peabody,' I said. 'He could off whoever he wanted, and given the slightest excuse, everyone would assume that it had been Morgan.'

'Not only Peabody,' the Gatekeeper said. 'Any of our enemies might have taken advantage of it the same way.'

'And it also explains why he came to Chicago after I dropped that challenge on the Council. He probably thought that the fake informant was Anastasia. He had to go there to find out if his brainlock was holding.' I shook my head. 'I mean, he never needed to come through that Way since he already knew one out to Demonreach. Christ, I got lucky.'

'Also true,' the Gatekeeper said. 'Though I would suggest that your forethought allowed you to make your own luck.' He shook his head. 'If Morgan had not acted so quickly, things might have been even worse. Luccio would have stood accused as well, and neither of them would have had any idea what had happened. Accusing Morgan was bad enough – the Wardens would not have stood for both the Captain and her second to be placed under arrest. It might have begun a civil war all on its own.'

'Morgan . . . he loved Luccio,' I said.

The Gatekeeper nodded. 'He wore his heart on his sleeve for quite a while when he was younger. But she never let anyone close. In retrospect, it was a personality shift that should have been noted, though she kept her relationship with you discreet.'

I snorted quietly. 'Easy to expect tampering when someone turns into a foaming maniac,' I said. 'When someone changes by becoming happy, it's sort of hard not to be happy for them.'

He smiled, a brief flash of warmth. 'Very true.'

'So she's . . . I mean, when you help her start fixing the damage . . .'

'It's already begun. Her subconscious has been struggling against the bindings placed in her mind for some time. Even if she'd felt something before, the fact that it was forced upon her will cause a backlash.'

'Yeah,' I said. 'Things got sort of tense between us, I guess, after this whole situation got going. I mean, I sort of figured we'd already broken up, but . . .'

But this wasn't a case of having loved and lost. She had never loved me. Madeline's kiss, when she'd buried me in an avalanche of bliss while she took a bite from my life force, had proved that. Anastasia hadn't ever been in love. Maybe she hadn't ever really liked me. Or maybe she *had*. Or maybe it was all of the above.

Whatever it had been, it was over now, before it could grow into anything else, and neither of us had been given much of a choice in the matter.

I hadn't expected it to hurt quite as much as it did.

Rashid put his hand on my shoulder. 'I'm sorry,' he said. 'I thought you deserved to know.'

'Yeah,' I said, my voice rough. 'Thank you. I guess.' I found myself letting out a bitter little laugh.

The Gatekeeper tilted his head.

'I've been trying to work out why no one used magic on anyone at LaFortier's murder.'

'What is your conclusion?'

'You can't do anything with magic that you don't really, truly believe in,' I said. 'Some part of Luccio had to recognize that killing LaFortier was wrong. So she used a knife. Morgan could no more have unleashed magic upon a lawfully serving Senior Council member or onto his commanding officer than he could have apologized for how he's treated me. And LaFortier never saw it coming from Anastasia. He probably died confused, never had a chance to use a spell.' I looked up at the Gatekeeper. 'It wasn't some big arcane, mysterious reason. It was because everyone was human.'

'In my experience,' he said, 'that is more than mystery enough.'

I was gathering my things to leave and go back home when Ebenezar appeared in the doorway. 'Hoss,' he said calmly. 'Figured I would walk you home.'

'Appreciated, sir,' I told him. I had already sent Mouse home with Molly, and it was always a good idea to avoid walking the Ways alone. We started walking through the tunnels. I was heartily sick of them. I'm not claustrophobic or anything, but I think you'd need some kind of groundhog gene to enjoy living at White Council HQ.

We hadn't gone far when I realized that Ebenezar was taking a roundabout route to the Way, through tunnels that were largely unused and unlit. He conjured a dim red light to his staff, just enough to let us see our way, and in the color least likely to be noticed.

'Well,' he said, 'we filled LaFortier's seat on the Senior Council today.'

'Klaus the Toymaker?' I asked.

Ebenezar shook his head slowly. 'Klaus didn't say it, but I suspect the Merlin asked him to decline. Gregori Cristos got the seat.'

I frowned. The seats on the Senior Council were awarded geriocratically. Whoever had the most years of service in the Council was offered the position of leadership, though there was nothing that required a wizard to accept a seat when it was available. 'Who the hell is that? He's not up at the top of the seniority list.'

My mentor grimaced. 'Aye. A Greek, and an unpleasant bastard. He's lived all through southern Asia over the past couple of centuries. Distinguished himself in the battle with that rakshasa raja the Council took on recently.'

'I remember when it happened,' I said. 'I heard it was pretty crazy.'

Ebenezar grunted. 'He was LaFortier's protégé.'

I took that in, processing the logic. 'I thought that bloc had been appeased.'

'When someone wants power, you can't buy him off,' Ebenezar said. 'He'll take what you offer and keep on coming. And Cristos as much as told the Merlin that he and his allies would secede from the Council if he didn't get the seat.'

'Jesus,' I said quietly.

He nodded. 'Might as well give the Red Court the keys to all our gates and let them kill us in our sleep. Fewer bystanders would get hurt.'

'So the Merlin made a deal,' I said.

'Didn't have a lot of choice. Cristos's people gained a lot of support after they lost so many at the trial. He'd have taken a third of the Council with him.'

'Screw the selection process, huh?'

Ebenezar grimaced. 'It's never been codified by anything but tradition. Oh, the Merlin made a show of adhering to it, but I guarantee you it was arranged behind the scenes,

Hoss.' He shook his head. 'The Senior Council has issued official positions on LaFortier's assassination.'

'Let me guess,' I said. 'Lone gunman.'

He frowned at that for a moment, and then nodded. 'Oh, Kennedy. Yes. It was an act of individuals motivated by profit. There is no evidence to suggest the presence of an organized conspiracy. There is no Black Council.'

I stared blankly at Ebenezar. 'That's . . . *stupid*.'

'Damn right,' he said. 'But they had a majority. The Merlin, Cristos, Mai, Martha Liberty, and the Gatekeeper.'

I shook my head. 'What the *hell* does he think he's accomplishing?'

Ebenezar shrugged. 'He's never been easy to read. And I've known him since I was sixteen years old. Two or three explanations come to mind.'

'Like, maybe he's Black Council.'

Ebenezar walked for several steps in silence. Then he said, 'Aye.'

'Or maybe Peabody got to him harder than we all think,' I said.

'Improbable,' Ebenezar said. 'The drugs he slipped the Senior Council let him nudge them . . . us. But we're all too crusty to bend more than that.'

'What then?'

'Well, Hoss,' he said, 'maybe Langtry's worried about the consequences of officially acknowledging the Black Council.'

I felt a little chill glide over the nape of my neck. 'He's worried that if enough people knew that the Black Council was real, they wouldn't line up to fight them. They'd join.'

'Everyone loves a winner,' Ebenezar said. 'And we haven't been looking too good lately. People are afraid. Cristos is building his influence on it.'

I stopped in my tracks and all but threw up on the cold stone floor.

Ebenezar stopped, putting his hand on my arm, and frowned in concern. 'What is it, boy?'

'Sir,' I said, hearing my voice shake. 'When Peabody came to the island . . .'

'Yes?'

'He wasn't alone. Someone else came with him. Someone we never saw.'

We said nothing for a long minute.

'That's only one explanation, Hoss,' Ebenezar said. 'It's not even a calculated estimate. It's a flat-out guess.'

There was no conviction in his voice, though. Ebenezar felt the same thing I did. A hard gut feeling that left me certain – not pretty sure, but *certain* – that I was right. Besides. We were talking in whispers in an out-of-the-way corridor of our own damn stronghold. If that didn't tell you something was seriously wrong with the White Council, I don't know what would.

'They're inside,' I whispered.

My mentor faced me gravely.

'That's why they whacked LaFortier. To get their own man into position.' I leaned against the wall and shook my head. 'They won.'

'They won the round,' he said. 'Fight isn't over.'

'It is for Morgan,' I said.

'But not for you,' he said with harsh intensity. 'Morgan thought that saving your life was worth losing his own.' Ebenezar took a deep breath. Then he said, very quietly, 'Hoss, it ain't over. Some of us are going to do something about it.'

I looked at him sharply. 'Do something?'

'It's just a few, for now. Some wizards. Some key allies. People we know we can trust. I'm the only one who knows everyone involved. We've got to take this fight to the enemy. Learn more about them. Determine their goals. Shut them down.'

'Fight fire with fire, eh?'

Ebenezar smiled wryly. 'In denying the existence of one conspiracy, Langtry has necessitated another.'

'And got himself a twofer with a side order of irony,' I said. 'If the Black Council finds out about us, they're going to jump for joy. They'll expose us, call *us* the Black Council, and go on their merry way.'

'"Us" already, is it?' His eyes gleamed as he nodded. 'And given what we'll be doing, if the White Council finds out, they're going to call it sedition. They'll execute us.'

See what I mean? *Just* like Disneyland.

I thought about it for a minute. 'You know that in every objective sense, we're making a Black Council of our own.'

'Aye.'

'So where does that leave us?'

'With pure hearts and good intentions,' he answered. 'Our strength shall be the strength of ten.'

I snorted loudly.

Ebenezar smiled wearily. 'Well, Hoss, we're not going to have much choice other than to be walking down some mighty dark alleys. And doing it in mighty questionable company. Maybe we should think of ourselves as . . . a Grey Council.'

'Grey Council,' I said. We started walking again, and after a few minutes, I asked him, 'The world's gotten darker and nastier, even in just the past few years. Do you think what we do will make a difference?'

'I think the same thing you do,' Ebenezar said. 'That the only alternative is to stand around and watch everything go to hell.' His voice hardened. 'We're not going to do that.'

'Damn right we're not,' I said.

We walked the rest of the way to Chicago together.

Murphy drove me down to get my car out of impound, and I caught her up on most of what had happened on the way.

'You're holding out on me,' she said, when I finished.

'Some,' I said. 'Sort of necessary.'

She glanced at me as she drove and said, 'Okay.'

I lifted my eyebrows. 'It is?'

'You are beginning to deal with some scary people, Harry,' she said quietly. 'And people are trusting you with secrets. I get that.'

'Thanks, Murph.'

She shook her head. 'I don't know, Harry. It means I'm trusting you to come to me when you've got something that intersects with my responsibilities. I'm a cop. If you screw me on something I *should* know . . .' She shrugged. 'I don't know if we could ever patch something like that up.'

'I hear you,' I said.

She shook her head. 'I never really cared for Morgan. But I wish it hadn't ended that way for him.'

I thought about that for a minute and then said, 'I don't know. He went out making a difference. He took out the traitor who had gotten hundreds of wizards killed. He kept him from getting away with God only knows what secrets.' I shrugged. 'A lot of Wardens have gone down lately.

As exits go, Morgan's was a good one.' I smiled. 'Besides. If he'd been around any longer, he might have had to apologize to me. *That* would have been a horrible way to go.'

'He had courage,' Murphy admitted. 'And he had your back.'

'Yeah,' I said.

'Did you go to his funeral?'

'No one did,' I said. 'Officially, he was *corpus non gratus*. But we had a kind of a wake, later, unofficially. Told stories about him and came to the conclusion that he really was a paranoid, intolerant, grade-A asshole.'

Murphy smiled. 'I've known guys like that. They can still be part of the family. You can still miss them when they're gone.'

I swallowed. 'Yeah.'

'Tell me you aren't blaming yourself.'

'No,' I said, honestly. 'I just wish something I'd done had made more of a difference.'

'You survived,' she said. 'Under the circumstances, I think you did all right.'

'Maybe,' I said quietly.

'I went through that phone you sent me.' She meant Madeline's phone, the one Binder had given me.

'What did you find?' I asked.

'The phone numbers to a lot of missing persons,' she said. 'Where's the owner?'

'With them.'

She pressed her lips together. 'There were a lot of calls to a number I traced back to Algeria, and another in Egypt. A couple of restaurants, apparently.' She took an index card out of her pocket and passed it to me. It had the names and addresses of two businesses on it.

'What are they?' she asked.

'No clue,' I said. 'Maybe Madeline's contacts in the Black Council. Maybe nothing.'

'Important?'

'No clue. I guess we'll file this under "wait and see".'

'I hate that file,' she said. 'How's Thomas?'

I shrugged and looked down at my hands. 'No clue.'

My apartment was a wreck. I mean, it's never really a surgical theater – except for right after Morgan had shown up, I guess. But several days of frantic comings and goings, various injuries, and serving as Morgan's sickbed had left some stains not even my faerie housekeepers could erase. The mattress wasn't salvageable, much less the bedding, or the rug we'd transported his unconscious body on. It was all soaked in blood and sweat, and the various house-keeping faeries apparently didn't do dry cleaning.

They'd taken care of the usual stuff, but there was consid-erable work still to be done, and moving mattresses is never joyful, much less when you've been thoroughly banged up by a supernatural heavyweight and then stabbed, just for fun, on top of it.

I set about restoring order, though, and I was hauling the mattress out to tie onto my car so that I could take it to the dump, when Luccio arrived.

She was dressed in grey slacks and a white shirt, and carried a black nylon sports equipment bag, which would hold, I knew, the rather short staff she favored and her Warden's blade, among other things. The clothes were new. I realized, belatedly, that they'd been the sort that she'd favored when I first met her, wearing another body.

'Hey,' I panted. 'Give me a second.'

'I'll give you a hand,' she replied. She helped me maneuver the mattress onto the top of the *Blue Beetle*, and then we tied it off with some clothesline. She checked the knots, making sure everything was just so, and then leaned on the car, studying my face.

I looked back at her.

'Rashid said he talked to you,' she said.

I nodded. 'Didn't want to push.'

'I appreciate that. Quite a bit, actually.' She looked off to one side. Mouse, now that the work was done, came out of a shamelessly lazy doze he'd been holding in the doorway and trotted over to Luccio. He sat down and offered her his paw.

She smiled quietly and took it. Then she ruffled the fur behind his ears with her fingers, the way she knew he liked, and stood up. 'I, ah . . . I wanted to be sure you were recovering.'

'That's very responsible of you,' I said.

She winced. 'Ah. Dammit to hell, Dresden.' She shook her head. 'I spent almost two hundred years *not* getting close to anyone. For damn good reasons. As can be evidenced by what happened here.'

'Can it?'

She shook her head. 'I was . . . distracted, by you. By . . . us, I suppose. Maybe if I hadn't been, I'd have seen something. Noticed something. I don't know.'

'I kind of thought that you were distracted by the mind mage who had you twisted in knots.'

She grimaced. 'They're separate things. And I know that. But at the same time, I don't know that. And here I'm talking like some flustered teenager.' She put her hands on her hips, her mouth set in annoyance. 'I'm not good at this. Help.'

'Well,' I said. 'I take it that you came here to let me know that you weren't going to keep pursuing . . . whatever it is we had.'

'It's not because of you,' she said.

'I know,' I said. 'Never was, was it?'

She exhaled through her nose, a slow sigh. Her eyes lingered on me. 'I've always liked you, Dresden. For a long time, I thought you were dangerous. Then I saw you in action against the Heirs of Kemmler, and I respected you.' She smiled slightly. 'You're funny. I like that.'

'But?' I asked.

'But someone pushed me toward you,' she said. 'And that pisses me off. And . . .' She started weeping, though her posture and her voice didn't waver. 'And I thought that maybe I had broken through some kind of . . . scar. Or old wound. Or something. That I had grown closer to you, and maybe would keep growing closer to you, and it made me feel . . .' She shook her head as her voice finally broke. 'Young. It made everything feel new.'

I walked around the car to stand in front of her. I reached a hand toward her shoulder, but she raised hers in a gesture of denial. 'But it was a lie. I'm *not* young, Harry. I'm not new. I've seen and done things that . . . that you can't understand. That I pray to God you'll never need to understand.' She took a deep breath. 'This is ridiculous. I should be better at handling this.'

'What's wrong?' I asked quietly. 'I mean, other than the obvious.'

'I got to have *sex* again,' she snarled. 'And I liked it. I *really liked* it. I had forgotten exactly how mind-numbingly incredible sex is. And right now I'm having trouble forming complete sentences because I want to rip your shirt off and

bite your shoulder while you're still sweating while you—'
She broke off abruptly, her cheeks turning bright red. 'You're
not even *forty*.'

I leaned against the car, looking at her, and started
laughing quietly.

She shook her head, scowling ferociously at me, her dark
eyes bright. 'How am I supposed to give you orders, now?'
she asked. 'When you and I have . . . done all the things
we've done.'

'Well. What if I promise not to put the pictures on the
Internet.'

She blinked at me. 'Pictures . . . you *are* joking, Dresden?
Aren't you?'

I nodded.

'Because I had *quite* enough of that during my first
young adulthood,' she said. 'Italy may not have had an
Internet back then, but you'd be shocked how quickly
pictures can circulate even when they're painted on canvas.'

'Ana,' I said quietly.

She bit her lip and looked at me.

I reached out and took her hands. I squeezed them.
Then I lifted them to my lips and kissed them each once,
gently. 'Whatever the reason, I'm happy to remember the
time we had.'

She blinked her eyes several times, looking up at me.

'I get it,' I said. 'Things have changed. And maybe that
time is over. But you'll be okay. And I'll be okay. You
don't have to feel guilty about that.'

She lifted my hands to her lips and kissed them, once
each, just as I had. A tear fell on my knuckle. 'I'm sorry,'
she said.

'It'll be okay,' I said. 'It's okay.'

She nodded and looked up at me. I could see the calm, collected strength of the Captain of the Wardens, ready to assume its guiding role. I could see the uncertainty of Anastasia, who hadn't been close to anyone in a long time. And maybe I could see something lonely and sad that was a part of who she had been when she was a young woman, well over a century before I was born.

'Goodbye, Harry,' she whispered.

'Goodbye, Ana,' I said.

She squeezed my hands and turned to walk away. She stopped after half a dozen paces and looked back.

'Dresden?'

I looked at her.

'Rashid doesn't talk much about the night Morgan died. I barely remember anything myself, after Peabody said what he said.'

I knew what she was after. 'He wasn't alone,' I said. 'I was with him. And he knew that he'd found the traitor. He was content.'

Something tight in her shoulders eased. 'Thank you,' she said.

'Sure.'

Then she turned and strode purposefully away.

I looked at the bloodstained mattress on the *Blue Beetle*, and sighed. I didn't feel like driving it anywhere. It was early. It could wait a few hours. I turned to Mouse and said, 'Come on, boy. I need a beer.'

We descended out of the summer heat into the relative cool of my basement apartment.

Maybe I needed two.

It took Justine more than two weeks to get me that meeting

with Thomas. When she called, she was speaking in her official secretary tone again. She stipulated a public meeting place, where both of us would have the protection of the need to maintain a low profile. It was a precaution that the White Court had required of me, given how tense things had been between the Council and the White Court's leadership, of late.

I met Thomas on a Saturday afternoon outside the Great Cat House at the Lincoln Park Zoo.

As I came up, I spotted a pair of Lara's security guys, trying to blend in. Thomas was leaning on the rail that looked into this big pit where they keep a couple of tigers. He was wearing tight blue jeans, and a big loose white shirt. Every woman there and a large chunk of the guys were looking at him, with various degrees of lust, longing, interest, and seething hatred. I walked up and leaned on the rail beside him.

'Hey,' I said.

'Hey.'

We stood there watching the tigers for a few minutes.

'You asked for the meeting,' he said. 'What do you want?'

I arched an eyebrow. 'Thomas, I want to see you. Talk to you. Be sure you're okay. You're my brother, man.'

He didn't react to my words. Not at all.

I studied his profile for a few moments. Then I said, 'What's wrong?'

He moved one shoulder in a careless gesture. 'Nothing is wrong, per se. Unless . . . it was me.'

'You? Were wrong?'

'I was an idiot to try to live the way I've been living,' he said.

I looked at him sharply. 'What?'

He rolled a hand in a lazy gesture. 'The boutique. The constant nibbling, never sating myself. The . . .' He shrugged. 'All of it.'

I stared hard at him. Then I asked, very quietly, 'What did the skinwalker do to you?'

'He reminded me of what I really am.'

'Oh?'

Thomas turned to look at me with calm deep grey eyes. 'Yes. It didn't take him long, once he set about it.'

I felt sick to my stomach. 'What happened?'

'He hung me up by my heels,' Thomas said. 'And ripped strips of skin off of me. One at a time.'

I shuddered.

'It's agonizing,' he said. 'Not terribly dangerous to one of us. My demon didn't really have any trouble regenerating the skin — but it did become hungry. Very, very hungry.' His eyes suddenly gleamed paler silver and he looked back at the tigers, which were now restlessly prowling the pit. 'He'd taken a female kine to the lair where he had me prisoner. And he fed her to me.'

'Hell's bells,' I breathed.

Thomas watched the tigers pace. 'She was lovely. Sixteen or so? I don't know, exactly. I didn't ask for her name.' He spread his hands. 'It was a fatal feeding, of course. I don't think I've ever really explained to you exactly what that is like.'

'What is it like?' I asked in a quiet rasp.

'Like becoming light,' he said, his eyes drifting closed. 'Like sinking into the warmth of a campfire when you've been shivering for hours. Like a hot steak after a day of swimming in cold water. It transforms you, Harry. Makes you feel . . .' His eyes became haunted, hollow. 'Whole.'

I shook my head. 'Thomas. Jesus.'

'Once she was gone and my body was restored, the skin-walker tortured me again, until I was in the same desperate condition. Then he fed me another doe.' He shrugged. 'Rinse and repeat. Perhaps half a dozen times. He gave me young women and then put me in agony again. I was all but chewing out my own innards when he took me to the island. To tell you the truth, I barely remember it.' He smiled. 'I remember seeing Molly. But you've taught her enough to protect herself, it seems.'

'Thomas,' I said gently.

He smirked. 'If you ever get tired of her, I hope you'll let me know.'

I stared at him, sickened. '*Thomas.*'

He looked at me again, still smirking – but he couldn't hold it. Once again, his eyes looked hollow, touched with despair. He looked away from me. 'You don't get it, Harry.'

'Then talk to me,' I said, urgently. 'Thomas, Jesus Christ. This is *not* you.'

'Yes, it is,' he spat, the words a bladed hiss. '*That's* what it taught me, Harry. At the end of the day, I'm just an empty place that needs to be filled.' He shook his head. 'I didn't *want* to kill those girls. But I did it. I killed them, over and over, and I *loved* how it felt. When I think back on the memory of it, it doesn't make me horrified.' He sneered. 'It just makes me hard.'

'Thomas,' I whispered. 'Please, man. This isn't what you want to be. I know you, man. I've seen you.'

'You've seen who I wanted to be,' he said. 'Who I thought I was.' He shook his head and looked around at the people around us. 'Play a game with me.'

'What game?'

He nodded toward a pair of young women walking by holding ice-cream cones. 'What do you see when you look at them? Your first thought.'

I blinked. I looked. 'Uh. Blonde and brunette, too young for me, not bad to look at. I bet the blonde paid too much for those shoes.'

He nodded and pointed at an old couple sitting on a bench. 'Them?'

'They're fighting with each other over something and enjoying it. They've been together so long, it's comfortable for them. Later, they'll hold hands and laugh over the fight.'

He pursed his lips, and pointed at a mother chivvying a trio of small children of various sizes along the zoo. 'Them?'

'She's got an expensive ring, but she's here at the zoo alone. Her kids all have matching outfits. Her husband works a lot, and she doesn't look as good as she used to – look how the shoes are biting into her feet. She's worried that she's a trophy wife, or maybe an ex-wife in progress. She's about to start crying.'

'Uh-huh,' he said. 'Can I give you my first thoughts?'

I nodded, frowning at him.

Thomas pointed a finger at the young women. 'Food.' He pointed a finger at the old couple. 'Food.' He pointed a finger at the mother and her children. 'Food.'

I just stared at him.

He rolled his head, inhaling deeply and then exhaling. 'Maybe it was all those kills together like that. Maybe he drove me insane with the torment.' He shrugged. 'Honestly, I don't know. I just know that things seem a lot simpler now.'

'What are you trying to tell me?' I asked. 'That you're happy, now?'

'Happy,' he said, scorn ringing lightly in his voice. 'I'm . . . not wandering around blind anymore. Not trying desperately to be something that I'm not.' He looked back down at the tigers. 'Something I can never be.'

I just stood there, shaking my head.

'Oh, empty night, Harry,' he said, rolling his eyes. 'I'm not some kind of ravaging monster. I'm not some kind of psychotic rampaging around the city devouring virgins.' He waved a hand in a casual gesture. 'Killing when you feed feels fantastic, but it's stupid. There are far too many advantages in ensuring that the kine survive. Not only survive, but grow and prosper.' He smiled a bit. 'You know, I really think I might have something to offer the world. I never could have exerted any kind of influence on my kin as a moping exile, trying to be human. Maybe this way, I actually can accomplish something. Promote a more responsible standard of relations between humanity and my kind. Who knows?'

I stared at him and said, 'Gosh, that's noble.'

He eyed me.

I hit him with my heaviest sucker punch. 'What does Justine think of it?'

He straightened and turned toward me, and there was imminent violence in the set of his body. 'What?' he asked. 'What did you say to me?'

'You heard me,' I said, without changing posture or rising to the threat.

His hands closed into fists, knuckles popping.

'Still stings, doesn't it?' I said quietly. 'Still burns you when you try to touch her?'

He said nothing.

'And you still remember what it was to hold her. Like you did the night you trashed Madeline at Zero.'

'Jesus Christ, Harry,' he said. He turned to face out, away from the tigers, and his voice was full of weariness. 'I don't know. I just know that it doesn't *hurt* so bad all the time anymore.' He was quiet for a long time. Then he said, in a very quiet voice, 'I have bad dreams.'

I wanted to put my hand on his shoulder, to give him some support. But some instinct warned me that it wouldn't be welcomed.

'You took a beating,' I said quietly. 'What that thing did to you . . . ? Thomas, it knew exactly how to get to you. How to torment you the most. But it won't last. You survived. You'll get past it.'

'And go back to that miserable half life I had?' he whispered.

'Maybe,' I said quietly. 'I don't know.'

He looked at me.

'You're my brother,' I said. 'Nothing will ever change that. I'm here for you.'

'You're a damn fool,' he said.

'Yeah.'

'It would be easy to use you. Part of me thinks it's a fantastic idea.'

'I didn't say you weren't an asshole. I said you were my brother.'

The bodyguards stirred. Nothing big. They just sort of animated and moved toward the exits.

Thomas grimaced. 'Lara thinks I've made great progress. She's . . .' He shrugged. 'Proud of me.'

'I liked you better the other way,' I said. 'So did Justine. Maybe that should tell you something.'

'I've got to go. She's afraid you'll think I'm all brain-washed. Didn't want to risk you trying to deprogram me when I haven't been programmed.'

'I confess. The idea occurred to me.'

'If someone had gotten into my head, I don't think there'd be so many doubts,' he said. 'This isn't something you can help me with, Harry.'

'Maybe,' I said. 'Maybe not. Either way, you're still my brother.'

'Broken damn record,' he said.

I held up a fist.

He stared at it for a couple of silent beats before he made a fist of his own and rapped my knuckles against his.

'Don't call me,' he said.

'I'll be patient,' I said. 'But not forever.'

He hesitated and then nodded once more. Then he thrust his hands into the hip pockets of his jeans and walked quickly away. The bodyguards fell in behind him. One of them said something while he had one hand pressed against his ear.

Purely from petty malice, I waved a hand and hexed his radio, or phone. Sparks flew out of his ear and he all but fell over trying to get the earbud out.

Thomas looked back.

He grinned. Not long but real.

After he was gone, I turned to regard the tigers. I wondered if I knew them for what they really were, or if all I could see were the stripes.

I'd missed Kirby's funeral while I was in the infirmary in Edinburgh. A couple of weeks had gone by after that, and I'd talked to Will and Georgia by phone occasionally.

Gaming night came along, and as I had most weeks for the past several years, I showed up at Will and Georgia's place. I had my Arcanos rule book with me, and a Crown Royal bag filled with dice. I was wearing a black T-shirt that had a monochrome image of several multisided dice and said, in block print, 'COME TO THE DORK SIDE. DO NOT MAKE ME DESTROY YOU.'

Will answered the door and smiled at me. 'Hey, Harry. Wow, your face is . . . manly.'

'Chicks dig scars,' I said.

'Who is it?' came Andi's voice. It sounded limp, life-less.

'It is I, Harry Dresden,' I said solemnly.

Georgia appeared behind Will, smiling. 'Harry.' She looked at my shirt, and my gaming stuff. 'Oh . . . we weren't really going to . . .'

Kirby had been the one who ran the game for us.

I stepped aside, grabbed the geek standing behind me, and tugged him forward. 'This is Waldo Butters,' I said. 'And his geek penis is longer and harder than all of ours put together.'

Butters blinked, first at Georgia and Will, and then at me. 'Oh,' he said. 'Um. Thank you?'

Will looked from Butters to me, his eyes searching. 'What is this?' he asked gently.

'Life,' I said. 'It keeps going. Butters says he can handle an Arcanos game. Or he can run a bunch of other ones if we want to try something new.' I cleared my throat. 'If you like, we can go over to my place. Change of view and so on.'

Georgia looked at me and gave me a small and grateful smile.

Will looked at me uncertainly. Then he turned back into the apartment. 'Andi?'

She appeared beside Georgia. Andi looked absolutely withered. Multiple broken ribs and major surgery will do that to you. She was on her feet and moving, but it was clear that she'd been staying with Will and Georgia so that they could help care for her until she recovered.

I smiled at Andi and said, 'I don't think Kirby would want us to stop playing completely. What do you think? I mean it won't be the same game, but it might be fun.'

She looked at me and then at Butters. Then she gave me a little smile and nodded.

Will swung the door open wide, and we went inside, where I introduced Butters to everyone and produced several bottles of Mac's best ale.

See, here's the thing. Morgan was right: you can't win them all.

But that doesn't mean that you give up. Not ever. Morgan never said that part – he was too busy living it.

I closed the door behind me, while life went on.

Author's Note

When I was seven years old, I got a bad case of strep throat and was out of school for a whole week. During that time, my sisters bought me my first fantasy and sci-fi novels: the boxed set of *Lord of the Rings* and the boxed set of Han Solo adventure novels by Brian Daley. I devoured them all during that week.

From that point on, I was pretty much doomed to join SF&F fandom. From there, it was only one more step to decide I wanted to be a writer of my favorite fiction material, and here we are.

I blame my sisters.

My first love as a fan is swords-and-horses fantasy. After Tolkien I went after C. S. Lewis. After Lewis, it was Lloyd Alexander. After them came Fritz Leiber, Roger Zelazny, Robert Howard, John Norman, Poul Anderson, David Eddings, Weis and Hickman, Terry Brooks, Elizabeth Moon, Glen Cook, and before I knew it, I was a dual citizen of the United States and Lankhmar, Narnia, Gor, Cimmeria, Krynn, Amber – you get the picture.

When I set out to become a writer, I spent years writing swords-and-horses fantasy novels – and seemed to have little innate talent for it. But I worked at my writing, branching out into other areas as experiments, including SF, mystery, and contemporary fantasy. That's how the Dresden Files initially came about – as a happy accident while trying to accomplish something else. Sort of like penicillin.

But I never forgot my first love, and to my immense delight and excitement, one day I got a call from my agent and found out that I was going to get to share my newest swords-and-horses fantasy novel with other fans.

The Codex Alera is a fantasy series set within the savage world of Carna, where spirits of the elements, known as furies, lurk in ever facet of life, and where many intelligent races vie for security and survival. The realm of Alera is the monolithic civilization of humanity, and its unique ability to harness and command the furies is all that enables its survival in the face of the enormous sometimes hostile elemental powers of Carna, and against savage creatures who would lay Alera in waste and ruin.

Yet even a realm as powerful as Alera is not immune to destruction from within, and the death of the heir apparent to the Crown has triggered a frenzy of ambitious political maneuvering and infighting amongst the High Lords, those who wield the most powerful furies known to man. Plots are afoot, traitors and spies abound, and a civil war seems inevitable – all while the enemies of the realm watch, ready to strike at the first sign of weakness.

Tavi is a young man living on the frontier of Aleran civilization – because let's face it, swords-and-horses fantasies start there. Born a freak, unable to utilize any powers of furycrafting whatsoever, Tavi has grown up relying up on his own wits, speed, and courage to survive. When an ambitious plot to discredit the Crown lays Tavi's home, the Calderon Valley, naked and defenseless before a horde of the barbarian Marat, the boy and his family find themselves directly in harm's way.

There are no titanic High Lords to protect them, no Legions, no Knights with their mighty furies to take the field. Tavi and the free frontiersmen of the Calderon Valley must find some way to uncover the plot and to defend their homes against the merciless horde of the Marat and their beasts.

It is a desperate hour, when the fate of all Alera hangs in the balance, when a handful of ordinary steadholders must find the courage and strength to defy an overwhelming foe, and when the courage and intelligence of one young man will save the Realm – or destroy it.

Thank you, readers and fellow fans, for all of your support and kindness. I hope that you enjoy reading the books of the Codex Alera as much as I enjoyed creating them for you.

—Jim

About the Author

A martial arts enthusiast whose resumé includes a long list of skills rendered obsolete at least two hundred years ago, **Jim Butcher** turned to writing as a career because anything else probably would have driven him insane. He lives in Independence, Missouri, with his wife, his son, and a ferocious guard dog. You can visit Jim's website at www.jim-butcher.com

Find out more about Jim Butcher and other Orbit authors by registering for the free monthly newsletter at www.orbitbooks.net